Spring 2024
Blockbuster

Spring 2024 Blockbuster

SUSAN MALLERY

JOANNE ROCK

JO McNALLY

MICHELLE DOUGLAS

MILLS & BOON

SPRING BLOCKBUSTER 2024 © 2024 by Harlequin Books S.A.

HALFWAY THERE
© 2013 by Susan Macias Reedmond
Australian Copyright 2013
New Zealand Copyright 2013

First Published 2013
Second Australian Paperback Edition 2024
ISBN 978 1 038 92348 6

Joanne Rock is acknowledged as the author of this work
HER TEXAS RENEGADE
© 2020 by Harlequin Books S.A.
Australian Copyright 2020
New Zealand Copyright 2020

First Published 2020
Second Australian Paperback Edition 2024
ISBN 978 1 038 92348 6

A MAN YOU CAN TRUST
© 2019 by Jo McNally
Australian Copyright 2019
New Zealand Copyright 2019

First Published 2019
Second Australian Paperback Edition 2024
ISBN 978 1 038 92348 6

MISS PRIM'S GREEK ISLAND FLING
© 2019 by Michelle Douglas
Australian Copyright 2019
New Zealand Copyright 2019

First Published 2019
Second Australian Paperback Edition 2024
ISBN 978 1 038 92348 6

Published by
Mills & Boon
An imprint of Harlequin Enterprises (Australia) Pty Limited (ABN 47 001 180 918), a subsidiary of HarperCollins Publishers Australia Pty Limited (ABN 36 009 913 517)
Level 19, 201 Elizabeth Street
SYDNEY NSW 2000
AUSTRALIA

MIX
Paper | Supporting
responsible forestry
FSC
www.fsc.org   FSC® C001695

® and ™ (apart from those relating to FSC®) are trademarks of Harlequin Enterprises (Australia) Pty Limited or its corporate affiliates. Trademarks indicated with ® are registered in Australia, New Zealand and in other countries. Contact admin_legal@Harlequin.ca for details.

Printed and bound in Australia by McPherson's Printing Group

CONTENTS

Halfway There

Susan Mallery

Believe in love. Overcome obstacles. Find happiness.

To my Facebook friends Brandy T of Pittsburgh, PA, and Brandy T of Clinton, UT, who love Fool's Gold. I think you're both terrific!

CHAPTER ONE

"THE BABIES ARE COMING! The babies are coming! Someone call nine-one-one!"

Ryan Patterson glanced up from his computer as a petite blonde raced past his open office. She was wide-eyed, with her hands waving in the air. She looked to be on the verge of complete panic, in case the screaming hadn't been enough of a clue.

He had to admit, even running around like a deranged chicken, she was kind of cute. He liked how she wore her skirt just short enough to be interesting. Her hazel eyes were big, her mouth full. Early to mid-twenties. Yup, except for the shrieking, she was what his father would call a damned fine example of a woman.

Ryan stood and stepped out of his small glassed-in office. The woman made a complete circuit of the larger central space, then raced back toward him.

"Did you call?" she demanded, wringing her hands together. "I feel sick to my stomach. It's too soon. At least I think it is. I thought we had another week." She sucked in air. "Did you call?" she asked again.

"I will, ma'am, as soon as I confirm there's a pregnant woman in the building."

It was still early. Just after eight in the morning. Ryan had arrived at six and had been focused on his work. He hadn't even heard anyone walking into the building. Other than the blonde, of course.

A quick look around the office confirmed that they seemed to be alone. Ethan Hendrix, Ryan's new boss, didn't believe in paying his engineers to sit around. Most of them were already on job sites or up at the manufacturing facility just outside of Fool's Gold. Because Ryan was working on a new design, he was in the main office. He'd been on the job all of a week. Ethan had mentioned something about hiring a temp to handle the phone, but hadn't given Ryan a name or ETA.

The woman stared at him blankly. "There's no pregnant person," she said, as if convinced he was an idiot. "It's Misty. I'm cat sitting, and she's pregnant. I told Ethan I couldn't leave her alone, so he said to bring her in to work with me. I didn't think it would be a problem because Charity, her owner, said she wasn't due for a week and they'd all be back by then. They're in Florida for a charity bike race that Josh is—"

The woman drew in a breath. "None of this matters. Misty is giving *birth*. We have to get help."

Ryan shook his head. "Most cats give birth just fine on their own. They know what to do. If there's a problem, we can contact a local vet."

"Won't it be too late then?" She turned and sprinted for the desk by the front door. "I have to do something." She disappeared behind one of the partitions.

Ryan followed her and found her crouched by a box containing a short-haired tabby and what looked to be one squirming newborn kitten.

"It's happening!" the woman shrieked. "Misty, stop, please! I'll call a vet. I can find a vet."

Misty shot him a look that begged for privacy, along with peace and quiet.

"Okay, then," he said, grabbing the woman by the elbow and tugging her to her feet. "You need to step back and breathe."

"How is that going to help? Misty needs me."

"Misty's doing fine on her own. Come on."

He thought about easing her toward the break room, but it seemed like the last thing the blonde needed was caffeine. She was plenty wired on her own.

Instead he took her to his small office and settled her in the visitor's chair. He took his seat and settled his hands on the computer keyboard.

"Do you know a vet around town?" he asked.

She stared at him. "What? Yes. Of course. Cameron Mc-Kenzie. He's the local vet."

Ryan typed the name into the search engine and got the link to the veterinary practice. "Here's the phone number. They opened at seven, and they'll be there until five." He studied the address. While he hadn't been in town long, he thought the office couldn't be very far away.

The woman twisted her fingers together. "We should go *now.*"

"So this is about you, not Misty, right? Because she's doing fine."

Those big hazel eyes narrowed considerably. "Excuse me? Are you saying I'm being selfish while Misty is doing all the work?"

"Pretty much."

He leaned back in the chair and prepared himself for a heated discussion. He'd always believed you learned a lot about a person by how she handled a disagreement. When tensions ran high, true character was revealed.

The woman sucked in a breath. He braced himself for shrieking and was surprised when she sagged back in the chair and nodded slowly.

"I've never been around a cat giving birth before," she said with a sigh. "I still think she belongs in a feline maternity ward, but your point is a good one. She seems to be doing fine on her own. I guess I can check on her every five minutes and if she seems to be handling it, leave her to become a mom in her own time."

"That seems like a plan," he said, impressed by her ability to be rational and only a little disappointed there wasn't going to be a show. "I'm Ryan, by the way."

Those beautiful eyes widened again, and color flooded her face. "Oh, no. We haven't met, have we? You're the new guy, and now you're worried you're trapped with a crazy person."

He grinned. "I'm pretty sure I can handle myself."

He looked like he could, Fayrene Hopkins thought as she stared into amused brown eyes. Ryan was close to six feet, with broad shoulders and dark hair. He wore a plaid shirt tucked into jeans and cute rimless glasses.

"You're saying if I came at you with a letter opener, you'd be comfortable wrestling me to the ground?" she asked.

"Are you going to?"

"I'm not into violence. It doesn't move me forward on my four-year plan. I'm Fayrene. Fayrene Hopkins."

She rose and offered her hand. They shook. His skin was warm, and for a second, as she gazed into his eyes, she felt a slight *zap* of electricity.

She settled back in the chair and told herself no zip, zap or tingle was going to get in the way of what she wanted. In the office alcove of her small apartment she had large sheets of poster paper tacked up on the walls. Each was covered with a graph or a chart or a list. She was a big believer in taking responsibility of her own happiness, and for her that meant getting her business up and running. Zaps tended to derail young women pursuing financial and business success.

"You have a four-year plan?" he asked, his tone slightly amused. "Not a five-year one?"

She raised her chin. "It was a five-year plan, but I'm wrapping year one now."

"How many pregnant cats does it include?"

She laughed. "Hopefully Misty is my last one. I'm a pet sitter. My company provides temporary employees and pet-sitting services."

"That's eclectic."

"I have a degree in business," she told him. "I spent eighteen months working for a bank and hated every minute of it. So I quit and spent a month figuring out what I wanted from my life."

"Which is?"

"I want to own my own business."

"You've already done that."

"Sure, my name's on the door, but I'm struggling. I want to be financially successful. I'm twenty-four. By the time I'm twenty-eight, I want four employees, all working full-time."

"That's a lot to take on."

"I know, but like I said, I have a plan. When I did my analysis, I saw there was a real need for good pet-sitting services in town. Not just someone to come in and feed the fish, but a person willing to be there 24/7 if necessary."

"That explains the pregnant Misty."

"Exactly." She smiled. "Charity didn't want to leave her alone. So I'm taking her with me. Although she wasn't supposed to be giving birth so soon."

"And the temp side of things?"

"I fill in. Right now I'm spending a couple of weeks here at Ethan's office while his regular receptionist is on vacation. There are a lot of small businesses in Fool's Gold. They need extra help but don't always want to hire someone full-time. I fill a gap."

Starting her business had taken every penny of her savings and a loan from her older sister. Dellina had handled the family finances ever since she'd turned eighteen and had taken over the responsibility of raising her two younger twin sisters. Each sibling had a small trust fund left by their parents' life insurance. Fayrene's loan was against that.

Ryan stood and held out his hand. "Come on," he said. "We'll go check on our girl."

Fayrene wasn't sure about touching Ryan again. She'd already felt that one zap. But maybe it had been static electricity and not anything chemical.

She took the outstretched hand and held her breath. The second their palms touched, she felt it. A distinct shivery sensation working its way up her spine. *Uh-oh.* This wasn't good. Her four-year plan didn't include time for romance.

Ryan, however, appeared unmoved. He gave her a quick smile, then led the way back to Misty's box under the receptionist desk.

Three tiny kittens nestled against their mother. Misty carefully licked them, dampening their fur. Their tiny eyes were closed, their miniature paws kneading slightly. Fayrene pulled free of Ryan and dropped to a crouch.

"They're beautiful," she murmured. "Do you think she's done giving birth?"

"Cats can take a break for up to twenty-four hours," he told her. "She's not in discomfort, so just let her be."

Misty might not be upset, but Fayrene felt the whole world kind of shift to the left. She wondered if she was about to faint for the first time in her life.

"T-twenty-four hours?"

"It's not that unusual. The fact that the first three came so quickly might mean she's done, but there's no way to know for sure."

She stood slowly, one hand on the desk for support. "I can't go through this for twenty-four hours," she murmured. "It's too stressful."

"Misty's doing great," Ryan told her.

Easy for him to say. He wasn't the one who would be watching over her for the next twenty-four hours. *Work now,* she told herself. *Panic later.* So the night would be long. She would make it through.

"Thank you for your help," she said, glancing at him. "You've been great, and now you probably want to get back to whatever it was you were doing."

He flashed her a grin that made her knees nearly give way. "I'll be in all day if you and Misty need any help."

"We might have to take you up on that."

She appreciated that he didn't point out the cat was doing great and didn't seem to need much of anything. She, on the other hand, could use a hug. Her gaze slid to Ryan's retreating back. She would bet he was a great hugger. She liked that in a guy. When he held on tight, as if he would never let go. Although not in a scary, stalker kind of way.

Not that she was interested in Ryan. She had goals and a plan. Part of that plan was to avoid romance for the next four years. There would be plenty of time for fun later.

CHAPTER TWO

RYAN SAVED HIS work on his program, then stood and stretched. It was after five. This was his second week working for Ethan. As the job was only for a couple of months and he didn't know anyone in town, Ryan had been working until at least eight. But tonight was different. All day he'd been conscious of Fayrene sitting at the front desk in the office. She'd answered phones, typed on her keyboard and checked on Misty about every fifteen minutes. From what he could tell, she was efficient and a bit of a worrier. Now that she wasn't running around screaming about the cat, he'd noticed she had the sexiest walk he'd seen in a while. Or ever.

He grabbed his leather jacket. While the early spring days were warm in Fool's Gold, the nights could be cool. He was staying at Ronan's Lodge—a nice hotel in town. It meant he could walk back and forth to work. It also meant dealing with the weather.

Now he moved toward Fayrene's desk. She'd gathered her belongings and looked ready to bend down to collect the box containing Misty and her three kittens.

"I'll get her," he said, stepping around the desk and lifting the box. "Taking her home for the night?"

Fayrene nodded. She was pale with worry. He could see the

strain in her eyes. "I spoke to Misty's owner, Charity. The bike race was today, so they're coming back tomorrow to be with her. I just have to get through until then." She bit her lower lip. "You really think she might have more kittens?"

"It's possible."

"That's a long time to be in labor."

"I don't think she's in pain."

Misty lay with her kittens snuggled close. Her eyes were half-closed, and she was purring.

"I guess not," Fayrene said.

Ryan surrendered to the inevitable and put the box on the desk. "I could stay with you and sit up with her, if that would help."

Fayrene stared at him. "I don't think so. I barely know you. You can't come over to my place."

If he hadn't been holding the cat and her babies, he would have raised both hands in a gesture of surrender. "I wasn't suggesting anything. Just offering. We could stay here, if you'd feel safer."

"You'd spend the night in this office to help me watch over the cat?"

"Sure."

"That's very nice of you, but I don't think so."

He couldn't read her tone, so he wasn't sure if she was paying him a compliment or mocking him. "It's how I was raised."

She studied him for a second. "Wallet in your back pocket?" she asked.

"Sure, but what—"

His question was cut off when he felt her fingers tugging the wallet free. She flipped it open and then picked up the phone and dialed.

"Police Chief Barns, please. It's Fayrene Hopkins."

"You're calling the police?" he asked, thinking his grumpy uncle had been right. No good deed went unpunished.

"Hi, Alice," Fayrene said with a smile. "I need you to run

a background check on someone." She explained about Misty and the kittens and his offer. "His name is Ryan Patterson. He's from Washington State." She gave Alice his date of birth and license number, then glanced back at him. "Nice picture."

"Thanks."

She covered the mouthpiece. "I dated Alice's oldest when I was in high school. We went to prom. She's always liked me."

He couldn't decide if Fayrene's actions impressed him or made him want to recant his offer. He supposed a little of both. He respected her need to protect herself, even as he was uncomfortable being investigated by the police. Not that he had anything to hide, but still.

Fayrene pointed to the bowl of jelly beans on her desk. "Want one?"

"No, thanks."

She picked out a couple. "Green apple. I haven't been eating much fruit lately."

He stared at her. "That's a jelly bean, not fruit."

"I think it still counts."

"Are you sure about that?"

"Duh." She uncovered the mouthpiece and listened for a minute. "Uh-huh. Okay, thanks. I'll tell him. No, I haven't heard from Jim. Alice, you have to let it go." She paused, then smiled again. "That's sweet. I'll let you know if anything changes. Bye."

She hung up. "Alice says I'm her favorite of her Jim's girlfriends, and she would like us to get back together."

"That going to happen?"

"No. We had fun, but we outgrew each other a long time ago." She tucked a loose strand of blond hair behind her ears and grabbed more jelly beans. "You have no arrests, but you have two speeding tickets on your record. Police Chief Barns wants me to remind you that local law enforcement takes the speed limit very seriously here in Fool's Gold."

"Good to know."

She studied him for a second. "If you're serious about staying with me tonight, that is not going to happen. However, I would appreciate you stopping by for a few hours, just in case more kittens arrive. But I want to be clear I'm inviting you over as a friend. I'm not sleeping with you."

Ryan laughed. "Thanks for clarifying. I wasn't planning on more than cat sitting, by the way."

She flushed. "I realize you hadn't asked, but I've learned it's best to get everything out in the open so there aren't any mis-understandings."

"A wise philosophy."

"Now you're making fun of me."

"Maybe a little."

She was an interesting combination of hysterical and ca-pable, he thought. She might not be comfortable around Misty in labor, but she was willing to call the local police chief and check on him.

He shrugged into his jacket. "How far's your place? I left my car at the hotel."

"I drove because of Misty." She picked up her purse. "I wasn't planning on company for dinner. Is pizza okay?"

"Pizza is my favorite."

Fayrene dropped her skirt to the floor and slid into her jeans. She'd left Ryan in the living room with Misty and the kittens. He didn't seem the type to snoop, but it had been so long since she'd brought a guy home, she felt strange leaving him alone. Who knew you could forget how to date?

Not that this was a date—he was a friend, helping her out. But he was also a man and nice-looking and there was the whole *zap* thing.

She pulled on her sweatshirt and shoved her feet into flats. Her curly hair was a mess, but then it usually was. She'd learned to ignore it. Less than two minutes after she'd left him to get changed, she was back in the living room. Where Ryan wasn't.

She stared at the empty space. His backpack was still on the floor by the door, and his coat was on the small rack. She paused and listened, then heard a distinct *meow* from the alcove that was her kitchen.

She followed the noise and found Ryan opening a can of cat food. Misty was out of the box and tracing a figure eight around his ankles.

He looked up and smiled. "I thought she might be hungry," he said. "She's had a tough day."

He scooped food into a bowl and set it on the floor. Misty hurried over and started eating. He poured out some dry food, then filled her water bowl.

"You're good," Fayrene told him. "You've taken care of pets before."

"I grew up on a farm."

Fayrene stared at him. "Seriously?"

He covered the rest of the canned cat food and put it in her refrigerator, then closed the door and leaned against the counter.

"Why is that surprising? You live in a small town."

"But not on a farm."

She led the way into the living room. The coffee table had a small drawer where she kept her favorite takeout menus. When they were both seated on the sofa, she handed him the stack.

"I owe you, so you get to pick. It doesn't have to be pizza. Other places deliver."

He chuckled. "You sure know how to spoil a guy."

He flipped through the various offerings before choosing pizza. Fayrene phoned in the order, adding a six-pack of beer to the pizza. Because all she had in her refrigerator was a jar of mustard and Misty's breakfast.

"So where is the family farm?" she asked, angling toward him.

"A place you've never heard of. Colville, Washington. It's

north of Spokane. My dad runs a few hundred heads of cattle and twenty acres of hay. We raised chickens, goats, rabbits. The usual."

She laughed. "The usual? Not for me. No wonder you were comfortable with Misty's delicate condition. Nothing you haven't seen before."

He shrugged. "I've had my share of birthing babies."

"How did you get from there to here?"

His dark gaze settled on her face. "Why aren't I still that farm boy?"

She nodded.

"It's a hard way to making a living. There are a few manufacturing jobs in town, but I didn't want that, either. I'd always been interested in how things worked. I would take things apart and try to put them back together." His mouth curved up. "When I was younger, I wasn't very good at the putting them back together part. My parents were really patient with me."

"So you always wanted to be an engineer?"

"Pretty much. When I was fifteen, my dad bought a wind turbine to generate electricity." The smile widened. "That's a windmill for you city folks."

She laughed. "Thanks for explaining. So that's what you studied?"

"My degree is more general. Alternative energy sources, but I've specialized in wind turbines. I've been working on some designs of my own, and I've modified existing designs. Efficiency is significant. Getting an extra kilowatt may not seem like much, but over time, it adds up."

He spoke with enthusiasm and got technical pretty quickly. In a matter of a minute, she had no idea what he was talking about. But she liked the sound of his voice and how he was excited about what he did. A lot of guys her age were just coasting. They wanted to be the next Steve Jobs without doing the work.

Not Ryan, she thought, respecting his desire to get ahead.

She also liked how his dark hair fell across his forehead and the way his glasses made him seem more approachable.

She found herself wanting to move closer. To lean into him and—

She slammed on mental brakes. That was so not happening, she reminded herself. She was the girl with a plan. She had dreams to fulfill. Getting involved would only distract her. Dreams first, romance second.

Oh, but he was tempting.

"...which was where I met Ethan," he was saying.

She'd been listening enough to know he'd been talking about a conference. "He convinced you to come here?"

Ryan hesitated. "Not exactly. My contract with him is for six weeks. He wanted some design modifications, which is what I'm doing now. I have a job offer in Texas."

That was news. "Are you going to take it?"

"I don't know. It's a good offer. There's a lot of cutting-edge work being done there. North Texas gets a lot of wind."

While she wasn't happy with the idea of him leaving, it did simplify the problem. If Ryan wasn't staying, then he couldn't interfere with her plan. And sitting just a little closer on the sofa was perfectly safe...

And maybe a little bit dangerous.

CHAPTER THREE

SEVERAL SLICES OF PIZZA, a couple of beers, two handfuls of jelly beans and some interesting conversation later, Ryan found himself wishing Fayrene hadn't been quite so clear on the "I'm not sleeping with you" front. She was bright, funny and sexy. Under other circumstances, he would be making his move. Only this wasn't that kind of situation. She'd asked him over to help her babysit a cat—not because she was interested in him. But a guy could dream.

They lingered at the small table by the kitchen. Misty had gone to sleep after her dinner and showed no signs of stirring or giving birth. If he had to guess, he would say she was done delivering. But admitting that meant telling Fayrene there was no reason for him to stay, and he didn't want the evening to end just yet.

"My mom came here to go to school," she was saying. "My dad had just been promoted to assistant manager of Ronan's Lodge. It was a big deal. He was thinking of taking some business classes to help him get ahead. They met on campus." She sighed. "It was love at first sight."

He rested his elbows on the table and leaned toward her. "You're remembering being told that story when you were a kid."

She nodded. "They told it every year on their anniversary. How Mom was in a hurry and Dad wasn't looking where he was going. They ran into each other, and her books went flying. By the time they'd picked them up, they knew."

"So you believe in love at first sight?"

"No. I mean it happened to them, but I think love grows over time. You need shared interests and a similar belief system. You have to want the same things."

He agreed with her, but he suspected she might read too much into him saying that. "So you don't think opposites attract?"

She wrinkled her nose. "I'm sure it's exciting and dramatic, but I don't want drama in my life. I like things organized."

"Like your plan."

She nodded. Her hazel eyes darkened slightly, then she looked at him. "They died. My parents. They took their first trip alone when Ana Raquel and I were fourteen. Dellina, our older sister, was nearly seventeen."

Ryan hadn't expected her to say that. He reached across the table and took her hand in his. "I'm sorry."

"Thanks. It was so hard. We didn't have any family in town, so we had to go live with our aunt in Arizona. She and my uncle were really nice, but everything was different. We lost our parents and our home and our friends in a single week. When Dellina turned eighteen, she took custody of us and moved us back here."

"You and your sister are twins?"

Fayrene nodded. "Ana Raquel and I tried to be good for her. You know, not make any trouble. But we were teenaged girls. It didn't always go well. Dellina hung in there. She got a job and was really careful with the life insurance money. We still had the house where we grew up."

"Why don't you live there now?"

"It's a huge four-bedroom place with a big yard. We lease it out. Some of the rent money is put in a fund to cover maintenance, and we split the rest of it." She gave him a faint smile. "During the lean months, it makes a difference."

He released her hand because it seemed the polite thing to do, but what he really wanted was to walk around the table and draw her into his arms.

"Your sisters are still here in town?"

"Dellina is. Ana Raquel is a chef in San Francisco, but she comes home a lot. It's nice when we're together." She shifted in her seat. "I admire Dellina for what she did. What she gave up. Ana Raquel went to culinary school in San Francisco, and I went to college in Santa Cruz. But she stayed here. She was our anchor. She worked jobs she didn't like because the hours were good and she couldn't risk not having a steady income. It's only in the past couple of years that she's felt comfortable enough to start her own business."

He put the pieces together. "You think she was trapped."

"Some."

Because of circumstances, Dellina had been forced to grow up fast and take on more responsibility than was comfortable. Fayrene had learned from that. She didn't want to risk her dreams to the unexpected.

"You think if you have a solid enough plan, you won't be surprised."

Her mouth twisted. "Is it that obvious?"

"It's not a big leap. Don't get me wrong. I understand what you're doing, and I respect it. You're strong and determined."

Fayrene wished there was a way to unwind the past few minutes of conversation. She hadn't meant to share so much with Ryan. She'd barely known the guy twelve hours and already he knew more than most.

"It's not that I don't want a family," she murmured. "I do, of course. Just not now."

He leaned back in his chair. "You don't have to explain yourself to me," he told her. "I'm the guy who swore he'd never marry before he turned forty."

"You're just saying that to make me feel better."

He shook his head. "Scout's honor."

"Ha. Like I know if you were a boy scout."

"Don't I look the part?"

He looked mostly sexy and earnest. A very appealing combination.

He stood. "Come on. Let's check on our new mother."

Fayrene followed him into the living room. Misty was still sleeping, her three tiny kittens curled up next to her.

"She looks good," he said.

"Thanks to you."

He flashed her a smile. "Misty did most of the hard work."

They settled on the sofa to watch a movie. Fayrene was careful not to sit too close, even though she wanted to. She was confused by how comfortable she felt around Ryan. It was as if she'd known him for years. At the same time, she was on alert—her body poised to tingle at a moment's notice. The juxtaposition confused her.

They argued playfully about which movie to watch. Her selection was mostly chick flicks. Finally they found a not-too-grisly action movie on pay-per-view and settled in.

She picked through the jelly beans left in the bowl. They were her "thing," as much for the childhood memories as for the sweetness without too many calories. She loved the taste and she could still fit into her clothes in the morning. Unfortunately, they weren't quite enough to distract her from the hunky guy sitting next to her on the sofa.

Was it her or had it gotten hot in here?

When the movie was over, Ryan stood and stretched. She allowed herself an eye-candy moment of admiring his broad chest and narrow waist before reminding herself it was impolite to stare.

"Whoa, look at that," he said when he'd lowered his arms to

his sides. He moved to an old boom box she kept on the bottom shelf of her bookcase. Most people didn't even notice it was there. He moved the dial back and forth until he managed to tune in one of the local stations.

"Great antique," he said when he saw her.

"It was my dad's. I know it's huge and hideous, but it makes me think of him."

He stood. "I like it."

On the radio, a low, masculine voice spoke. "This is Gideon, and we're going to play oldies tonight. Like we do every night. I thought I'd start with a song that reminds me of a beautiful woman from my past. To the smartest woman I ever met. And here it is, by the Drifters."

Fayrene was trying to figure out which song he was going to play. While she'd never been a fan of the oldies, her dad had liked them. He complained he'd been born in the wrong decade. That he would have been happier in the fifties, with great music and muscle cars. Then her mom would tease him about how he would have been too old for her.

She felt her throat tighten as blurry memories tried to focus. But it had been too long, she thought sadly, and she couldn't see much more than shadows. Before she had to start fighting tears, Ryan pulled her close and started to dance with her.

"Who's Gideon?" he asked, moving in time with the beat. He held her just tight enough to make her want to snuggle closer and loose enough that she didn't feel pressured.

"He's new in town," she said, aware the memories were fading and content to let them retreat for the night. "There are a lot of rumors about him. Everyone says he was in the military and did some really dangerous things."

"I like his taste in music."

Ryan's shirt was soft under her fingers, his body warm. Being next to him made her forget everything else—her past, her plan. There was only the gentle sway of the dance, the rhythm of the song and an unexpected yearning.

His dark gaze settled on her face; then he lowered his head a few inches and lightly kissed her.

The brush of his mouth against hers was light as breath. He didn't push, didn't claim. He teased, then drew back and put his hand on the back of her head, so she rested her cheek on his shoulder.

Fayrene closed her eyes. Wanting spun through her, igniting nerves and making her long for more than the chaste kiss. But instead of reacting to that, she stayed where she was, enjoying the sense of being taken care of. Of being safe. Even if it was just for the night.

But when the song ended, Ryan drew back. He gave her a quick smile, murmured "good night" and was gone before she could figure out if she wanted him to stay or not. And wasn't that just like a man?

CHAPTER FOUR

FAYRENE WAS PLEASANT, friendly and distant for the next three days. When she went out for sandwiches, she brought one back to Ryan. She warned him about the warring hair stylists in town when he asked where to get his hair cut, and she explained he would have to alternate his business between House of Bella and Chez Julia unless he wanted to start a boatload of trouble. Even so, she was careful not to spend more than a minute or two in conversation at any given time because it was both smarter and safer.

But on Friday morning she arrived at work to find Ryan being interrogated by two very determined older women. Eddie and Gladys—both long past the age of eligibility for Social Security—stood in his office.

"I heard you're an engineer," Eddie was saying. "I have a new all-in-one printer I need help with. You know, hooking it up to my Wi-Fi network. You could come over this afternoon."

Ryan shifted on his feet, his expression both trapped and desperate. "I'm not a computer engineer, ma'am," he told her. "I work with wind turbines."

"Still, you're young and, from what I can see, very strong. You should be able to figure it out."

Gladys grinned. "Eddie keeps her place a little warm, so

you might want to wear a T-shirt. A tight one. I really like the glasses. They're kind of sexy."

Ryan flushed. Fayrene was both impressed and shocked by the older ladies' determination. She'd heard rumors about their tactics but had never seen them in action before.

She cleared her throat.

Eddie and Gladys both turned toward her. Eddie grinned. "Fayrene. There you are. Tell your friend here that he needs to come help me this afternoon."

"No."

Eddie's smile faded. "Excuse me?"

"I said no. You need to leave Ryan alone. If you don't, I'm telling Josh you're bullying Ethan's favorite engineer."

Eddie's expression fell. She'd worked for Josh for years and loved him like a son. She bossed him around, and he looked out for her. But he was also Ethan's best friend and wouldn't appreciate Eddie messing with work stuff.

"I wasn't bullying him," Eddie said, a whine in her voice.

"I can handle this," Ryan added, apparently realizing he was getting protection from marauding near-octogenarians.

Gladys tugged on her friend's arm. "We'll find someone else to help us. Maybe that nice young man on the radio. Gideon. I saw him at the gym the other day. He has a great butt."

Eddie nodded. "I like a good butt just as much as a good chest."

The two women left.

When the front door closed, Ryan shook his head. "That was the most surreal experience of my life. When they first came in, I told myself it was all a misunderstanding."

Fayrene didn't bother hiding her amusement. "Not if they were talking about seeing you naked and asking if you liked older women in a sexual way. They're legendary. Mostly they're harmless, but you have to be willing to stand up to them. I'm going to guess you weren't raised to talk back to grandmother types."

"It's not a skill set I thought I was missing. Anything else I need to know about the town?"

"How much time do you have?"

Something flashed in his eyes. A flash of male admiration with a hint of stalking predator thrown in for fun. But as quickly as it had shown up, it was gone, leaving behind the mild-mannered Ryan she knew and liked.

Fayrene's breath quickened a little. She'd been avoiding him for very sensible reasons. This proved that. Yet she also found herself wanting to throw caution to the wind and pick up where Eddie and Gladys had left off.

"Thanks for the rescue," he said, moving back to his desk. "Your arrival was well timed. I'll do my best to be more surly the next time I run into those two."

He was backing off because she'd made it clear that was what she wanted. The downside of being sensible, she thought.

But after nearly a week with Ryan, she knew he was both sweet and funny. Polite, smart and possibly interested in her. Did it get better than that?

"You're arguing with yourself about something," he said.

She nodded. "You."

He'd reached for his chair, but now he let his arm fall to his side as his eyebrows rose. "What about me?"

"I'm torn. I have a plan, and I'm clear on my goals. Getting involved would mess up everything."

"It would."

She appreciated that he didn't point out he hadn't actually said he was interested in her.

"But you're leaving," she continued. "In a way, that makes things safer. There's a time limit, so even if we did get involved, it wouldn't be for very long."

"Lessening the distraction factor."

"Are you making fun of me?" she asked.

One corner of his mouth curved up. "Maybe a little."

"I suppose I deserve it. You're right. It doesn't have to be that complex. There's an Easter Egg Drop tomorrow. Want to go?"

"An Easter egg what?"

She laughed. "People decorate raw eggs and bring them to city hall. Then we drop them."

"Raw eggs?"

"It's fun and strangely satisfying."

"It's a little disgusting."

"Maybe. You in?"

"Absolutely. What time?"

"I'll pick you up at ten. You're at the Lodge, right?"

He nodded. "I'll be waiting in the lobby."

The Lucky Lady Casino Resort was north of Fool's Gold, nestled on over a hundred acres at the foot of the mountains. Through time and rain and probably a few earthquakes, a pass had been created a couple of miles due east of the land where the casino sat. On the other side of the mountain were more mountains, each with its own unique shape.

With changing temperatures and perfectly placed canyons and valleys, there was a constant difference in barometric pressure, otherwise known to the layperson as what created wind.

For Ryan the unique placement of the casino and the land meant a sweet two-acre spot that was always blustery. It was the perfect place for wind turbines.

He stood with Ethan at the foot of the massive machines. Ethan downloaded the most recent readings onto his tablet, then tapped to get them in chart form.

His boss shook his head. "Well, damn. You were right. We've increased efficiency by three percent just this week."

"A small sampling of what's happening," Ryan pointed out. "We need more data over time to be sure the modifications are working, but it looks promising."

"Modest?" Ethan asked.

Ryan shrugged. "I like to be sure."

He was confident about his calculations, but he had learned that what worked on a computer program didn't always translate to the real world.

"Caution is good," Ethan told him. "What about the blades themselves?"

"I'm still working on that. I should have new designs ready in the time we agreed on."

He was tasked with modifying the existing blades for the turbines. The steady high wind by the casino meant more electricity could be generated with a higher degree of certainty. Maximizing that was why he was here. First with program tweaks, then with the physical blades.

"I have a lot of customers who are interested in what we're doing here," Ethan told him. "It's going to be difficult to get them all in to talk to you before you leave."

"I'll fit them in as best I can."

Ethan studied him for a second before nodding slowly. Their arrangement had been clear from the beginning. Ethan wanted a project completed, not a new employee. Ryan had needed time to figure out his next career move. So this had worked for both of them.

The job in Texas gave him a lot of what he wanted. Great pay, interesting work, a chance to advance in his field. Everyone he'd met on his interviews had been friendly, and there was a lot to be said for how pretty the girls were in the Lone Star State.

But he wasn't sure. Maybe because the company was so large, or it was located so far from his family in eastern Washington State. Whatever the reason, he'd put off accepting the offer.

Now that he'd been in Fool's Gold a couple of weeks, he found himself liking it more and more. It was a small town without being too small. Fayrene was part of the appeal, he admitted to himself. But she'd made it clear she was only looking for temporary. Which meant staying or going had to be his own decision—not based on his feelings for her.

"You take that job in Texas yet?" Ethan asked.

"No. I have six more weeks until I have to give them an answer."

Ethan turned off his tablet, and they headed for the truck. "That's a long time to wait for you."

Ryan grinned. "I like to think I'll be worth it."

Ethan chuckled. "I'm sure you do."

CHAPTER FIVE

"SEE," FAYRENE SAID as she and Ryan went down the front stairs of city hall and out onto the street. "Wasn't that satisfying?"

Ryan chuckled. "Strangely, yes. I didn't expect it to be."

"You have good aim." While her eggs had drifted off course, Ryan had hit the bull's-eye nearly every time.

Now that she'd made the decision it was okay to have a casual relationship with him while he was in town, she was able to relax and enjoy the tingles and zaps she felt in his company. When they reached the street and he took her hand in his, she hung on tight.

This was nice, she told herself. Four years was a long time to go without dating. She should do this more often. Hang out casually. All she needed was a series of interim guys. Although to be honest, she couldn't imagine any of them being better than Ryan. Not just in the looks department, but in how he acted. She supposed there was a reason people said that character mattered.

"Where to now?" he asked.

She glanced at her watch. It was nearly noon. "We have time to get lunch and still find a good place to watch the parade. Because it's Easter tomorrow, there are a lot of bunnies."

"Live bunnies?"

"A few of those, but mostly people in bunny costumes. Dozens of them. Entire families dress up like rabbits. It's pretty cool."

"Seriously?"

"How could I make that up?" she asked. "You're going to see the parade. And there's the Bonnet Brigade."

"I don't think I want to know what that is."

"Women in bonnets, of course. Some are handmade, a few are bought. They're all lovely. And huge."

"These aren't regular hats?"

"Not exactly. You'll have to see for yourself."

"I can't wait."

They walked down Katie Lane to Fourth and reached the park. Food vendors were set up along the parade route. They debated the traditional burger or hot dog versus more exotic street food.

"This is what my sister's been talking about," Fayrene said as they waited in line for the first elephant ears of the season. "Having a food cart of some kind."

"She's a chef, right?"

She nodded. "She found a trailer on eBay and is thinking of putting in a bid. She would have to remodel it pretty quickly to be up and running for the summer."

"Good for her. You come from a line of strong women."

"The town inspires us."

With their parents dying so unexpectedly, there hadn't been much choice. Either they would get strong and survive or be sucked under by grief.

Ryan handed her an elephant ear. The confection was still warm and covered with powdered sugar. She juggled the paper plate and napkin, then led the way to a bench in the sun. Although it was sunny, the temperatures were still cool in the shade.

"We probably should have started with something more nutritious," she said before taking a bite.

"So says the jelly bean queen."

She grinned. "I'm not their queen. It's more about worship."

He chuckled. "Tell you what. We'll have salad later."

"You're lying. Guys don't eat salad on purpose."

"Yeah, but saying it sounds good and, with luck, you'll forget."

"So you're playing me."

His humor faded. "I'd never do that, Fayrene."

She wanted to believe him. So far Ryan had shown himself to be one of the good guys, and she didn't want that to change. He was smart, handsome and single. Why wasn't he married? Or at least in a committed relationship?

"Did you have a girlfriend back home?" she asked.

He finished chewing and swallowed. "No. I dated in high school but nothing serious. I did have someone in college."

Fayrene would guess Ryan was only a couple of years older than her, which meant college hadn't been all that long ago.

"What happened?"

"We were engaged." He shrugged. "She cheated."

"I'm sorry," she said automatically. "How did you find out?"

"I was friends with the guy. One afternoon I went to go see him. It was strange because we didn't hang out all that often. I just wanted to go to his dorm room. Maybe subconsciously I sensed what was going on. I don't know. When I walked toward his door, she stepped out. They were kissing, and it was pretty obvious what they'd been doing."

She winced. "That's awful."

"I was heartbroken. She apologized and said it had been a onetime thing, but I didn't believe her."

Fayrene touched his arm. "I don't get it. Why cheat? Why not just break up?"

"That's what I said. She kept telling me I was the one. But we both knew she was lying. I ended things."

"Ever tempted to get back together with her?"

"No. I don't revisit the past. I graduated and moved on. I was recruited to work for a large alternative energy company in Kansas. I was there about three years. But it wasn't a good fit. I quit and went back home to think about what I wanted. I had a lot of interviews. Now there's a job waiting for me in Texas when I'm done here."

Because he was moving, she thought. That was the point of this. Ryan was safe because he wasn't permanent.

"You move around a lot," she said. "I haven't lived out of the state."

"I think I'm looking for where I want to settle down," he admitted.

They finished their elephant ears, then went and explored what was new at Morgan's Books. While the rest of the world had embraced e-readers, in Fool's Gold, Morgan's store was going strong.

Fayrene pointed out the display of books by local mystery author Liz Sutton, who was married to their mutual boss, Ethan. With Ryan's hand still holding hers, they made their way to the parade route.

The sidewalks were crowded with locals and tourists. People were setting up chairs and settling on curbs, waiting for the parade to start.

"The best place is back by the library," Fayrene told him as they walked back up Fourth. "You can sit on the stairs until it's time, then stand up and have a great view because of the elevation."

"Always with the plan."

She laughed. "My parents used to bring us here when we were kids. It's kind of a tradition."

"Are your sisters going to join us?" he asked.

"No. Ana Raquel is in San Francisco, and Dellina is working today."

They wouldn't be together long enough for him to meet her sisters, which was kind of too bad. She had a feeling both of them would like him.

He tugged her to a stop. People moved past them as Ryan stared into her eyes.

"Thank you for trusting me with the Hopkins family parade spot," he said, before lightly kissing her.

She leaned into him as she felt the warmth of his skin against herself. The touch was brief—just enough to get her tingling all over. Then he stepped back and they were walking again.

As Fayrene had promised, from the library steps they could see the whole street. There were bunting and flags. Religious symbols comfortably shared space with images of rabbits and eggs. Fool's Gold welcomed all, Ryan thought, sitting next to her as more people filled in around them.

The scent of barbecue mingled with the sweetness of spring flowers. Everywhere he looked there were families or groups of friends, all anticipating the parade to come.

"Which is first?" he asked. "The rabbits or the hats?"

"The rabbits. There are more kids in that part of the parade, and they don't wait well." She turned to him, her hazel eyes bright with amusement. "One year my parents rented bunny costumes for all of us and we were in the parade."

"I'd love to see the pictures."

"I could show them to you."

Her mouth tempted him, but he knew he couldn't indulge again. Every time he kissed Fayrene, he wanted to take things a little further. This was a family event, he thought with a grin. Having sex on the steps of Fool's Gold Public Library was out of the question.

"Where does a family of five rent rabbit costumes?" he asked.

"There's a costume and party store in town. They have a big storage facility filled with rabbit costumes. One year there was a fire in the warehouse, and everyone panicked. For a while we thought the costumes had been ruined. But they were fine. All they needed was a little airing out."

"I have this vision of the parade route being lined with clothes racks filled with rabbit costumes."

"It was the parking lot."

"I'm glad they were saved," he told her.

He still had her hand in his. He looked down and took in the sensible short nails and the absence of any rings. Fayrene wore earrings most days but didn't seem to feel the need to jingle and clink when she walked. There were no half-dozen bracelets or necklaces. For work she dressed professionally and for play…

He tried not to picture her heart-shaped butt in the tight jeans she wore today.

"What are you thinking?" she asked.

A question he couldn't answer, he told himself. Not honestly. "What happens in three or four years?" he asked instead. "When you have your business where you want it and you're ready to settle down. Are you planning on getting married?"

"I hope to," she told him. "I want the usual things. A husband, a couple of kids."

"Interesting, because I have no interest in a husband."

She laughed and leaned against him. "You know what I mean. I like the idea of being part of a family."

"Renting rabbit suits for the parade?"

"That would be fun. What about you?"

"The same. Except maybe for the rabbit suits. If I'm not in Fool's Gold, people will be confused." He put his arm around her. "My mom bugs me regularly for grandchildren. We have a lot of extended family up where they are. I spent summers with my grandparents pretty much until high school. She's already talking about when she has grandkids to spoil over the Fourth of July."

"That's a lot of pressure."

"I can handle it. Plus I'm the youngest, so she's really focusing on my older brothers. Jeff is married, but Neil isn't and is he going to be in trouble if he hits thirty without a bride."

He paused and kissed the top of her head. "Does it bother you to hear me talk about this?"

She looked up. "Because of my parents? No. It's nice. I think I'd like your mom."

"She's the one who holds us all together. My dad isn't much of a talker, so Mom was always the one who checked on us and made sure we were okay." He smiled as memories vied for his attention.

"When I was fifteen, I *borrowed* the farm truck and promptly plowed into a tree. My mom was hysterical, alternating between making sure I was going to be okay and trying to come up with ways to punish me. My dad told her he would handle it and led me to the barn."

Fayrene winced. "Did he hit you?"

"Not him. That would have been too easy. Instead he led me to where all the farm equipment was stored. It was dirty from the last hay harvest that had ended a few days before. He told me I had to clean all of it. By myself. And while I was doing it, there wasn't to be any music. I was to work in silence and think about what I'd done."

He remembered that discussion. "At the time I was furious. I thought my dad was being unfair. But by the time I was done, I'd learned my lesson. Both the punishment and the thinking had been good for me. I guess my dad thought so, too, because he came out the last couple of days and helped me."

She smiled at him. "Okay, I think I'd like your dad, too."

"He'd like you. He's always had a thing for blondes. And he is a big believer in schedules and organization."

She angled toward him so that their knees touched. "Why do you want to be away from them?"

"I don't. But you can't do what I do from Colville. I have some ideas for wind turbine design. I want to make them more efficient. I want to experiment with different blades. Small changes can make a big difference. For that I need a company—or at least their money."

"You're an artist rather than an entrepreneur," she said.

"An artist?" While he liked the sound of that, it wasn't exactly true. "I'm more a geek than an artist."

Her hazel eyes widened slightly. "I wouldn't say you're geeky."

"Thanks. You're right about the rest of it. I have no drive to open my own business. I don't like all the logistics that go with it. The day-to-day details aren't interesting. I'd rather spend my time with the design work or out in the field doing the testing."

"Not me," she told him. "I like all of it. I even like paying my bills. I use a computer program that keeps track of income and expenses. I can compare my monthly billing to my projects and see how much I'm growing. It's exciting."

She obviously meant what she said. Her eyes were bright, her pupils dilated. Desire grew, but he ignored the sensation of heat and hunger.

"You're strange," he told her.

She laughed. "I accept my failings."

"It's not a failing. It's kind of cute."

"You're kind of cute, too."

Her gaze promised while her mouth called. But they were surrounded by families, and the library steps were getting more crowded by the second.

He leaned close. "You're tempting, Fayrene. I'll give you that."

"I don't mean to be."

He tightened his hold on her hand. "Yes, you do."

She smiled. "Okay. Maybe just a little."

CHAPTER SIX

"HE'S CUTE," CHARITY Golden said as she arranged the bruschetta on a plate. "Is it serious?"

Fayrene picked up the bottle of red wine and two of the three glasses. "Yes, he's cute, and no, it's not serious."

Charity, a pretty woman with curly brown hair and a quick smile, laughed. "Okay, I'm sorry. I don't mean to pry. It's just you're an adorable couple."

As a thank-you for looking after Misty during the birthing process, Charity had invited Fayrene over to dinner and told her to bring a date. Fayrene had invited Ryan to join her. Now she was wondering if maybe that had been a mistake. Not that Ryan wasn't handsome, and he was great company. It's just now there were going to be lots and lots of questions.

"His stay in town is temporary," she said, because that made more sense to most people than her saying she was the one driving the "this is going nowhere" bus. Not that Ryan had said he wanted more. It was too soon for anyone to want more, and for all she knew he was into the fling idea as much as she.

"Enough said," Charity told her. "I can't imagine anyone wanting to leave Fool's Gold. I'm glad we're not going to lose you."

Charity had moved to town a few years ago. She was Mayor

Marsha's long-lost granddaughter. Charity had been hired as the city planner. Within a few months, she'd fallen in love with Josh and gotten pregnant. Now they were a happy family. Josh was a famous, now-retired cyclist. The town adored him for his easygoing ways as much as his athletic exploits. He also owned several businesses and made it a point to always give back.

Fayrene would never admit it to the man, but Josh had been a role model for her. She doubted she would ever have his net worth, but she admired and wanted to emulate his business practices.

Charity took the other wineglass along with the tray of bruschetta and led the way into the spacious living room. The guys were already seated on the sofa, arguing about whether the San Francisco Giants or Los Angeles Dodgers would have the better season.

The second Josh saw his wife, he stood and took the tray and glasses from her. He shifted on the large sectional so there was room for her next to him, and then set the tray on the oversize coffee table.

For a few seconds he looked at her as if there wasn't anyone else in the room. They'd been together three years, and they were still at the "in love" stage of their relationship. Fayrene felt her chest tighten a little. Because that's what she wanted—when she finally had the chance to settle down and start a family, she wanted it to be with a man she could be "in love" with for the rest of her life.

She took the chair next to the sofa and smiled at Ryan. "There's a pretty big divide in town between the Giants and the Dodgers. They're rivals, and people here are evenly split. While you're here, you're going to have to decide which camp you fall into."

"Hey, I'm from Washington State. I'm a Mariners fan."

Charity wrinkled her nose. "No way. If you insist on saying that, you're going to have to drink your wine on the porch."

Ryan chuckled. "This is a tough crowd."

"You have no idea," Josh told him.

Fayrene poured the wine while Charity passed around the plate of bruschetta.

"Where are the kids?" Fayrene asked, then turned to Ryan. "The Goldens have a son and a daughter."

"I'm a good breeder," Charity joked. "They're with my grandmother. Marsha loves her time with the kids. I swear, she'd take them every night if we asked."

"That's not going to happen," Josh told her. "We need those kids around." His expression filled with pride. "This is Hunter's first night away from us since being born last month."

"Are you panicked about him being gone?" Fayrene asked.

"A little nervous," Charity admitted. "But my grandmother is very capable, and it's time to get him used to going other places. We were pretty much cocooned here for the past couple of months, so I'm excited about having a social life again."

Fayrene started to pour wine into all four glasses. Charity stopped her.

"None for me. I'm still breast-feeding."

Josh got up and went into the kitchen. When he returned he had a glass of sparking water with a fresh wedge of lime. "For you," he said, handing it to his wife, then sitting beside her.

Ryan looked at Fayrene. "I checked in with Misty. She says hi."

"Did she? How's she doing?"

"Great. The kittens have their eyes open. You should see them before we leave."

"I'd like that."

"You can take a couple with you, if you want," Josh offered.

Charity patted his arm. "He doesn't mean that. He's a little overwhelmed with a newborn and kittens in the house at the same time."

"There's a moratorium on pregnancies," Josh muttered,

reaching for another piece of bruschetta. He glanced at Fayrene. "What are your plans for the summer?"

Ryan raised his eyebrows. "I don't think I like that question."

Josh looked confused while Fayrene and Charity laughed. Josh chuckled a second later.

"Sorry. I wasn't linking those topics. I've been meaning to call you," he told Fayrene. "There's going to be a summer program at my cycling school again. There are more people interested than there were last year. I was swamped then, and I don't know how I'm going to handle it this year."

"So he's made the decision not to," Charity said.

"She's right. I want to hire you to manage the whole program. Let's set up a meeting to figure out what I need done and how many hours it will take. The workload is pretty heavy."

"I can handle it," Fayrene told him, doing her best to sound confident. "I'll call you tomorrow and set up an appointment for us to talk."

"Thanks."

Talk turned to the rapidly approaching tourist season and how the number of festivals seemed to grow every year. Charity excused herself to check on dinner and Josh went with her.

Ryan touched Fayrene's arm. "You still with us?"

She'd been thinking about work rather than participating in the conversation. "It was obvious I wasn't listening?"

"Only to me. Was it the new job with Josh?"

She nodded and held on to his hand. "This is a big opportunity. Not just because it's going to be a lot of work, but because Josh knows everyone in town. He's really connected in the business community, so if he's happy with my work it could be a real boost to my business."

She thought about what she already had scheduled. "Wow—if he wants me more than fifteen hours a week, I'm going to have to hire someone part-time to help. That would be so great."

"I'm dating a tycoon."

"Not yet, but one day."

* * *

Fayrene sat cross-legged on her sister's sofa. Dellina stared toward the kitchen.

"She takes this too seriously. It's lunch." Dellina leaned back in her chair. "Why do you have to take this so seriously?" she yelled toward the kitchen.

"Because I'm talented and you're not appreciative enough," Ana Raquel yelled back.

Dellina cocked her head. "Really? So if I was more appreciative, you'd take this less seriously? You know that doesn't make sense."

An exasperated choking sound came from the kitchen. "You know what I meant," Ana Raquel yelled.

"I do, but it's not what you said."

Fayrene laughed. Being with her sisters always made her feel better. Dellina had been their rock ever since their parents had died. It had been the three of them dealing with the tragedy. While they'd always been close, the accident had drawn them even more together.

Now they were living their separate lives. While Dellina was in town, they were both busy, and Fayrene rarely saw her. Ana Raquel only got back every few weeks.

"Okay," her twin said, coming out with three plates balanced on her arm. "This is an experiment. I've made three different salads, and I want your honest opinion."

She handed them each a plate with three scoops of what looked like some kind of chicken or turkey salad, some cut up fruit and slices of French bread.

Looking at Ana Raquel was almost like looking in the mirror, Fayrene thought. They were both blondes with hazel eyes. Dellina had taken more after their father. She had brown hair and brown eyes. She was also the tallest of the sisters. Not that five-five was extraordinarily tall.

Ana Raquel picked up her fork. "Turkey salad with dried

cranberries and toasted walnuts. I think I'm almost there with this one, but I'm going to try to make it more creamy." She pointed to the second salad. "Curried chicken. It's perfect. If you don't like it, there's something wrong with you. Then a second chicken salad. No curry. I'm thinking it's the perfect picnic food."

Dellina studied the plate. "You want our honest opinions?"

"Yes."

Fayrene took a bite and felt her taste buds do the happy dance. "Delicious. You should really get serious about that trailer. Wouldn't you rather be working for yourself instead of in a restaurant?"

"Yes, but a trailer is expensive. I don't have enough of a credit history to get that much in financing, and I would still need money to remodel it."

Dellina scooped turkey salad onto the bread. "Want some of the money from the trust fund?"

They each had money left over from their parents' life insurance policies. It had paid for college and Ana Raquel's culinary school with some left over. Dellina had invested it wisely, and they were all benefiting.

"Fayrene has a point. Wouldn't you rather work for yourself? You could rent a small place here in town. Your share of the house lease could cover most of your living expenses." Dellina studied her sister. "I'm not pushing, I'm offering."

"Remember, I took a loan against the trust, and it's really helped me," Fayrene said. "I'm making a payment every month, paying back principal and interest."

"I've thought about, but I'm not sure." Ana Raquel sighed. "I have so many ideas. I love the idea of street food, but starting my own thing is scary." She smiled at them. "Not that you two haven't already done it."

"Being your own boss is a trip," Dellina said. "I was hired by Clay Stryker to plan his wedding, then fired by his bride-to-be, who informed me she doesn't want a big wedding."

Fayrene shook her head. "It's been what? Nine months since they got together? They need a plan."

"They'll come up with one," Dellina said. "But there are days I think a nice office job would be a whole lot easier."

"Not many," Fayrene told her.

Dellina grinned. "That's true."

Ana Raquel drew in a breath. "Let me get some numbers together. Maybe I could get a loan and use some of the trust fund money. That way I still have some put away for an emergency."

Because they'd all learned that life was nothing if not uncertain.

Fayrene took a bite of the curried chicken and moaned. "I love this."

"See?" Ana Raquel's expression turned smug. "Now imagine that in a very soft crustless bread at high tea. Delicious."

"You don't get to have a trailer and a teahouse," Dellina told her. "You have to pick."

"You mean it's time to settle down?" Ana Raquel asked, then turned to Fayrene. "So who's the guy I keep hearing about?"

Fayrene speared a strawberry and did her best not to blush. "You've been back in town fifteen minutes. How do you know about any guy?"

"I have sources. As long as it's not Greg Clary."

Dellina rolled her eyes. "Seriously? Are you still obsessing about him?"

"I don't obsess. The man is annoying. He's been annoying since the second grade."

"Ignore her," Fayrene said, having listened to literally *years* of her sibling's complaints about Greg. "She's secretly in love with him, and one day when she's mature enough, she'll admit it."

"I totally agree," Dellina said.

Ana Raquel shook her head. "I can't hear either of you." She turned to her twin. "And don't think I didn't notice how you changed the subject when I asked about your guy."

"I didn't mean to." Fayrene thought about Ryan.

"Oooh, did you see that?" Ana Raquel asked. "There was definite glowing."

"I saw it," Dellina dug her fork into the turkey salad. "I thought you weren't getting serious about anyone for years? You have a plan."

"We're not serious, and I do have a plan. We're just having fun. He's not staying in town permanently, so nothing is going to happen."

Although when he kissed her, she felt a lot of potential.

"It's a fling," she added. "Temporary and fun."

"Sounds dangerous to me," Ana Raquel said. "What starts out as something simple can get complicated really quickly."

"She would know," Dellina teased. "She's been in a long-term relationship since the second grade."

Ana Raquel groaned. "I'm serious. I really, really don't like Greg Clary."

"Uh-huh," Fayrene told her. "Keep telling yourself that and maybe one day it will be true."

CHAPTER SEVEN

"I'M IMPRESSED," ETHAN SAID, studying the data they'd downloaded from the computer system linked to the wind turbines.
"The data is consistent. There's an average of a twenty percent
increase in generating power without any increase in wind.
You're getting more electricity from the same wind."

Ryan nodded. "That was the goal."

His boss looked at him. "Okay, I'll admit it. I didn't think it
could be done."

Ryan grinned. "You didn't think I was that good."

"I'd hoped, but you're right. I lacked faith. Not anymore.
If your designs are half as efficient as the tests show, this is a
game changer." Ethan checked the computer, then turned back
to him. "I'd like you to stay on permanently. Is that an option?"

Ryan didn't try to conceal his surprise. "I didn't think you
wanted to take on research. It's not cheap."

"I don't have unlimited resources, but the company's doing
well and I have some wealthy investors."

Ryan wondered if Josh was one of them.

"You'd have access to our customers' facilities for testing.
I've talked to most of them already, and they're interested. Plus,
we'd share a percentage on any licensing of patents."

That got Ryan's attention. Generally when an employee developed technology while working for a company, the company owned the patent and any income derived from it. After all, developing the technology was the job description. If a product did well, there could be a bonus of some kind, but that was it. To be offered a percentage was significant. Over time, that could be real money. Assuming Ryan was able to come up with something they could market.

"I'm intrigued," Ryan admitted. "Give me a couple of days to think about it?"

"Sure. Get back to me Monday. If you're interested, we'll talk numbers. In the meantime, why don't you go look at houses in town? Check out the town and see if this is somewhere you'd enjoy living."

"I will."

There was also someone he wanted to talk to. Someone who made the idea of sticking around even sweeter. Only Fayrene had a plan, and he wasn't sure how she would react when he told her he might not be a short-term fling after all.

Fayrene looked at her dining room table and nodded with satisfaction. Dellina had sent her specific instructions on how to set up the table to look both romantic and casual. Apparently it was all about the layers. A tablecloth with a runner and placemats, done in pretty colors. She'd added a few flameless candles and some fresh flowers.

In the kitchen, the salads were done and she'd prepared chicken with mushrooms and white wine. For the meal, she'd called Ana Raquel. Her twin had sent her several recipes that were delicious but didn't challenge Fayrene's undeveloped cooking ability. Or as her sister had put it: "Even you can't mess these up."

Fayrene hoped her sister was right. She wanted Ryan to relax and maybe have a bit too much wine. Because she'd made a decision—tonight she was going to seduce him.

It had been several weeks of fun dates and interesting conversation. Plenty of hand-holding and light kisses. If he was trying to seduce her with his warm eyes and gentle touch, he'd done a heck of a job. She was primed. Beyond primed. She was antsy and hungry, and she wasn't talking about dinner.

But the meal was an important part of her plan. She was going to lull him, feed him and then rip off his clothes. She'd thought ahead enough to have a box of condoms waiting in her nightstand drawer.

She'd chosen her outfit carefully. She wanted to look pretty and sexy without being obvious. There was also the issue of being easily undressable. To that end she'd picked a sleeveless blouse and a skirt. They were feminine, and there weren't any hidden closures. She'd painted her toes, used scented body lotion and put on a matching thong and bra set. While she didn't actually like wearing a thong, desperate times and all that.

Now she glanced at the clock. Three minutes to six. Ryan was always on time—yet another characteristic she liked about him. He would be here and they would kiss.

Just the thought of his firm, teasing mouth on hers had her thighs heating, but she knew she couldn't dwell on the image of his large hands roaming her body. There was a meal to get through. She wouldn't think about him cupping her breasts or the feel of his mouth on her tight, aching—

The doorbell rang.

She jumped and hurried toward it. Ryan stood on the tiny porch of her small apartment. She smiled and let him in.

"Hi," she said as she raised herself up on tiptoe to kiss him.

"Hi, yourself."

He handed her a bag of jelly beans.

"Fruit only," he teased.

She laughed, but before she could say anything, he kissed her. Just one soft brush that had her nerve endings swooning. Did they really have to have dinner? Maybe if she shrugged out of her shirt he would get the message and simply take her right there on the entryway floor. Or they could move to the sofa. She'd never done it on the sofa, but she'd seen scenes in movies and it looked doable for ordinary people. She was less sure about the whole standing, him supporting her position, although at this point, she wasn't about to be picky.

"Something smells good," he said.

For a second she thought he meant her, but then she remembered the simmering entrée. "I hope it lives up to the hype. Come on. I have some wine."

"Wine would be good."

She went into the kitchen to pull the bottle out of the refrigerator. He followed, which made her eye the counters. They could do it in here, she thought. They were the right height and—

"Fayrene, I need to talk to you."

Something in his tone had her turning around to look at him. His dark eyes were serious, his expression almost stern. Desire fled, leaving behind worry. Something had happened, she thought, putting down the bottle of wine. Something important.

Possibilities crowded her brain. He was leaving sooner than he'd planned. He didn't want to see her anymore. He'd found someone else.

In that moment, with her stomach writhing and her chest tight, she understood that Ryan leaving was going to be more difficult for her than she'd planned. That while he was supposed to be a fling, he'd somehow become a little bit more. Okay, a lot more. While she'd been busy having fun with him, she'd also been falling in love.

"What is it?" she asked, her lips suddenly dry.

He moved toward her and took her hands in his. "Ethan offered me a job. Full-time. He wants me to stay in Fool's Gold."

She pulled free of his hold and stared at him. "A job here? You're not leaving?"

"I haven't decided yet. I wanted to talk to you about it."

Relief battled with fury. Because she knew what would happen. She was going to have to give up *her* dream. She was going to get married before she was ready and somehow her business wouldn't get off the ground and she would never have her four employees and it was all Ryan's fault.

One corner of his mouth turned up. "Whatever you're thinking, you have to stop. I can hear the wheels turning from here."

"No," she said, stomping her foot. "It's not fair. I have a plan, and while that might seem silly to you, it's really important to me. I want to get my business going. I want to be successful."

She paused for air. "I'm not stupid. I get all the psychological reasons. I lost my parents when I was young. It was horrible and unexpected and ever since then I've tried to control everything so I never feel so out of control again. So what? It's my emotional scar, and I accept it. I want to start my business."

She consciously lowered her voice to something slightly less shrill. "It's not that I don't like you. I do. A lot. But that's not the point. You have to do what you have to do. It's your decision. But I don't want you to go and I'm scared of what will happen if you stay. I'll get distracted by you and my feelings. We'll get really serious and then we'll get married and there will be kids and what about my career? What about what I want? Because when people get married, the woman is usually the one who compromises. I don't want to lose my dream because of some guy. Even if that guy is you."

She pressed her lips together and replayed her outburst. Heat burned her cheeks as she realized that, yes, she had discussed them getting married *and* having children, all while saying that wasn't going to work for her, when all he'd done was tell her Ethan had offered him a job.

"I have to go throw up," she said, spinning toward the bathroom.

He reached for her and pulled her close. "You're a handful—you know that."

At least he wasn't running, she told herself. So maybe she hadn't scared him too much. His arms felt good around her. Warm and strong and safe.

He eased her toward the living room, then settled her on

the sofa. He sat next to her, her hand in his, his gaze locked on her face.

"Let's take your concerns one at a time," he said.

"Oh, let's not." She touched her cheek with her free fingers. "I shouldn't have said all that."

He shook his head. "One of the things I admire most about you is how determined you are and how honest. You say what you think. I *want* you to be honest."

He gave her a gentle smile. "I know your goals are important to you. I understand you need to be successful and I'm impressed you're self-aware enough to know why. We're both young, so there's no reason to move fast in this relationship."

"Are you talking emotionally or about sex?" she blurted out before she could stop herself. "Because I'm open to…"

Another blush flared.

His eyebrows rose. "Sex, huh?"

She thought about the back part of the thong digging into her butt. "You have no idea," she muttered.

"Good. We'll get to that in a second. But let's finish up with my job offer. Do you love me?"

She bit her lip and gathered all her courage, then nodded slowly. Admitting it while calm was much scarier than announcing it in the heat of a rant.

"I love you, too. I think you're the most intriguing woman I've ever met. But you need to focus on your business, and I need to get settled with Ethan. Why don't we do this—we'll date exclusively for the next three years. Then I'll propose. We'll be engaged for a year and get married when you're twenty-eight."

Emotions flooded her. Warm, happy feelings that had her blinking to hold back tears. "You'd do that for me?"

"I'd do anything for you, Fayrene. I'm going to spend the rest of my life proving that to you."

She flung herself at him. He caught her and held her close. His mouth claimed hers with a kiss that promised her his heart.

He slipped his hand to her knee and moved his fingers up the back of her thigh.

"Now about this sex thing," he said, his voice teasing.

Then he reached the top of her thigh and the absence of panties. His whole body stiffened. She opened her eyes and found him staring at her. He swore under his breath.

"What are you wearing under that?"

She smiled. "I'm not sure I should tell you."

"You could show me instead."

"I suppose I could. But what about dinner?"

He stood and pulled her to her feet. "Dinner can wait," he muttered as he guided her into the tiny hall and toward the only bedroom.

Later, when they'd made love and eaten the only slightly ruined dinner and had the wine, he took her in his arms again. "I don't know how I got so lucky," he told her. "Finding you like this."

She smiled, bubbling with happiness. "It was all part of a plan."

* * * * *

Her Texas Renegade

Joanne Rock

DESIRE

Scandalous world of the elite.

Joanne Rock credits her decision to write romance after a book she picked up during a flight delay engrossed her so thoroughly that she didn't mind at all when her flight was delayed two more times. Giving her readers the chance to escape into another world has motivated her to write over eighty books for a variety of Harlequin series.

Books by Joanne Rock

Dynasties: Mesa Falls

The Rebel
The Rival
Rule Breaker
Heartbreaker

Texas Cattleman's Club: Inheritance

Her Texas Renegade

Visit her Author Profile page at
millsandboon.com.au,
or joannerock.com, for more titles.

Dear Reader,

It's always a thrill to return to Royal, Texas, where passions run high and romance is around every corner. I found so much to admire about Miranda Dupree, a heroine who has been misjudged by the world and disappointed by her marriage. Underneath all her fierce ambition, she has a huge heart.

And that's something she needs to protect around tech wizard Kai Maddox! Just when she thought no one could ever tempt her to love again, she's faced with the man who broke her heart—and maybe the *only* man who stands a chance of fixing it.

I hope you'll enjoy the conclusion to the Texas Cattleman's Club: Inheritance series, and please don't forget to visit me at joannerock.com.

Happy reading,

Joanne Rock

For Marcie Robinson,
whose books I can't wait to read.

PROLOGUE

Five months ago

MIRANDA DUPREE BLACKWOOD took deep breaths before the
meeting with her ex-stepchildren where they would learn
the contents of Buckley Blackwood's last will and testament.
Miranda had flown from her home in New York City to Royal,
Texas, because of Buck's highly unorthodox last wishes. Knowing what her wily ex-husband had planned for today made her
ill, but she understood the role he wanted her to play, and she
wasn't going to turn her back on it.

"Are you sure you want to be there for this?" Kace LeBlanc,
Buckley's lawyer, asked her as the hour drew near for the meeting that she imagined would be like facing a firing squad. "You
don't have to attend in person."

Miranda was upstairs in her former marital home, Blackwood Hollow, where she was trying to make herself comfortable again after a three-year absence. Kace had been kind to
stop by early to check in with her. She'd received the attorney
in the upstairs den, the space she'd used as her office during her
marriage to the wealthy finance mogul. So much had changed
since she'd left Royal after her divorce. One thing that remained
the same, however, was the animosity of her adult stepchildren,

who would soon hate her more than ever once they understood the terms of their father's will.

"I'm committed," she assured herself as much as Kace, knowing that behind Buckley's unconventional strategy, his heart had been in the right place when he set up his terms. "I just wish he didn't have to be so damned secretive about his motives."

Kace shook his head, pacing in front of one of the windows overlooking the front gates of the sprawling ranch estate. "I urged him to make peace with his kids before his death, but he insisted this was the only way. You know how tough it was to argue with him."

How well she remembered. Miranda hugged herself tighter, bracing for the role she would have to play over the next few months until Buck's real motives made themselves apparent.

She'd had zero interaction with the Blackwood family since leaving Royal. Which, no doubt, was how all three of Buck's grown children preferred it. Their combined venom toward Miranda for marrying their wealthy father in the first place hadn't subsided, not even when she left the marriage behind without taking anything of the Blackwood estate with her. She'd walked away with the same assets that she'd entered into the union, thanks to an ironclad prenup that they'd both wanted. Miranda did just fine for herself, and she preferred it that way.

"It's going to be a rough few months," she murmured, seeing a glint through the front window and guessing that the guests were already starting to arrive for the meeting. "I'll do my best to support Buckley's wishes, but you know there may be an uprising in the office once you tell them what the will says."

"I'm aware," Kace told her grimly, turning away from the window. "Just remember that Buckley believed in you. He saw what you were doing with Goddess and he was impressed. He knew you'd be a good steward for his estate until his kids are ready to take over."

She nodded, taking some comfort from that, at least. If only the family knew that they would receive their inheritances eventually. That one day, Miranda would hand everything back to the Blackwoods once each of his children was more settled. From the bank to the house, none of it would remain hers, although Buckley had donated an incredibly generous sum to her charity, Girl to the Nth Power, for her time and trouble in overseeing the distribution of his estate. She was humbled by the trust he'd placed in her, even if she hated that he was being so secretive with his true heirs.

Buckley may not have been the best husband, but he'd always supported her efforts to build her own business and their split had been amicable. Without his encouragement, she might not have driven her Goddess line of health and lifestyle centers into the level of nationwide success they now experienced. She'd pushed her way onto the *Forbes* list last year.

Now that she would be staying in Royal for at least the next several months, she had told her producer she couldn't be in New York when filming started for a new season of *Secret Lives of NYC Ex-Wives*, a reality show that had spurred the Goddess brand to huge new heights.

But Nigel had told her not to worry. She had a feeling he was making plans to film the show down here if he could talk her castmates into making the move. Which would bring a whole other level of chaos to an already complicated time in her life.

Still, she was going to forge ahead. First she just needed to get through today. Buckley Blackwood was about to deliver a devastating blow to his offspring, robbing them of everything he'd promised since they were children.

A cold sweat dotted Miranda's head. Buckley's children had called her the "step-witch" when she'd joined the family. What would they think of her today when they learned their father had left every shred of their inheritance to her?

CHAPTER ONE

Present Day

MIRANDA HAD HOPED today's brunch could be a girls-only affair for her friends from the *Secret Lives of NYC Ex-Wives* show, but producer Nigel Townshend had convinced her he needed some footage at a more intimate gathering. Since the show had started filming in Royal, Texas, thanks to Miranda being tied to the town, their schedule had been packed with big, glitzy parties.

Especially engagement parties. Romance seemed to be in the air in Royal. Her stepson Kellan was now married with a baby on the way. Kellan's sister, Sophie, had married Miranda's producer, Nigel, just a few weeks ago. Their brother Vaughn had just gotten engaged, as had two of Miranda's castmates. And Darius Taylor-Pratt, her new business associate, had managed to find love, too—after he'd come to town to learn the stunning news that he was Buck's illegitimate son. The discovery had been a shock, but the love he'd found—or rather, rediscovered—with his former sweetheart, Audra, had softened the blow.

Weddings were all anyone wanted to discuss anymore. Even now, Miranda's castmate Lulu Shepard used the time as an opportunity to discuss plans for her nuptials to Kace LeBlanc, Buckley's lawyer.

"Do you have a venue in mind for the wedding, Lu?" Miranda asked her newly engaged costar.

They were seated at a table under the extended eaves that shaded the outdoor entertaining area near the guesthouse pool at Blackwood Hollow. In the five months that Miranda had spent in Royal since the reading of the will, she'd come to feel even more at home here than she had during her marriage to Buckley. Now that she and Kace had told the siblings about how their father had actually chosen to divide up his estate, her work here was almost done. That was why she was staying in the guesthouse at the ranch—the property belonged to Kellan and his wife now. She'd been surprised and touched when he'd invited her to stay in the guesthouse for as long as she needed while she wrapped things up in Royal. Her real inheritance had been the opportunity to mend her relationships with the Blackwood heirs, something she'd genuinely enjoyed.

Even if it involved enough weddings and engagements to make the most reluctant romantic a little envious.

"You *have* to marry in New York," Rafaela Marchesi announced, flipping dark, cascading waves over one shoulder to ensure her good side was visible to the camera. A five-time divorcee on the hunt for husband number six, Rafaela thrived on troublemaking and she played the diva for all it was worth. "Bring the party back where we belong."

Henry the cameraman lingered on the resident diva while Sam swiveled his second camera for a reaction shot from Lulu.

"No." Lulu tilted her champagne glass in Rafaela's direction, pointing it at her and showing off her amazeballs new diamond at the same time. "We're getting married in Royal, that much I know."

"Good," Miranda interjected, not wanting the brunch to turn into a snipe-fest. Audiences might love that kind of thing, but Miranda wouldn't let popular demand turn Lulu's wedding preparations into nonstop bickering. "It's only fitting to celebrate here when it all began in Royal for you two lovebirds."

Never let it be said Miranda didn't have a soft side, even if romance hadn't worked out well for her. She and Buckley had split on friendly enough terms, but the dissolution of her marriage still felt like a failure on her part. And lately, her thoughts were full of the man who'd held her heart before Buck.

Kai Maddox, the cybersecurity expert she needed to review the digital encryption measures at Blackwood Bank. No doubt that's why her long-ago lover had taken up residence in her brain this week after years of doing her best to forget him. Well, that and the fact that they'd shared a searing kiss the first time she'd asked for his professional help—right before he'd refused her outright. She'd have to swallow her pride and try asking him again. He might have a sketchy past, but no one could argue the man excelled at his job. Besides, his new company, Madtec, was local, based in nearby Deer Springs, where he'd grown up.

"Cheers to being a Texas bride, Lu." Zooey Kostas, the youngest one of the ex-wives at thirty years old, lifted her glass to toast their friend, her diamond-encrusted bangles sliding down her slender wrist. Her honey-colored hair and green eyes gave her a fresh-faced appeal in spite of her hard-partying ways. "I want you to get married here anyway."

The five women at the table, including Seraphina "Fee" Martinez, who was also due to marry a local, lifted their glasses automatically to toast the bride. Miranda sipped her mimosa, savoring the fresh-squeezed oranges even more than the champagne, while Rafaela rolled her eyes.

"Zooey, darling, you've lost your mind," Rafaela declared, leaning in and piling on the drama for a good sound bite. "Why should we waste ourselves on cowboys in the Lone Star State when we can have our pick of Wall Street billionaires in Manhattan?"

Miranda slouched in her seat, so done with Rafaela Marchesi. Was this what her life had amounted to, trading barbs with frenemies over cocktails?

Lulu looked ready to fire off a comeback, but Zooey surprised them all with a wicked laugh that bordered on a cackle.

"Waste ourselves? You're just jealous you haven't bagged a rich Texan the way Lulu and Fee have." Zooey tossed her napkin on the table and then stood, her cream-colored halter pantsuit draping beautifully as she moved. "Excuse me, ladies, but I've lost my appetite."

The sudden diva-exit was so un-Zooey-like that Miranda and Lulu turned to one another at the same time, with Lulu looking as shocked as Miranda felt.

"Bitch," Rafaela muttered, studying her manicure. "Clearly, she's not getting laid enough if she's acting like such a shrew."

Miranda smothered a laugh while Lulu went back to brainstorming good places to exchange vows with Kace. No doubt the production team had filmed all the footage they needed for this week's episode anyway. And since the show had plenty of juicy moments for viewers, maybe Miranda stood a chance of sneaking away from the camera crew and Blackwood Hollow for the afternoon.

She needed to meet with Kai Maddox sooner rather than later to convince him to take on Blackwood Bank as a client, even though thinking about another confrontation with her former flame tied her in knots. What had she been thinking to allow that damned kiss to happen in the first place? Kai was the only man to ever shred her restraint so thoroughly.

Now that Vaughn knew he'd inherited the bank, it was time to pass everything over to him officially—but first, she needed someone to check into the irregularities she'd noticed while going over the books. She owed it to Buckley's family to pass over the reins of the company in good standing, especially now that she was only just starting to form real relationships with them. But she had no intention of letting her television audience see her fork up a bite of humble pie with her sexy-as-sin ex-lover to ask for his help.

Again.

He'd practically thrown her out on the street the last time she'd approached him. Right after the kiss that set her on fire every time she remembered it. Things were going to be complicated with Kai.

Assuming she even made it past the front door of Madtec.

This time, she'd simply have to make him an offer he couldn't refuse.

Kai Maddox strode across the rooftop terrace of Madtec's recently built headquarters in Deer Springs, lingering near the half wall and glass partition that overlooked the parking area as his afternoon meeting broke up. A light breeze blew from the west, but it did little to cool the afternoon heat. Soon, the days would be too warm for terrace meetings, but Kai planned to take advantage of the outdoor spot for as long as he could, knowing the benefit of fresh air and green space. He'd learned to make his health and mental wellness a priority since his teen years when he'd all but fallen into his computer screen, spending every waking moment honing his skills as a coder, a developer and, yes—occasionally—as a hacker.

Nothing prepared a coder for building the best digital encryption quite as well as breaking down someone else's.

Madtec had moved into its Deer Springs location shortly after the new year, as soon as work crews had finished the custom-designed, high-tech office building. With five floors and the rooftop terrace, it was more square footage than the Maddox brothers currently needed for their growing tech business, but the cost of real estate here was reasonable and Kai had faith that Madtec would only grow.

Even if he didn't return Miranda Dupree's phone calls. He was doing just fine without taking business from a woman who'd dumped him the moment someone richer came along.

"Did you need anything else, Kai?" his personal assistant called to him from the steel-beam pavilion in the middle of the rooftop as he packed up his notes and tablet. Amad was new to the job, but the guy was efficient and eager to learn.

"No, thank you. I've got a meeting with Dane soon, but first I'm going to review the data penetration tests again." Kai and his brother, Dane, had new fraud-protection software almost ready to take to market, but first he'd asked his old hacking buddies to try to crack it.

So far, the issues in the software they'd uncovered had been minor, but he wanted to ask for one more opinion. He refused to rush the product to market without thorough testing.

"Sure thing, boss." Amad jammed everything in a leather binder and headed for the door leading back into the building, but he paused to look down at his phone before opening it. "The main desk says you have someone here to see you. Miranda Dupree? She's not on your schedule."

He cursed silently.

Miranda had cornered him at his hotel in New York last month and things had spiraled out of control fast. How he'd ended up kissing her was still a mystery to him, but that's just what had happened, even though he'd spent ten years hating her.

As much as he would have preferred to ignore her forever in light of their nasty breakup a decade ago, Kai suspected the knee-jerk reaction would be too damned self-indulgent. Bad enough that he'd been ignoring her calls. Now that she'd shown up in person, sending her away would be too visible, and might reflect badly on the company. She was a respected business-woman. She'd made the *Forbes* list. He would at least do her the courtesy of a meeting before he refused whatever the hell she wanted from him.

"I'll meet her in my office," he said, deciding the quickest way to end this would be face-to-face—and one-on-one. He sure as hell didn't want anyone else around to see the chemistry that still sparked between them. "You can send her up in five."

"Will do." Amad shoved his phone in his pocket before he left the rooftop.

Kai followed him down to the penthouse office a few moments later. He shared the top floor with Dane, the two copresident suites separated by an executive conference room. Both Maddox brothers had private terraces on opposite sides of the building. On a clear day, Kai could see the roof of the humble house where he'd grown up.

There were a lot of unhappy memories in Deer Springs, but some good ones, too—and the hope for more in the future. Madtec had brought hundreds of jobs to the community that had shaped him, and that gave him a lot of satisfaction. Far more than he was going to get from this meeting with Miranda.

By the time Kai arrived in his office through the private back entrance, Amad was just opening the double doors to admit his guest in the front.

And damn, but she still had a potent effect on him.

Her fiery-red hair was cut just above her shoulders, with her curls tamed so that her hair swooped over one eye. She was dressed in a fitted black suit that showed off her figure— although not quite as much as the strapless red dress he'd seen her in last time. That dress had been... Damn.

Fantasy worthy. He was grateful to today's suit for covering more of her. She remained toned and athletic thanks to her lifelong commitment to yoga, and she had the lean limbs of a dancer. But her generous curves were more the pinup variety, giving her a silhouette that made men of all ages stop and stare. Including him, damn it.

He forced his gaze to her ice-blue eyes.

"Hello, Kai. Thank you for seeing me on such short notice." She smiled warmly at Amad before Kai's assistant left the room.

"You didn't leave me much choice," he informed her shortly, gesturing to one of the two wingbacks in front of his desk. "Please, have a seat."

She disregarded the offer, remaining on her feet as he did. Even in heels she was half a foot shorter than him, but her cool demeanor still commanded attention and exuded authority along with her smoking-hot sexiness.

She'd gained confidence along with over-the-top wealth from her marriage to Buckley Blackwood. Besides a national fitness empire and popular television series, he was certain that Miranda had access to a level of financial support that Kai had to wrestle and scrabble for from investors. The Blackwood name had unlocked a whole world for her. Kai's courtship, on the other hand, had consisted mostly of diner dates and motorcycle rides whenever he'd had a free moment from the endless stream of work that had claimed most of his time.

"You could have ignored me, the way you've snubbed my phone messages." She peered around the office.

He'd purposely kept it clutter-free and impersonal, a mostly soundproof haven for him to think. The walls were all gray stone except for the windows behind the desk. Lights ringed the tray ceiling, hidden in the molding to mimic the effect of daylight at any hour. His desk was glass-topped with steel underneath. Industrial and functional. He wondered briefly how it looked through her eyes.

If he was being honest, he wondered how *he* looked through her eyes, too. Ten years ago, he'd been knee-deep with the old hacker crowd, and skirting the law as he unraveled the most complex facets of data encryption. Miranda had been older than him, with a drive and ambition he admired and an ease with her sensuality that he'd found sexy as hell.

But she'd turned her back on him the moment she met Buckley Blackwood and his millions. And he wasn't about to take a trip down memory lane with her, even if memories of that rogue kiss in New York had put her in his thoughts all too often lately.

"Deer Springs is a small town, Miranda." He rounded the desk to stand closer to her, noting the way her eyes followed him. "I wasn't about to feed the local rumor mill with stories about me refusing to see the town's most illustrious native."

She laughed but it was a brittle sound. "Please. Deer Springs is practically Silicon Valley compared to Sauder Falls."

He'd forgotten she was technically from the next town over, a fact never referenced in her bio since Sauder Falls was a dingier town that had never recovered from a mill closing many years prior. When they'd met, Miranda had been working part-time at a diner in Deer Springs while she ran a local yoga studio and gave classes at another fitness center in Royal. Her big dreams and hard work to achieve them had captivated him since he understood that thirst to do something more.

"Nevertheless, your name is well-known around here." He was close enough to her to catch a hint of her fragrance, the same scent that made him think of night-blooming flowers. The sooner he sent her on her way, the better. There wouldn't be any surprise kisses this time. "And now that you've got your audience, what is it you want from me? I thought I made it clear I wasn't interested in doing business with you the last time we met."

Her lips compressed into a thin line at the reminder of their last meeting. After the kiss that had been so damned unexpected, he'd recovered by assuring her he wouldn't so much as cross the street for her anymore. Harsh? Not considering the way she'd dumped him.

No sense pretending they had much to say to one another anymore.

"I'm temporarily managing Blackwood Bank," she began, coming straight to the point as she tilted her chin. "And I need to update the security before I pass over the reins to the Blackwood heirs. You wouldn't be doing business with me so much as with the Blackwoods."

Surprise registered. He'd thought maybe she wanted help with Goddess, her line of fitness studios. Blackwood Bank was a client of a whole different caliber. Encryption for a financial institution was extremely complex. It might have been tempting, if not for the woman who made the offer.

She was tempting, too. But in all the wrong ways when he needed to focus on his business.

"But as you pointed out, you're managing the bank right now. You honestly expect me to work for you?" Folding his arms, he leaned against his desk. Waiting. Willing his thoughts to stay on business and his boots to stay firmly planted.

No touching. No thinking about touching.

Even though the pulse at the base of her throat leaped frantically, drawing his eye and making him wonder what would happen if he ran his tongue over that very place. He'd be willing to bet she'd burst into flames. But then, he would too, and he'd be damned if that happened.

"Not for *me*. For the bank." Opening her purse, she removed a manila folder and placed it on his desk. The movement put her body in dangerously enticing proximity to his. "I have a contract ready, but if the terms aren't to your liking—"

"No." He didn't need to look at the terms.

"No?" She left the folder on the desk and her blue eyes met his. "Kai, this is a very good offer. The bank deserves the kind of data protection your company specializes in, and since you're local—"

"Madtec is busy." He was being abrupt. Borderline unprofessional. But he didn't like the way she affected him and didn't intend to tempt fate by spending any more time together than was absolutely necessary.

She gripped the leather of her designer purse tighter, her short nails and simple French manicure oddly reminding him she wasn't quite as high maintenance as the other women on her reality television show. There was still something more down-to-earth about Miranda.

Not that he'd ever watched more than a two-minute clip.

"I understand," she told him finally, inclining her head with the grace of a medieval queen. "But I'll leave the contract here and hope you'll reconsider. Perhaps Dane would feel differently."

Dane would kick his ass for turning down a client like Blackwood Bank. But Kai said nothing.

Realizing he was probably staring her down like a street thug, Kai shook off the frustration and straightened.

"Thank you for thinking of us," he said with too much formality, ready to get back to his work. "My assistant can show you out."

Not that Miranda Dupree had ever needed help walking away.

"I could assign someone else to be the point person for the bank." She tossed out the compromise, clearly sensing he wasn't going to budge. "You'd never have to see me once you agreed to the job."

He wasn't about to let her see that the offer had appeal. He managed a cool smile. "Afraid you'd end up in my bed again if we worked together, Miranda?"

"Not at all." She folded her arms and peered up at him like she knew exactly what he was thinking. "Are you, Kai?"

She let the question hang between them for a long moment before she turned on her heel and walked out of his office with the same quiet confidence that had accompanied her through the doors in the first place. Kai didn't breathe again until she was out of sight. And hell, he couldn't help but wonder if she had a point. Because she still tempted him like no woman he'd ever known.

Even if he couldn't trust her.

Shoving aside the contract she'd left behind, he pulled out his laptop from a hidden drawer in one gray stone wall, and got to work.

Humble pie tasted even worse when choked down with no results.

Miranda fumed on her way out of the Madtec offices, thoroughly irritated with herself for wasting time driving to Deer Springs only to have Kai Maddox reject her offer without even stirring himself to look at it. He'd been more concerned with making sure she knew how easily he could ignite the old attraction between them.

And she couldn't very well dispute it. The heat rolled off him in waves, melting her defenses like they'd never been there in the first place.

She took the stairs—she preferred stairs whenever possible to up her steps, especially when there was anger to be stomped out—and was surprised to discover the Madtec stairwell seemed to be designed for employee wellness. Motivational phrases were painted on the walls, and the stairs were wide enough to accommodate several people at once. There was even a "runners' lane" painted in red to one side. With vinyl walls and ventilation fans, the staircase implemented some of the same techniques she used in her fitness centers to keep the space clean and well aired.

And how frustrating was it to find something to admire about Kai when she wanted to stay furious with him?

"Ms. Dupree?" A young woman with a swinging ponytail yanked her earbuds free as she locked eyes with Miranda and halted on her way up the steps. "I love your show so much. Is it true the *Secret Lives of NYC Ex-Wives* is leaving Royal soon? It's been so fun seeing sites close to home on TV."

"Thank you." Miranda smiled warmly, knowing the importance of connecting positively with viewers who invested their time in the program. "We will be filming in Royal for at least a few more weeks," assuming Lulu and the show's production team could pull together a big wedding in time, "but next season we'll be returning to New York."

"We'll really miss you," the woman said sincerely, digging in her messenger bag and pulling out a pen and paper. "Especially since you grew up around here and have ties to the area. May I have an autograph?"

"Of course." Miranda signed the back of the woman's grocery receipt before they went their separate ways, her thoughts snagging on the fan's words about being native to the region.

Miranda hadn't visited her mother since she'd been back in Texas. Nor had her mother come to Royal to see her, which was even more surprising in light of how thoroughly Virginia "Ginny" Dupree loved Blackwood Hollow. And how hard she'd once lobbied to have a role on *Secret Lives of NYC Ex-Wives*. She'd been angry at Miranda for not giving her that chance. Although not as angry as she'd been at Miranda for leaving her marriage in the first place. It had made her furious that Miranda signed a prenup—and walked away with nothing from Buck.

How stupid can you be? she'd shouted at Miranda over the phone, her diction sloppy from a prescription painkiller addiction that ebbed and flowed according to what was going on in her life at the time.

Breathe in. Breathe out.

Yoga, and all the mindful breathing that went with it, had been helping keep Miranda grounded her entire adult life. The teachings of Goddess centers everywhere weren't just about being physically fit. All that breathing definitely helped her emotional and mental health, too.

By the time she reached the main floor of Madtec, Miranda didn't feel quite as annoyed with Kai. Looking around at the design touches in the building, from the vintage video game posters that decorated the café walls to the courtyards and green spaces that seemed to give employees plenty of options for working outdoors in mild weather, Miranda had to admire the employee-centered corporate environment he'd given his workforce.

Kai Maddox might be a former hacker who'd skirted the law in the years he'd worked to learn the computer security business from the inside out, but there was no denying he'd turned his knowledge into an incredibly successful undertaking. Moreover, he'd given back to his hometown by building his corporate headquarters here. She'd read an article about a community center he'd built close to the diner where she used to work.

Where they'd met.

She wouldn't be driving by that on her way out of town, however. Shoving out the front doors of Madtec into the late afternoon sunlight, Miranda had enough thoughts of Kai crowding her head for one day. He'd packed on more muscle since they'd dated a decade ago, but there was no mistaking the always-assessing, smoldering green eyes and the scar on his jaw where he'd collided with the road on one of his motorcycle tours. The tattoos she remembered had been covered up by his custom Italian suit, but she found herself remembering every swirl and shadow of the intricate ink.

Stop.

She told herself not to give the reformed bad boy another thought. Clearly, he'd put her in his past and had no intention of spending more time with her than was absolutely necessary, no matter that she'd been prepared to pay him well.

She'd simply have to find someone else to review the Blackwood Bank digital security since Kai was determined not to help her. She'd been a fool to expect anything else. Maybe while she worked on bringing the cybersecurity of the bank up to snuff, she would have firewalls installed on her heart, too.

CHAPTER TWO

"WHAT THE HELL is the matter with you?" Dane Maddox stormed into Kai's office the next afternoon, a stainless-steel mug of coffee in one hand, and a sheaf of papers in the other.

Or, it *was* in the other hand until he slid the packet across Kai's desk.

The contract with the logo from Blackwood Bank emblazoned on the top pinwheeled across the glass surface before a corner lodged under his laptop.

Recognizing there wasn't a snowball's chance in hell of getting any work done until he addressed whatever had his brother fired up, Kai closed his computer and shoved back from the desk to meet Dane's glare. Dane might be two years younger than Kai, but he had all of Kai's tech smarts and a level of business savvy worthy of someone who'd been in the corporate world for twice as long. Kai was proud of him, even when he was being a pain in the ass.

"Let's see," Kai mused aloud, humoring him. "Depending who you talk to, it could be the chip on my shoulder. Or that I'm too much of a workaholic. And the whole thrill-seeking thing rubs some people the wrong way—"

"I'll tell you what your problem is," Dane continued, jabbing a finger on Kai's desk. "You're too damned bullheaded to recognize *this*—" he jabbed the contract twice more "—is everything we've been waiting for."

Tension bunched up the muscles in his shoulders, twisting its way along his neck.

"Madtec is thriving," Kai reminded him. "There's no need to affiliate ourselves with—" How to phrase his reservations about Miranda? About *himself* when he was around Miranda? "—people we don't care to work with just to make a buck."

Dane paced around Kai's office, his dark brown hair overdue for a cut and giving silent testament to how many hours he'd been putting into the new software testing.

"This contract is not with *people*." Dane loosened his tie a fraction although it wasn't even noon yet. "This is a contract to partner with one of the top ten privately held banks in the country, Kai."

He hardly needed to be reminded. But the knowledge didn't ease the knot in his throat at the thought of seeing more of Miranda. She might be easy on the eyes, but she'd been hell on his heart. Worse, Kai had been so thoroughly distracted by their affair and the thought of losing her that he'd taken his focus away from a project he'd been working on with his brother. The job had required a large-scale "almost" hack, since the first step toward preventing hackers from gaining access to any system is to learn how hacking is done. Quietly breaching a system—with zero malicious intent—had been a delicate task with devastating consequences if it was mishandled, but Kai had let Dane step up his role, confident his brother had the skills to monitor the program while Kai wooed Miranda.

The fact that Dane had done prison time for Kai's mistake would weigh on him forever. But bringing that up now would only tick off his agitated brother even more.

"When we started this company," Kai reminded him instead, "we agreed we would take the work we *wanted*—"

"I'm going to stop you right there." Dane charged toward the desk again to retrieve the paperwork. "When we came up with our mission statement, we agreed to work with companies that shared our values wherever possible, and I stand by that. But that doesn't mean we're suddenly going to turn down the chance to work with a reputable financial institution because an old flame happened to deliver the offer."

His brother laid the sheaf on top of his laptop and placed a heavy silver pen nearby.

"Does this mean you want us to take the project, even when we're already running at full capacity to get the new software to market?"

"We're only running at capacity because we haven't filled all the positions the new place can accommodate. We built this space to grow, and the Blackwood Bank account will allow us to do just that," Dane pointed out reasonably.

Kai blew out a frustrated breath, hating that his brother was right. Hating that he'd thought about Miranda almost nonstop since she'd walked out of his office the day before.

"Kai, you know that a partnership with Blackwood Bank would give Madtec that final stamp of legitimacy we've been looking for." Dane finally dropped into the seat across from Kai's desk. Dane sat forward in his chair. "CEOs from major corporations across the country would be willing to take a cue from an institution as prestigious as Blackwood to take a chance on a business founded by a couple of ex-hackers."

"The affiliation would take us mainstream," Kai admitted, knowing he couldn't deny Dane this opportunity to cast off the last taint of his jail time.

How ironic that Miranda had been the one to give them that chance.

"You'll sign?" Dane pressed.

Kai picked up the pen for an answer, seeing no other choice. He'd bring the signed contracts to Miranda personally. Maybe then, he'd figure out a way to broker a peace between them long enough to fulfill Madtec's obligations to Blackwood Bank.

Dane was right about the need to accept the offer. But the

sooner the job was done, the sooner Kai would put Miranda Dupree back in his past, where she belonged.

Miranda clutched a letter from Buckley Blackwood in her hands, eyes moving over the text. This was the third and final missive Buck had written to be delivered to her after his death. The first had explained the true intentions behind his will and the role he'd needed her to play. The second had included instructions on how to find his illegitimate son, Darius, and bring him into contact with the rest of the family. Now this letter included the last of his requests. She reread her ex-husband's final missive for her.

Dear Miranda,
Thank you for hanging in there with me to take care of these last tasks—the jobs I couldn't seem to pull off myself when I still had time. I hope this one last request will be a little easier than the others. I'd like you to organize a send-off for me, but not some schmaltzy memorial service—you know I hate things like that. I'm picturing an epic charity event, something like "Royal Gives Back," and I want you to organize it as only you can. I was thinking the proceeds ought to go to the Stroke Foundation or maybe the Heart Association since they study the underlying causes of strokes. It still weighs on me that my children lost their mother too soon because of a stroke. I wasn't the husband I should have been to Donna-Leigh before our divorce, but I'd like to do this in her honor. Now that I've been exposed for a philanthropist do-gooder, I might as well go all out one last time, right? I know you won't disappoint me. After this last favor, you can go back to your life in New York, and I'll rest easier. Yours, Buck.

Miranda returned Buckley's last letter to the small secretary desk in the guesthouse's second bedroom that served as her temporary office. She mulled over what it meant as she sat in front her laptop to review her work email for Goddess. Kace LeBlanc had hand delivered the note this morning, assuring her it would be the final note from Buckley.

That had been both good and bad news for her. While she was relieved there would be no more surprises from her ex, she would also miss Royal. She'd grown close to her stepchildren, people who felt more like her family these days than her mother ever had. Her gaze shifted away from her laptop screen to a new framed photo of the Blackwood heirs from Sophie's wedding—Sophie, Kellan and Vaughn with their half brother, Darius. Buckley would be so proud to have them all together at last.

Miranda felt glad she'd played a part in making that happen. Buckley hadn't been a great father, but he'd cared. Miranda's father had died when she was three, too young to be sure she remembered him, although sometimes she imagined she recalled his laugh or a feeling of being hugged by him. At first, her mother had worked two jobs after his death to provide for them, but she'd given up by the time Miranda was ten. The house fell into disrepair. The electricity was shut off more often than not. Miranda had only ever worn other girls' cast-off clothes. None of which was as troubling as her mother's decision to spend the little bit of money she brought in on a prescription pill addiction.

Ginny Dupree was a mean addict. She didn't hit, but she threw things, and she was verbally cruel. Some of her more cutting words had continued to hurt Miranda long afterward, which was why she drew firm boundaries with her now. But as she saw the Blackwood family healing, Miranda couldn't help a twinge of envy for the kind of companionship and support that came with family relationships.

The love.

She suspected that lack of love in her childhood home had been one of the driving forces behind her strong feelings for

Kai Maddox. Being with Kai had opened a whole new world
of possibilities for her heart.

Until he'd started to withdraw from her. She'd never understood it, but she'd felt his retreat in the weeks before their split.
He might blame her for their breakup, but he'd pulled away long
before she'd ended things.

Buckley Blackwood might have been richer and worldlier
than Kai. But in many ways, she'd settled for him when she'd
married him, telling herself maybe her quieter, steadier feelings for him were what more mature love felt like.

Lesson learned.

Except Kai Maddox was back in her thoughts now, stirring
up feelings she'd thought she'd put to rest long ago. And stirring up a hunger for him that she couldn't possibly deny. She'd
dreamed about his hands all over her the night before, bringing her intense pleasure while he whispered wicked, sugges-
tive things in her ear. She'd awoken edgy and breathless, her
heart beating fast.

Maybe organizing this charity event for Buckley was just
what she needed. Instead of spending her final month in Royal
working side by side with an old lover she couldn't stop thinking about, she would spend it planning something worthwhile.

With a frustrated sigh, she shut her laptop and changed into
her workout clothes, knowing she'd never get anything accomplished with her thoughts spinning this way.

Lying on her belly in cobra pose, Miranda arched her spine
and pulled her shoulders back while she moved through her
afternoon yoga workout in the studio of the Blackwood Hollow guesthouse. She inhaled deeply and slowly, matching her
breath to her pose. The cycle of postures in the sun salutation
was grounding for her during times of stress, and it took all her
effort to focus on her breathing when memories of Kai clung
to her thoughts.

With her mat positioned near the studio's big front window

overlooking the grounds, she held the pose for five deep breaths, turning her head to one side and then the other as she tried not to think about how it had felt to stand near him. She would force his smoldering image from her mind by sheer will.

Except, was that him pulling into the driveway of the guesthouse? Parking a sleek silver sports car in front of the double bay detached garage?

She forgot all about her breath in the scramble to her feet as Kai emerged from a Jaguar F-Type coupe. Dressed in a deep blue jacket with a light blue shirt underneath, he looked more casual than the day before and every bit as compelling. Awareness and anticipation tingled over her skin. She had to remind herself that her sexy dream about him hadn't been real. That she couldn't afford to indulge those kinds of thoughts around him. She hurried toward the door, dismayed that instead of being dressed to impress, she wore capri-length leggings and a drapey tank shirt for her workout.

Not that there was any help for it now.

Slipping on a pair of beaded sandals by the front mat, Miranda opened the door of the studio attached to the rest of the guesthouse by a covered breezeway. The smooth stone path connected the buildings, outlined by native plants and shrubs. When she stepped outside, Kai's green gaze swung toward her.

He changed the trajectory of his stride, turning away from the main house toward the studio building. She hadn't realized until then he carried a small box with an all-too-recognizable logo on it.

One that stirred nostalgia.

"Hello, Miranda. I hope I didn't interrupt you." He stopped a few feet from her under the shade of the breezeway, the spring air still fragrant with almond verbena.

Her breath caught to be close to him again, her heart rate picking up speed.

"I'm surprised to see you." She remembered how curt he'd been the day before, but if he was here to tell her he'd reconsidered, she couldn't afford to refuse. Still, there was no reason to make it too easy for him. She'd had to scarf down humble pie the day before—it wouldn't kill him to have a bite or two of his own. "I got the distinct impression you didn't want to cross paths again when I left your office yesterday."

"For that, I apologize." He lifted the white box in his hands. "I brought a peace offering."

Her gaze shifted to the parcel with the Deer Springs Diner label, a million memories bombarding her all over again. She used to waitress there, depending on the money to finance her first yoga studio. She'd met Kai there. They'd spent time plotting to take over the world from their favorite booth in the corner, and had shared many breakfasts there after long nights of lovemaking. Tentatively, she lifted the lid.

She suspected what would be inside before she even peeked under the top.

"Half lemon meringue, half caramel apple," she confirmed, the scent of their two favorites stirring nostalgia and longing she couldn't afford to feel around this man. Part of her wanted to send him away, escape what he made her feel. But she still needed him on a professional level. "Would you like to come in for a slice?"

She peered up at him and realized how close they stood. Close enough for her to touch the short bristles he'd always worn along his jaw. Close enough to breathe in the light spice of soap on his olive-toned skin and remember the taste of him. Hastily, she released the box top and took a step back.

"Thank you. I'd like that very much." His green eyes missed nothing. "We can celebrate our new venture together since I have a signed contract to give you."

The surprises continued.

"That's excellent news." For the bank, of course. But for her, the prospect of working with him proved equal parts tempting and daunting. "Although I'll admit I'm curious what made you change your mind after you seemed so adamantly opposed yesterday. Was it the prospect of me stepping aside?"

Turning, she led the way to the front door of the guesthouse, aware of his nearness every step of the way.

"No. That won't be necessary. I can separate my personal life from my business obligations." He sounded sincere. And yet both times she'd visited him recently, there had been enough sensual tension simmering to burn them both. Did he plan to ignore it?

Giving herself a few heartbeats to shore up her boundaries, she entered the cool interior of the guesthouse and paused in the entryway as Kai pulled the door closed behind them. The dark wood floor and white walls were simply furnished with rustic elegance. Sturdy leather couches and heavy iron pendant lamps were softened by an abundance of natural light, pale rugs and oversize yellow throw pillows. Drinking in the calming effects, she glanced at him.

"I didn't expect a warm reception after how we parted ten years ago," she admitted, pulse skipping erratically as she continued toward the open kitchen to retrieve plates and forks. "And how you reacted to seeing me in New York."

She hoped discussing it would dismiss the elephant in the room. They needed to put their old relationship behind them, so it didn't interfere with the bank's business.

Kai joined her at the kitchen island, setting the pie box on the white quartz countertop.

"That's all in the past now. I was needlessly abrupt yesterday, especially when you came to discuss a significant opportunity for Madtec." He reached into an interior pocket of his jacket and retrieved a folded packet of papers. He laid them on the counter, as well. "Dane and I look forward to a thorough review and revamp of the bank's digital security."

Miranda retrieved two bottles of sparkling water from the refrigerator and placed them on a bamboo serving tray along with the plates and silverware. While it would be easy to eat indoors at the kitchen counter, she thought sitting under the pergola in the backyard would help her keep boundaries in place. Especially when lemon meringue and caramel apple pie slices had the power to catapult her back in time to that diner with Kai. Feeding each other bites. Sitting so close her thigh pressed against his.

She would *not* think about his thighs.

"Dane convinced you to give this a chance?" she guessed aloud, her cheeks warm from the vivid thoughts she was trying to stifle.

"He was livid I hadn't already signed the papers," Kai acknowledged. As she moved to pick up the tray, he took over the task, his warm hand brushing hers momentarily. "Lead the way."

She felt that brief touch long afterward. *Breathe in. Breathe out.* She opened the French doors to the patio where coral honeysuckle hung from the deep pergola. Hummingbirds bobbed around the vibrant trumpet-shaped blooms. Kai set the tray on the wrought iron dining table, then pulled out a cushioned chair for Miranda.

"Thank you." She tried to recall the thread of the conversation to distract herself from all the ways his nearness affected her. "I hope that Dane's insistence doesn't mean you're conflicted about working with us."

"I have no trouble opposing my brother when the situation calls for it." Kai took the seat next to her at the round table. "But in this case, Dane's instincts were correct. The software we're developing is tailor-made for a complex financial platform like Blackwood Bank."

Grounding herself in mundane tasks, Miranda laid out napkins and divvied up the waters while Kai opened the pie box and slid thin slices onto their plates. One of each kind for each of them. But rather than soothing her with routine, the familiarity of that simple act, something they'd done countless times and yet not for so many years, crowded her chest with feelings she wasn't ready for. Swallowing past the swell of emotion, she took her time smoothing the napkin over her lap.

"I have followed the rise of Madtec with interest. I suspected your company was a good fit for this role, Kai, or I wouldn't have approached you." She appreciated how the conversation anchored her in the purpose of the meeting. Because this was just business.

Something they both excelled at. Unlike personal relationships.

"I know that," he conceded, lifting his water bottle and clinking it lightly to hers. "Thank you."

Her gaze flicked to his as he held the pale green bottle in midair. She followed suit, clinking hers to his in a friendly toast that felt like a fresh start.

At least, professionally speaking.

"Here's to a successful partnership." Kai's green gaze lingered on hers, and she couldn't help but think she saw something simmering in their depths.

Old frustration over how things had ended? Or a hint of the lingering attraction that she'd been grappling with all day?

Neither one boded well for their venture. But she licked her lips before raising the bottle to her mouth. One way or another, she would figure out how to work with Kai Maddox for the sake of Blackwood Bank. "To new beginnings."

CHAPTER THREE

SHE HAD THE sexiest mouth he'd ever seen on a woman.

Kai tried not to stare at it, the top lip slightly fuller than the bottom in a perfect cupid's bow that made her look perpetually ready for a kiss. But the more he tried not to think about that incredible mouth of hers, the more he pictured it doing wicked things to him.

Being seated across from Miranda on a property that had once belonged to his rival for her affections felt damned surreal.

Kai had made the trip into Royal with his best professional intentions, hoping to make peace enough to take care of business together. But one look at her in the afternoon sunlight with no makeup on, wearing her yoga clothes, had stolen the breath from his lungs. Miranda was a beautiful woman no matter what. Full stop. Yet seeing her relaxed in her temporary home had reminded him of the woman he'd known, before she was a business mogul in her own right. The sight had catapulted him a decade backward in time, right down to wishing he could invite her for a ride on the back of his motorcycle, her slender thighs hugging his hips.

Except they were far different people now, no matter if he still saw shades of the woman he'd once loved in Miranda.

That woman had been a myth—an illusion fueled by incredible chemistry. She'd made that clear when she left him for Buckley.

"We should discuss our next steps," he suggested as he pushed aside his plate. "The contract put a very condensed timeline in place for updating the bank's cybersecurity."

He glanced around to ensure their privacy. The patio behind the Blackwood Hollow guesthouse had a large, covered area for entertaining, complete with fireplace and outdoor kitchen. The table under the vine-covered pergola looked out over the pool shared with the main house. There was no one in sight.

Miranda nodded, bringing his attention back to the moment. To her. A few tendrils of red hair slipped from the clip holding the rest at her nape. "Because I have a reason to worry about it. Most aspects of the bank have been well managed since Buckley's death, but the internal data security director has flagged several concerns that haven't been addressed."

"The outside company Blackwood contracted with prior to us has had a few incidents in the past two years, which suggests to me they are failing to stay up-to-date." Kai had spot-checked Blackwood's system before making the trip to Royal to start familiarizing himself. "Our service niche requires continual, aggressive measures to keep current in a quickly changing marketplace."

"You and Dane have done incredibly well for yourselves, especially—" Her tone suggested she'd been about to say more but she stopped abruptly, then glanced back down at her plate. She speared her fork through a morsel of lemon meringue pie.

"Especially for former hackers?" he supplied, knowing he'd guessed accurately by the slightest tinge of pink in her cheeks. "You can't be a success at preventing cybercrime without knowing how the criminal element works."

"Madtec's rapid rise has been formidable," she amended before sliding her dessert dish to one side. "But remembering how protective you were of Dane, I know that it had to be hard for you when he got into legal trouble."

His jaw tightened. While he felt a small amount of satisfaction that she'd noticed Dane's arrest even as she'd been celebrating her engagement, Kai couldn't dodge the sting of resentment, too. He'd been solely responsible for his brother since their father died of pancreatic cancer when Kai was seventeen and Dane was fifteen. Their mom had been exhausted from the hardship of caregiving and her own grief, and she'd taken off to recover, leaving Kai in charge. She never returned.

"Mostly, I regretted that I hadn't been giving him my full attention in the months before his arrest. He'd only just turned eighteen." Instead of working with his brother on the weekend of the hacking incident that had first flagged an investigation into his brother's activities, he'd taken Miranda to Galveston for a few days at the beach even though her mother had already told Kai that Buckley Blackwood had started coming around the Dupree house. Kai had thought maybe devoting more attention to her would sway things in his favor, but in the end, he couldn't compete with Buckley's money.

Did she remember the timing of the events leading to Dane's arrest? It had been some months after the investigation began, but surely she remembered he'd been concerned about his brother's activities when Kai hadn't been around to keep an eye on him.

Her blue gaze broke away from his. Retrieving her water bottle, she took a long drink. "Dane was a prodigy. When someone is so gifted intellectually, it's probably easy to lose sight of their youth."

Leaning back in his chair, he weighed her answer. Told himself not to ruminate on the past. And still found himself asking, "Speaking of family, how's your mother?"

Her lips pressed together momentarily. A fleeting reaction from this self-contained woman, but he didn't miss it. He'd never understood the dynamic between her and her mom, but then again, Miranda had been more focused on her future than her past when they'd dated.

"Honestly, I'm not sure." She folded the linen napkin that had been on her lap, matching the corners and smoothing the fabric. "She has battled an addiction to prescription painkillers over the years, and that's made it difficult for us to maintain a relationship."

"I'm so sorry to hear it." The news was unexpected. Jarring, even, considering Ginny Dupree had been the one to warn Kai away from her daughter. Had she been an untrustworthy source of information? "I never saw any sign of that kind of problem when we were dating."

"She used to hide it better than she does now," Miranda told him drily, moving the folded napkin to the table and laying it over her plate. "But the problem dates back to when I was a preteen. I started working at a young age since a lot of her paycheck went toward her problems."

His understanding of their past together shifted, the pieces falling together in a different way. Had Miranda's financial situation pushed her toward Buckley? Or had her mother seen a payday when the wealthy rancher had come calling?

It didn't matter now since their breakup had been so long ago. But damn.

"I always admired your ambition, but I didn't realize that it was partially driven by necessity." He reached across the table to lay his hand on hers before considering the wisdom of it, the movement instinctive.

Her blue eyes darted to his, awareness leaping between them when he'd meant only to offer empathy. Understanding.

"Circumstances help make us who we are—good or bad." She didn't move her hand beneath his fingers, but he could feel the leap of her pulse at the base of her thumb. Her skin was so soft. "I'd like to think I used her problems as a push in a positive direction for myself."

He forced himself to release her, but it took more effort than it should have. And he may have glided a touch along the pulse point of her wrist before letting go completely, wanting her to remember the way they could set each other on fire.

Her eyes darted to his. Aware. He didn't know what to make of the current sparking between them. No matter how much he wanted to tell himself this next phase of their relationship needed to be all business, he was still undeniably drawn to her. He wanted to know more about her and how she'd spent the last ten years, but since he suspected she wasn't any more eager to talk about her past than he was willing to revisit his, he let go of the topic.

"That sounds like some of the inspiration for your nonprofit." While Kai hadn't watched much of her reality television show, he had pulled up a speech she'd given about her charity when he'd seen a mention of it online a year ago. "I read about Girl to the Nth Power."

She'd organized the group five years ago and had since received national service awards for her efforts to create supportive environments for young women. In her speech, she'd referred to her organization as a girls' club for a new generation, complete with mentors in disciplines from the arts to STEM, with access to workshops on friendship and self-care.

Her whole face changed, her expression lighting with some of that ambition and passion he remembered from those conversations in the diner where they'd shared their dreams. "While I'm incredibly proud of the work I do at Goddess, Girl to the Nth Power is where my heart lies. It's exciting to make a difference in teens' lives."

He couldn't miss the spark in her eyes. The commitment to her cause.

"If your schedule permits, you should come down to the community center in Deer Springs sometime. Check out the afterschool program." He thought she might be interested in the operation because of her work with teens. Not because he wanted her to spend more time near him.

"I read something about the community center." She stacked

their dishes back on the tray they'd used to carry everything outside.

Taking his cue from her, he lifted the tray and followed her back inside the house, his gaze dropping to her curves as she moved. A butterfly tattoo on the back of one ankle was a colorful new addition that called him to explore the rest of her. He placed the tray on the island and shoved his hands in his pockets to remind them not to wander.

"Dane and I built one at the same time we broke ground on the Madtec headquarters. We thought it would give back to the town and make it more inviting for potential employees." He liked the idea of giving local teens more support and opportunities than he and Dane had.

"Smart thinking of you." She slid the remnants of the pie in the refrigerator while he loaded the plates in the dishwasher. "And thank you for the invitation. I'd like to see the community center."

Sensing their time together was coming to an end, Kai wouldn't linger. It was enough to give her the signed contract and pave the way for a working relationship. No need to rehash the past.

"Excellent. We'll be in touch with the Blackwood Bank data security director today and get to work installing new encryption precautions." He should shake her hand and leave. Or maybe just leave.

Except spending time with her today had stirred up too much. His feet didn't move as he watched her lean a hip against the kitchen island.

"I'm glad you changed your mind about handling the cybersecurity, Kai," she admitted. "Thank you."

Walk away, his brain told him.

But he didn't think he could keep this facade of civility between them every time they saw one another if he didn't address at least one of the issues that still bugged the hell out of him after all this time.

"Kai?" Her brow furrowed as she looked up at him questioningly.

Standing there together in that quiet kitchen could have been any one of a hundred times they'd been alone. The past and the present merged.

"There's just one more thing." He shifted closer, lowering his voice. "It's strange for me to be in Blackwood Hollow with you after how things ended for us. But how does it feel for you to be living in Buckley's guesthouse and overseeing his estate surrounded by his sons and daughter?"

She bristled visibly. "I'm not their enemy. Buckley arranged for me to play a role helping them through the aftermath of his death."

"Still loyal to him even after the divorce?" The question came out crueler than he'd intended. But he couldn't help wanting to know.

Her eyes narrowed and she straightened from the island.

"That's not any of your business," she told him coolly, making it clear that he'd effectively erased any progress he'd made smoothing things over between them.

"You're right, it isn't," he agreed, suspecting he'd need Dane to be the one to interact with Blackwood Bank if Kai couldn't refrain from poking at the past this way. "But that doesn't take away the fact that things are bound to be awkward between us while we're finding our footing to make this deal work."

Her full lips pursed. She gave a clipped nod and leaned toward him.

"In that case, let me assure you that living here again is beyond strange for me." She stabbed one manicured finger into the quartz countertop to make her point, a diamond tennis bracelet quivering with the movement. "Discovering my ex-husband trusted me with all his worldly assets during this transition of power to his kids has been even more bizarre." Another finger stabbing the quartz. "But given how much time has passed since you and I shared a history, I don't think there's any need for *awkwardness*. I'm thirty-six years old, Kai. I don't do awkward."

He welcomed the passionate outpouring from her, another facet of Miranda he recognized better than the self-possessed control she'd exhibited in his office and throughout some of their talk today. He stifled the urge to smile at the reemergence of her fiery side.

"Point taken. I've long envied your maturity," he told her with 100 percent honesty. "But for what it's worth, I think what I'm labeling 'awkwardness' might be more accurately called *attraction*." He gave her a moment to process that, knowing he owed her the truth even if it made a working relationship more difficult to navigate. "I'll be on my best behavior with you, Miranda, but I think it's obvious the fire is still there."

This time, she had no comeback, her lips parted in surprise.

Hell, he'd shocked himself too with that admission. But he wasn't the kind of guy to sidestep the facts. He plowed straight through.

Now, he watched as her jaw snapped shut and she straightened.

"Then maybe we should wait for things to cool off and revisit this at a later date." She stalked past him toward the front door, clearly done with him for the day. She pulled it open and stood to one side of the exit, studying him. "Goodbye, Kai."

Had he overstepped the bounds of professionalism?

He didn't think so. She knew him well, no matter that their shared history was ten years old. She couldn't be too surprised that he would speak plainly about his feelings. The attraction was still there—it would be ridiculous to pretend otherwise.

Closing the distance between them, he moved toward the door. He stopped before stepping over the threshold, their gazes meeting.

"Come to Deer Springs," he urged, awareness of her inching over his skin. "If we can come to terms with the history between us, then we can get some closure. Maybe then the attraction will fade and it will be easier to work together."

Her breathing quickened, the stroke of each warm puff stirring an answering heat inside him. But he didn't wait for her to agree. He strode by her toward his vehicle, needing to put Miranda in his rearview mirror. Not just today.

This time, for good.

Three days later, Miranda sat outside on the guesthouse patio with her morning coffee and set aside her work to organize the Royal Gives Back gala that Buckley wanted. Instead, she scrolled through the latest photos from Sophie Blackwood Townshend's European honeymoon. Sophie, the baby of the Blackwood family, had married Miranda's producer last month and was living it up in Paris, Morocco and—most recently— Florence. The backdrop in every picture was stunning, but what captured Miranda's eye most was how in love the happy couple looked. Sophie had met Nigel while working under a false identity at Green Room Media in New York in an effort to dig up dirt on Miranda. Happily, she'd found nothing and had finally come to terms with their relationship. It touched Miranda's heart to be included on the family's message group each day and see what Sophie was up to.

Although, settling her phone back on the wrought iron table, Miranda had to admit that even as her comfort with the Blackwoods grew, the contrast made her more aware of how she'd failed to heal the rift with her mother.

Maybe she didn't need to since her mom had betrayed the most basic rules of family loyalty in the past. But since Ginny Dupree was an addict, Miranda still held out hope one day it might be different between them.

Kai's suggestion she visit Deer Springs echoed in her mind— along with his reminder about the attraction that still simmered. At first, she'd been angry with him for stirring up trouble. Yet a part of her couldn't help but admire his willingness to wade headlong into the topics most people would dance around. It made things frustrating since it would be more comfortable to pretend the spark they'd shared was long buried. But was it true?

She couldn't deny the flare of heat when he'd touched her, even in a moment intended to offer comfort. Maybe he had a good point about trying to get closure. Surely then she could put all her feelings for him behind her. But every time she thought about him saying it was obvious the fire between them was still there, her belly flipped just like it had the first time they'd met.

Miranda had been holding down two jobs at the time, overloaded by the lunch crowd in the diner where she worked as a waitress, and panicked about the duct tape holding together a split seam in her uniform, a tear she hadn't gotten around to sewing the day before after getting into an argument with her mother. She'd never forget how it felt to arrive at Kai's table to take his order and having his heart-stopping smile chase away all the stress until it evaporated like summer dew.

He'd insisted he didn't want to order until she could join him for lunch. She'd brought him a soda anyway. He hadn't touched it until two o'clock when her shift ended. After she took a seat, it seemed like they didn't stop talking for months except to kiss and make love.

But Kai ended things.

Not in so many words, of course. But in his actions. He'd been the one to retreat.

She'd always thought it was stress of his own that had made him pull away. He'd worked even more hours than she had, and some of the jobs had been shady. And yes, that had bothered her, given how many times she'd been burned by her mother's brand of flexible ethics. She'd had enough instability in her life. She wanted steady. Even if predictable wasn't some people's idea of happily ever after, to her it had sounded blissful. Kai was six years younger than her, and he lived more dangerously than Miranda ever could. And yet she'd put up with all of that, compromising again and again, until she'd felt him pulling away. That was when she'd decided to stop trying.

He hadn't even argued with her when she'd decided to end things, the final proof she'd needed that things weren't right between them. Was it any wonder she'd been aggravated two days ago by his insinuations of loyalty to Buckley?

The marriage hadn't been perfect, but she'd given it her best shot.

Leaving her coffee cup on the patio table, Miranda grabbed her phone and put it in her pocket. She wasn't going to get anything accomplished on the Royal Gives Back event with her thoughts straying time and again to Kai.

He'd invited her to Deer Springs to put the past behind them, hadn't he? She intended to take him up on it.

CHAPTER FOUR

LULU SHEPARD RAISED her fist to knock on the door of the guesthouse when Miranda opened it wide.

"Lulu." Miranda smiled warmly, wrapping her in a friendly
hug that carried a whiff of subtle perfume. "I wasn't expecting
you. Is everything okay?"

Stressed and anxious about her wedding plans, Lulu hoped
Miranda could help her. Sometimes she wondered if the other
woman had ever experienced a moment's indecision. She
seemed so perpetually poised.

Designer purse in hand, Miranda wore a fitted navy blue
suit with wide lapels. Raspberry-colored sling back heels were
a nice touch. Miranda always managed to look feminine and
badass at the same time.

"I'm fine. I just wanted some wedding advice, but I won't
keep you if you're on your way out." Lulu stepped back, giving
her friend room to join her on the porch.

Pulling the door closed behind her, Miranda pointed to a
couple of Adirondack chairs to one side. "I always have time
for you. Let's sit."

Relieved, Lulu dropped into one of the seats. "Thank you. I'm
in a dilemma about the bridesmaids for my wedding. I worked
out the details with your stepson and then Nigel texted me

confirmation that we can have the wedding here at Blackwood Hollow, which is great. But he sent around a memorandum to the crew that our next episode will be shopping for bridesmaid dresses for all of the *Secret Lives* members."

"I remember seeing that," Miranda confirmed. "And I'm glad you're getting married here, but I do remember thinking that it's going to seem forced for you to have us in your wedding. The audience knows we're not all best friends."

Lulu bit her lip, hoping she hadn't offended Miranda, whom she'd grown close to over the last two seasons. "I want Fee, of course, and I'd love to have you in it, but Rafaela? Come on. Why would I ask her to stand up with me after some of the stunts she's pulled?"

Earlier in the season, Rafaela Marchesi had snapped a photo of Seraphina's fiancé, rancher Clint Rockwell, without his prosthetic leg and sent it to the media in an obvious bid for ratings. Fee had been hurt and furious, of course, so as Fee's best friend, Lulu had been doubly outraged. She still was. She'd go to the mat for Fee.

"You have every right to decide who you want in your wedding," Miranda assured her in no uncertain terms, stabbing the arm of the chair with an emphatic finger. "That's a given. But it occurs to me that maybe Nigel is setting us up for the usual show drama by putting you in the position of having to tell the others yourself—on camera."

"Meaning you think he wants a bridesmaid shopping show to turn into a bitch-fest about exactly that kind of thing?" Lulu hadn't considered that, but it made perfect sense.

"If I've learned one thing from doing this series, it's that we live or die by the sound bites." Miranda shrugged a shoulder. "That's why I don't get as much screen time. I'm less interesting for viewers because I don't go from zero to sixty with my emotions."

"Or with your mouth," Lulu added, thinking how grounded Miranda seemed. How unlikely to fly off the handle. Whereas the others—Lulu included—were all apt to say whatever came to mind. They didn't hold back.

"Exactly," Miranda agreed, leaning back in her seat with a thoughtful expression. "Still waters might run deep, but they don't make for good television. I'm okay with that, though. I'm grateful to be a part of the show for the friendships. I hadn't realized until I got involved with *Secret Lives* how lacking my life has been in female friendships."

Touched, Lulu squeezed Miranda's hand. "I'm glad to have you in my life, too," she told her honestly, appreciating the different perspective. "What would you do about the bridesmaids if you were me?"

"The simplest option would be to just go along with it. You wouldn't be the first woman to fill up her wedding photos with frenemies. At least with us, you'll be aware of what to expect. How many friends do you know who were coerced to put cousins they hardly knew in their ceremony in order to placate an aunt or mother—only to then get in trouble anyway when the cousin couldn't stand the other bridesmaids? We've gotten through a few seasons and haven't killed each other yet, so you'll be safe on that score." Miranda shrugged, making it all sound so reasonable. "Personally, I don't think it's a big deal to have Rafaela in your wedding photos, but it's not about me, Lu. It's your day. Yours and Kace's."

Lulu's heart warmed all over again at the thought of marrying Kace. Having the day free of drama and artifice had become so very important. This was about their future. Their love. Not ratings.

"And at the end of the day, that's all that really matters, isn't it?" Lulu felt a tension slide away at Miranda's gentle wisdom and she decided she needed some more of that brand of Zen in her life. Or maybe she was already experiencing it now that she felt loved and appreciated by a man she wanted to spend the rest of her life with. "At my first wedding, I got all spun up about the details—seating arrangements and a whole lot of superficial stuff that didn't really matter."

"What counts is the marriage, not the wedding." Lulu caught the shadows in her friend's eyes. Was she thinking of her own marriage to Buckley?

Lulu knew Miranda hadn't had an easy road, no matter how much of a placid facade she tried to present to the world.

"I'm going to do it right this time," Lulu agreed, already imagining the future she'd have waking beside Kace every day. "The marriage, that is."

Miranda nodded approvingly, a few darting birds chirping a happy echo to the sentiment. "I know it's right when I see you two together. I think it's obvious to everyone around you."

Lulu held tight to the knowledge. She didn't need anyone else's approval, but she liked the idea that her friends backed her decision. "He makes me happy." It was as simple as that. "And the wedding can be as over-the-top as Nigel wants it."

"Are you sure?" Miranda asked, leaning forward, a diamond pendant swinging out and reflecting the sun. "Because you can tell him that you don't want Rafaela—or any of us—in it."

"I'm sure." At peace with her decision, she accepted that the wedding was a one-day party. The marriage was what would last a lifetime. "I wouldn't have met Kace without this show, and I don't mind celebrating that. Once the reception is over, I'm going to have a good man in my life forever, and that's what counts."

Standing, she thanked Miranda for helping her think things through. Before she left, however, she couldn't help but ask, "Where are you headed? That suit looks stunning on you."

Even before Miranda answered, Lulu's instincts told her Miranda was going to see a man. There was a hesitation. The briefest moment of uncertainty that Lulu didn't remember ever seeing before in this supremely poised woman.

"I'm heading to Deer Springs to speak with the tech com-

pany helping me bring Blackwood Bank's security up to speed."
Miranda rose, walking Lulu to her rental car.

"My female intuition is screaming that there's a person of
interest on the other end of this meeting," Lulu said lightly,
not expecting much of a reply. Trying to pin Miranda down
wouldn't yield results anyway.

Opening the driver's side door, Lulu remembered clearly
how it felt to be circling Kace when they were getting to know
one another. How alive she felt. She still did, just thinking
about him.

She hoped Miranda's mystery man was worthy of her.

"He's interesting, all right," Miranda admitted, standing by
the tall pots of flowering trees that lined the porch. "I'll give
him that."

Lulu whistled low under her breath as she started the car,
intrigued at the thought of Miranda navigating a new relationship. "For what it's worth, you look sizzling hot. Thank you for
the advice, Miranda."

"Always," Miranda assured her, closing the driver's door before blowing her a kiss as Lulu put the car in Reverse.

Her heart felt happy. She would have Seraphina as her maid
of honor in her wedding. As for Rafaela, Lulu knew Miranda
would be right there next to her to intervene if their fame-
chasing costar stepped out of line. Because while the audience
might see Miranda as the grounded one who didn't cause a stir,
Lulu had no doubt that her quieter friend would do whatever
was necessary to make sure the wedding went smoothly. She
just hoped Miranda knew that her friends would have her back
in return, no matter what she was going through on her own.

Kai had just finished helping one of the kids in his coding class
at the community center when a teen in the back of the room
let out a quiet wolf whistle.

"Is there a problem, Rhys?" he asked the boy seated closest

to the window. The teen's eyes were fixed on something outside in the parking lot.

Normally, Kai had the blinds lowered since the first-floor tech room had a view of people coming and going from the building, but today he'd opened one to let in some natural light.

"Sorry," Rhys muttered, swiveling in his chair to face his laptop screen. "Got distracted."

The teen went back to work without Kai having to say anything else, and Kai was about to dismiss the class when he spotted a feminine figure striding closer to the building's front doors.

Miranda.

Anticipation fired through him, even as he experienced a moment of understanding for the teen student's loss of focus. No doubt, Miranda had the power to distract. She entered the community center's front doors, out of sight once more.

"We'll finish our projects next time," Kai announced. "The tech lab will remain open for another hour if anyone wants to keep working."

Kai nodded his thanks to the lab's afternoon monitor, a local graduate student earning some internship credits. About half of the students gathered their backpacks and dispersed to the gym or the game lounge, but the rest stayed behind, including the wolf whistler.

Kai clapped Rhys on the shoulder before leaving the class. "Whistles and catcalling can make women uncomfortable," he reminded. The kid was working on a sophisticated program for someone his age—but when it came to emotional maturity, he still had a lot to learn. "A definite no-go."

"It won't happen again," Rhys assured him quickly, straightening in his chair.

Nodding, Kai let the kid off the hook, then headed toward the door to find Miranda. He could only assume she was here because she'd taken him up on the offer to put the past behind them in the town where they'd met. The town where their affair had set them both on fire.

He spotted her just outside the tech lab door, her fitted blue suit skimming her memorable curves, the skirt revealing toned legs. Hunger for her stirred. Not just because she was an extremely attractive woman. Some of his best memories were with her at his side.

"Hello, Kai." She tucked a slim handbag under one arm, her gaze fixed on his.

"I wasn't sure you'd come." He'd been waiting for days, wondering if he'd overstepped by suggesting they had unfinished business between them.

"I wasn't either," she admitted, her gaze taking in the huge common area of the community center. Couches were filled with groups of teens talking and laughing. The area was ringed by meeting rooms, a game room, gym and a snack counter. "When it comes to a business decision, I'm sure of myself. But the way forward in my personal life never seems quite as clear."

He appreciated her honesty, and repaid her in kind. "I'm glad you're here."

While it might be easier for them both, from a business perspective, to ignore their history for the sake of Blackwood Bank, Kai found himself wanting more resolution with Miranda. Or did he just want to bring her home with him and forget all the animosity to lose himself in her one last time? He couldn't deny that his thoughts about her ranged from sensual to explicit, and those thoughts were more and more frequent.

"You've done an amazing job with this place," she observed, not paying attention to the small commotion she was creating with her presence. A few girls seemed to have recognized Miranda's famous face, and the news spread in audible whispered conversations from group to group.

"Thank you. But it seems I've underestimated your show's popularity with the teen crowd. Looks like I created quite a stir by inviting you here." He slid a hand under her elbow, guiding her away from the lounge toward an unused meeting space in the back of the building. "Would you consider continuing our discussion at my house? I live close by."

She glanced over her shoulder briefly, as if to gauge how much of a commotion she was causing. Yet she never slowed her step, allowing him to lead her away.

A surge of misplaced possessiveness—or perhaps it was simple desire—made him want to wrap her in his arms. Tuck her even closer.

"Perhaps that would be for the best," she agreed, her voice quiet beside him so that he had to lean nearer to hear. "I'm parked out front."

"I'll drive you," he assured her, as he quickened his pace through the empty room sometimes used for local speakers or book clubs. There was a back entrance that opened onto a separate parking area. "My vehicle is right outside."

Today, no one else was in the rear lot as there were no special events planned for the evening, so they arrived at his Jaguar quickly enough.

"This is the second time I've seen you without a motorcycle," Miranda observed lightly while he unlocked the passenger door and opened it for her. "I will confess I'm surprised to see you behind the wheel of a car."

Watching her lower herself gracefully into the leather seat, Kai latched onto the topic of discussion to distract himself from her legs.

"While the Bluetooth systems available in helmets have come a long way, it's still easier to conduct a business call from a car," he admitted, closing her door and then letting himself into the driver's side. He started the engine once they were buckled in, heading west toward his house through the relatively quiet streets. "However, if you have an urge to roam Deer Springs on the back of a bike, it would be a pleasure to take you for a ride. I still keep two of them in the garage for when the restless urge strikes."

He shifted into a higher gear, remembering the feel of her arms wrapped around him, her breasts pressed against his back when they used to ride together. As her throaty laugh floated between them, he wondered if she was recalling some of those same times.

"I thought we were going to put the past to rest, not relive it." She slanted a glance his way, blue eyes assessing.

That's what he'd thought, too.

But his relationship with Miranda had never lacked for complications. And he found himself tossing out a far thornier solution.

"There's more than one way to fix a simmering awareness." He knew better than to label the chemistry "awkwardness" this time. She'd been very clear about that. "We could appease it."

Just saying the words made the idea shimmer with real possibility. If she agreed, they could indulge themselves as much as they wanted. Let the heat consume them both. Visions of her naked and eager for him practically crowded out his view of the road.

"I don't think I can appease your restless urges, Kai." She shifted in her seat, crossing one leg over the other in a way that snagged his gaze. "I never was very effective at that. And now that we're older…"

She let the thought slide, as if he knew the rest of what she'd say. He had to refocus on the words since his brain lingered on her legs. He wanted to part her thighs and lay between them. Kiss her until they were both breathless.

"Now that we're older, what?" he prompted, needing her to spell it out for him while he battled enticing images in his head. He turned down a side street that led to his private drive.

"If I couldn't keep your attention when I was a twenty-six-year-old, chances are good I won't be enough of a diversion for you at thirty-six." Her words were so unexpected—so unwelcome and wrong—that he pulled to a stop the moment he turned onto his private driveway even though they hadn't reached the house yet.

He shoved the car in Park.

"You were all I could think about when you were twenty-six, Miranda." Hell, thinking about her to the exclusion of all else was what had cost Dane his freedom. That had been the final blow to their faltering relationship. "Holding my attention has never a problem for you."

Surprise colored her eyes, her expression thoughtful for a moment before she spoke.

"You checked out on our relationship long before I ended things," she reminded him.

"Only because I knew we were a lost cause once your mother told me Buckley Blackwood had started coming around." He'd never forget the force of that blow. The kindness shaded with pity in Ginny Dupree's eyes when she'd informed him he had a powerful—rich—rival for Miranda's affections. "Six weeks later, we were finished. Dane was under investigation. Buckley Blackwood was shopping for diamonds and you were out of my life for good."

He heard Miranda's quick gasp. Saw her brow furrow. But she knew how that story turned out as well as he did, so he couldn't imagine what she seemed surprised about now.

For his part, he welcomed the reminder that this meeting between them wasn't about appeasing the damnable attraction that hadn't faded. Better to confront it. Shred it apart if necessary.

One way or another, he was putting Madtec and his brother first this time. He wouldn't let his attraction get in the way. If it was a problem for her, then Miranda would have to figure out how to work with him. She'd always been good at prioritizing the bottom line ahead of everything else.

Miranda had come to Deer Springs to put the past to rest.

The idea had sounded a whole lot more peaceful than the process was turning out to be.

She'd made a misstep marrying Buckley—she could admit that now. Had it been rooted in her relationship with Kai? She'd forgotten how being with Kai had always felt like someone turned the flame on high beneath her normally mild emotions. With him, feelings were more intense. Anger and passion were hotter. Pleasure deeper. Hurts more painful. She'd have to sequester herself in her yoga studio to breathe through all the tumultuous sensations pinballing around inside her.

But the revelation that her mother had intervened with Kai— effectively chasing him off the moment Buckley had shown up at the Dupree house to ask if he could see Miranda privately— had rocked her. Kai had never told her about that before, but it made so many other perplexing moments from the past suddenly make sense.

Not that it mattered now.

As Kai drove the Jaguar the rest of the way down a winding drive and through a wrought iron gate flanked by brick columns, Miranda reminded herself to focus on the present. She needed to smooth things over with the copresident of Madtec and pave the way for a good working relationship with Blackwood Bank. That was why she was here.

Not to contemplate motorcycle rides with a hot guy from her past. Not even when he'd told her that she had been all he could think about back when they'd dated.

Pull it together.

"Here we are," he announced pulling around a copse of trees so she could see a house.

An incredible, modern marvel of a house. Because as the car arrived in the driveway, the lights around the place—inside and out—turned on.

"It's beautiful, Kai," she told him honestly, taking in the expanses of glass between sleek black stone walls.

The lights—perhaps motion-detection or connected to whatever security system he had in place—made the whole place glow. She could see into the huge rooms decorated in minimalist style. Designed in an L shape, the house wrapped around a pool that became visible only as he drove deeper into the property toward a detached garage. He didn't open any of the bays, however, leaving the sports coupe parked outside while she took in the details of the house.

A second-floor deck with a firepit and hot tub overlooked the pool area. From master suite to kitchen, guest rooms to office, the whole floor plan was visible thanks to the windows and abundant light.

"Thank you." He shut off the engine and came around to help her out of the car. "I worked on the design for almost a year before I was happy with it."

She braced herself for his touch before placing her hand in his, that current of awareness ever-present. Rising to her feet, she withdrew her hand quickly, but the memory of how he felt lingered long after.

Her only consolation was that Kai seemed ready to drop the idea of acting on their attraction after their conversation in the car.

"You designed this?" She shouldn't be surprised. She'd always known he was a gifted Renaissance man, his agile mind hopping from one project to the next, fascinated by the inner workings of things and studying them until he found answers that satisfied him.

"It was easier that way." His hand landed at the base of her spine briefly, guiding her toward a walkway leading around the pool. "At first, whenever I wanted to modify someone else's design to use recycled materials, I got a long song and dance about why it wouldn't work."

The feel of his touch called to her. She refocused on the house, grounding herself in the physical space to keep her thoughts off the ever-present awareness of the man.

"So you developed your own design instead." She admired the black, glittering stone walls, idly wondering where he'd sourced the material.

Small talk was a whole lot easier than what she'd come here to discuss.

"It's my home. Why should I compromise?" A hint of a smile curved one side of his lips. "Although my builder did call my blueprints the most obnoxiously detailed he'd ever seen, I took it as a compliment that the end product is exactly what I'd envisioned."

He stopped in front of a sliding door that opened into the kitchen, and de-armed the security system with an app on his phone. The system chimed twice before he slid the door wide, then wider still, opening the wall to the outdoor area and letting in a warm breeze. The lights that had flickered to life while they were still in the driveway dimmed now, leaving only the pendant lamps in the kitchen, which Kai had flicked on with a conventional switch.

"You did an incredible job. Your house, Madtec, the community center—they're all a testament to how much you've invested in Deer Springs. The town must be very happy with you." She set her purse on a padded barstool with sleek chrome legs that was tucked under the marble island.

Kai retrieved a pair of small bottles of seltzer from the built-in refrigerator and set them on the island near two glasses.

"This community was good to Dane and me after our father died and our mother left." He'd never spoken much about his family when they'd dated, but Miranda knew that his mom had taken off not long after their father had lost his protracted battle with cancer. "I had a lot of anger about my dad's passing and the responsibilities that came with my mom's departure, but the people here gave me room to work through it, overlooking a few screwups, helping out when they could."

"You've paid them back and then some," she assured him. "You've done good work here."

He dismissed her words with a curt shake of his head as he poured their drinks and passed her a glass while she thought back to their first meeting. It had been only three years after losing his parents, but he'd been so sharp. Mature beyond his age. Ready to take on the world.

She hated to think her mother had helped sabotage things between them when Kai already had so much on his plate. He'd had big dreams to build his company and advance his software. Except he'd had to look out for his younger brother.

Of course, Kai could have opted to fight for their relationship, and he hadn't. Sipping the bubbling water, Miranda's eyes met his over the rim of her glass. The bubbly sensation shifted from her lips to her belly, the awareness of him tickling over her skin.

It made no sense that he could make her feel like that from nothing more than a shared look. No doubt it had to do with the way he affected her, turning up the intensity of everything she felt. She set her glass aside abruptly, trying to rein in her emotions.

"Speaking of good work." He rested his glass on the counter beside hers and covered her fingers with his. "How do you suggest we move forward, Miranda, when the thought of kissing you crowds out everything else?"

CHAPTER FIVE

MIRANDA STILLED.

He felt that stillness where he touched her, an unmoving wariness that lasted a long, breathless moment before her pulse jumped hard enough for him to feel the kick of it under his thumb.

"You were never one to mince words," she said finally, her blue gaze tracking his, probing deeper as if she could pluck his thoughts from his mind.

"We're here to have a conversation about it," he reminded her gently, stroking his thumb over that telltale vein. "So we might as well come to the point."

He hadn't meant to rekindle this spark with her, but it leaped to life of its own free will whenever they were near one another. It seemed foolish to pretend otherwise.

Her gaze lowered, settling on the place where their hands touched. "I think I had a different idea about what it would mean to settle our differences."

"Why don't you tell me what you hoped to accomplish today," he pressed. "You're not a woman who minces words either. So be honest with me. How do you suggest we go forward from here?"

She remained quiet for so long he wondered if she was going

to answer. A breeze blew through the kitchen, stirring her red hair, a strand stroking along her cheek the way his hand longed to. When she lifted her chin, there was a determined glint in her eyes.

"With dogged resolve not to repeat the mistakes of the past."

He couldn't help but admire her, but he'd be damned if he was going to let her off the hook when he knew he wasn't the only one feeling tempted by what they'd once shared. "I couldn't agree more. But I can't say I ever viewed touching you or kissing you as a mistake. Far from it."

"That brand of thinking isn't going to solve the problem." She withdrew her hand from underneath his, but her restless gaze roamed over him in a way that eased the sting of rejection.

The caress of her eyes was far bolder than his hand had been.

"Neither is ignoring what we both want." He folded his arms, daring her to contradict him. Craving the chance to prove her wrong.

Miranda didn't oppose him, however. "As temporarily satisfying as it might be to indulge ourselves, Kai, I think we have too much painful and complicated history for any good to come from falling into old patterns. We can't just pretend the hurtful parts didn't happen."

Had it been hurtful for her, too?

Her expression seemed to confirm it, but at the time, he'd viewed their breakup as one-sided. She'd moved on without him, turning her affections toward someone more successful. He'd thought he'd been doing her a favor by giving her up. The idea that there might have been more to it gnawed at him.

"You think renewing our affair is too risky." He summarized her point, winnowing it down to the bottom line. He paced away from her as he thought it over, his gaze shifting to the silent spill of water at the edge of the infinity pool on the patio.

"Yes." She sounded relieved that he seemed to understand.

But a good negotiator always had a backup plan.

"I disagree." He strode toward her again, liking the vision of her here, in his home. "We're both older and wiser. We wouldn't fall prey to the false illusions we had about one another ten years ago."

He stopped just short of her, his chest so close to her he could feel the heat radiating off her, the heat of their desire for each other. Except she looked ready to argue again.

"What about a compromise?" he suggested, before she could speak, still not touching her even though the ache for her was a tangible thing inside him.

She arched an auburn brow, questioning.

"One last kiss," he suggested, presenting his real agenda.

For now.

"I think that's a bad idea," she said quickly, reaching for her water glass again. She took a sip, then kept the cut crystal in one hand, a barrier between them.

Her lips glistened with moisture. His heart slugged faster.

"Is it?" He leaned closer, but didn't touch her. "Let me tell you why I think it's the best idea."

"Um." She shifted, her knee grazing his as she moved.

The brief feel of her stoked a fire inside him, but still he didn't touch her, needing her to make the decision. "It would let us end on a good note. Give closure to that chapter."

She set her glass on the counter, the tumbler clinking unsteadily on the granite. "I don't think so. And I'm not sure this is a fair discussion."

"Good debate calls for supporting arguments." He eased back enough to look into her eyes, a far deeper blue than the pool outside. "But if you're not interested in hearing how a kiss might clear away the thoughts that cloud my head when you're around—"

She closed her eyes for a moment, and he thought she was trying to shut down the conversation. But then she nodded. It was a gesture so slight it was almost imperceptible, but he'd seen it. Somehow that nod told him she was conceding the point. His pulse sped.

"If we're going to do this, make it count." Deliberately, she curved a palm around his neck and lowered his mouth toward hers.

She began by brushing her lips over his with a feather softness that made him groan.

Or maybe it was the feel of her luscious curves pressing into him that tore the sound from his throat. Either way, the sweet satisfaction of her hands on him, urgently gripping his shirtfront to draw him closer, was the best possible outcome.

Her lips parted, welcoming him, and he took his time savoring her, licking his way inside. He lingered in the places that made her breath hitch, remembering what she liked, reminding her what they could do to one another. He wrapped her in his arms, sealing her to him, positive no man could make her feel the way he could. The orange-jasmine scent of her skin fired through his senses while her fingers skimmed over his shoulders and down his back.

He tried telling himself it was just a kiss. That he couldn't handle any more than that. But the soft swell of her breasts against his chest, the shift of her hips muddled his thoughts. Her hips rocked, seeking, and he was lost.

The kiss went wild. Out of control. The needy sound she made in the back of her throat undid him. Her hands slid over his shirt and then her fingers made quick work of the buttons. She slipped one hand along the heated flesh of his bare chest, her nails lightly scoring. He forced himself back, knowing he needed to end this. Remembering she hadn't signed on for more than a kiss.

But before he could pull away completely, she captured his lower lip with hers, drawing on it in a move so sexy he had to grind his teeth together to keep from leaning her over the kitchen counter and pulling up her skirt.

"Miranda." He said her name, almost in a plea—needing her help if he was going to regain control.

Her blue eyes sprang open, but she didn't move away from

him. Their heartbeats pounded wildly against his chest, and for a second, he couldn't have said which rhythm belonged to him. Need for her crowded out rational thought for long moments afterward.

Finally, her hands fell away from his chest.

He mourned the loss of her touch even as he said a prayer of thanks that he'd enlisted her aid. He'd never lost his head so fast for a woman.

Except with Miranda the first time.

Hell.

"I did warn you it was a bad idea," she reminded him, stepping back enough to give them both some breathing room.

She combed restless fingers through her red hair and then gave her suit jacket a tug, straightening it. A bright emerald cocktail ring on one finger was a welcome reminder that she was no longer the ambitious waitress with dreams of a big future.

This Miranda was independent and successful, with a whole life waiting for her in New York. And she'd made it clear she didn't want to retread their past.

"We have very different ideas of bad." He was in no mood to argue now. Not until he had his head screwed back on straight. "Because what just happened there was so damned good it hurt. You know it was."

"You wanted a last kiss. You got it." She finished her seltzer water and walked over to deposit the glass in his sink. "Now we can close that chapter and focus on the bank's business."

He slanted her a sideways glance as he refastened a few of his shirt buttons. "You realize how ludicrous that sounds. I think it's safe to say I was dead wrong about a kiss settling the tension between us."

She peered out over the patio area, a warm breeze filtering in. Her cheeks were flushed pink, her lips softly swollen from his kiss. Huffing out a sigh, she turned back toward him.

"Until we figure out what that means, why don't you show me the highlights of the house while we shake off the aftereffects?"

* * *

Her legs still felt shaky.

One kiss and she'd been ready to peel off all her clothes to relive the past with Kai. The rush of adrenaline must be what was making her skin buzz now. Maybe she should have just told him to take her back to her car.

But Miranda hadn't grown her business by being a quitter, and it bugged her to leave Kai's place without accomplishing what she'd come here for—to resolve the past so they could move forward with their professional partnership.

So even though the memory of the out-of-control kiss was still simmering in her veins, she followed him through his home, taking in the details of upcycled materials that had been used to achieve the sleekly modern aesthetic. Maybe her subconscious would tackle the problem of the kiss while she tracked the work Kai had done over the years.

She wasn't sure what impressed her most—the solar panels and collection of rainwater that made him far less dependent than most on conventional utilities, or the repurposed stone collected from teardowns around central Texas. He opened the last door on the bottom floor for her now, gesturing her inside a pale gray office space or lab of some kind, full of humming computers, a huge locked server cabinet and monitors everywhere.

"And this is my tech room," he announced, following her inside across the travertine floor. "I work on new software and gadgets in here. It's not so much an office as grown-up play space."

Her brain supplied a whole different set of visuals for a play space with Kai. She squeezed her legs together against the ache for him, but that only made it worse. Huffing out a pent-up breath, she focused on what she was seeing instead of what she felt.

"It looks a little high-tech for play," she observed, noting the electronic parts in various states of assembly at a counter along the far wall. There was a huge overhead lamp on one swing arm for easy movement, and a magnifying glass the size of a dinner plate on another.

"I come here when I get burned out on coding," he admitted, following her deeper into the room as if drawn forward by his favorite things. "I love my work, but when the thing you're passionate about becomes your primary means of income, it robs you of a good creative outlet."

Surprised by the keenness of the insight, she remembered another thing she'd enjoyed about Kai. No matter their other differences—his bad-boy ways that flirted with danger while she stayed firmly on the straight and narrow—they were both wired for high productivity and ambition. They'd been able to share their dreams and their passion for their work.

"I couldn't agree with you more." Walking through the space, Miranda recognized shades of the man she'd known. An artist's rendering of a futuristic-looking motorcycle hung on one wall. A framed photo of the groundbreaking for Madtec's headquarters rested on another. "I couldn't wait to share the peace I take from yoga with other people, and I get to do that in a big way with Goddess. But the business means I don't get to be in the studio as much I would like."

She felt his presence close to her shoulder, her whole body keyed in to his no matter how hard she tried to forget about that kiss in the kitchen.

He didn't linger by her, however. Instead, he moved toward the door as if ready to move on. He waited there for her. "We're lucky to have those kinds of problems. But I hope you make taking care of yourself a priority, too."

The simple sentiment lodged in her chest, touching her, affecting her as much as his touch. When was the last time someone in her life had urged her to put her wishes first? Even Buckley—a great champion of her ambition—had measured her success by her profit margin. Shaking off the draw of the old bond with Kai, it occurred to her that relating to him physically was a whole lot simpler than acknowledging the deeper chemistry.

"I try." She strode toward the door as he made way for her in the gray stone corridor.

He nodded. Leaned a shoulder into the doorframe as he considered her, his arms folded. "The only places left to show you on the tour involve...beds." His green eyes darkened. Even the word sounded silky on his lips. "Places I don't dare take you with the aftermath of that kiss still singeing my insides."

She did that to him?

Her gaze dipped to where the fabric of his gray dress shirt went taut around his biceps. Tendrils of desire teased her, tangling around her legs and rooting her feet to the floor.

Breathless at the thought of him needing restraint around her, she posed to him the question she couldn't answer herself. "What do *you* think we should do to fix this?" She hesitated. "To get us to a regular working relationship, that is."

"I wish I had a clear answer for that." Sincerity colored his words, leading her to believe he'd thought long and hard about it, too. "But all I know is that ignoring the attraction is only making it worse."

Her heart beat so hard it felt like her whole body pushed her inexorably toward him. Fighting what she wanted demanded all her energy. All her focus.

The memory of what it felt like to be in his arms roared through her. The seductive answer to her question seemed impossible to ignore when he stood so close to her, more appealing than any man she'd ever met.

"At least we agree on what's *not* working," she murmured, as much to herself as to him.

"Why don't you let me make you my priority for the rest of the day, Miranda?" he suggested, reaching out to skim a knuckle along her cheek.

The touch melted any argument she might have made, any thought she might have had that didn't involve being with him.

Closing her eyes, she let herself focus on the place where his skin brushed over hers, the scent of him stirring her need while he continued to speak.

"We could step away from the problem of work for a while," he added, spinning a vision too enticing to resist. "And just... be."

Being with him would be so much more complicated than he was making it sound. But when was the last time she'd put what she'd wanted ahead of everything else? Her whole life had been about work and responsibility for years.

Opening her eyes, she found his.

"Yes." The affirmation of what she wanted felt like a step off a precipice, but it also felt damned good. She would take ownership of her choice. "I want to do more than see a room with a bed. I want to be in one. With you."

His knuckle stilled against her cheek as he seemed to absorb the words. Process them. And then, all at once, both hands cupped her face, lifting her chin for his kiss.

She stepped closer to him, wanting no space between them, needing Kai to deliver on the sensual promise he'd made. Now that she'd committed to this, she was going all in.

His mouth covered hers, claimed hers. His tongue stroked her lower lip, teasing a shiver that coursed through her whole body. She wrapped her arms around his neck, wanting to feel him everywhere.

He lifted her against him, his body a sensual friction against hers as her feet left the ground. She steadied herself with her hands on his shoulders while he turned them down a hall and up a stairway, his thighs stroking hers as he walked with her in his arms. His chest a warm weight against her breasts, his hips rolling against hers as they moved together.

Flames licked their way up her body, anticipation making her ready to come out of her skin by the time he shoved through a door into the master suite dominated by a platform bed with a padded leather headboard. He set her on her feet a moment before he leaned down to jab a remote. On cue, electronic blinds lowered to cover the windows while sconces flickered to life near a stone hearth on one wall, the low golden glow turning Kai's olive-colored skin to warm bronze.

The sight only fired her urge to see more of it. For the second time that day, her fingers went to work on his shirt buttons, desperate to feel him. Taste him.

"Miranda." Her name on his lips made her insides quiver. "I've missed your single-minded focus."

A startled laugh bubbled free, but it didn't come close to distracting her.

"You know how I am about goal setting," she teased, bending to kiss his sculpted pecs, his skin clean and his scent woodsy.

"And I enjoy being the focus of your goals." His hands were steadier than hers, quickly undoing the jacket of her suit. "But I did promise to make you my priority, remember?"

The cool air of the room, stirred by an overhead fan, sent a pleasurable shiver through her before he flicked a bra strap off one shoulder. The emerald green silk tickled before he lowered a kiss to her collarbone.

She forgot everything else but how that felt, gladly giving herself over to his touch. His mouth. She'd tried to bury the memories of what it had been like to be with him, but the knowledge leaped to life now, adding to the anticipation coiling tighter inside her.

She lost track of how his skillful hands freed her from one piece of clothing after another, but her skirt slid down her hips even before her jacket fell away from her arms.

Kai edged back to look at her, his green eyes missing nothing while she tried to catch her breath.

"You're so incredibly beautiful," he informed her, shrugging out of his shirt. "It's unfair to other women."

Feminine pleasure danced through her at his over-the-top flattery. She toed off her high heels and then moved toward him, her bare feet silent on the cool stone floor.

"It's far more unfair that you get to see me, and I can't see you." Hooking a finger in his belt, she slid the leather through the buckle before unfastening his pants, his skin hot to the touch where her knuckle grazed his abs.

He bent to kiss her again, distracting her with a flick of his tongue. She wavered on her feet and he lifted her once more, turning to deposit her on his bed. The downy navy-and-white-striped duvet felt cool against her skin while Kai remained standing. She watched him strip off his socks and shoes before shedding his pants. His boxers.

Her throat went dry at the sight of him. At the reminder of how much he wanted her. A helpless, needy sound tore free from the back of her throat before she could stifle it. He covered her with all that warm, heavy muscle, and the pleasure of it nudged her closer to the edge of fulfillment. Every nerve ending vibrated. One strong thigh sank between hers and she gasped at the feel of it.

Her fingers flexed against his shoulders, drawing him down to her, but he wouldn't be hurried as he unfastened the front clasp of her bra. Sensation tingled and tightened, making her ache. He soothed it with his tongue, circling the tip of her breast, drawing on her until she pulsated with need between her legs.

That too he cared for, fingering her lightly at first, then harder, through the thin silk of her panties until she writhed for more. She was so close to finding release. So close.

Dimly, she thought of telling him. But before she could form words, his breath warmed her ear.

"Come for me," he urged her, the whisper of sound coinciding with a sweet, devastating stroke of his finger up the very center of her.

The orgasm spun through her like a whirlwind, seizing all of her and twisting pure pleasure from her. The sensations pulsed over and over, as if she hadn't found release in all the years since he'd last touched her. She gripped his wrist, holding him there, even though she knew she didn't need to. Somehow, he still understood her body so very well.

When her quivers subsided, he drew her panties down and off. Speechless still, she kissed him hard, pouring the feelings she couldn't name into passion. She felt him reach into the nightstand drawer and knew he returned with a condom. Not trusting her trembling hands, she let him take care of it.

Just the way he took care of her.

The thought captivated her for a moment as he slid inside her. Then, his green eyes met hers and she didn't think about anything but making him feel as good as he'd done for her.

Rolling him to his back, she rained kisses down his neck as she moved over him, rolling her hips into him. Softly at first. Then harder.

He wasn't the only one who remembered their old rhythms. She found the pace he liked as naturally as breathing. Desire built all over again. As if he hadn't just delivered a toe-curling climax for her moments before. Her hunger for him returned. Redoubled.

They moved in sync. Perfect. Blissful. Harmony.

Kai rolled her to her back, taking over with an urgency she recognized. The pleasure boiled over, seizing her once more, even harder than before. Only then did he let himself go, the shudder of his powerful body a testament to what he felt.

When he slumped to her side, dragging pillows under both of their heads and wrapping a quilt over their cooling bodies, he stroked her face and kissed her forehead.

He'd always been the most tender, caring lover she could imagine. And right now, he'd awakened feelings inside her that she couldn't begin to pick through with drowsy contentment weighing down her limbs.

"It's early yet," he said into her ear, skimming her hair away from her face. "You have a lot of hours of pleasure ahead before you're allowed to have any second thoughts."

It seemed he still knew how to make her melt with his words as much as his body, too.

"Ten years have made you a wiser man," she observed lightly, knowing she'd need to retreat to her own space before she could figure out what this time with Kai meant in the big scheme of things.

No sense overthinking it now when she was in a muddle.

"Ten years have made you sexier," he returned without missing a beat. "Do *Forbes* list executive women still like postsex backrubs?"

Already his fingers were trailing light circles around her shoulders.

"You know my weakness," she groaned, rolling over to give him better access.

For one night, she could indulge herself, couldn't she?

Closing her eyes, she promised herself she'd wade through the confusing questions in the morning. There would be time enough to figure out a way to work with Kai then so she could leave for New York with Blackwood Bank in good hands.

Too bad a little voice in the back of her mind told her that ten years hadn't made her one bit smarter when it came to resisting this man.

CHAPTER SIX

AS THEY PULLED up to Natalie Valentine's bridal shop in downtown Royal later that week, Miranda asked the driver to give her a moment to refresh her makeup before she exited the car.

She should have done it on the way to the shop, but she'd been preoccupied with thoughts of Kai—the same way she had been pretty much every minute since the unforgettable night they'd spent together. So much for hoping that giving in to the attraction would help tame her runaway feelings.

With one hand, she raised the mirrored case of her eye shadow palette, and with the other, she swept powder over her nose. One of the perks of her role on *Secret Lives of NYC Ex-Wives* was having access to a makeup artist, and it had been kind of fun to sit back and let someone else do the work for the first few episodes, but as a woman with a lot of goals to tackle every day, Miranda soon found the time in the makeup chair felt excessively indulgent. As long as her face didn't shine and she had some mascara on her lashes, she was good enough. Why feed into the idea that women needed to spend hours on their makeup? Besides, she couldn't help but remember how nice it had felt to wash her face in the master suite at Kai's house the night they'd spent together and have him kiss every inch of her clean cheeks, swearing she'd grown lovelier in the last ten years.

She might have written it off as empty flattery except that his eyes had been sincere. His hands and mouth positively worshipful in their attention to every part of her...

Was it any wonder she couldn't keep her attention on something as mundane as what shade of lipstick matched her dress? Maybe time spent filming the show would help her corral her thoughts. She needed to tie up loose ends in Royal and head back to New York. Maybe it was just being back in Texas that had stirred all the old feelings for Kai. If that was the case, then leaving Royal should help her forget.

Satisfied she looked acceptable for the afternoon filming at the bridal shop, Miranda shoved the compact and makeup brush back in her bag and thanked the driver for waiting before she stepped out onto the sidewalk.

"Over here!" Seraphina called from beside the cameramen. She and Lulu looked like they were comparing shoes, their toes out like they were in ballet first position, their designer heels side by side.

"We're twinsies today," Lulu announced as Miranda got closer. "Fee bought the new Jimmy Choos in leopard print, and I snapped up the metallic silver."

"You'll set the new bridal trend for animal prints and glitter. I like it."

Lulu laughed, tossing her dark hair. "My wedding, my way, right?" She sounded more at peace with it since their talk earlier that week. "No sense going too conventional."

"Good for you." Miranda gave her a one-armed hug. She was thrilled for Lu, even if that meant being the tiniest bit envious. Who wouldn't want that kind of happiness in a marriage?

Miranda had tried marriage, putting all her considerable ambition and effort into making her union with Buckley a success, and it still hurt that it had been the biggest failure of her life.

A wicked smile curved Fee's lips. "You could do metallic cowgirl boots under your wedding dress and make all the bridesmaids match you. Rafaela would spontaneously combust at the thought."

Miranda relaxed into their chatter, soaking in the joy of being around her friends while they ramped up to the show's season finale. Rafaela and Zooey joined them a few minutes later and they took the wedding party into the bridal shop. Even Rafaela seemed impressed by Natalie Valentine, the knowledgeable shop owner whose inventory ranged from couture to vintage with plenty of interesting designers in between. Lulu spent a lot of time trying on international bridal gowns inspired by wedding traditions from around the world.

Miranda sipped champagne poured over fresh raspberries while she perched on a settee beside Zooey, watching Lulu twirl around in a beaded mermaid-style gown. The odd sense of envy nipped again, bugging Miranda, because she wanted to be a better friend than that to Lu.

Besides, it's not like Miranda believed she needed a man in her life to be complete. Far from it. If anything, she'd known greater contentment in her life since her divorce from Buckley, spending her time on friends and projects that were important to her. That fulfilled her spirit and nurtured her soul. So why the unrest now when her friend practically bubbled with joy?

Kai Maddox.

The man's face appeared in her mind's eye, distracting her all over again, assuring her that her mood today was entirely because of him. All at once, it occurred to her that some latent romantic part of her heart was craving something more with Kai.

It was a thought so startling she reared back from the starry-eyed romanticism of it, nearly spilling her champagne. Only Zooey noticed.

"You don't like the dress?" Zooey started to ask after Lulu disappeared to try on the next gown. Zooey turned toward Miranda on the settee. As she saw Miranda's face, she frowned, her honey-colored hair dipping over one eye as she leaned closer. "What's wrong?"

One of the camera crew rolled closer to them. Maybe someone else had noticed Miranda's sudden unease.

Crap.

She could practically hear the camera zoom button whirring, knowing her face was coming into sharp focus. Any lie she attempted about would be dissected by viewers.

Knowing she wasn't ready to confide her thoughts about Kai to anyone, let alone their million viewers, Miranda trotted out the one other truth beneath her melancholy mood today and hoped it would be enough.

"It just feels like the end of an era, doesn't it?" She swallowed over the emotions causing a lump in her throat, focusing on the bubbles in her champagne. "Seraphina's staying in Texas with Clint. Lulu and Kace are tying the knot, and I'm betting they'll be here more often than New York, too."

Nearby, Rafaela and Fee were scrolling through their phones to read more about a bridal gown designer, though they looked up when they saw the second camera moving toward Miranda and Zooey.

"Like high school graduation," Zooey offered, the comparison making Miranda smile at the reminder of how young she was. "Happy and sad at the same time because things will never be quite the same. Plus, you know you'll never have the same amount of drama."

Maybe the high school comparison was more apt than she'd realized.

"Exactly like that," she admitted, her eyes lifting to include Fee and Rafaela as she set aside her drink. "I'm going to miss the girl time."

Lulu stepped out of the dressing room just then, wearing a simple white sheath dress that was understated enough to put all the focus on her. She stopped short on the pedestal, surrounded by mirrors and her bridesmaids, peering around at their faces.

"What did I miss?" she demanded. "Something good?"

"We're getting all sentimental about the wedding feeling like a last hurrah for us," Fee told her, hopping up on the raised platform to link arms with Lu before slanting a glance toward Rafaela. "Remembering that we like each other…most of the time."

Rafaela sniffed, but didn't argue, which was practically agreeing for her.

"I'm the *bride*," Lu reminded them, squeezing Fee's arm tighter. "You can't get sentimental without me. Save all gooey love talk for when I can be here to savor it."

Miranda set down her champagne and moved closer to the dressing platform, fluffing the bride's skirt. "This one gets my vote, Lu. You look amazing."

"I like this one, too." Zooey stood, smoothing a hand over her green floral minidress that made her hazel eyes more emerald. "But don't let Miranda deflect. She was all *verklempt* about this being the end of an era."

Rafaela sighed. "So does that mean we have to group hug? Because I just had a blowout and I don't want it crushed." She flipped her long dark hair over one shoulder as she came to her feet.

"Get up here, you ungrateful wench," Fee blustered, holding out a hand.

Miranda wasn't sure if Seraphina and Rafaela had made nice for the bride's sake, or if they were genuinely burying the hatchet, but she was glad for the peace among the group as they all joined the bride on her pedestal. The five of them looped arms around each other's shoulders, and she looked around at the other four faces of the women she'd plotted with, laughed with and cried with on more than one occasion.

"This is more like it," Miranda said. "If it's our last hurrah, ladies, let's make it a good one."

The cameras loomed, a boom mic hovering overhead, the intrusion oddly startling since she'd been so focused on her friends.

"We're going to rock this wedding," Fee added, squeezing Lu even closer.

"Do you think this is what guys talk about in their football huddles?" Zooey asked, narrowing her green eyes. "They look just like this when they're on the field."

"Except their asses are more fun to look at," Rafaela deadpanned.

Her phone buzzed in Miranda's pocket even though she'd set it to not disturb her. Very few contacts could override that and get a notification through. Excusing herself as she waved to her friends to continue the fitting, she moved to a quiet corridor just outside the dressing area of the bridal shop.

She was surprised to see a text from Kai on the screen.

Major security breach of Blackwood Bank data during transition to Madtec's new software. Need to see you ASAP.

A chill ran through her. Of all the ways she'd been fantasizing about seeing him again, this wasn't one of them.

"Vaughn." Miranda blurted her stepson's name, grateful to have gotten through to Buckley's son and the inheritor of the bank as she fastened her seat belt in the back of the town car. She'd already told the driver to head to Deer Springs. "We need to talk."

She'd left the bridal fitting immediately, knowing her friends understood the demands of running a business. And right now, she wasn't just in charge of Goddess. During the transition of the Blackwood assets to the rightful heir, she was still responsible. The weight of that felt heavy on her shoulders while she contemplated the possibility of exposing customer financial information to hackers.

"I've already heard about the breach," Vaughn informed her, his voice brusque. "From what I can tell, Dad's in-house security team has been running on fumes for too long. I can't say I'm surprised."

She stared out the window, focusing on her breathing to settle taut nerves as they hit the outskirts of Royal, the homes giving way to fields and farmland.

"I'm heading to Madtec now to assess the damage." She knew that hiring Kai had been the right move, but had it been too late to protect the bank's clients?

"Good. In the meantime, I'm going to have to call a press conference to get on top of this." Vaughn might have spent most of his life ranching, but he had the same good head for business as his father. "News like this leaks fast."

"Do you want me to be there for the press conference?" she offered, needing to make herself available to Vaughn. Kellan and Sophie had been the toughest of the Blackwood heirs to convince that she wasn't the step-monster they all once thought, but while Vaughn hadn't been as focused on fighting her and contesting the will, he'd been the most withdrawn of the siblings. In fact, he'd barely set foot in Royal over the past few months. It wasn't until he'd come back for Sophie's wedding and reunited with his sweetheart—and their surprise child—that he'd opened up to Miranda at all. Their relationship was friendly now, but still fragile, and Miranda wanted him to know that he could count on her.

"No," Vaughn answered quickly. "I'd rather have you at Madtec being our ears to the ground. Please loop me in on whatever measures they're taking to counterbalance this attack."

"Of course." She hesitated as her driver left Royal behind, heading south toward Deer Springs. And Kai. "I still feel sure that hiring Madtec was the way to go. The Maddox brothers are excellent at what they do."

There was a beat of silence before his reply.

"I'll admit their client list is impressive. But we're their first big financial customer, and they do have a hacking background—" Vaughn swore on the other end of the phone. "Look, Miranda, I'd better go. My public relations department is up to their ears in calls."

"We'll make this right," she assured him before disconnecting.

Grip tightening on her phone, she tried to gather her thoughts before seeing Kai.

She trusted him, despite the Maddox brothers' reputation as the bad boys of tech. She worried her lower lip, remembering how Kai had mentioned his regret over not giving Dane his full attention in the months before Dane to jail. She'd understood what he was saying. Kai been distracted wooing her.

No doubt Kai and Dane had something to prove.

Maybe she did, too. She might have failed at her marriage, but she would at least succeed in business. Blackwood Bank wasn't hers permanently, but she was in charge of it for now, and she would fight for this company to make sure it thrived.

She'd hired Kai because she believed he was the best. So if there was anything she could do to help him avert disaster, she was all in.

"Ms. Dupree to see you, Kai," Amad's voice came through a speaker in the on-site lab at Madtec.

"I'll be right out," he informed his assistant.

At any other time, Kai would have been glad to see her. But with the cybersecurity breach weighing on him like a lodestone, dread balled in his gut. This was no personal call. On this visit, Miranda represented Blackwood Bank, and the news from all sides was grim. He'd been pulled out of his bed at 5:00 a.m. on his day off to deal with the breach, alerted by Dane, who'd been on-site with one of the techs when the drama started to unfold.

Now, twelve hours later, Kai's eyes were beginning to cross from the stress and exhaustion of securing the site, assessing the damage and implementing a new system.

"I'll be back," he assured Jerrilyn, the systems engineer in charge of revamping the bank's cybersecurity. "Call me if you find anything."

"We're fine," she assured him, never looking up from her screen. "We'll take care of this."

The hum of the electronic equipment and cooling fans was

broken only by the occasional keystrokes of technicians scouring every inch of the breached site. In a lab of fifteen workstations, three computers were projected onto big screens so all the techs could track the progress of the new security data's installation, a slow process considering the massive undertaking. The initial installation had been interrupted by the breach, and they'd needed to do some cleanup on the site before they could try a second time.

Kai's gaze went to the central screen before he walked out to find Miranda. The new software would take all night to install, and that was running at the absolute fastest possible capacity. Madtec hadn't been prepared for this level of client demand so quickly into the relationship with Blackwood Bank, but at least—so far—the bank's internal tech team had taken the blame for the breach. They knew their security measures had gradually fallen apart before Madtec came on board.

But what would Miranda think?

It bugged Kai how much that mattered to him right now. After taking the elevator to his office, he walked past Amad's desk and into his office. Miranda's back was to him as she studied a photo on his bookshelves. No doubt she recognized the backdrop since it came from their long-ago trip to the beach in Galveston. The photo showed only his motorcycle, but the two helmets on the seat never failed to remind him of who'd been with him that day.

A silent reminder to him not to let himself get distracted again.

Miranda replaced the framed photo, her movement drawing his attention to the sweep of her blue chiffon dress sprigged with daisies. It was an ultrafeminine choice, reminding him he'd bothered her on the weekend when she'd no doubt been enjoying herself outside work. Memories of being with her at his place—never far from his mind this week—redoubled. For a moment, the urge to speak to her on a personal level, to pull her into his arms, was damn near overwhelming.

He ignored it, knowing his first loyalty had to be to his business.

"Thank you for coming." He shut the door behind them, ruthlessly reining in the need to touch her. "I'm sorry to interrupt your Saturday."

She turned, the hem of her dress swishing softly around her knees as her blue gaze locked on him.

"I'm grateful you phoned," she assured him, shrugging off his apology. "The only reason I'm still in Royal is to oversee the distribution of the Blackwood assets. There is nothing more important to me than this."

While he appreciated her commitment to the project, the reminder where her loyalties lay still stung. But it was just as well to remember their reunion had happened only because of business.

He gestured to the high-backed leather chairs in front of his desk. "Please, have a seat, and I'll walk you through what's happening."

Miranda smoothed the full skirt of her dress before lowering herself into one of the chairs. Kai took the other, hitting a button on a remote to reveal a built-in projector screen on a wall between the bookshelves. When not in use, the black background broadcast a digital clock, but now it mirrored his laptop, where he had multiple tabs open to demonstrate the damage done by late-night hackers into the bank's system.

The frustration of seeing the bank's data compromised helped keep him focused on the task at hand instead of Miranda's nearness, her rapidly shifting sandaled foot the only indication of the tension she felt as he explained how many customers' financial data might have been compromised. No matter what life threw her way, the woman remained cool. Composed.

Always looking for her next move.

Throughout the briefing he gave her, she asked few questions, but those she did were thoughtful insights, demonstrating her attentive eye for business. Not that he was surprised. She'd always excelled at extrapolating pertinent information, utilizing her resources to propel her work forward. Whether she was scouting locations for a yoga studio in downtown Royal the way she'd been doing when he first met her, or listening to a post-mortem on a cybersecurity incident, Miranda could home in on the key points and carry forward a vision for her next move. That cool head of hers was always thinking, always working ten steps ahead so she didn't miss a thing.

All of which made her a formidable businesswoman, but it made her tough as hell to read on a personal level. And it made him wonder where the passionate woman who'd been in his bed earlier that week still lurked inside this self-possessed head of America's biggest fitness empire.

"So the hackers could have accessed financial data for up to ninety thousand customers." Miranda summarized the bottom line as she stared up at the projected screen. Then she turned to him. "How are we fixing that? What steps do we tell them to take, and what are we doing on our end to ensure it won't happen in the future?"

Tired from spending all day addressing the dumpster fire that was Blackwood Bank's cybersecurity, Kai knew he wasn't at his best. He couldn't restrain some frustration that she didn't seem rattled about the ninety thousand people who'd had their data exposed to fraudsters.

"For starters, tell the bank's customers they weren't being adequately protected by the last system, and that Madtec was brought into an impossible situation to try to fix it overnight," he pointed out, losing patience with the job, but also with Miranda's cool veneer that didn't reveal a hint of what they'd shared.

A frown pulled at her lips, and Kai rose out of his seat to stalk behind his desk, needing some distance from her.

"While I obviously can't do that, I realize this situation isn't of your making, Kai," she assured him, too damned reasonable to tell him he was being irrational and defensive.

Always a professional. And gorgeous. So desirable he ached to have her again.

He hauled his gaze away from the tempting sight of her and leaned a shoulder against the window looking out over a first-floor courtyard with the central fountain.

"The rest of the tech world won't be so gracious, I assure you." He ran a hand through his hair, blinking gritty eyes. "Madtec has put everything into steering our image away from our past, so a breach like this on one of our clients—our fault or not—is a huge setback if we can't get on top of this."

He needed to pull it together. The job. The meeting.

The desire for this woman who revealed so damned little of herself.

"You will," she said simply, rising from the leather armchair with the graceful movements that punctuated her every step. "I have every faith in you and Dane. But I can see you have your hands full with this situation right now. Should I leave you to do your job?"

How was it she could just shut down the attraction that still threatened to set him ablaze just looking at her? Nerves frayed and tension radiating through him—from work and personal things—he felt as overcharged as a live wire and yet exhausted at the same time. More than anything, he wanted to hold her, and the realization that he needed her with a tangible, physical hunger was more than a little daunting.

"No." He ground his teeth together to hold back words that might reveal the depth of that need.

When he didn't say anything else, she shifted her weight from one foot to the other, toned calves flexing. He thought he saw a hint of uncertainty in her eyes.

"Are you sure?" she asked, her manicured fingernails lightly resting on the black leather seatback, a bright blue cocktail ring winking in the slanting afternoon sunlight.

Something about her chiffon dress, so different from what she normally wore for work, gave him an idea. A way to appeal to her that might slip around those damned professional boundaries of hers.

"Actually, if it's just the same to you, the head of Blackwood Bank can leave." He straightened from his spot at the window, facing her head-on. "As for the woman I slept with? I'd like to speak to that Miranda right now."

CHAPTER SEVEN

A SPARK LEAPED between then, arcing in the quiet air of Kai's office.

Miranda exhaled as she stood next to his desk, some of the tension sighing from her lungs at his clear-cut directive.

She understood it. Empathized, even, because she felt the strain of reining in her feelings around him. No doubt he was exhausted. Stress and fatigue hung heavy on him, making her long to offer him some kind of comfort. But she could also see how dialed in he was to the task at hand. How engaged.

Leaving her leather bag on the back of the armchair, she circled the massive steel-and-wood workstation to face him, stopping just inches short of him.

"Speaking as the woman who slept with you," she began, threading her fingers through his because she couldn't resist touching him another moment, "you're seriously lacking imagination if you can't see past the bank executive to who I am underneath."

His green gaze darkened as he looked down at her. He shifted an inch closer, until there was just a hair's breadth of room between them.

"I can imagine every inch of the woman beneath. Vividly." His voice hit a gravelly note. "That may be part of the problem."

He lifted their joined hands to his face and stroked the back of her fingers against his jaw. "But the other part of it is that you're the last person I want to let down right now, Miranda. Not because of the bank. Because of what's happening between us."

The honesty of those words sent a shiver of worry through her, because she didn't know where this relationship was headed either. Anxiety constricted her rib cage, a sharp confusion she still wasn't sure how to resolve. The uncertainty about Kai's expectations made it hard for her to simply enjoy the feel of him, even though she had an urge to lean into him, too.

She wasn't used to relying on anyone, and the neediness she felt scared her.

"Is there anything I can do to help…with the fallout from the cyberattack, I mean?" she asked, pulling her attention from his face to the big office around him, wary of falling into his arms while they were in the middle of a work crisis. If he noticed her dodging the subject, he didn't comment on it. "Vaughn is going to hold a press conference, but I told him I would update him once I knew more."

Unthreading their fingers, Kai stepped back, distancing them again. Her relief at sidestepping a thorny talk was overshadowed by disappointment at the loss of his touch. His expression shuttered, and she had the sinking feeling she'd disappointed him.

But she didn't know how to walk this line they were treading. She couldn't keep indulging a physical relationship when the business was her priority.

"Right." Kai nodded, moving past her to close his laptop. "In a perfect world, I would send someone to the press conference to represent Madtec, but unfortunately I need every available body on-site working on the Blackwood Bank problem." His gaze locked on hers, and there was no hint of the tender lover she remembered from their night together. "I've got to return to the tech lab to oversee things. Why don't you make yourself comfortable here, and I'll send up our PR rep to help you coordinate a statement from us for Vaughn. She can provide ideas for how to frame the news for your customers."

She bit her lip as she watched him retreat from her. Not just physically. She remembered how he'd withdrawn from her before they'd broken up ten years ago. It shouldn't hurt anymore, now that she'd stopped hungering for a romance to complete her.

And yet, the pang in her chest was undeniable.

"Kai—" she began, wanting to be more supportive of his work. Wondering if there was a middle ground for a relationship she wasn't seeing.

But he was already pushing through the double doors and out of his office. She glimpsed him leaning over his assistant's desk to give instructions before the heavy double doors swung shut again.

Later, she would figure out a way to make it up to him for not knowing how to be his lover in these circumstances. She was a better professional colleague anyhow. She wasn't leaving Madtec until she could see with her own eyes that the new security software was up and running. She would set up camp for the night in an office and provide whatever updates she received to Vaughn.

For now, she'd do what she did best. Take care of business.

"You should head home," Kai told his brother, Dane, eight hours later. "You look like roadkill."

Dane had just walked into the tech lab, his thick brown hair standing on end, his focus going straight to the overhead screen that broadcast the progress made on installing the new security software for Blackwood Bank. They'd wanted to test it further before rolling out the installation, but the breach had robbed them of that chance. They didn't have the luxury of time anymore.

Setting aside a fresh cup of black coffee, Kai swiveled in the ergonomic leather office chair at the center of the room, pushing back from his workstation. Three other systems analysts remained in the area with him, overseeing their own responsibilities in the implementation process, but the installation had all gone smoothly so far.

"You're just jealous you can't rock a beard like mine," Dane said absently, stroking a hand over the facial hair while he glanced at one of the other analysts' monitors on his way to the center of the room.

"Dude, you've been here so long there are probably small life forms setting up colonies in that thing," Kai returned, relaxing a bit at Dane's easy demeanor. It reinforced Kai's own sense that the crisis was abating.

If Dane was still worried about Blackwood Bank's system, he would be wired, no matter how little sleep he'd had. The zombie-like trudge of his brother's steps was reassuring as Dane reached the chair beside Kai's and lowered himself into it.

"Possibly. But if looking like roadkill keeps me out of the media, I'll take it." Dane tapped the screen to life at the workstation in front of him, refreshing a tab tracking the day's business news. "We're going to have to give in and get more aggressive about defending the Madtec image though, so someone will have to start speaking on behalf of the company."

A bad feeling crept up the back of his neck.

"What do you mean?" Kai asked.

"I mean we should have sent someone to the bank's press conference instead of just issuing a statement, because Vaughn Blackwood wasn't prepared for the technical questions about the breach." Dane hit a button to fast-forward a clip from the local network news, stopping when it reached the last third of the video.

The camera captured a weary-looking Vaughn looking like a deer caught in the headlights as he fielded detailed inquiries from journalists about the nature of the breach, the party responsible and the kinds of measures being taken to address the problem. He kept returning to his note cards, reiterating talking points that only partially answered the questions.

"Shit," Kai muttered as he stared down at Dane's screen, wondering if he should have encouraged Miranda to be there for the press conference. No doubt she would have done a better job holding her own. "I had our lone press relations expert working with Miranda on the statement. That mistake is on me."

Before Dane could respond, the news coverage swapped to footage of the Madtec headquarters, where news vans were camped outside with a graphic marked "Live" next to the images. A reporter told viewers that they would obtain answers "as soon as possible." Kai had no idea they were out there since there were no windows in the tech lab at the center of the building.

"The vans only arrived about an hour ago," Dane informed him, switching off the tab to open a different program he'd been working on. "But since it's after business hours, they haven't been able to enter."

"No one told me." Kai wondered if Miranda knew. They'd exchanged a few texts over the last eight hours, but he hadn't gone back to his office since they'd parted ways. She'd settled in for the night, requesting periodic updates on the security installation, then feeding the information to Vaughn.

She'd refused to leave until Blackwood Bank was secured again.

Which Kai understood. But her rebuff had stung. Maybe it had been unfair of him to ask for his lover instead of his colleague though, given how important the fate of Blackwood Bank was to her. When she'd arrived, he'd already had hours to come to terms with the breach, but the news had still been fresh—and upsetting—for her.

"You might consider holding an impromptu meeting with the press of your own," Dane suggested, waving over an intern who'd just stepped into the tech lab with a fresh pot of coffee and a stack of cups.

Normally, they didn't allow food or drink in the lab, but the crisis of the big client breach had temporarily relaxed their standards.

Kai shook his head, even though he knew that meeting the media was inevitable. "No wonder you look like death warmed over," he observed wryly, understanding Dane wanted no part of the spotlight.

Grinning, Dane took a steaming cup from the local college student and set it carefully on his desk. "Method, meet madness."

Conceding the point, Kai was about to go up to his office to speak to Miranda about it when the woman herself burst into the tech lab, her cell phone in hand.

"Kai, I'm so sorry to disturb you." She hurried over, walking so fast that her lightweight skirt sailed behind her a bit. Face pale, her features were drawn into a frown. "It's Sophie Blackwood. She's been rushed to the hospital."

Concern for Miranda, for her family, quickly shifted his focus.

"Why? Is she okay?" Kai was already on his feet, alert to Miranda's distress. He understood the importance of family.

"I don't know. Nigel just texted the family to let us know. They were just returning from their honeymoon and she fainted at the airport—"

"I'll take you," he told her shortly, steering her toward the door. He knew she hadn't gotten any more sleep than he had, so there was no way he was letting her go alone. He nodded to his brother, knowing Dane would oversee things. "Let's go."

Grateful for Kai's certainty about the decision, Miranda gladly let him lead her out a private entrance to the building. The warmth of his hand on the small of her back was a comfort even more than a pleasure, and she stayed close to him.

The last hours had been exhausting, monitoring the implementation of the new data security while exchanging calls with Vaughn about Madtec's progress. And then, there was the media interest and customer outcry. The media she didn't care about so much. But she was frustrated on behalf of the bank clients and wanted to do better for them.

Although none of that compared to her worries for Sophie. She'd just repaired her relationship with Buckley's only daughter. And while she'd never fooled herself that she could be a stand-in mother for the fiercely independent woman who was only a handful of years younger than her, she meant to be the most supportive friend possible.

"What about the news vans?" Miranda asked Kai as she stepped outside the building, peering in the dark to try to orient herself. "The press is camped out waiting to talk to you."

Long after midnight, the executive parking area was quiet, with only three vehicles visible.

"They're on the other side of the building," he assured her, pointing to their left where the glow of fluorescent streetlamps cast a bluish glow.

No sooner had they gone five steps than a spotlight popped on a few yards away from them, accompanied by the rush of footsteps and a rolling camera dolly. Miranda had been around enough of them to become intimately acquainted with the sound.

"Ms. Dupree!" a woman shouted as the sound of high heels pounded nearer, a camera eye winking to life beside her as a red light flashed a recording signal. "Is it true you chose Madtec to provide digital security because of your romantic involvement with Kai Maddox?"

Beside her, she felt Kai tense as he muttered under his breath. "I should have had security escort us. I don't know how they got through the fence." Then, holding up an arm to bar the camera's view of her, he continued to hustle her toward his car. "This is private property," he informed the camera crew. "You're trespassing, and there's no statement at this time."

"It's okay," she assured him, seeing their way blocked by a second duo of journalist and camera operator. She turned to speak into Kai's ear so as not to be overheard. "If we give them two minutes, they might leave. It might be faster than if we try to bulldoze through them."

His green eyes met hers, his face clearly visible in the bright wattage of the media lights as he seemed to decide whether or not to agree with her. Finally, he lowered his arm from where it had been shielding her face from view.

Miranda looked directly into the camera, knowing what she wanted to say after having spent hours working on potential statements with Vaughn. "Blackwood Bank has full confidence in Madtec. We are grateful to be the first financial institution to benefit from their new encryption software, and it couldn't have come at a more opportune moment."

"Will your relationship with the Madtec copresident be a storyline on *Secret Lives of NYC Ex-Wives*?" the woman asked, jarring Miranda since she didn't know how Kai felt about the show or his company's potential connection to it.

"No storyline is needed because there is no relationship," Kai shot back, spurring Miranda into motion again as he resumed a determined pace toward the silver Jaguar sports coupe. "No more questions."

The light and camera crews followed them, a second group joining the first in shouting provocative questions meant to incite a reaction. One of the women asked Kai if he hoped Miranda would move back to Royal, while another asked Miranda if Kai's "bad boy" reputation in the tech world had appealed to her. A man's voice wanted to know if Miranda's marriage had ended because of her previous relationship with Kai.

But by then, Kai had opened the passenger side door for her, and as she lowered herself into the seat, she saw two security officers dressed in Madtec uniforms rounding the building. No doubt they would ensure the journalists were relocated to the front parking lot where the other vans were.

Freed to move faster with the arrival of the guards, Kai pulled open the driver's side door and started the engine.

"That wasn't the business media, that's for damned sure," he observed darkly, driving quickly out the back gate and distancing them from the building.

"Probably tabloids. There are paparazzi down here following the show. I recognized one of the women from a seedy outlet that reports on celebrity scandals." She hugged herself, the run-in more disconcerting since it had happened with Kai at her side. And because the real story was supposed to be about Blackwood Bank, not a relationship between her and Kai.

Which, according to Kai, they didn't have anyhow.

His words harkened back to her now, along with the cold tone he'd used. No doubt he'd been irritated to be caught on camera in the first place, which she understood. Except she'd thought that he was angling for more of a relationship.

Wasn't he?

The silence between them stretched as he navigated through the vacant Deer Springs streets in the predawn hours, toward the highway to head north to Royal.

When he didn't speak, she glanced over at him. His jaw flexed, his mouth set in a flat line.

"I hope it wasn't a mistake to speak to the media. It didn't occur to me that anyone would ask about the show, or anything personal." Although even as she said it, she realized how naive she'd been to think she could keep her personal life separate from the Blackwood Bank trouble. "I should have anticipated it, however."

He seemed to weigh her words before answering carefully, "For someone as determined as you are to keep your professional image at the forefront at all times, I'm surprised you decided to do that show in the first place."

The highway unfurled before them in an endless-seeming gray path outlined in yellow and white. No other cars were on the road, the farms dark and silent on either side of them. Inside the luxury sports vehicle, the dashboard lights were minimal, highlighting the angles of Kai's handsome face.

Miranda wasn't sure if she should be offended about his implication that the show was the opposite of "professional." She supposed she could understand why he'd feel that way.

"The show may be over-the-top, but the relationships are real. And viewers relate to seeing how we handle crises of friendship." She remembered the young woman on the stairwell in the Madtec building who'd asked for her autograph. "I think we give women hope that life can be rewarding and fulfilling even if romance doesn't work out. We have plenty of things to be passion about. And we have each other."

"From the promos, it looks more like the show is about catfights and competitive shopping." He adjusted the air conditioner, and she felt the chilly breeze around her legs subside.

A different kind of coolness ran through her at his words, though.

"Marketing hooks don't always reflect the substance of a product," she retorted, miffed at the way people could write off feminine art. And yes, what they created was a kind of art, even if she was too tired to march out that particular argument tonight. "That doesn't mean the substance isn't there."

"Fine." His words were clipped as he acknowledged the point. "I was just curious why you did the show. Now I know."

"I hated failing at my marriage, that's why," she told him honestly, too irritated and out of sorts to hold back the way she normally would. "*Secret Lives* shows another side of life for women. Not just their dating. But their businesses. Their friendships."

Frustration simmered as she remembered the way Kai had denied they had a relationship. Even though she'd been the one to ensure that new boundaries went up between them since their night together, his slight had still hurt tonight. She told herself it was probably because she was also worried about Sophie. She hadn't heard any updates since that first text from Nigel.

"Then it's a good thing I told that reporter we don't have a relationship," Kai mused as they saw a sign for the exit for Royal. "Since it's clear you don't plan on having one."

She couldn't argue with that.

She'd thought as much herself, hadn't she?

And yet, as they drew closer to Royal Memorial Hospital, Miranda couldn't deny that she'd thought about Kai—and romance—every moment since she'd left his house earlier that week. The idea that he didn't see it as the start of a relationship caused an ache in her chest to deepen, and she didn't have a clue how to make the hurt stop.

CHAPTER EIGHT

AN HOUR LATER, Miranda sat on the edge of the creaky vinyl chair in the emergency room waiting area, checking her phone for updates on a business meeting she needed to delay with AMuse, a rival fitness chain. When she'd agreed to the meeting, she'd hoped to be back in New York next week, but between the Blackwood Bank crisis, the Royal Gives Back gala she still needed to plan, Lulu's wedding and not knowing what was wrong with Sophie, Miranda didn't think the timing would work out.

She would just have to juggle things as best she could from here, delegating as much as possible to her staff while she waited for news about Sophie. Just as she started typing a message to her assistant to reschedule, Kai strode back into the waiting area. And how was it that even when she should be engrossed in work, she felt his presence? A cup of coffee in each hand, he dodged a toddler pushing a truck around the floor while the boy's grandmother read a paperback. That was all the action in the waiting room right now, since it was three in the morning. Vaughn had fallen asleep after the press conference, so she'd been unable to reach him. Kellan and Darius were both out of town, but she'd spoken to them both briefly to let them know about Sophie. Kellan hadn't wanted to wake Irina at this hour unless it was an emergency, but he'd promised to call her once the sun rose so she could be with Sophie either way. An ambulance had rushed in someone earlier, but there'd been no family with the older man.

How much longer until Nigel appeared with an update about Sophie fainting?

"Thank you." She took the cup Kai offered her, then met his weary green eyes. "You must be running on fumes."

"I'll sleep soon enough." He took the seat beside her, winking at the adventurous toddler who was slaloming his truck between chair legs now. "Dane said the download just finished. He's going to work for another hour and then he'll crash, too. We're in good shape."

Testing her coffee, Miranda tasted the soy milk she preferred. "Yum. You've got a good memory, Kai Maddox. Thank you."

How strange that something so small could make a person feel so well cared for.

"We shared enough breakfasts that I ought to remember," Kai said before he tried his own drink.

A nurse peered into the waiting room and then hurried back out, calling something to an orderly with a wheelchair. The loudspeaker squawked, paging a doctor. All normal activity.

Except life was far from normal for her right now.

Miranda's attention returned to Kai as she mulled over his words. "I shared more than a few meals with Buck, but he wouldn't have known my favorite color or song, let alone how I like my coffee."

"Green. And Sinatra's version of 'Summer Wind.' Or at least, it used to be." Kai pulled her favorites from his brain as easily as if he were citing multiplication table facts. "I never did understand what you saw in Blackwood beyond his money."

The warmth she'd been feeling toward him dissipated. Defensiveness prickled and she was tempted to snap at him, but another nurse appeared in the waiting room. Miranda's heart stuttered in anticipation. Kai shot to his feet. But the nurse waved over the grandmother and little boy. Leaving Miranda and Kai alone.

He sank back into his chair with a lengthy exhale.

"It was never about his money." She set aside her coffee, wishing Nigel would make an appearance soon and tell them what was going on with Sophie. "How could you think that? I married Buck because I thought our goals and interests were aligned. On paper, we made good, practical sense. He encouraged my business ideas. I helped him grow his empire. I thought we'd be a good team."

Kai shook his head before slanting her a sideways glance. "And you and I didn't make sense?"

His tone was challenging. But then they'd never cut each other any slack before. Why should now be different?

Did she *want* it to be different?

"We were passionate, not practical." She'd been happy with passion at first, but then she'd believed the passion must have been fading—on his side, at least—when Kai had withdrawn from her. She'd been devastated. Brokenhearted. Not that she'd ever confess the depth of that hurt to him.

"We were lovers and friends, too," he reminded her, his dark eyebrows furrowed. Clearly her view of the past didn't line up with his. "We had both."

Old regrets tugged at her, but she hadn't made the decision to end things lightly.

"You might have been enthusiastic about my ideas for Goddess, but you were more wrapped up in your coding world than anything." She smoothed the wrinkles from her filmy skirt. "I think you saw me as an escape from work, whereas I wanted to share my professional journey with you, and I wanted to know more about yours, too."

"You wanted a business partner?" he asked drily, stretching his arm along the back of her chair, his hand grazing her shoulder. "Being lovers and friends wasn't enough to get the job done?"

Had she expected too much from their relationship? Maybe. She'd been so in love with Kai, there was a chance she'd lost herself with him a little. Lost her bearings. Passion was exciting and heady, but it could be overwhelming, too. The realization—and the worry that she might have subconsciously pushed him away because of it—robbed her of a reply.

Just then, the double doors to the patient rooms opened, and Sophie Blackwood's new husband, Nigel Townshend, walked through them. Though he was impeccably dressed as always, the Green Room Media studio executive's expression appeared tired and—happy?

"Miranda." He gave her a slight smile as he caught sight of her and headed their way. The normally unflappable Brit looked decidedly worse for wear in his wrinkled suit. His tie was gone and his hair stood on end as if he'd raked fingers through it a few too many times. "Thank you for coming."

"How's Sophie?" she asked, coming to her feet. Then, as Kai rose beside her, she introduced the two men. "Nigel, this is Kai Maddox. Kai, Nigel Townshend works for the studio that produces *Secret Lives*."

The two men shook hands briefly, nodding acknowledgment. Then Nigel spoke.

"Turns out Sophie's fine," he explained, his blue eyes still a bit dazed. "The doctor thinks she got dehydrated because she's pregnant—"

Miranda drew in a breath, ready to celebrate the news, when Nigel finished his sentence.

"—with twins."

The news left her stunned, but overjoyed at the good news. Relief streaking through her that Sophie was all right, Miranda hugged Nigel, then turned to hug Kai without thinking—only to stop short. "That's wonderful news."

Kai cleared his throat and agreed, "Yes, it most certainly is." He shook the father-to-be's hand again. "Congratulations, man."

"Thank you," Nigel said with genuine joy. "I couldn't be happier. Although I really do need to return to my wife so we can process the big news together."

"You're sure you don't need us to do anything for you, Nigel?" Miranda asked, ticking through the possibilities in her mind. "You came here straight from the airport. Do you need food? Or should we stop by your house and get Sophie some clothes?"

"The doctor isn't admitting her." Nigel ran a hand through his light brown hair, his Patek Philippe watch glinting in the fluorescent lighting. "We're just getting a referral to be sure she can see an obstetrician tomorrow, and then I'll take her home."

A silence took hold in the wake of Nigel's departure, leaving her standing alone with Kai. Clearing his throat, he gestured toward the door.

"Should we go?" he asked, startling her from her thoughts of babies and marriage. New beginnings.

"Of course." She nodded, happy for Sophie even as she wondered what kind of relationship she would have with the Blackwood family once she left Royal.

She wanted to meet the twins. More than that, she wanted to hold them. Be a part of their lives.

She blinked past the rush of feelings, telling herself she was just tired.

Leaving the hospital together, Miranda saw the sun was just rising as they reached Kai's silver sports car.

"I'm thrilled for Nigel and Sophie, but I've lost all track of time," she murmured, exhaustion kicking in now that she didn't have worry and stress driving her forward. And yet Kai had been awake for longer. She couldn't let him drive all the way back to Deer Springs. "I can't imagine how you're still coherent."

"I'll be fine. And I'll have you home soon," he promised, holding the door for her as she took her seat and buckled up.

Her eyes followed his broad-shouldered frame as he strode

around to the driver's side, her hungry gaze tempered by the realizations in the hospital waiting room.

Had she given up on passion prematurely when she broke things off with Kai? Yes, he'd pushed her away, but now she knew why. Her mother had been moving him around like a chess piece to ensure Miranda ended up with Buckley. Miranda could have found that out back ten years ago—but she hadn't asked. She'd felt Kai stepping back, and she'd just let him go.

It was difficult to accept that what she had with Kai was well and truly over when she still felt so drawn to him.

As he settled into the driver's seat and started the car, she watched his movements. She could see the flex of his forearms where his shirtsleeve remained rolled up from working. His broad, capable hands wrapped around the steering wheel, and she was transfixed by the memory of what his touch did to her.

He caught her staring.

"I'm curious what you're thinking right now." He didn't put the car into gear, his gaze wandering over her.

That simple attention stirred her insides, her nerve endings flickering to life.

"It occurred to me that you can't possibly drive back home tonight. You can stay at the guesthouse." She would have made the offer even if she hadn't been genuinely concerned for his safety. There were no two ways about it. She wanted Kai in her bed. "With me," she added, her voice grazing over a husky note.

Desire darkened his eyes. She shivered from the awareness tickling over her skin.

"And just like that," Kai spoke softly as he put the car into gear, "I'm not the least bit tired."

Fifteen minutes later, Kai held Miranda snugly against his side, nuzzling her neck as she entered the security code on the guesthouse.

A night breeze blew through the filmy skirt of her dress, lifting the fabric enough to brush his pant leg. A touch so subtle he shouldn't have been able to feel it, except that his nerve endings were wound tight, his senses keenly attuned to this woman.

The scent of her shampoo mingled with the light fragrance she wore that smelled like jasmine. Her red lacquered fingernail hovered over the buttons on the security panel, as if she was unsure what to press next. He wondered if she was distracted by the same fire in the blood that roared inside him.

While she searched for the next numeral to input, Kai bent closer to taste the skin exposed along the back of her neck. A breathy sigh erupted from her lips, her head tipping toward him as she leaned into the kiss.

As much as he couldn't wait to explore the rest of her, to indulge himself in her sweet responsiveness, he also knew they needed to be inside the house for what he had in mind.

"Did you forget the code?" he asked, sliding a hand around her waist as he kissed his way to the hollow beneath her ear.

"No." She hit another number and he skimmed his touch higher, brushing the underside of her breast. With a sharp intake of air, she jabbed the last number hard. "Just distracted."

The alarm chimed an agreeable tone, allowing her to open the door and step away ahead of him. He followed her inside, trying not to think about the fact that this place once belonged to Buckley Blackwood, the man who'd stolen Miranda from him.

The man he'd believed Miranda wanted more than him.

Thoughts of the man stilled Kai. Tonight, he'd learned that she hadn't been wooed by his wealth. Yet ten years ago, Kai had been quick to believe the worst of her, probably because of his own insecurity about the hardscrabble kind of life he would have been able to give Miranda back then. He'd given her up too easily.

A mistake he wouldn't repeat.

Miranda called to him from the kitchen while he still stood in the entryway. "Can I get you a drink? Something to eat?"

The sound of her voice spurred him back into motion.

"No. Thank you." He followed her into the kitchen where he'd brought her pie from the Deer Springs Diner.

She was already at the island, a hip leaning against the white quartz countertop, pouring two glasses of water from a green bottle before returning it to the refrigerator. Kai paused by the island long enough to tip the beverage to his lips, his eyes following her movements as she ran a hand through her gorgeous red hair.

"I'm not hungry either," she agreed, joining him at the counter to pick up her glass for a sip of the sparkling water.

"Who said anything about not being hungry?" he asked, setting aside his drink before he bracketed her hips in his hands. He walked his fingers down her thighs, lifting the fabric of her skirt as he moved, baring more of her legs to his gaze. "I'm starving for a taste of you."

A stillness took hold of her as her blue eyes locked on him while he rucked up the skirt. Then, lowering her glass, she steadied herself with her hands on his shoulders. He traced the lace fabric of her panties with his finger while she sucked in a gasp.

His temperature spiked. And then their hands were all over each other, roaming and exploring. She smoothed a touch over his chest and shoulders. He pressed his palm between her legs and her hips arched into him. He kissed her deeply, liking the small sounds of pleasure that hummed in the back of her throat. He was so damned greedy for her, he all but forgot where they were. When she stepped back, it took him a moment to blink through the hunger for her and remember they were standing in the kitchen.

She drew him forward by the hand, and he recovered his wits enough to follow the hypnotic sway of her hips as she moved down a lengthy hall toward a bedroom. He could see the king-size platform bed through an open door. A gray coverlet that looked like crushed velvet beckoned.

As they crossed the threshold, the scent of fresh flowers

wafted from the nightstand where a vase of coral honeysuckle and daylilies rested. Behind the bed, a black-and-white print of downtown Houston took up a whole wall. But these were details he only half noticed as Miranda peeled down the top half of her dress, letting the silky fabric fall to her waist. A statement clear as a gauntlet dropped, and he'd be damned if he'd leave it unanswered.

Stress from the last twenty-four hours evaporated. All thoughts and doubts faded. The only thing he felt now was hunger for her.

"Let me help," he insisted, reaching for the buttons on her skirt. "I want to feel you as I undress you."

"I'd like that." She shifted her fingers to his shirt, working her way down the placket. "I want to feel you, too." She rolled her hips in a way that shifted her thighs against his. "All of you."

His body responded instantly.

"Happy to oblige." He tugged her dress down and off, leaving her in just a whisper of silk and lace that shielded her from view.

He shrugged out of his shirt as soon as she undid the final button, then shed his pants, socks and shoes, tossing them in easy reach of the bed.

Her eyes followed his movements, locking on his body in a way that was damned flattering. And burned away his last reserves of patience.

Lifting her against him, he carried her to the bed and laid her down in the center. Taking only a moment to admire how beautiful she looked with her fiery-red hair in the center of the gray velvet, Kai fell on her like a starving man. He kissed his way down her neck to her breasts, nipping and licking her through the thin silk barrier of her bra. She wriggled out of one strap and then the other, tugging the cups lower to give him full access. Gladly, he savored her bare skin, finding the source of her jasmine scent in the valley between her breasts. When he kissed his way lower, he dragged her lace panties down with his teeth, listening to every nuance of her breathing as he touched the sweet, hot center of her.

He glanced up for a glimpse of her face. The flush spreading across her chest told him she was so close to release already, as on fire for him as he was for her. He licked her and kissed her, loving the taste of her. Her release hit suddenly, surprising him with how quickly she flew apart in his arms.

A few hammering heartbeats later, he took his time retrieving his pants where he'd tucked a condom in his wallet, needing a moment to regain his self-control. But Miranda took over the task, ripping open the packet and sheathing him with eager hands.

Which totally worked for him.

Everything about her turned him on. Turned him inside out. When she reversed their positions, she climbed on top of him to straddle him. His breath came in a harsh rush, his heart slamming hard against his chest. He looked up at her in all her feminine glory and forgot everything else but being inside her.

And then he was.

Moving slowly at first, and then faster. She raked her nails lightly down his chest, a welcome counterpoint to the feelings that threatened to send him hurtling over the edge too soon. He rolled with her, putting her on her back so he could enjoy her that way, too.

"You feel so good, Kai," she murmured, her eyes half closed as she writhed beneath him.

It might have been the movement or her words, but something about the moment sent him hurtling toward completion long before he wanted. The realization slammed into him that he hadn't brought her to that precipice with him, yet at the same moment, her legs wrapped around his waist, and she found her own release with him. Fulfillment rocked him even as he acknowledged how thoroughly she made him lose control.

As the sensations continued to ripple through him, Kai

couldn't remember the last time he'd been so consumed by passion. Probably, it had been with Miranda ten years ago.

Sliding to the side of her, he felt a wave of tenderness for the woman in his arms. A feeling he had no business having for Miranda given how soon she'd be out of his life again. But he ignored that thought as he wrapped her in the soft coverlet and tucked a pillow under her tangled red hair, thinking she'd never looked more appealing to him.

Emotions crowded his chest, but he pushed them aside for now and simply kissed her on her forehead. She had to be tired. And he was, too. He hoped that was why he felt the urge to invite her to Deer Springs and spend more time pursuing a relationship. He knew that would never work since she had a whole life away from him in New York.

He shouldn't trust her anyway, based on how fast she'd put him out of her life the first time.

They didn't make sense on paper, she said.

And no matter how much he might wish it otherwise, they still didn't.

CHAPTER NINE

MIRANDA PACED THE floor of the guesthouse office the next morning after slipping from the bed she'd shared with Kai. She hadn't wanted to wake him, knowing his sleep deficit had far surpassed hers when they'd finally dozed off. She'd done her morning yoga poses out in the detached studio, then she'd returned to the office where a pewter pitcher full of purple coneflowers and sunflowers rested on the narrow secretary desk by her laptop. She carried a mug of mint tea to the desk and took a seat, hoping to use this time to somehow untwine her messy knot of feelings for the man sleeping just a few rooms away.

She'd told herself that she could resist his charm enough to prevent herself from falling for him again, but the more time she spent with him, the more she wondered if that was possible. History seemed to be repeating itself. And with that thought, she realized it might help to call her mother.

A crazy idea, maybe, she acknowledged as she pulled out her cell phone and scrolled through her contacts.

But the need to reconnect with her mom—to confront her about interfering in Miranda's relationship with Kai ten years ago—had preyed on her mind ever since Kai had revealed the role Ginny had played.

Leaning back in the leather office chair, Miranda tried to

breathe through her nervousness as the call rang. And rang. She was about to hang up when her mother's voice sounded in her ear.

"Hello?"

Even from that lone word, Miranda could hear the husky rasp of exhaustion in her mother's tone.

"Hi, Mama. It's Miranda. Did I wake you?"

"Miranda?" Shuffling noises sounded on the other end of the call. A brief coughing spell ensued before her mother returned. "I'm surprised to hear from you."

Guilt pinched, but not for long. They hadn't parted on good terms the last time they'd spoken.

"How are you feeling?" she asked, knowing her mother always had a litany of health complaints—and yet her mother's ailments only increased the more "medicine" she took. The prescription pill problem ebbed and flowed over the last fifteen years, compounded by Ginny's refusal to get help.

"Since when do you care how I feel?" Her mother's words came wrapped around a cigarette, spoken out of one corner of her mouth. Miranda knew her mother so well, the small distortions of her words familiar to her after living with her for over twenty years. The flick of a lighter sounded, then a long exhale. "I seem to recall you didn't want me anywhere near you the last time I came for a visit."

Defensiveness pricked along her skin.

Ginny had arrived on the set of Secret Lives of NYC Ex-Wives during the first season, determined to be a part of the show. Miranda had refused. She had enough trouble navigating a relationship with her mom privately, let alone having the bond subject to public scrutiny.

"I would have been happy to spend time with you," she reminded her, glancing over her shoulder to ensure the door to her office remained closed. She didn't want to wake Kai. "But I got the idea you were only interested in visiting if our time together was televised."

Ginny sniffed. "I forgot you only show the world your cleaned-up side."

Miranda clutched her mug of tea, inhaling the minty scent and focusing on her breathing to ease the sting of the gibe that hurt more than she would have expected, maybe because there was some truth in it. But she'd worked hard to become the person she wanted to be. Why should she have to dwell on the unhappy pieces of her past that refused to heal?

Her mom had chosen her path—and continued to choose it, over and over again. Speaking of which, Miranda had a question to ask, and hedging only increased the nervous tension.

"Do you remember me dating Kai Maddox? Back when I still lived at home?" She'd remained in Deer Springs well into her twenties, determined to help her mother get clean.

It took a long time for her to learn that no one could help an addict who wouldn't help herself.

"The motorcycle guy who was too young for you?" Another puff on her cigarette, the exhale a long, protracted sigh. "Sure I do."

Closing her eyes against the wave of frustration she felt, Miranda traced the rim of the stoneware mug with her fingertip.

"I never thought he was too young for me," she reminded herself more than her mom. Only six years separated them, a difference no one would blink at if the older party happened to be male. "And I cared for him a great deal." She'd loved him. "Do you remember why things didn't work out for us?"

Her mother snorted dismissively. "Seriously? Buckley Blackwood and his millions came calling, Miranda. No one would blame you for having your head turned."

Clinging to her own memories of the past, Miranda felt sure that hadn't been the way it had happened. Buckley had liked her from the first—that much was true. He'd come to her yoga studio not long after his divorce from his first wife, Donna-Leigh Westbrook. He'd immediately asked Miranda out, but she'd declined. Unperturbed, he'd continued to take classes with her.

He'd sent flowers. He'd been a gentleman, but he'd also been persistent, sending her invitations to exclusive local events and introducing her to a few key members of the Texas Cattleman's Club who'd been instrumental in building her business.

But she'd been in love with Kai.

"My head wasn't turned by his wealth." She couldn't swallow back the defensiveness, remembering how careful she had always been to make sure the world knew she hadn't married him for his money. "I signed a prenup, remember? When we divorced, I walked away with nothing." She'd been determined to prove to the world she could make it on her own after her marriage fell apart, and she had. But she hadn't phoned her mother to talk about that. With an effort, she breathed through the simmering resentment and asked, "What I want to know is did you say something to Kai to send him away? To make him think I cared about Buckley and not him?"

As soon as she asked the question, she regretted it. She knew Kai wouldn't lie to her about something like that. Yet it upset her to think her mom had quietly upended Miranda's life like that without her knowing.

Her fingernails bit into her palm.

"That was a long time ago," Ginny informed her after a long pause. "I don't think I ever had much to say to the motorcycle-riding boyfriend."

This was a mistake. Closing her eyes, Miranda heard sounds emanating from the kitchen and inhaled the scent of frying bacon. She grappled for a way to end the phone call that was only frustrating her and not providing any answers. She dragged in a breath, but her mother spoke again before she could get a word out.

"Although now that you mention it," Ginny continued, "there was one time when he stopped by just as the floral delivery truck left. He asked me about the huge arrangement, and I remember being frank with him about Buckley having his eye on you. Why all the interest in Kai now?"

Miranda needed to end the call. With the hint of fresh coffee wafting in the air, she knew Kai was awake. She just hoped she could still enjoy their time together now that talking to her mother had her tense and stressed all over again.

"No reason," she lied, feeling twitchy and anxious. "I'll call again soon, Mama."

Disconnecting the call, Miranda tried to shake off the knowledge that her mother had poisoned her relationship with Kai ten years ago. Understanding the role she'd played helped her to forgive—a little bit anyway—Kai's withdrawal. Now, anticipation curled through her belly and it didn't have anything to do with the food. Being around him made her feel like a twenty-something again, full of starry-eyed romantic notions that she knew better than to believe.

Didn't she?

As she padded barefoot toward the kitchen, she really questioned how much she'd learned from her previous relationships. She knew she shouldn't count on something as fleeting as passion, and she couldn't expect any man to be a full-fledged partner in her life. Yet with Kai, she found she was wrestling back the persistent beast of hopefulness all the time.

The thought gave her pause, slowing her steps just as she reached the archway leading into the kitchen. Was it too late to retreat?

"Good morning," Kai greeted her, making any attempts to escape a moot point. "I hope you're hungry."

Hungry? Absolutely. For more than food. The enticing man standing at the stove was most definitely a feast for her eyes as he carefully flipped an omelet in one frying pan while monitoring a second omelet and bacon in another. He wore his jeans and a black unisex T-shirt emblazoned with the Goddess fitness logo that she'd left out for him the night before. With his hair damp from his shower and his face unshaven, he looked clean and roguish, like a man who would taste delicious.

Shivery sensations tripped over her skin thinking about what they'd shared the night before. And not just in a physical sense. His presence at the hospital, his insistence on driving her there to check on Sophie, touched her. Finding him in the kitchen, making them both breakfast, reminded her of when they'd been a couple.

"It smells great. How can I help?" She was already moving toward the coffeemaker, pulling mugs out of the cupboard and wondering how she was going to find her equilibrium with him today.

She might be tempted to lean into his warmth and support as a lover and a friend, but where would that leave her if he pulled away from her again? Her mother may have played a role in their relationship's demise, but Kai had never let Miranda weigh in on that conversation either.

She needed to be careful.

"Just butter the toast and we'll be good to go." He slid crispy slices of bacon onto two plates, each decorated with an orange slice. Fresh juice was already poured in glasses on the kitchen table. "Have you been awake long? I saw you were on a call before I started breakfast."

After taking care of the toast, Miranda poured two cups of coffee, finding it far too easy to fall into their old rhythms of working together. Had she been wrong to write off what they'd shared as purely passionate and therefore impractical?

"I woke up about an hour ago and felt like I should touch base with my...office." That much was true as she'd checked in with her assistant at Goddess before she'd called her mom. But she wasn't ready to share about her uneasy conversation with Ginny. Instead, Miranda carried the mugs to the table, noticing Kai had already put the creamer she preferred beside her place setting. "I've been in Royal for so long. I feel guilty about leaving my staff, but they've handled what they can really well."

He brought over their plates. "That sounds to me like there are tasks you haven't given them to manage. Are there things you need to be there for personally?"

He held her chair for her, silently inviting her to sit. She told herself to relax and enjoy Kai's attentiveness while it lasted.

"I need to meet with my biggest competitor, AMuse." Settling into her chair, she laid her napkin in her lap while he took the seat across from her. Their knees bumped and the jolt of electricity had her skin tingling. "Their CEO has called twice in the last month and I'm curious what that's about."

"Do you think they might try to buy you out?" He sipped his black coffee, his green gaze finding hers over the rim of the stoneware mug.

"I wouldn't think so, but either way, I'd never sell." She had to look away from his assessing eyes, unsure where she stood with him today or what the night before had meant for him. Instead, she thought back to the early beginnings of her business and how hard she'd worked to grow it. "Building Goddess helped me find my own strength. Every setback taught me something."

"I feel the same way about Madtec." He pulled out his phone between bites of the omelet and tapped a few buttons on the screen. "I double-checked with my pilot—the Madtec jet is available. We could be in New York before the close of day. Why don't we go check on things at Goddess and put your mind at ease?"

The suggestion caught her off guard.

"Really?" While her own business was thriving, she had never had the need for a jet or regular pilot service, but she could certainly see the appeal. "What about the bank? Should we be overseeing anything more with the hacking incident?"

Nibbling on a bacon slice, she ran through a mental checklist of all they needed to do in Royal. Beyond ensuring Blackwood Bank and its customers were now well protected, she still had details to oversee with the Royal Gives Back gala that Buckley had requested, and she wanted to be available for Lulu as the wedding date neared.

"The new data protection software is in place for the bank." He spoke with reassuring confidence. "We can send out a joint press release about that as soon as you or Vaughn approve the copy my PR department submitted for your review."

Mulling over the idea, she had to admit it sounded good to set her mind at ease about work. But she voiced the concern that held her back.

"Assuming we do this—and I appreciate the generous offer— what does it mean for us? It bears discussion as we start spending more time together." She wasn't sure about his expectations and she didn't want to confuse the issue. "That is, we haven't spoken about where this relationship might lead. You know I'm not staying in Royal."

Reaching across the table, he laid his hand over hers. The touch was tender, yet it stirred butterflies and memories, a wealth of feeling in that simple connection.

"What if we simply enjoy the time we have instead of worrying about what will happen at the end of the month?" His words cast a spell separate from his touch, tapping into the secret wishes of her heart and old, dangerous longings. "You've got a lot on your plate right now without adding me to the list of things you have to resolve."

It felt reckless to run headlong, heedless of consequences, into something that could cause her a world of hurt. And yet she found herself wanting to agree, just so their affair didn't have to end. She didn't know what she wanted long term, but the thought of ending things with Kai right now caused a pain that was almost physical. Could she trust him not to pull away from her the way he had the last time? Or would she be the one to pull away when she finished her duties in Texas and returned to New York? They had only a few more weeks before Royal Gives Back.

Surely she could keep her heart safe for just a little longer.

"In that case," she began, threading her fingers through his where their hands rested on the table, "I'd love to fly to New York with you."

* * *

"You went *where*?" Kai's brother's voice was curt over the phone. Dane sounded more than a little agitated.

Kai juggled the cell while he continued to work on his tablet in a chauffeured Range Rover. He sat in midtown traffic at rush hour, having dropped off Miranda at the Goddess headquarters. He was doing his damnedest to stay out of her way and let her use the time in Manhattan to conduct her business, but the moment she exited the private SUV, he'd begun making plans for their evening together.

His window of opportunity with her was narrowing as the end of the month approached, and he planned to pull out all the stops to romance her. That meant dinner and dancing at one of the most beautiful and exclusive rooftop bars in the city. He'd asked an assistant to review Miranda's episodes of *Secret Lives of NYC Ex-Wives* to learn any intelligence about her favorite places, and the Chelsea restaurant was a spot she'd exclaimed over in the first season. Kai had spent a small fortune to have the place to themselves on short notice. But before he could finish making preparations for the evening, he needed to deal with his brother.

"I flew to New York with Miranda," Kai explained. "Madtec has two clients I can see while I'm here."

"What about Blackwood Bank?" Dane swore on the other end of the call, and from the rhythmic thumping in the background, Kai guessed his brother was taking out his aggravation by running the green stairwell they'd installed in their building to use like a gym. "Reporters have been breathing down our necks all day."

"The situation is well in hand or I wouldn't have left the office yesterday." Kai leaned back in the leather seat, glancing out the window to see if they'd made progress. He had a meeting downtown in ten minutes. "The joint press release went out, so if the newshounds want a story, just keep referring back to the talking points. The data breach is old news."

"Is it, though?" The thumping on Dane's end of the call slowed and then stopped. He was breathing hard now. "I don't like the resentful tone I'm picking up in the tech community about the way we rolled out the new software during a PR crisis."

Kai frowned, his nerves drawing tight with foreboding. "What do you mean?"

"Face it, Kai. The bank data breach might have catapulted our cybersecurity software into national recognition if it ends up working as well as we think it's going to." Dane huffed out a long breath and then lowered his voice. "There are bound to be detractors who'll suggest we pulled some kind of unethical stunt to put ourselves in the position to be the white knights—and gain lots of publicity—given our...er, *my* history."

Kai knew Dane was referring to his stint in jail—to their shared hacking history that had been well publicized. Yet he still couldn't believe what he was hearing. He double-checked the partition window between him and SUV's driver, stabbing it hard with his finger to ensure it was sealed tightly.

"Are you suggesting that people are saying we organized a major breach of one of our own clients in order to draw media attention to our bringing a new protection software product to market?" The repercussions of that kind of publicity nightmare could be devastating for a fledgling business. Madtec was only just beginning to realize full legitimacy in the tech marketplace. This could ruin their credibility with any business that might be thinking of hiring them.

For that matter, what would Miranda think of the rumors? She'd never been comfortable with the idea that many successful tech gurus had skirted the law to learn the business, testing the bounds of cybersecurity by quietly hacking it. Her opinion mattered to him, and not just because of their business affiliation.

"I'm saying it's an excellent possibility." Dane sounded weary and more than a little ticked off. "It's already being speculated about among the tech elite. It's probably only a matter of time before a story like that finds traction with a wider audience."

"We need to track those rumors and put a stop to them." Kai opened a new screen on his tablet and got to work, firing off a message to the overworked press relations advocate at Madtec. "I'll be back in Deer Springs tomorrow, but I'll see what I can find out from here to squash the story."

Disconnecting the call, Kai realized the SUV was slowing outside his appointment with the city's major public transportation provider. He'd been working with them for months to increase their cybersecurity and had been glad to wrangle a last-minute meeting today. But it would take a superhuman effort to redirect his thoughts to this project right now when the fear of negative repercussions from the Blackwood Bank scandal threatened Madtec.

And his relationship with Miranda.

More than anything, he simply wanted to focus on making tonight a memorable experience for her. Because somehow, she'd slid straight past his defenses for the second time in his life, and he refused to waste this opportunity to woo her and win.

Stepping inside the custom closet in her Brooklyn brownstone that evening, Miranda took pleasure in the sight of her full wardrobe for the first time in months. Being able to dress for her date tonight with Kai would be all the more enjoyable for having access to her things. Because yes, she wanted to knock his socks off. To feel feminine and desirable after the failure of her marriage and the loneliness of the years that followed.

Peering over the rows of shoes carefully stored in protective clear bins, Miranda couldn't shake the unsettling truth that her New York home felt strange to her after spending so much time in Royal. Lonelier, somehow, since she'd formed tentative bonds with Buckley's children.

Not to mention the much more exciting connection she shared with Kai.

Inspired by a pair of sunshine-yellow high-heeled sandals, Miranda turned toward the rack where she kept her gowns to thumb through them for a draped silk gown in a creamy color, printed with greenery and yellow flowers. Kai had texted that he was sending a car for her at seven and would meet her for dinner at a surprise location. He'd indicated the dress was formal for a special evening out, a caveat that only added to her enjoyment in getting ready.

In the days when they'd been a couple in Deer Springs, their dates had been diner visits where they'd sneak a few moments together on her breaks, or rides on his motorcycle. They'd always had fun together without spending money neither of them had, but she looked forward to seeing Kai in a tuxedo and standing next to him in the kind of couture gown she'd once only dreamed of owning. It had taken her a lot of years to give herself this Cinderella moment, but she couldn't deny she took pride in herself for the hard work that made it possible to slide into handmade Italian leather shoes and fasten a bracelet of tiny yellow diamonds around one wrist.

When the sleek black Cadillac arrived for her half an hour later, the driver greeted her warmly but only smiled when she asked for a hint about her destination, ratcheting up the suspense, anticipation...desire.

What did Kai have in mind?

She was glad to think about the night ahead instead of her earlier meeting with her competitor, AMuse. The offer they'd made for a joint venture to go global had been exciting, but it also added a new complication to her already uncertain future. There'd been a time when she wouldn't have had to think twice about an offer like that. The opportunity to take the Goddess brand to other countries was exciting. A natural extension of her business plan. Yet it would make seeing Kai all but impossible down the road. Bad enough she was based in New York and he was based in Texas. But if she began traveling internationally to make the new venture with AMuse happen, she wouldn't ever have time to work on a relationship.

Not that Kai had hinted he wanted to continue seeing her once she left Royal. For tonight, she simply wanted to enjoy whatever Kai had planned.

The driver slowed down in front of a brick building in Chelsea, and it took Miranda a moment to recognize the plain black awning and black double doors with a discreet pineapple insignia beside them. Anticipation swelled when she recognized the facade to her favorite rooftop venue in Manhattan. How had Kai guessed?

A warm spring breeze teased her bare shoulders as she emerged from the vehicle, and a doorman appeared to escort her inside. This time, she didn't try to pry hints from him. She merely stepped into the elevator he indicated, surprised that the building seemed quiet at this hour. The lower floors were home to a unique, immersive theater experience and the restaurant and bar on the upper levels were usually packed, especially when the weather was this ideal.

Reaching the top level, the elevator doors slid open to reveal the rooftop bar swathed in green just the way she remembered. Lightweight vines climbed high structural arches. White lights wound through the greens and stretched overhead to put a network of tiny stars almost in reach. Live violin music—more formal than the sounds of the usual bar scene—played softly from a duo in a far corner.

But, strangely, the bar was otherwise empty until a devastatingly handsome man stepped out from behind a row of potted flowering trees. His face was illuminated by the white lights overhead and the hurricane lamps that crowded a nearby table.

Kai.

Her heartbeat quickened at the sight of him. Clean-shaven and dressed in a tuxedo custom fit to his athletic frame, he looked like a man born to the finer things in life. Desire for him, and all the delectable ways he could make her feel, curled warmly in her belly.

"You look incredible, Miranda." He walked forward to greet her with a debonair kiss that lingered on the back of her fingers. He held her gaze as his mouth grazed her skin.

The feel of his lips on her skin stirred fresh longing. Tingly sensations zipped up her spine and back down again.

"Thank you." She noticed he didn't let go of her hand, keeping her fingers wrapped in his. Her gaze wandered over the lines of his black silk jacket where it skimmed his broad shoulders and tapered to his narrow waist and hips. "The tux suits you, Kai. I wasn't expecting such a special night when you offered a spur-of-the-moment trip."

"I thought it was time to make my intentions toward you known," he countered, leading her farther from the musicians to a spot near the edge of the rooftop terrace.

They had a clear view of the lighted spires from skyscrapers in lower Manhattan when he took her in his arms for a slow dance. Her body followed his easily, one hand landing on his shoulder while he kept hold of the other.

"What intentions might those be?" Her pulse hammered harder, uncertain what she wanted or hoped to hear.

She thought she knew better than to get involved with Kai again, and yet here they were, unable to stay away from each other.

"I want to remind you how good it can be between us, Miranda." His forehead tipped toward hers. "Last time we were together, I let outside influences come between us."

A chill feathered through her as she remembered the way her mother had interfered, planting the seeds of doubt in Kai's mind about their future together.

As much as she wanted to make the most of their evening and push aside outside concerns, she found her current doubts harder to ignore. The offer from AMuse circled around her brain.

"What happens when I leave Royal at the end of the month?"

she asked, peering deep into his green eyes, desperate for answers that had proved all too elusive to her. "I have a whole life in New York. And today, my competitor suggested a joint venture that would take Goddess global."

Kai's smile was as unexpected as it was unmistakable. "That's fantastic, Miranda." He squeezed her gently. "Congratulations. You deserve this."

"Thank you." A surge of pride swelled. After all the times she and Kai had sat in the Deer Springs Diner together, figuring out how to make their dreams come true, it felt like she'd come full circle to savor this business victory with him here, dancing on a rooftop under the twinkle of white lights and the glow of the city's skyline. "I've been so focused on how it would work that I haven't taken a moment to really celebrate the achievement."

"That changes now," he insisted. "I hope you'll let me celebrate with you over dinner. We'll see what the server can find for a fitting champagne to toast the moment."

The lilting tune they'd been dancing to shifted, slowing down a bit. Kai's steps matched the cadence, easily guiding her while she tried to put her finger on what was bothering her about celebrating the news with him.

"I appreciate that. And I'd love some champagne. But I wonder how hard this would make things for work and—" she hesitated as her hair blew softly against her cheek "—for me, personally. It would mean a lot more travel."

She didn't spell out her concerns about seeing him after she left Texas, mainly because she wasn't sure if he saw her departure as an obvious end date for their affair.

"There was a time when we wouldn't have let logistics dictate our future." He seemed unconcerned. But did that mean he wasn't counting on a long-distance relationship in the first place?

She didn't ask because she didn't know what she wanted either.

"And yet we both have too much at stake to walk away from

businesses we've worked hard to create." The fact that they were even discussing it worried her a little. But it excited her too, stirring a forgotten hopefulness.

Could they find a way to make it work?

The distant sounds of New York nightlife drifting up from the street provided a soft background to the violins' romantic melody.

"For tonight, it's enough if I can just prove to you that we were meant to be together." He twirled her under his arm as the music stopped altogether. When it ended, he pulled her against him for a long, slow, thorough taste.

She sank into him, wanting to burn the memory of this moment into her brain to preserve it forever. To look back on when she left Texas for good and resumed her life in New York without him. With the end of their affair in sight, she was eager to keep the outside world at bay, the moment sweetly dream-like with the soft breeze blowing her silk gown against her legs, and Kai's strong arms holding her close. His lips were soft and teasing at first, then lingered until she felt breathless.

When he eased away, she opened her eyes slowly.

"Is that why you went to all the trouble of booking this amazing venue just for us?" she asked, curious about what this over-the-top evening truly meant. "To show me how well you know what I like?"

"To show you there's nothing I wouldn't do for you, Miranda." His green eyes were serious, and her heart turned over in her chest.

Romantic words. They fluttered around her with teasing promise like the spring breeze. But could she trust them?

"For tonight, I just want to be with you," she admitted, not ready to think beyond the here and now.

Because after her failed marriage, she couldn't afford to be wrong about love again.

CHAPTER TEN

WITH THE TEMPTATION of Miranda Dupree seated beside him, Kai willed the driver to go faster as their private car sped over Manhattan Bridge later that night, leaving the New York skyline behind them. He'd enjoyed every moment spent with Miranda tonight, but the need to be really, truly alone with her burned hotter than ever.

"Thank you for celebrating with me tonight." Miranda turned her liquid-blue eyes on him as her fingers covered his on the expanse of leather seat between them. "Sometimes I get so caught up in achieving the next goal I forget to enjoy the milestones as they come. This was…nice. Better than nice, actually. It was an unforgettable night."

Her happiness made all the effort he'd put into the evening well worth it. He took his time threading his fingers through hers, relishing the simple connection even as he craved a far more intimate one. With his other hand, he stabbed the button to raise the privacy window to prevent the driver from overhearing them. Or seeing them.

"The celebrating isn't over, as far as I'm concerned." He lifted her palm to his mouth and pressed a kiss in the center. "I hope to make the night more memorable for you soon."

He heard her swift intake of breath as he kissed his way past her wrist. Over the delicate skin of her inner arm. The scent of her fragrant skin—soap and jasmine—teased his nose as she shifted closer, her knee brushing his.

Electricity crackled between them. He lifted his attention from her arm to the soft swell of her breasts over the low neckline of her cream-colored dress. Her chest rose and fell quickly. Her lips parted in silent invitation.

An invitation he couldn't afford to indulge until they were alone. Because once he started kissing her, he wouldn't stop. He settled for cupping her chin and running his thumb over the full softness of her mouth.

"How much longer until we reach your place?" he wondered aloud, thinking he could put the time to more satisfying use for them both.

She turned to peer over her shoulder and look out the window as they drove deeper into Brooklyn.

"My street is next," she replied, straightening in her seat. "We're in luck."

A damned good thing given the way the sparks between them flared hotter with each passing second. A few moments later, the vehicle slowed on a tree-lined street in front of a row of brownstones. After helping Miranda from the vehicle and exchanging a few words with the driver about the next day's itinerary, Kai forced himself to take an extra moment to admire her quiet neighborhood before following her up the steps to the tall, black double doors that served as the main entrance. No sense crowding or rushing her. She had to know how much he wanted her. She'd already disarmed the alarm on the keypad by the door.

He stood in the foyer while she locked and reset the alarm. The long, narrow foyer was dimly lit from the hall sconces, but Kai could see the whitewashed brick fireplace and pocket doors that gave the home a historic feel. The low, modern furnishings and industrial chandelier were obvious touches of the current owner, however.

Before he could compliment her on the house, Miranda was in his arms, reminding him exactly why they'd been in such a hurry to get here. Her arms locked around his neck, breasts pressed to his chest in a way that made him forget everything else. She kissed along his jaw while he molded her to him, his hands tracing her curves through the silky fabric of her printed gown.

"Where's your room?" he asked, his breath coming fast.

She unfastened two buttons of his shirt before pointing toward the staircase. "Second floor."

They ascended the steps together, her hand wrapped in his, legs brushing on the way up.

She led him to the left where the master suite awaited. Inside the open archway, her bed stood in front of another fireplace. Here, everything was white and gray. A color scheme that would normally be calming if he wasn't on fire to have her. A single orchid bloomed by the bed. The blinds over the bay windows were already lowered so that the room was lit only by the white glow spilling from the open door of the en suite bath.

A beautiful space for an even more beautiful woman. She had so damned much to be proud of. She was vibrant. Independent. Fearless. And Kai wanted her more than he'd ever thought possible to want any woman.

Not ready to vocalize that until he figured out what it meant for them, he tucked a finger underneath his bow tie and freed the knot before unfastening the top button of his shirt. Miranda's gaze heated. A small smile curved one side of her lips.

She answered him by slipping off the straps of her gown. First one. Then the other.

Damn, but he was crazy about her.

When he shrugged out of his shirt, she stepped out of her shoes, her toes disappearing in the thick white carpet beneath their feet.

"Turn around." He reached for her hips to bring her closer. "I'll unzip you."

She pivoted to present him with her back. He lowered the zipper slowly, stroking touches along each new square inch of silky skin he bared.

When the gown sagged and fell to her feet, he anchored her to him with an arm around her waist. Skimming her hair away from her jasmine-scented neck, he kissed a trail from beneath her ear to her shoulder and back again. Unhooking her pale green bra, he let that slip to the floor too, his attention fixed on the taut peaks of her breasts. She shimmied against him, her hips rocking back into his as a low moan vibrated through her.

The last shreds of his restraint disintegrated.

Miranda was on fire.

Spinning in Kai's arms, she couldn't undress him fast enough, desire fogging her brain and making her fingers fumble awkwardly with the fastening of his tuxedo pants. She needed him naked with an urgency she'd only ever experienced with him.

He peeled off her panties while she dragged down his boxers, their arms bumping and hooking. Not that it mattered. Nothing mattered but being with him.

He lifted her to deposit her in the middle of her bed, a smooth drop into the soft, thick comforter. She had a moment to savor the way he looked when he retrieved a condom from a pocket of the discarded clothing. His square shoulders were backlit by the light from the bathroom, the outline of him deliciously masculine. Unquestionably powerful. When he stepped closer, the rippled muscles of his abs caught her eye, but only for a moment before her gaze shifted to his hips and the rigid length of him that awaited her touch.

Yet when she reached for him, he pinned both her hands lightly, his gaze probing hers as he covered her.

"I need you too much to wait another minute." His ragged words made hot pleasure curl in her belly. "I've wanted you all night."

Anticipation and excitement twined together, rendering her breathless. Light-headed.

"No more than I've wanted you." She liked knowing what she did to him, relieved that she wasn't alone in this out-of-control hunger.

With his gaze locked on hers, he let go of her wrists to curve a hand around her hip, tilting her toward him. She bit her lip against the exquisite feel of him sliding inside her. Deeper.

When she realized her fingernails were digging into his shoulder, she let go, kissing the place where she'd left red crescent moons. Wrapping her arms around his neck, she held on to him, letting him set the pace while the rhythm of it carried her away. Each stroke was pleasure filled. Each breath brought her closer to a climax she wasn't ready for. Not yet.

She wanted this night to last and last. Not just because of how it felt to have him with her. In her.

But because she couldn't imagine letting go of Kai again.

The realization slid into her consciousness at the same time he whispered her name in her ear, the sound of it and the feel of his breath making her shiver. Sending her hurtling toward the release she couldn't possibly stave off another moment.

She clung to him, her body undulating with waves of sweet sensations she never wanted to end. In the midst of it, she registered that she'd taken him with her, her body teasing him to his own completion.

They held each other for long moments afterward, breathing raggedly, heartbeats pounding madly. When, finally, those slowed down, Kai settled on her right side. The overhead ceiling fan stirred cool air over them, but he tucked her closer. She felt around for the edge of the duvet and draped it over them both.

He sifted his fingers through her hair, relaxing her enough to chase latent worries about their future from her brain. She was almost asleep in his arms when he whispered to her.

"I hope you're going to take the deal with AMuse." He spoke

softly, but her eyes fluttered open to fix on his in the dim light. "It's the culmination of everything you've worked so hard for."

It definitely wasn't pillow talk, or sweet nothings whispered in her ear. She held her breath for a moment, wondering what it meant for him. Why he'd shared that thought with her now. Was it his way of setting her free after her time in Royal was done? Or was it a genuine encouragement for her to embrace the dreams she'd always had for her business? Seeing nothing but warmth and thoughtfulness in his eyes, she forced herself to let out her breath.

"I know," she admitted, tracing circles on his chest. She felt grateful at least that he understood her even if he wouldn't always be a part of her life. But thinking about a future without him in it hurt. "I probably will."

His nod was a fraction of movement. His eyes closed then, as if he felt his role in the decision was finished. He'd encouraged her to do what she wanted.

For the first time, she acknowledged that Kai was more than just a passionate lover. She'd been wrong to write off what they'd shared in the past as simple chemistry that wouldn't stand up to the tests of time. He was her friend. And he wanted what was best for her.

But was that enough to keep them together through a long-distance separation? Her chest ached at the idea of leaving, but she also couldn't possibly stay. So for now, she closed her eyes and told herself to keep breathing. One way or another, she'd have to figure it out.

Kai awoke to his cell phone vibrating.

He'd been so deeply asleep beside Miranda that it took him a moment to orient himself and realize that he was still in her Brooklyn brownstone after their impromptu trip to New York City. Sliding from the covers, Kai reached for his phone and answered it, even as he tucked the duvet tighter around Miranda.

He regretted leaving her side one of the few times he'd been able to sleep beside her.

He gathered up a fistful of clothes from the floor before he made his way into the adjoining bathroom so he wouldn't wake her. There, he closed the door silently before speaking.

"What's up?" he asked quietly, meeting his own gaze in the huge mirror over the marble vanity. He knew it had to be his brother since Dane's number was the only one allowed to ring through at this hour.

Well, Dane's and Miranda's. But obviously *she* hadn't phoned him.

"Disaster is what's up." Dane spewed the words like hot lava, voice raised and angry. "The rumors about Madtec orchestrating the Blackwood Bank breach have gone national. A major news organization picked up the story."

Dread enveloped Kai's gut. Juggling the phone, he stepped into his boxers.

"Rumors aren't news," he answered reflexively, hoping like hell his brother was overreacting.

"Seriously? Have you read what gets shared for news nowadays, man?" Dane spoke fast, each word punching through the phone. "It doesn't matter if it's true. The suspicions raised will cripple the business—"

"Hold up." Kai stepped into his pants, noting that the sun was rising, a low light filtering in through the stained glass window. He needed to get on top of this. Fast. "Send me a link where I can get up to speed, and I'll call you back."

His brother swore, but pinged him an address to read the story.

Disconnecting the call, Kai sank to the white tile tub surround and scrolled through the article along with the comments before checking a couple of social media platforms. Dane hadn't overstated the case. Madtec needed a full-scale response to the bad press if they wanted any chance of overcoming this.

He texted his brother and his head of public relations to set up a virtual meeting in an hour. First, he needed to wake Miranda. He needed to be back in Deer Springs. Regret that their night together had to end this way stung hard. But she would understand.

Tossing his phone aside, he sat on the mattress near Miranda and touched her shoulder through the covers. Her eyelids fluttered, and he wondered what it would be like to wake up beside this woman day after day. He was falling for her.

Hard.

The realization threaded through the tension of the day, tightening it all into a hard knot. He couldn't afford to think about long term with her yet. Not when she was going to be building her brand overseas and working out of Manhattan while he was in Deer Springs.

"Miranda?" He watched as she came upright in bed slowly, dragging the covers with her.

"What is it? Is everything okay?" Her blue eyes darted around him, taking in his clothes before shifting to the clock on the wall.

More than anything, he wanted to slide back into bed beside her. To relive their incredible night together. But that was no longer possible.

He flipped on the bedside lamp.

"I need to fly home. Madtec is under assault in the press because of rumors that we someone how orchestrated the Blackwood Bank breach." Sharing the words made it hit hard all over again. Just when he'd finally thought Madtec had gained the legitimacy and credibility they needed.

Fighting to prove himself over and over again was getting old.

"I don't understand." Miranda shook her head, a crumbled red curl wavering as she moved. "Why would anyone suggest your company would launch a cyberattack on the business you were hired to protect? It makes no sense."

Frustration flared. "I wouldn't think so either. But it's been suggested that we fabricated the security breach in order to show off our new software. Our detractors have gained traction with the idea that our saving a giant like Blackwood Bank was perfect—and free—advertising for the new encryption software."

Miranda's blue gaze faltered, a shadow passing through their depths. But then she seemed to hide her reaction, her lips pursing in thought before she spoke again. "That's ludicrous."

A moment passed as he tried to process what he'd seen. But it damned well looked like she doubted him.

"You can't think I'd do something like that... Do you?" he asked, feeling like the ground had been yanked out from under him.

He'd worked his ass off to prove himself in the business world. But it had never occurred to him that Miranda would question his ethics.

"Of course not," she assured him, as if he hadn't seen her doubt with his own eyes. Perhaps being so newly awake made it tougher to hide her real feelings.

She glanced down at the duvet where she picked at the white binding on the cotton cover. "It's just—for a moment—I was remembering what you told me about the tech community. That most of the giants who understand the industry best are the people who started like you and Dane—hacking."

The sense of betrayal shook him. He stiffened his spine against it.

"So you figured it was only natural we'd undermine our own clients for the sake of some good press." He understood now why total strangers could think it of him and Dane, when the woman he cared about so much could come to the same sickening conclusion about him.

"No." She sounded more certain now, but it didn't erase the flash of doubt. "I came to Madtec because you're the best, Kai. End of story."

Woodenly, he stood. He refused to think about how close he'd come to losing his heart to this woman all over again. Only to be stomped twice as hard as the first time.

"Either way, I need to return to Deer Springs." His problems had only multiplied by sharing them with Miranda. Funny, now the potential loss of his business reputation didn't feel nearly as daunting as the loss of her. "The pilot can be at the airfield in an hour, so I'll call a car as soon as you're ready."

For a moment, he thought she'd argue. Or somehow try to retract the way she'd just leveled him with her lack of faith in him.

But then, she simply nodded.

Kai turned on his heel and left her to get ready on her own. The sooner he got back to Texas, the better.

He belonged there. As for Miranda Dupree and her global success? She'd have to pursue her dreams without him, the same way she always had.

CHAPTER ELEVEN

A WEEK AFTER the disastrous conclusion to the New York City trip, Miranda stood on the front steps of the Pine Valley estate that Sophie Blackwood Townshend now shared with Nigel. Miranda clutched a bouquet in one hand and a basket of cookies and pastries from a local bakery in the other. She was overdue to congratulate Sophie on her pregnancy news in person, but it had been a long, heart-wrenching week since her misstep with Kai.

He'd barely spoken to her on their flight back to Royal. Of course, she'd understood he was in the middle of a business crisis with Madtec's reputation under attack. But she suspected that he'd been more upset by her moment of doubt than any of the rumors, and that had given her plenty of pangs of conscience since then.

It wasn't that she believed he was unethical. It was just... Well, she'd been waiting for the other shoe to drop from the moment they'd reignited their affair.

She shoved those thoughts to the side, however, as a young liveried housekeeper with a long blond ponytail opened the door of Sophie's pretty French country estate.

"Hello." Miranda smiled at the woman. "I'm here to see Sophie—"

"Thank God for a visitor," Sophie's unmistakable voice rang

out from the back of the house. "Tell her I'm in the kitchen, Josephine!"

The petite housekeeper grinned at the same time Miranda did.

"I'll find her." Miranda nodded her thanks while the housekeeper shut the door. "Thank you."

"Miranda, is that you?" Sophie asked, peering out of the kitchen, a glass of water in her hand. At twenty-seven years old, Sophie had long auburn hair and brown eyes. She had killer curves and a quick wit, always ready with a smile. As the baby of the Blackwood clan and the only daughter, she'd been beloved by all. "I'm so glad you're here. Nigel practically keeps me housebound on a steady diet of constant calories, so I don't faint again." Her gaze went to the basket. "Although I'll bet whatever is in that basket is the kind of calories I'll actually enjoy."

Warmth suffused Miranda's heart to be welcomed this way by the stepdaughter she'd once feared would hate her forever. Sophie had still been a teenager when Miranda married Buckley, and Sophie had strongly resented their relationship. After the reading of the will, Sophie had put all her considerable efforts into proving Miranda was up to no good by infiltrating Green Room Media in New York to dig up dirt on her ex-stepmother. Dirt she hoped to use to get the will overturned in court.

The fact that they were finally able to put those years of ill will behind them was nothing short of a miracle in Miranda's book. She would always be grateful to Buckley for giving her this second chance to be a family with the Blackwoods.

"I got your favorites," Miranda announced, remembering her own efforts to get to know Sophie as a young woman, attempting to buy her favor with treats. She set the basket down on the island of the gleaming white kitchen where Sophie seemed to be preparing a pot of tea at the coffee bar. "And some flowers to congratulate you on your amazing news." Miranda hugged her tightly.

"Thank you." Sophie sniffed the bouquet of hydrangeas and roses. "The flowers are gorgeous. Can I make you some tea?"

"Sure. But why don't you let me do it? You haven't been home from the hospital for very long."

Sophie turned a dark scowl her way before peering into the basket of pastries. "Don't you gang up on me too, Miranda. I'm pregnant, not ill." She withdrew an almond croissant. "Oh, this smells amazing."

While Sophie loaded a plate with some of the pastries, Miranda quietly found spoons and napkins, eager to get the two of them everything they needed so Sophie could sit and rest. Because no matter what Nigel's new wife said, Miranda had just visited the two of them in the hospital, so clearly Sophie needed to be mindful of her health.

Of course, thinking of that visit made Miranda remember how thoughtful and kind Kai had been to personally drive her to Royal that night. She'd missed him to the point of pain this past week, but she reminded herself to focus on Sophie as she carried the mugs and spoons to the breakfast bar in the huge, open kitchen.

"So what did the doctor have to say, Sophie?" she pressed, gesturing for the younger woman to take a seat on one of the padded leather stools. "Why did you faint at the airport?"

"Probably because we were going through customs in a crowded airport with a crush of other people and I hadn't eaten since the night before. I slept the whole flight." Sophie slid onto one of the stools while Miranda carried over the teapot and pastries. "If I'd known I was pregnant I would have packed a protein bar or something. But as it was...*whoosh*. Down I went. I scared Nigel half to death."

"I'm sure you did," Miranda mused as she took the stool beside Sophie, enjoying the vision of those two very different personalities spending their lives together. Sophie was so bubbly and warm, while Nigel was reserved to the point that he could be mistaken for aloof—unless, of course, you happened to see him when he was looking at Sophie.

Clinking the pot against Miranda's mug, Sophie lifted it to pour, the pointed sleeves of a colorful caftan trailing over her hand.

"But now he's completely overcompensating, expecting me to eat constantly and stay close to home." She rolled her eyes. "Although the honeymoon was so amazing, I guess I can forgive him."

A sly, happy smile curved her lips.

"I'm so glad for you both." Miranda felt another pang of envy for all the love and happiness around her while she floundered around trying to get her own life in order. She'd just finished celebrating one wedding and now Lulu's was the week after the Royal Gives Back gala. "I hope you'll both be at the Royal Gives Back event?"

"We wouldn't miss it." After pouring her own tea, Sophie slid into the leather counter stool beside Miranda. "I think of it as Dad's 'coming out' party, where the rest of the world will finally know his good qualities."

They drank their tea in silence for a moment, perhaps equally wrapped up in their own memories of Buckley Blackwood. He'd been a blowhard and a tough businessman, always hiding his softer side while he'd been alive, even with his family. And while Miranda was happy he was finally going to be celebrated for the good person he was underneath the unyielding facade, she knew it would have made a lot of people in his life happier if he could have been more giving—and forgiving—while he'd still been alive.

She didn't want to be the kind of person who made the same mistakes over and over again her whole life. And yet hadn't she ended up back in the same place with Kai as she'd been ten years ago? The new rift between them hurt even more than the first time.

Sophie broke the silence when she set her cup back on the

granite countertop, the scent of chamomile and lemon rising from the tea. "I heard from Vaughn this morning that things are running smoothly at the bank again after the security breach."

Miranda's breath caught, her thoughts flying straight back to Kai, the man who'd steered the bank through the chaos.

"We were fortunate to have Madtec helping us through that nightmare," Miranda said, missing Kai even more. She nibbled on a raspberry tart, wondering how she'd ever get over him.

Would he even speak to her again? Or had he checked out on her for good this time? She'd hoped he'd be at the Royal Gives Back gala, but maybe he wouldn't bother attending now.

"No doubt." Sophie slanted a sideways gaze in her direction. "How about you, Miranda? Did *you* feel fortunate to have Kai Maddox back in your life after so many years?"

Miranda didn't miss the arch note in Sophie's voice.

She spun to look at her.

"You knew I dated Kai?" she asked. Had Sophie just learned about this when the tabloids showed her and Kai leaving Madtec's offices together? Or had she known before? But no, surely if she'd known years ago, it would have come up when Miranda had first married Buckley.

Back then, Sophie had been so eager to do anything that might get under Miranda's skin.

"Of course. You forget how eager I was to see you trip up as Dad's new wife when he brought you to Blackwood Hollow." She didn't sound proud of the fact anymore. She stirred more sugar into her tea, the spoon clinking softly against the sides of the mug before she withdrew it and laid it on a napkin. "I made it my mission to learn whatever I could about your past. I hoped to catch you cheating, but nothing ever happened. You stayed loyal, even when things weren't working out in your marriage. Even I couldn't find fault with how you treated Dad, as hard as I tried. You were good to him, Miranda."

She released a pent-up breath, grateful she felt that way. "I tried to be. But I failed as a wife to Buckley. And it looks like I failed with Kai again."

Sophie swiveled in her seat to look at her head-on. "What do you mean?"

"I mean we were seeing each other again. Up until last week." Miranda hadn't told anyone about what happened with Kai. Not even the other *Ex-Wives*. But she felt the need to share it with someone, and Sophie had always been candid with her—even in the years when she hadn't been kind. Maybe she needed that candidness right now. "I was rattled when he told me about the scandal surrounding Madtec and the rumors that he and his brother had somehow engineered the breach for the publicity."

"You believed that?" Sophie's auburn eyebrow arched.

Clutching the warmth of her mug with both hands, Miranda felt like even more of a heel.

"Not really. But for a moment, I suppose, it sounded like something he might have done back in the days when he walked the knife's edge between right and wrong." He'd been so desperate to learn back then, even if it meant crossing some lines. But he wasn't that desperate kid anymore. She knew how much the reputation of his business meant to him. Not to mention the reputation of his brother, who'd gone to jail for something Kai felt like he should have prevented.

"So tell him you were wrong." Sophie underscored the advice by pointing at her with a fig cookie. "No one knows better than me that sometimes a big, fat apology is in order. I've had to give a lot of them since I've jumped to my fair share of wrong conclusions. But if you're sincere—"

"There are so many more things that aren't right between us though, Sophie. My life is in New York and his is here. I have the show, and an offer to take Goddess global—"

She halted herself abruptly as Sophie was shaking her head, her long auburn hair swinging. "That's all a smokescreen. And none of it really matters if you love each other. First you apologize. Then you can see if any of the rest of it has any bearing on your relationship. My two cents says that it won't."

Miranda wasn't so sure. But she understood what Sophie was saying.

Reaching for her, she squeezed Sophie's forearm. "When did you turn so wise?"

"A miracle, right?" Sophie laughed. "I guess I had to make my own share of missteps before I figured out how to be a better person. I hurt you, and I hurt Nigel with my headstrong ways, so convinced I knew it all. But part of being a strong person means learning to back down when you're wrong."

Miranda felt the unfamiliar prick of warmth in her eyes and she swallowed back a lump in her throat. She wasn't sure if the knot of feelings were for all she'd been through in her role as the Wicked Stepmother to Buckley's kids, or if it was because of how she'd handled things with Kai. But she appreciated Sophie's words.

She needed to decide if she was going to take the plunge and come to terms with everything she felt for Kai. She'd been hiding behind her defenses and her boundaries for too long. Maybe all of it was a smokescreen, after all.

"You're right." Miranda nodded, glad she'd come. "Thank you, Sophie."

"Of course. That's what families are for." Sophie winked at her. "Do you need any help with the gala? I'm really ready for a new project—"

"Nigel would have my head, and we both know it," Miranda reminded her. "I'll just be happy having you both there."

"We're looking forward to it," Sophie assured her.

An hour later, Miranda left Pine Valley and headed back to Royal to finish her preparations for Royal Gives Back. It would be her last task in town on Buckley's behalf, but she planned to stay for a week afterward for Lulu's wedding. The wedding would be the season finale of their show.

After that, there would be no excuse for her to remain in

Royal any longer. Unless, of course, she convinced Kai to take a chance on continuing their relationship. Something she couldn't deny that she wanted more than air.

Because she knew now—after this miserable week of hurting without him—that she loved him. Now, more than ever. She hadn't wanted to face it, fearing how much it might hurt, but she'd fallen for him anyhow.

Maybe she'd sabotaged things with him purposely so she wouldn't have to face the hurt of rejection a second time. Whatever her reason, she refused to let Kai think she believed the worst of him.

That wasn't fair to him.

She just needed to find the right time to tell him before the gala. Then, she'd hope for the best. No matter how much it hurt.

Kai ignored the phone messages from Miranda the day before the Royal Gives Back Gala.

Amad had walked into his office with two of them earlier in the week. And now, the day before the gala, there'd been another.

Kai couldn't say why he was avoiding her—out of a need to protect himself from hearing her say goodbye, or to maintain the anger he still felt that she'd believed the worst of him. Thankfully, he'd discovered the source of the smear campaign earlier in the week, and this afternoon he'd had the pleasure of seeing the same tech rival who'd started the rumors now under investigation for breaking the law himself. Alistair Quinn had been a thorn in the Maddox brothers' side for years, but it seemed he wouldn't be making trouble any longer. How ironic that he'd been charged with pulling the kinds of cheap stunts he'd accused Madtec of using.

It was damned satisfying to be vindicated. Madtec had two big job offers roll in just in the last day, their legitimacy cemented for good.

Now, shutting down his workstation for the night, Kai retrieved his jacket and slid his arms in the sleeves. He opened his office door to find Dane and Amad watching replays of a college basketball game on Amad's desktop computer, reviewing the video in slow motion to exclaim over a great basket.

The workday was done, and it was rewarding to see Amad stick around the office to socialize. That kind of atmosphere was what he and Dane had hoped for when they'd created a more employee-centered office space at Madtec. And now, the business was back in good stead with the public. It should have been a day of celebrating, capped off by the sight of his brother smiling and happy.

Except Kai's victory felt hollow without Miranda.

"Hey." Dane straightened as Kai walked into the outer office. "Ready to go out for a drink to celebrate the future of Madtec now that Alistair Quinn is under investigation?"

"I thought I'd take the bike out for a few hours." He hadn't ridden his motorcycle in weeks. Maybe the fresh air would clear out his head.

Ease the red-hot burn in his chest where his personal regrets lived.

Dane frowned. He strode with Kai toward the private elevator that led directly to the parking area. "Let me walk down with you."

Kai nodded, but said nothing. He felt like a countdown clock was ticking in the back of his brain, every second a reminder that Miranda was a moment closer to leaving Texas for good.

As soon as the elevators doors closed silently behind them, Dane turned serious eyes toward him. "What gives?"

"What do you mean? Why would something be wrong just because I want to take the bike out instead of going out for a drink?" Kai pulled his keys from his pants pocket, agitated.

"I mean, the news broke that the company was the target of a deliberately malicious smear campaign by a rival. We're vindicated and we got two big-money offers from huge companies. Our human resources department can't hire people fast enough." Dane ticked off all the good news on his fingers. "Yet you're dragging yourself through the office like you lost your best friend."

Kai stifled the urge to scowl and snarl because he didn't need Dane sniffing around his private life. As the elevator settled on the ground floor, he charged out into the parking area. The late afternoon sun glinted off a windshield, making him blink.

"It's all good news, but I'm fried. I've been working more than not for the past two weeks." He'd poured all of his energy into clearing his name—and Dane's, too.

And to keep himself from thinking about Miranda.

"I'm not buying it." Dane stepped in front of Kai, making him pull up sharply so he didn't run right into him. "Where's Miranda been? You two went to New York together, yet I haven't a heard a word about her or what went down."

The urge to scowl wouldn't be quieted this time. Kai narrowed his gaze.

"Since when do we trade stories about women? You don't see me inserting myself in your private life." He stepped around his brother and continued toward his car, popping open the locks on the coupe from the key fob.

The executive parking area was quiet, deserted. Heat sweltered off the tarmac even though it was almost six o'clock.

"I didn't say anything when you let her go the first time," Dane countered. "But I know you regretted it then, and you're probably going to regret it this time, too."

Kai ground his teeth together, his jaw flexing. "She's the one walking away," he said finally, the words spilling out in spite of him. "She turned her back on what we had then, and she's never believed we could last this time either."

"How convenient you never have to put yourself on the line with her," Dane observed drily, folding his arms over his chest. "I guess if you don't really try, you can't ever fail. Good thinking, Kai."

The sarcasm dripped from his words. Shaking his head, Dane pivoted on his heel to leave.

"I've tried," Kai retorted. But even he had to cringe at the sullen tone in his voice.

Hell.

Dane spun toward him, arms spread wide. "Have you? Because from my point of view, it looks like you've been dodging her since that first day she showed up here with a business opportunity."

He flinched a little at the direct hit.

"True. But I had my reasons." He stalked away from his vehicle, thinking and pacing. "Since then, I've committed to showing her we could be good together."

He'd driven her to the hospital when her family needed her. Flown her to New York. Supported her global expansion.

"I believe you showed her. But that doesn't mean she understood your message as anything other than being helpful." Dane leaned a hip into Kai's car. "Have you *told* her how you feel? Or have you even worked out for yourself whether you love her or not?"

Kai quit pacing, stunned. The words called everything in him to a halt.

Did he love Miranda? Was he *in love* with her?

He'd never acknowledged the idea openly, maybe because he'd been trying his damnedest not to have his heart shredded a second time. But his love for her was so damned much a bedrock of everything he felt that he couldn't believe he'd never brought the feeling up into the sunlight where he could appreciate it. Share it.

Tell her about it.

Hell yes, he loved her.

"I've got to go." He charged toward his car, his feet fueled with purpose.

"Is that a yes?" Dane drummed his fingers on Kai's hood, assessing his brother.

"She's everything to me," Kai told him simply, the truth settling over him with new clarity. "And I've got to make sure she knows it."

He didn't miss Dane's smug smile as he backed up a step while Kai started the car.

Later, he would thank Dane for helping him figure out what to do next. Right now, he needed to get to the Texas Cattleman's Club before the gala kicked off. He wasn't sure of the logistics for how he'd tell Miranda he loved her, and he didn't know if the sentiment would be returned.

But he understood one thing now thanks to Dane. Kai would regret it forever if he didn't at least try to win her back.

CHAPTER TWELVE

JUST OUTSIDE THE kitchen of the Texas Cattleman's Club, Miranda consulted with the head of catering an hour after the Royal Gives Back gala began. She was grateful to lose herself in the details of the evening to escape the heartbreak of her rift with Kai. She'd been at the venue for two hours before the event kicked off to ensure things ran smoothly, taking a break only to slip into a black crepe cocktail gown with subtly sexy keyhole cutouts at the waist and shoulder.

Once she approved two minor menu changes, Miranda left the caterer to return to the party, walking through an archway draped with white and gold flowers. A few attendees stood in front of the wall of petals taking photos of each other, and Miranda smiled at them as she passed. The musicians were playing a short set of big-band music in the warm-up hour before Miranda took the stage to thank the guests and make a few announcements about Buckley Blackwood's legacy.

She had her notes waiting on the podium, and she had a few surprises to share with the guests. But for now, she took a few moments to peer around the great room that had been outfitted for the night's gala.

Looking for Kai.

She'd counted on seeing him here so she could apologize

in person for doubting him. Even though she knew it wouldn't change the pain she'd caused him. Her words would come too late anyhow, since he'd already been cleared of any wrongdoing. She wished she'd driven to Deer Springs earlier in the week— before the news story broke about his tech rival organizing a smear campaign against Madtec. Then, her apology might have meant more. Might have changed things.

Either way, she had to see him tonight once her obligations at the gala were complete. She owed him the words.

Swallowing hard, she tried not to think about him tonight when she had this one final task to manage for Buckley. With an event planner's eye, she went over the room again, noting the huge white and yellow-gold flower arrangements on the tables, with white roses, daffodils and ranunculus dominating the tall sprays. Black accents kept the theme quietly elegant, the wrought iron candelabra and chair backs picking up the more masculine decor that dominated the remodeled building of the Texas Cattleman's Club.

Couples milled around the tables and admired the appetizer stations while cocktail service circulated regularly with specialty drinks of the evening. Kellan Blackwood and his bride, Irina, circled the dance floor along with the other couples. Russian-born Irina had been the quiet beneficiary of Buckley's kindness when he'd given the down-on-her-luck former mail-order bride a job as his maid to help her obtain a work visa while she divorced an abusive ex. The woman's green eyes sparkled now as she clearly enjoyed Kellan's expert moves on the dance floor, a purple spotlight winking off the bangles on her fringed red dress. She must be nearly four months pregnant by now, but Miranda would have never guessed if she hadn't heard the good news from Kellan two months ago.

While Miranda watched the utterly devoted couple, Kace LeBlanc, Buckley's lawyer and the executor of his will, drew up to her side. "I'd call this an unmitigated success," he announced quietly. The attorney was an interesting match for Lulu with his by-the-book, quiet competence. "You did an outstanding job with the gala. Buckley would be pleased."

"Thank you." Miranda had been grateful to throw herself into the preparations over the last week when she ached with all she'd lost, missing Kai every moment. And yes, she'd truly wanted to offer up this last tribute to her ex-husband, to give herself much-needed closure to move forward with her life. If only there was a gala she could throw that would somehow fix the way she'd left things with Kai. "I'm thrilled with the turnout, but even more excited about the donations. I think Buckley's kids were all pleased he wanted to support the Stroke Foundation."

Donna-Leigh Westbrook had died too young from a stroke, and her three children—Kellan, Sophie and Vaughn—had reeled from the loss for long afterward. Miranda had witnessed the hurt in their family firsthand.

"And you can double that amount," Kace confided, leaning closer to make the comment for her ears alone. "Nigel Townshend just told me Green Room Media wants to match whatever we raise tonight. You can announce it when you take the podium."

"That's fantastic news." She was pleased and overwhelmed. If only she didn't feel like she was missing a piece of herself tonight with Kai's absence. "Are you set for the wedding next weekend?"

A smile curved Kace's lips, his normally serious expression transforming. "Honestly? I can't wait."

As if on cue, Lulu hurried over to them, her hands already outstretched to take Kace's, her diamond engagement ring flashing under the lights.

"Hello, gorgeous Miranda," she drawled, even though she never glanced Miranda's way. She twirled in front of Kace, her sapphire-blue gown fanning around her ankles at the kick-pleat. "I must borrow my man for a dance."

"Lulu—" Kace sounded like he wanted to protest, but he

stretched his hands out to hers and let Lulu tug him toward the dance floor.

Faced with all these happy couples, loneliness hovered over Miranda like dark clouds, even in the midst of all the partygoers. Actually, maybe being among these happy, smiling people only increased her own sense of loss. She'd hoped to see Kai here, but now that it seemed like he wasn't going to show, she suspected she could slip away unnoticed from the party after her announcements were made.

She would drive to Deer Springs and speak to him in person. She had an apology to make and some news to deliver about a decision she'd made about her future.

Course set, she spun away from the dance floor and headed toward the podium. She was about to give the bandleader a nod to end the set when Kellan Blackwood intercepted her. Dressed in a tuxedo, Buckley's oldest son had dark brown hair that he'd always worn short, with blue eyes that crinkled at the corners. He looked happy tonight.

"Great party, Miranda." He folded her in a quick hug that reminded her how far she'd come with the Blackwood heirs in the last few months. There'd been a time they'd been certain she was a gold digger. "I'm bringing Irina something to eat, but I wanted to let you know we found out that she's having a boy."

Touched that he'd sought her out to share the news with her, Miranda smiled, genuinely happy for them. They deserved every bit of happiness they'd found together and she refused to let her own sadness taint their joy. "I'm thrilled for you both, Kellan."

"We're going to name him Trevor Buckley Blackwood," Kellan continued, his blue gaze growing serious. "In memory of all that Dad did for Irina."

Kellan excused himself while Miranda battled to get her emotions under control. She was so happy for Buckley's family. So why did she feel on the verge of tears?

Breathe in. Breathe out.

Standing off to one side of the raised platform where the podium had been stationed, Miranda focused on her breathing while the bandleader brought the song to a close. The partygoers clapped, and Miranda climbed the carpeted steps to take her place in front of the gala guests. Her small perch looked out over the dance floor, and to the rest of the great room beyond. The lighting was a dim violet, but she could still discern the faces in the gala, even as a spotlight snapped on over the podium.

"Good evening." She spoke into the microphone, pausing a moment to let the crowd take notice and tune in before she continued. Once more, she searched for Kai and didn't see him anywhere, his absence emphasizing the emptiness inside her.

Part of her short speech was just for him.

Swallowing hard, she told herself to forge ahead anyhow so she could go find him once she was done. Clearing her throat, she spoke into the microphone.

"Thank you all for being here at Royal Gives Back. I organized this benefit at the behest of Buckley Blackwood, a secret philanthropist who came to understand that all the millions he made during his lifetime couldn't compare to the joys of doing good for others." Her gaze traveled over her notes and then lifted to the attentive crowd. "And his wealth certainly couldn't compare to the rewards of his family."

The room seemed to go even more silent as if everyone gave her their full attention now, even the servers and musicians. Miranda bit her lip to keep her emotions in check, knowing the importance of giving Buckley a proper send-off. The weight of responsibility he'd given her settled on her shoulders one last time, and she hoped she proved worthy of his trust.

"Buckley found it hard to admit his mistakes in life. But before he died, he came to terms with the things he'd done wrong, and he chose to leave a legacy of philanthropy that we're celebrating tonight. It's my pleasure to announce that every cent we raise at Royal Gives Back will be matched by Green Room Media, thanks to Nigel Townshend." She waited while the assembled guests whooped and applauded. The engineer working the lights searched the crowd to find Nigel beside Sophie at a table in the back, and the producer waved a good-natured hand.

Sophie beamed proudly beside him.

Miranda remembered her stepdaughter's advice about Kai. *First, you apologize.* Then she'd worry about the rest. All the more motivated to wind things up so she could get to Deer Springs, Miranda read the segment of her speech that was in memory of Buckley's first wife, then talked briefly about how the fundraising efforts would aid stroke research.

Then, Miranda tucked her notes to one side.

She was just about to conclude her remarks with a personal addendum when she thought she heard a stirring of movement at the back of the room. A shuffle of feet. Low murmured voices.

Movement in the crowd alerted her to a dark-haired man walking closer to the front of the podium.

Kai Maddox stopped in the middle of the dance floor, separated from her by only a few couples in black tie. Her heart pounded so hard she was sure the microphone would pick it up and amplify it through the venue. His green eyes gave away nothing. She felt shaky as she started to speak again.

"Finally," she continued, pulling in a deep breath and willing herself to get this part right. For Kai. "I am grateful to Buckley for giving me this opportunity to return to Royal. While I was as stunned as any of you at the initial terms of his will, I hope I have grown as a person over these last five months—" Her throat closed up. She had to pause for a moment. "And I'm so glad to feel like I have a family here. Now that Blackwood Bank and the other Blackwood assets are in the hands of their rightful heirs, I could officially head back to New York."

Her gaze locked on Kai's handsome face. The face of the man she loved more than she could have ever imagined possible.

"But overseeing Buckley's estate has taught me not to take for granted the time with family and loved ones. So I'm going to stay in Royal a little while longer to open a local Goddess fitness center." There was a murmur of surprise in the audience. Guests turned to one another. But Kai remained motionless, his face a mask. Miranda dug deep, pulling out the words that were meant for him alone. "Besides, I have unfinished business with a certain technology CEO who means the world to me. A man who—I hope—understands the value of a second chance."

He made his way across the room and the crowd began to part for Kai, his gaze locked on her with every purposeful stride. A spark of hope ignited inside her as she wondered if there could be a way forward for them after all. Maybe putting her heart out there for him to see could be enough. Perhaps he could hear the genuineness of her apology and her love.

Kai took the stairs two at a time to reach her. To tell her he wasn't ready to give her that chance? Or to tell her that he wanted to work things out with her, too? Uncertainty made her hands shake as she switched off the microphone and the crowd applauded.

When Kai swooped her up into his arms, the applause redoubled to become thunderous. Miranda looped her arms around his neck, holding tight. He hadn't spoken yet, but surely the action—his being here and holding her—meant something.

"I'm so sorry I doubted you," she told him, hoping against hope that he liked the idea of a second chance. "Kai, I want to do everything I can to make things work between us."

"In that case, we can't possibly fail." His strong arms flexed beneath her, lifting her a fraction so that his forehead tipped to hers while the band resumed playing nearby and the spotlight faded from the speaker's podium. "I happen to know you can move mountains if you set your mind to it, Miranda."

Closing her eyes, she gave herself a moment to soak in the feel of his arms tightened around her, the warmth of his forehead where it rested against hers. She breathed in the scent of his aftershave. Then, Kai straightened and carried her through the parted curtains that led to a small backstage area where extra tables and chairs were kept for events. He ignored the sign that said No Exit on a rear entrance and backed them through it, landing them in the parking area of the Texas Cattleman's Club, close to one of the side gardens.

Lowering Miranda to her feet, he took her hand and led her down a stone path to a secluded garden bench near a fountain.

"When I didn't see you earlier tonight, I was afraid you weren't coming. I planned to drive to Deer Springs right after I spoke so that I could apologize to you in person."

"I'm glad." Kai threaded her fingers through his, one by one as he let out a ragged sigh of relief. He pressed the back of her hand to his lips for a moment, his eyes sliding closed before he looked up again, his eyes open now and alive with desire. "Not that I needed the apology, but it makes me happy to hear you were making it a priority to talk to me. I know I haven't done a good job communicating what's important to me in the past, but I'm determined to do better with you in the future."

Hope sprang to life inside her, green and bright. He'd spoken exactly the kinds of words she'd longed to hear from him so many years ago.

"You're thinking about a future together, too?" she asked, turning more fully toward him on the bench so her knee bumped his.

He took her breath away in his tuxedo, his broad shoulders filling out the black silk and casting her in shadow as she gazed up at him. Music from the gala seeped through the walls and windows, a lively country tune that would have the whole crowd two-stepping in their tuxes and gowns.

"I'm doing more than thinking about it," Kai promised, his thumb rubbing over the back of her hand and making her shiver from the simple pleasure of it. "I'm going to do everything in my power to make sure the logistics of our relationship will work."

A relationship. Something lasting. He was meeting her halfway in this, the way a real relationship worked.

"I really do want to stay in Royal for a while," she assured him, eager to do her part, make their commitment a two-way street that would pay off so beautifully for both of them. She'd given a lot of thought to bringing a Goddess fitness center to town, and she knew it was the perfect way to spend more time cementing what she had with Kai. "I've been so happy here— except for the past week, of course. I've missed you every minute we weren't together."

"I've missed you, too. I knew I was missing the big picture, but it took Dane rattling my cage a little to make me see I was never going to be happy until I took a risk and laid my heart at your feet." He cupped her cheek with his free hand, stroking along her jaw. "Tonight, I'm doing just that. I love you, Miranda, so damn much."

Her heart soared. A smile curved her lips, relief and joy wrapping around her like a hug.

"Oh, Kai." Leaning into him, she kissed him gently, taking her time to feel the exquisite pleasure of this man's lips on hers, a pleasure she looked forward to revisiting as often as she wanted. "I love you, too. I regret that I didn't work harder to make things right between us the first time, but I'm not going to take what we have for granted ever again."

She'd meant every word of her speech at the podium. Seeing her first husband's mistakes up close and personal had helped her see that she would never be happy pursuing her business goals at the expense of everything else. She would make time for love in her life, even if it sometimes felt riskier than her career.

She trusted Kai with her heart.

When he eased back to look at her, his feelings were all right there for her to see. Full of love and a promise for the future.

"Maybe we both needed the time to grow and appreciate what we had to make it work this time," Kai reassured her, his words a soft whisper over her lips. He kissed her again with slow thoroughness that left her breathless. Then, he nipped her lower lip and backed away again. "But I promise you, we'll get it right now that we have this second chance."

"Even with you based in Deer Springs and my company in

New York?" She didn't mind flying back and forth, but he'd said something about taking the logistics into account, and she was curious what that meant.

"Listen," he began, releasing her hand to cradle her face between his palms. "I want you to take the deal with AMuse and follow all your dreams, Miranda. I can open a Madtec office in New York so we can have a life together there, too. We don't have to choose. We can have it all."

She believed him.

More than that, she believed in *them*.

Together, they could take on the world.

"I like the idea of sharing all our future plans." She remembered sitting in the Deer Springs Diner all those years ago, telling him about the life she'd imagined for herself. Listening to him spin lofty goals of his own. "We were always good at dreaming big."

"Now that we've established that we're sticking together forever, would you like to go back inside and dance with me?" Kai's green gaze tracked over her. "You look stunning tonight."

Her pulse quickened.

"Actually, I was already plotting my escape after my speech," she told him honestly. "I'd rather you take me home and make love to me all night long."

With a husky growl of approval, he drew her to her feet, a hand curving possessively around her waist, landing on the bare patch of skin where her dress had a cutout.

"I drove my motorcycle tonight. Can you manage the bike in that dress for a moonlight ride?"

"Are you kidding?" She began to walk backward toward the parking lot, tugging him with her. "I've been dying for an excuse to wrap my arms around you. Lead the way."

His teeth flashed white as he stepped ahead of her, guiding her through the parking area toward their future. It promised to be a wild and incredible ride.

EPILOGUE

One Week Later

"DO YOU, LULU SHEPARD, take this man…"

Kai listened to the officiant's words at the wedding ceremony, but his eyes weren't on the bride as he stood under the huge white canopy erected near the pool at Blackwood Hollow for the televised nuptials of Lulu Shepard and Kace LeBlanc. Granted, the bride was a beauty in her simple white gown that showed off the natural beauty of her glossy black hair and almond-shaped brown eyes. But Kai's eyes kept straying to one of the lovely bridesmaids. He could manage only to glance over to the couple in question.

Miranda's costar from *Secret Lives of NYC Ex-Wives* glowed, rushing to answer the question with an emphatic, "I do."

Her groom looked at her like he'd won the wife lottery.

Kai noted their happiness—and then returned his focus to the redheaded bridesmaid. Miranda stood with Lulu's other costars at the front of the canopy, the hem of her pale yellow bridesmaid's dress blowing gently around her legs thanks to the cooling fans placed around the tent for the sunset exchange of vows. She carried a small bouquet of purple violets. As always, Miranda captivated him.

She was everything he'd ever wanted in a woman—smart and ambitious, but tender and kind. She devoted herself to her charity and her loved ones even more than she committed herself to her work. Considering how far she'd come as a businesswoman, that was saying something. Kai's heart damned near burst with love for her as a quintet of musicians launched into a triumphant wedding recessional. Lulu and Kace led the way, holding their joined hands up in victory as a newly married pair, but Kai's attention stayed on Miranda where she walked through the aisle, each step bringing her closer to him.

The television cameras moved smoothly with the wedding party, tracking their every step while keeping out of the way. The ceremony was informal enough that the bride and groom were skipping a reception line since the party would start straight away. Photos had already been taken before the vows, so Kai looked forward to Miranda being free for the rest of the evening.

Her blue eyes found his among the guests milling about to admire the wedding cake on a table at the back of the tent. A space for dancing was set up as a country band readied to take over for the chamber musicians now that the formal part of the evening was finished. Flashes popped on cell phones as guests all hurried to capture the bride and groom in their first moments of married life.

All of that activity around him was just a backdrop for his night with Miranda, the most important woman in the world to him.

He pulled her to him as soon as she reached him, indulging in a brief kiss to her cheek and neck, her jasmine scent an aphrodisiac after the tantalizing nights they'd spent together.

"Well, hello to you, too," Miranda murmured warmly, clutching his shoulder with one hand while she still held her bouquet with the other.

"Public displays of affection are allowed at a wedding, right?" He forced himself to step back a fraction, but he wound an arm around her waist, his fingers gliding along the pale yellow silk of her gown.

"Absolutely." Her smile lit her whole face as she gazed up at him. "It seems only appropriate to celebrate a new love match with a kiss."

She set down her flowers on a nearby folding chair.

"Would you like to step outside for a minute?" he suggested, nodding toward the pool area visible on the other end of the tent. "It's a beautiful night."

"Sounds good." She threaded her arm through his so he could escort her among the folding chairs to a spot where they could exit the canopy.

The spring Texas air was warmer, even with the sun going down and a breeze stirring. The landscape lights reflected in the pool and violet stars winked overhead in the fading twilight. Kai followed the smooth stone path behind the water feature. Here, trees arched over the path, their leaves fluttering softly.

The country band launched into its first tune, and a whoop went up inside the canopy.

"Are you sorry to see your show end for another season?" Kai asked as he twirled her under his arm in a silent invitation to dance.

Miranda fell into step with him easily, as if they'd been together for a lifetime. He still couldn't quite believe his good fortune finding her again after the past ten years apart. This time, nothing would come between them. He felt it with unswerving certainty.

"No." She shook her head, the red strands of her silky hair catching the moonlight. "The whole season has felt like a finale to me, not just the wedding episode. I've loved my time with the women on this show, but I think I'm ready to turn my attention to other things in the coming year."

He'd sensed the same thing in the way she'd talked about the other cast members. With both Seraphina and Lulu getting married and moving to Texas, the group seemed to be moving on. He smoothed a hand up her spine and back down, savoring the feel of her. Grateful as hell to hold her in his arms.

"You know I'll stand behind whatever decision you make," he assured her. "But if I have my way, you won't be an 'ex-wife' for much longer."

He didn't want to rush Miranda, but he also knew that he wanted forever with this woman.

Her breath caught and she blinked twice before a smile curved her lips. "Something tells me it's going to be an exciting year."

Kai tipped her chin up with his knuckle, looking deep into her eyes.

"Have I told you today how much I love you?" He leaned in to kiss her and they swayed together, lips locked, for a long moment.

"No." Her eyes simmered with blue fire. "But I'm going to have you show me tonight instead."

With pleasure, Kai vowed to do just that.

* * * * *

A Man You Can Trust

Jo McNally

Special EDITION

Believe in love. Overcome obstacles. Find happiness.

Jo McNally lives in coastal North Carolina with one hundred pounds of dog and two hundred pounds of husband—her slice of the bed is very small. When she's not writing or reading romance novels (or clinging to the edge of the bed), she can often be found on the back porch sipping wine with friends while listening to great music. If the weather is absolutely perfect, Jo might join her husband on the golf course, where she tends to feel far more competitive than her actual skill level would suggest.

She likes writing stories about strong women and the men who love them. She's a true believer that love can conquer all if given just half a chance.

You can follow Jo pretty much anywhere on social media (and she'd love it if you did!), but you can start at her website, jomcnallyromance.com.

Books by Jo McNally

Harlequin Special Edition

Gallant Lake Stories

A Man You Can Trust

Visit the Author Profile page
at millsandboon.com.au for more titles.

Dear Reader,

Welcome to Gallant Lake, New York! This fictional lakeside town nestled in the Catskill Mountains has definitely seen better days. But the newly renovated Gallant Lake Resort is back in business. That means the *town* is back in business, too. New faces. New jobs. New opportunities...for love.

Nick and Cassie have each come to Gallant Lake for a fresh start, and they end up working together at the resort. Cassie is a jumpy, defensive bundle of nerves. Nick is loud and restless, always off kayaking or hanging from some mountain cliff. After a pepper spray incident, Nick, an ex-cop, offers to teach Cassie self-defense, which puts them in close, sweaty contact. When Cassie's past threatens to send her on the run again, they both have to set their fears aside to take a stand for love.

I'm so excited to bring the setting of Gallant Lake to Harlequin Special Edition! The town got its start in my Lowery Women series for Harlequin Superromance, and some familiar characters make an appearance in this book. If you want to know their stories, please check out *She's Far From Hollywood*, *Nora's Guy Next Door* and *The Life She Wants*. I look forward to sharing more Gallant Lake Stories with you in the coming months.

In this book, Cassie is a victim of domestic abuse—and so is Nick, in a way. This subject is extremely important to me personally. If you or someone you know is in an abusive relationship, *please* reach out for help. Don't let anyone steal your sense of security and self-worth.

Wishing you forever love,

Jo McNally

This book, with a Genuine Good Guy as a hero, is
dedicated to the memory of a Genuine Good Guy—
my dad. He was quietly, yet fiercely,
devoted to the people he loved.

I love and miss you, Dad.

CHAPTER ONE

THE RESORT PARKING lot was quiet.

That was hardly surprising, since it was seven o'clock on a Monday morning.

But Cassandra Smith didn't take chances.

Ever.

She backed into her reserved spot but didn't turn the car off right away. She didn't even put it in Park. First, she looked around—checking the mirrors, making sure she was going to stay. Pete Carter was walking from his car toward the Gallant Lake Resort. He waved as he passed her, and she waved back, then pretended to look at something on the passenger seat as she turned off the ignition. Pete worked at the front desk, and he was a nice enough guy. He'd offer to walk her inside if she got out now. And maybe that would be a good idea. Or maybe not. How well did she really know him?

Her fingers tightened on the steering wheel. She was being ridiculous—Pete was thirty years her senior and happily married. But some habits were hard to shake, and really—why take the chance? By the time she finished arguing with herself, Pete was gone.

She checked the mirrors one last time before getting out of the car, threading the keys through her fingers in a move as natural to her as breathing. As she closed the door, a warm breeze brushed a tangle of auburn hair across her face. She tucked it back behind her ear and took a moment to appreciate the morning. Beyond the sprawling 200-room fieldstone-and-timber resort where Cassie worked, Gallant Lake shimmered like polished blue steel. It was encircled by the Catskill Mountains, which were just beginning to show a blush of green in the trees. The air was brisk but smelled like spring, earthy and fresh. It reminded her of new beginnings.

It had been six months since Aunt Cathy offered her sanctuary in this small resort town nestled in the Catskills. Gallant Lake was beginning to feel like home, and she was grateful for it. The sound of car tires crunching on the driveway behind her propelled her out of her thoughts and into the building. Other employees were starting to arrive.

Cassie crossed the lobby, doing her best to avoid making eye contact with the few guests wandering around at this hour. As usual, she opted for the stairs instead of dealing with the close confines of the elevator. The towering spiral staircase in the center of the lobby looked like a giant tree growing up toward the ceiling three stories above, complete with stylized copper leaves draping from the ceiling. The offices of Randall Resorts International were located on the second floor, overlooking the wide lawn that stretched to the lakeshore. Cassie's desk was centered between four small offices. Or rather, three smaller offices and one huge one, which belonged to the boss. That boss was in earlier than usual today.

"G'morning, Cassie! Once you get settled, stop in, okay?"

Ugh. No employee wanted to be called into the boss's office first thing on a Monday.

Blake Randall managed not only this resort from Gallant Lake, but half a dozen others around the world. It hadn't taken long for Cassie to understand that Blake was one of those rare— at least in her world—men who wore their honor like a mantle. He took pride in protecting the people he cared for. Tall, with a swath of black hair that was constantly falling across his forehead, the man was ridiculously good-looking. His wife, Amanda, really hit the jackpot with this guy, and he adored her and their children.

Blake was all business in the office, though. Focused and driven, he'd intimidated the daylights out of Cassie at first. Amanda teasingly called him Tall, Dark and Broody, and the nickname fit. But Cassie had come to appreciate his steady leadership. He had high expectations, and he frowned on drama in the workplace.

He'd offered her a job at the resort's front desk when she first arrived in Gallant Lake. It was a charity job—a favor to Cathy—and Cassie knew it. It took only one irate male guest venting at her during check-in for everyone to realize she wasn't ready to be working with an unpredictable public. She'd frozen like a deer in headlights. Once she moved up here to the private offices, she'd found her footing and had impressed Blake with her problem-solving skills. Because Blake hated problems.

She tossed her purse into the bottom drawer of her desk and checked her computer quickly to make sure there weren't any urgent issues to deal with. Then she made herself a cup of hot tea, loaded it with sugar and poured Blake a mug of black coffee before heading into his office.

He looked up from behind his massive desk and gave her a quick nod of thanks as she set his coffee down in front of him. Everyone knew to stay out of Blake's way until they saw a cup of coffee in his hand. He was well-known for not being a morning person. He took a sip and sighed.

"I was ready to book a flight to Barbados after hearing about the wedding disaster down there this weekend, but then I heard that apparently *I*—" he emphasized the one-letter word with air quotes "—already resolved everything by flying some photographer in to take wedding photos yesterday, along with discounting some rooms. Not at *our* resort, but at a *competitor*. I hear I'm quite the hero to the bride's mother, but I'll be damned if I remember doing any of it."

Blake's dark brows furrowed as he studied her over the rim of his coffee cup, but she could see a smile tugging at the corner of his mouth. The tension in her shoulders eased. Despite his tone, he wasn't really angry.

"The manager called Saturday looking for you," she explained. "Monique was in a panic, so I made a few calls. The bride's mother used the son of a 'dear family friend' to organize the wedding, instead of using our concierge service. The idiot didn't book the rooms until the last minute, and we didn't have enough available, which he neglected to mention to the bride's mom. Then he booked the photographer for the wrong date." She smiled at the look of horror on Blake's face. "We're talking wrong by a full month. It was quite a melodrama—none of which was our fault—but the bride is some internet fashion icon with half a million followers on Instagram. So we found rooms at the neighboring resort for the guests we couldn't handle, and convinced the wedding party to get back into their gowns and tuxes for a full photo shoot the day *after* the wedding, which was the fastest we could get the photographer there. Mom's happy. Bride's happy. Social media is flooded with great photos and stories with the resort as a backdrop. I assumed you'd approve."

Blake chuckled. "Approve? It was freaking brilliant, Cassie. That kind of problem-solving is more along the lines of a VP than an executive assistant. You should have an office of your own."

She still wasn't used to receiving compliments, and her cheeks warmed. When she'd first arrived, she'd barely been able to handle answering calls and emails, always afraid of doing something wrong, of disappointing someone. But as the months went by, she'd started to polish her rusty professional skills and found she was pretty good at getting things done, especially over the phone. Face-to-face confrontation was a different story.

This wasn't the first time Blake had mentioned a promotion, but she wasn't ready. Oh, she was plenty qualified, with a bachelor's degree in business admin. But if things went bad back in Milwaukee, she'd have to change her name again and vanish, so it didn't make sense to put down roots anywhere. She let Blake's comment hang in the air without responding. He finally shook his head.

"Fine. Keep whatever job title you want, but I need your help with something."

Cassie frowned when Blake hesitated. "What is it?"

"You know I hired a new director of security." Cassie nodded. She was going to miss Ken Taylor, who was retiring to the Carolinas with his wife, Dianne. Ken had taken the job on a temporary basis after Blake's last security guy left for a job in Boston. Ken was soft-spoken and kind, and he looked like Mr. Rogers, right down to the cardigan sweaters. He was aware of Cassie's situation, and he'd made every effort to make sure she felt safe here, including arranging her reserved parking space.

"Nick West starts today. I'd like you to work with him."

"Me? Why?" Cassie blurted the words without thinking. She laughed nervously. "I don't know anything about security!"

But she knew all about *needing* security.

Blake held up his hand. "Relax. I'm not putting you on the security team. He'll need help with putting data together and learning our processes. I need someone I can trust to make sure he has a smooth transition."

"So... I'm going to be *his* executive assistant instead of yours?" Her palms went clammy at the thought of working for a stranger.

"First, we've already established you're a hell of a lot more than my EA. And this is just temporary, to help him get settled in the office." Blake drained his coffee mug and set it down with a thunk, not noticing the way Cassie flinched at the sound. "He's a good guy. Talented. Educated. He's got a master's in criminal justice, and he was literally a hero cop in LA—recognized by the mayor, the whole deal."

A shiver traced its way down Cassie's spine. Her ex had been a "hero cop," too. Blake's next words barely registered.

"I'm a little worried about him making the shift from the hustle of LA to quiet Gallant Lake, but he says he's looking for a change of pace. His thesis was on predictive policing—using data to spot trouble before it reaches a critical point." That explained why Blake hired the guy. Blake was all about preventing problems before they happened. He did *not* like surprises. "It'll be interesting to see how he applies that to facility security. His approach requires a ton of data to build predictive models, and that's where you come in. You create reports faster than anyone else here."

Cassie loved crunching numbers and analyzing results. She started to relax. If Blake wanted her to do some research for the new guy, she could handle that.

"I also want you to mentor him a bit, help him get acclimated."

"Meaning...?"

"Amanda and I are headed to Vegas this week for that conference and a little vacation time. Nick's going to need someone to show him around, make introductions and answer any questions that come up. He just got to town this weekend, and he doesn't know anyone or anything in Gallant Lake."

"So what, I'm supposed to be his babysitter?"

Blake's brow rose at the uncharacteristically bold question.

"Uh, no. Just walk him around the resort so he's familiar with it, and be a friendly face for the guy." He leaned forward. "Look, I get why you might be anxious, but he's the director of security. That's about as safe as it gets."

Her emotions roiled around in her chest. She hated that her employer felt he had to constantly reassure her about her safety. Yes, the guy in charge of security *should* be safe. All men should be.

"Cassie? Is this going to be a problem?" The worry in Blake's eyes made her sit straighter in her chair. What was it Sun Tzu wrote in *The Art of War*? The latest in a long line of self-help books she'd picked up was based on quotes from the ancient Chinese tome.

Appear strong when you are weak...

"No, I'm sure it will be fine. And the data analysis sounds interesting. Does he know...?"

"About your situation? No. I wouldn't do that without your permission. I only told Ken because you'd just arrived and..."

She was hardly strong now, but she'd been a complete basket case back then.

"I understand. I don't think the new guy needs to know. I don't want to be treated differently."

Blake frowned. "I don't want that, either. But I do want you to feel safe here."

"I know, Blake. And thank you. If I change my mind, I'll tell him myself." She was getting tired of people having conversations about her as if she was a problem to be solved, no matter how well-meaning they were. "When will I meet him?"

"He's getting his rental house situated this morning, then he'll be in. I'm planning on having lunch with him, then giving him a quick tour. He dropped some boxes off yesterday. Can you make sure he has a functioning office? You know, computer, phone, internet access and all that? I told Brad to set it up, but you know how scattered that kid can be."

Two hours later, Cassie was finishing the last touches in West's office. The computer and voice mail were set up with temporary passwords. The security team had delivered his passes and key cards—his master key would open any door in the resort. Brad, their IT whiz, had been busy over the weekend, and a huge flat-screen hung on one wall. On it, twelve different feeds from the security surveillance room downstairs were scrolling in black and white. It looked like a scene straight out of some crime-fighter TV show.

A familiar voice rang out in the office. "Hel-lo? Damn, no one's here."

Cassie stepped to the doorway and waved to Blake's wife. "I'm here!"

Amanda Randall rushed to give Cassie a tight hug. Cassie *hated* hugs, but Amanda got a free pass. The woman simply couldn't help herself—she was a serial hugger. She was also Cassie's best friend in Gallant Lake. They'd bonded one night over a bottle of wine and the discovery they shared similar ghosts from their pasts. Other than that, the two women couldn't be any more different. Amanda was petite, with curves everywhere a woman wanted curves. Cassie was average height and definitely not curvy—her nervous energy left her with a lean build. Amanda had long golden curls, while Cassie's straight auburn hair was usually pulled back and under control. Amanda was a bouncing bundle of laughing, loving, hugging energy. Cassie was much more reserved, and sometimes found her friend's enthusiasm overwhelming.

"I brought chocolate chip cookies for everyone, but I guess you and I will have to eat them all." Amanda held up a basket that smelled like heaven.

"You won't have to twist my arm. Come on in and keep me company."

Amanda followed her into the new guy's office.

"Wow—this is some pretty high-tech stuff, huh?" Amanda walked over to the flat-screen and watched the video feeds change from camera to camera. One feed was from a camera in front of Blake and Amanda's stone mansion next door to the resort. The private drive was visible in the view from above their front door. "I really need to talk to Blake about those cameras. I don't like the feeds popping up in some stranger's office."

"Hasn't resort security always been responsible for the house, too?"

"I was never crazy about that, but Blake insisted. And it was different when it was Paul, whom I'd known from the first week

I was here. And then Ken. I mean, he's like having a favorite uncle watching over the house. But some hotshot ex-cop from LA watching me and the kids coming and going?" Amanda shuddered. "I don't think so. Have you met him yet?"

"Who?"

"The new guy? Superhero cop coming to save us all? The one who has my husband drooling?"

"No, I haven't met him yet." Cassie set a stack of legal pads on the corner of the desk, opposite the corner Amanda now occupied as she devoured a cookie. "What do you know about him?"

"What *don't* I know? He's all Blake talked about this weekend. 'Nick is so brave!' 'Nick is so brilliant!' 'Oh, no! What if Nick doesn't like it here?' 'What if Nick leaves?'" Amanda acted out each comment dramatically, and Cassie couldn't help laughing. "But seriously, he *really* wants this guy to work out. You know Blake—he believes in preventing problems before they happen, and that wasn't Ken's strong suit. He's so anxious for this guy to be happy here that he actually suggested we skip our trip to Vegas so he could be here all week for *Nick*! That was a 'hell no' from me. We haven't been away together without the kids in ages." Amanda finished off the last of her cookie, licking her fingers. "And this girl is ready to par-tay in Vegas, baby! Whatcha doin'?"

"Blake said Nick dropped off these boxes. I'll unpack them, and he can organize later." Cassie pulled the top off one of the boxes on the credenza. It was filled with books on criminal science and forensics. She put them on the bookshelves in the order they were packed. Police work was usually a life's calling. What made this guy walk away from it?

She stopped after pulling the cover off the second box. It contained more books and binders, but sitting on top was a framed photo. She lifted it out and Amanda came around the desk to study it with her.

It was a wedding portrait. The tall man in the image looked

damned fine in a tuxedo, like a real-life James Bond. His hair was dark and cropped short, military style. His features were angular and sharp, softened only by the affectionate smile he was giving the bride. Her skin was dark and her wedding gown was the color of champagne. Her close-cropped Afro highlighted her high cheekbones and long, graceful neck. She was looking up at the man proudly, exuding confidence and joy. Cassie felt a sting of regret. When was the last time anyone thought that about her?

"Wow—are those two gorgeous or what?" Amanda took the silver frame from Cassie and whistled softly. "I wonder who it is." She turned the frame over as if there might be an answer on the back.

"I'm assuming it's Nick West and his wife."

"No. Blake told me he's single."

"Maybe she's an ex?"

Amanda rolled her eyes. "Who keeps photos like this of their ex? Maybe it's not him at all—could be a brother or a friend. But if it is Nick, he's hot as hell, isn't he?"

Cassie took the picture back and set it on a shelf. "I hadn't noticed."

"Yeah, I call BS on that. There isn't a woman under the age of eighty who wouldn't notice how hot *that* guy is. You'd better be careful, especially now that you're living in the love shack."

"The *what*?"

"Nora's apartment—we call it the love shack. First it was her and Asher. Then Mel moved in there and met Shane. And now *you're* there, so…"

Cassie's aunt had sold her coffee shop in the village to Amanda's cousin Nora a few years ago but still worked there part-time. The apartment above the Gallant Brew had been a godsend when it came vacant shortly after Cassie's arrival. But a *love shack*?

"I don't believe in fairy tales. And even if Nora's place *did* have magic powers, they'd be wasted on me." She started to pull more books out of the box, but Amanda stopped her.

"Hey, I'm sorry. I don't mean to push you. Sometimes my mouth gets ahead of my brain. But someday you're going to find someone…"

Cassie shook her head abruptly. "That ship has sailed, Amanda. I have zero interest in any kind of…whatever." She glanced back to the photo and studied the man's dark eyes, sparkling with love for the bride. Her heart squeezed just a little, but she ignored it. "I can't take the chance. Not again."

"Not every guy is Don. In fact, there are millions of guys who *aren't* Don."

Amanda meant well, but they were straying onto thin and dangerous ice here. Cassie had wedding photos, too. They were packed away somewhere, and they showed a smiling couple just like this one. She'd been so innocent back then. And stupid. She was never going to be either again.

"Look, I have a ton of work to do, and this guy—my *co-worker*—is going to be here any time now. No more talk about love shacks and hotness, okay?"

Amanda stared at her long and hard, her blue eyes darkening in concern. But thankfully, she decided to let it go. She picked up the basket of cookies. "Fine. I have to finish packing for the trip anyway. I'll leave these out on the coffee counter." She started to walk away, then spun suddenly and threw her arms around Cassie in an attack hug. "We leave in the morning, but we'll be back next week. If you need anything at all—*anything*—you call Nora or Mel and they'll be there in a heartbeat."

Cassie bit back the surprising rebuke that sat on the tip of her tongue. She was fed up with everyone hovering and fretting, but she knew it was her own damn fault. How many times had she called Amanda those first few months, crying and terror-stricken because of a bad dream or some random noise she heard? Sure, she'd changed her name and moved about as far away from Milwaukee as she could get, but Don was an ex-cop with all the right connections. That's why she kept a "go-bag" packed and ready at her door. She took a deep breath, nodded and wished Amanda a safe and fun trip. But after she left, Cassie was too agitated to sit at her desk. She ended up back in Nick West's office, unpacking the last box.

A little flicker of anger flared deep inside. It had been nudging at her more and more lately, first as an occasional spark of frustration, but now it was turning into a steady flame. She wanted her life back. She wanted a life where she could rely on herself and stand up for herself. She looked at the wedding photo again. She wanted a life where she smiled more. Where she didn't jump every time someone…

A shadow filled the doorway.

"Hey! Whatcha doin' in here?"

CHAPTER TWO

NICK WEST KNEW he'd startled the woman, but he was just trying to be funny. It was a *joke*. He figured the auburn-haired stranger would jump, then they'd both have a good laugh as he introduced himself. Humor was always a good icebreaker, right?

He never figured she'd send a stapler flying at his head.

He managed to swat it down before it connected with his face, but it ricocheted off the corner of his desk and smacked him in the shin.

"Ow!" He hopped on one leg. "Damn, woman! I was just kidding around." He rubbed his throbbing shin, unable to keep from laughing at the way his joke had backfired on him.

But the woman wasn't laughing. She was wide-eyed and pale, her chest rising and falling sharply. Her eyes were an interesting mix of green and gold. Her hair was a mix, too—not quite red, but more than just brown. It was pulled back off her face and into a low ponytail. She was pretty, in a fresh-scrubbed, natural way. Then he noticed her hand, which was clutching a pair of scissors like she was getting ready to go all Norman Bates on him.

The desk was still between them, but he raised his hands as if she was holding a loaded gun. He'd already seen how good her aim was.

"Whoa, there! Let's dial it back a notch, okay? I'm Nick West and this is my office... I think. Am I in the wrong place?" The thought didn't occur to him until he said it out loud. Shit. Had he just burst into some woman's office and scared the bejesus out of her? What if this was the boss's wife? He'd heard Randall's wife was involved in the resorts somehow. Even if it wasn't her, traumatizing a coworker wasn't a good way to start his first day here.

The hand holding the scissors lowered and color came back to her previously white knuckles. She lifted her chin, but it trembled, and there was genuine fear in her eyes. It made him feel like a jerk.

"Look, I'm sorry. I was kidding around. I do that sometimes."

"You scared the hell out of me, and you did it on purpose!" Those green-gold eyes flashed in anger. "Is that how you plan on introducing yourself to everyone here? Because I've got news for you—it won't go over well." She reached up to push her hair behind her ear and took a steadying breath. "This *is* your office, Mr. West. I'm Cassie...um... Smith, and I'll be working with you. I was setting up your desk."

Great. He'd never had a secretary before, and he'd just traumatized the first one he got. *Smooth move, West.* He grunted out a short laugh, rubbing the back of his neck as he tried to figure out how to fix this mess.

"Let's rewind and start over, okay? You're my first secretary." He stopped when her eyes narrowed. "What? What'd I say wrong now?"

"I am *not* your secretary. I'm Mr. Randall's executive assistant, and I'll be supporting you with some of your projects. I'll provide data. I'll run reports. But I don't take dictation and I won't be fetching your damned coffee."

Well, well, well. The jumpy lady had a backbone after all. Nick knew how to be a good cop. He had no damned clue how to be a good executive.

"Not a secretary. Got it. Like I said, I'm new at this corporate thing. In LA, I had a dispatcher and a desk sergeant. Something tells me you'll be closer to the latter." He nodded down to her hand. "I'd be a lot happier if you'd put those down."

Cassie looked down and appeared surprised to see the scissors still in her hand. She dropped them to the desk like they were burning her.

"Sorry," she mumbled. She continued to look down, lost in thought.

Her body language was all over the place, causing his cop's sixth sense to kick in. First she was jumpy and defensive. Then proud and outspoken. And now, as she apologized, she visibly shrank. He didn't like timid women. They reminded him of victims, and he'd had his fill of victims. But then again, victims didn't fling staplers at people's heads.

"Don't apologize," he said. "That was a juvenile thing for me to do. I gotta remember I'm not in a police precinct anymore." And he'd never be in one again. He rubbed his thigh absently. Shoving that thought aside, he flashed her a rueful grin. "I'll probably need your help monitoring my corporate behavior."

She nodded, not returning the smile, but straightening a bit. "I don't like practical jokes, but I'm sure you'll do fine here. It's a good group of people, and they like to have fun."

Interesting. She said *they* like to have fun, not *we*. He looked around the office. He'd barely noticed it yesterday, just dropping off his boxes and checking in to his room to crash after the long cross-country drive. The view of Gallant Lake was sweet. The giant flat-screen on the wall with all the changing camera feeds was even sweeter. He saw the photo on the bookshelf and blinked. Jada. It was her death that chased him out of LA and into this new life. The picture was a reminder of how quickly good things could go bad.

A large hand clamped down on his shoulder from behind, and Nick restrained himself from spinning around swinging. Old habits were hard to break. In this case, it would have been especially bad, since it was his new boss.

"Sorry I missed your arrival, Nick. We had a guest giving the desk staff a hard time about the five movies on his room bill. Turns out his ten-year-old has a thing for superheroes and didn't realize movies are fifteen bucks a pop." There weren't many men who could make Nick tip his head back and look up, but Blake Randall was one of them. He was a few years older than Nick, but he had no doubt Randall could hold his own in a physical challenge. Blake spotted Cassie on the other side of the desk. "Oh, good, you've met Cassie. You're going to want to treat this girl right because she's the one who can make or break you, man."

Nick met Cassie's gaze. Her moods were as changeable as her eyes. Now that Blake was here, she was clearly more relaxed.

...she's the one who can make or break you...

Even after Blake's warning, Nick couldn't resist teasing her.

"Oh, don't worry, Blake. Cassie's made quite an impression already." Her eyes narrowed in suspicion. "She's already throwing things… I mean…*ideas*…at me." Her hands clenched into fists, and he was surprised his skin wasn't blistering under the heat of her glare. "She even took a stab at trying to define her job responsibilities."

Blake was oblivious to the tension buzzing in the room. "Trust me, there is no way to define her job duties. Cassie's always surprising you by doing more than expected." Nick's smirk grew into a wide smile.

"Yeah, she's full of surprises. Oh, look, the stapler fell off the desk." He bent over to pick it up from where it had landed earlier. He couldn't help wondering if exposing his back to the woman, with scissors still nearby, was a good idea. "We don't want the boss to think you were throwing things at me, now, do we?"

"No, we don't." She watched as he set the stapler on the desk. Her voice was cold as ice. "But Blake knows me well enough to know I'd never launch an unprovoked attack."

Nick looked up in surprise. *Touché.* She was playing along. He winked at her, and a little crease appeared between her brows.

Blake chuckled behind him. "I can't imagine Cassie throwing things at anyone." Her cheeks went pink, but Blake didn't seem to notice. "Come on, Nick, let's grab lunch and I'll make some introductions. Would you like to join us, Cass?"

"No, thanks. I have work to do. You and Mr. West go ahead and…"

"Mr. West?" Blake looked at Nick and frowned. "We're on a first-name basis up here, Nick."

"No problem. Cassie and I were joking around earlier and she's just trying to get a rise out of me." Now it was her turn to be surprised. She looked at him and her mouth opened, but she didn't speak.

For the first time, Blake seemed to pick up on the undercurrent of…something…that was swirling around them.

"Really?" He looked at Cassie with clear surprise. Apparently she wasn't known for cracking jokes. She gave Blake a quick nod and smiled. It was the first smile Nick had seen from her, and it was worth waiting for, even if it was aimed at someone else. Her whole face softened, and her eyes went more green than gold.

"You two go on to lunch, and let me get back to work, okay?"

His curiosity was definitely piqued. Cassie Smith had a story.

On Thursday morning, Cassie was still trying to put a finger on her riled-up emotions. It started before Nick West's arrival, so she couldn't place all the blame on him for this low rumble of frustration and anger that simmered in her. In no mood to deal with her tangled hair, she pulled it into a messy knot on top of her head and frowned at the mirror. Simple khakis, sensible shoes and a dark green Gallant Lake polo shirt. Practical attire for a busy day. She was giving Nick a tour of the grounds today and wanted to be able to keep up with his long strides.

The man was always in motion, leaving her constantly on edge. He paced when he talked and bounced when he sat. He had a foam basketball that he tossed around his office when he was alone in there, and it drove her crazy. Yesterday she'd moved her computer so her back was to his door, trying to avoid the distraction of the ball flying through the air. Nick started laughing the minute he walked into the office and saw the new arrangement, and laughed every time he walked by. *Jerk.*

She went downstairs in the loft apartment and poured herself a cup of tea, adding three spoonfuls of sugar. She usually joined Nora in the coffee shop before heading to the resort, but Nora had her hands full watching Amanda and Blake's teenaged son and toddler daughter this week. Mel might be down in the shop, but it was more likely Amanda's other cousin would be enjoying her coffee with her fiancé on the deck of their waterfront home. So Cassie fixed herself a bagel and sat at the kitchen island, feeling almost as restless as Nick West.

Ugh! She'd known the man only three days, and he was in her head constantly. His big laugh when he was kidding around with employees—who all seemed to adore both him and his practical jokes. The way he started every conversation with a booming "Hey! Whatcha doing?" The way he rapped the corner of everyone's desk sharply with his knuckles every time he passed it. Except hers. After the first time he did it and she'd squeaked in surprise, he'd left her desk alone.

But she hadn't managed to stop his infuriating running joke of putting her stapler—the bright blue one she'd flung at him on their first meeting—in a different place every day. Monday afternoon she'd found it on her chair. Tuesday, it was next to the coffee maker. And yesterday, when she attended a meeting in the surveillance room with Nick and the entire security staff, the blue stapler was sitting on the circular console that faced the wall of monitors. She spotted it immediately and turned to glare at him, only to find him laughing at her. *Ass.*

Sure enough, when she walked into the office later that morning, the stapler was sitting next to a small vase of daffodils on her desk. Wait. Where did the daffodils come from? The sunny flowers were in a simple vase, which on closer inspection turned out to be a water glass.

"They reminded me of you, slugger."

Nick West was leaning against the doorway to his office. He'd taken his jacket and tie off and rolled up the sleeves of his dress shirt. That was his usual uniform during the day. He always looked ready for action.

"Excuse me?"

"You know—sunny and bright and happy?" He was baiting her. Yesterday, he'd asked her why she was so serious all the time. Deciding the misogynistic question didn't deserve an answer, she'd walked away, but she should have known he wouldn't drop it. She dropped her purse into a drawer and clarified her comment.

"I was referring to the 'slugger' part."

"Well, you've got pretty good aim with that arm of yours, and you're a fighter. Slugger seems to fit you."

Cassie's breath caught in her throat. He thought she was a *fighter*?

"And what should I call *you*? Ducky, for how fast you dodged the stapler?" He gave her an odd look, somewhere between surprise and admiration. Then his face scrunched up.

"Ducky is a hard pass. Let's stick with Nick."

She looked at the flowers. "Please tell me the director of security didn't *steal* these flowers from the garden in front of the resort."

Nick winked at her. He was a big winker. She did her best to tell herself those twinkling brown eyes of his had no effect on her. "They actually haven't left the property, so at best, the director of security has just *misappropriated* them. I think they look nice there, don't you?" She rolled her eyes.

"I'm sure a cheating accountant thinks misappropriated funds look *nice* in his bank account, too, but that doesn't make it any less a crime."

He barked out a loud laugh. "And here I thought I left all the attorneys back in LA. You missed your calling." He turned back to his office, but stopped cold when she called out.

"Oh, Mr. West?" His exaggerated slow turn almost made her laugh out loud, and she hadn't done that in a long time. He admittedly had a goofy charm. "Don't forget the stapler. You seem to prefer mine to the one you have in your office, so maybe we should switch." She picked it up and tossed it gently in his direction, surprised at her own moxie. He was equally surprised, catching the stapler with one hand. She nodded at the daffodils. "And thank you for the stolen goods."

He gave her a crooked grin. "Just following orders. Blake told me to treat you right, remember?"

Cassie rolled her eyes again and turned away, ignoring his chuckle behind her.

A couple hours later, Nick was surprisingly all business during their tour of the grounds, jotting notes on his tablet and snapping pictures. It was a gorgeous early May day, warming dramatically from earlier in the week. A breeze raised gentle waves on the lake, which were shushing against the shoreline.

They started by walking around the exterior of Blake and Amanda's home, a rambling stone castle named Halcyon, then worked their way down the hill past the resort, all the way to the golf course that hugged the shoreline. The entire complex, including the residence, covered over one hundred acres, and by lunchtime, Cassie felt as though they'd walked every one of them.

She rattled off anecdotes as they walked. Nick's security staff had been showing him around all week, but Blake instructed her, in his absence, to give Nick a tour that included the *stories* behind the business. This place, with lots of help from Amanda, had changed Blake's life. He wanted his employees to understand its importance. Nick listened and nodded, busy with his notes.

She told him the history of Halcyon and how close the mansion had come to being destroyed, along with the resort. The rebirth of the resort, thanks to Amanda's designer eye and Blake's hotel fortune. The coinciding growth of the town of Gallant Lake, where most of the employees lived and many guests shopped and dined. The upscale weddings the resort specialized in, often for well-heeled Manhattanites. And the new championship golf course, already home to several prominent charity tournaments.

He glanced at her several times as they headed back from the golf course, but she was careful not to make eye contact. His chocolate eyes had a way of knocking her thoughts off track. The waves were larger now that the wind had picked up. Above them was the sprawling clubhouse, a stunning blend of glass and timber, with a slate tile roof.

"Where's the best place to launch a kayak around here?"

"What?"

"I want to get my kayak in the water this weekend, and my rental doesn't have a dock yet. Does the resort have a launch site?"

Cassie stopped walking and looked at him, brushing away the stray strands of hair that blew across her face. She knew her mouth had fallen open, but it took her a moment to actually speak.

"You're asking *me* about kayaking?"

"You live in a mountain town. You must do *something* outdoors. Are there mountain bike trails here? Places to rock climb?"

Her chest jumped and it startled her so much she put her hand over her heart. That had been dangerously close to a laugh. She shook her head. "You are definitely asking the wrong person. I'm sure those things exist around here, but I don't know anything about them. You should ask Terry at the front desk—he's outdoorsy."

"Outdoorsy?" His shoulders straightened. "I'm not 'outdoorsy.' I enjoy outdoor activities. There's a difference."

"And that difference would be?"

Nick stuttered for a minute, then rubbed the back of his neck. "I don't know. But it's different, trust me. You've never kayaked here?"

"Uh…no. My idea of a good time is curling up with a book and a cup of tea."

He shook his head. "Well, that's just sad. I'll think of you tomorrow night when I'm out on the water taking in the scenery and you're stuck at home reading some boring book."

She turned away and started walking. "I'm working tomorrow night."

"Yeah? On a Friday night?"

"There's a big wedding this weekend, and the rehearsal dinner is tomorrow. One of our events people is on vacation, so I'm helping our manager make sure everything runs smoothly."

"The manager is Julie, right? I spent yesterday afternoon with her. She seems on top of things." Cassie nodded. Julie Brown was nice. If Cassie was sure she'd be staying in Gallant Lake, they'd probably be better friends. But she couldn't afford to get too comfortable. Nick, walking at her side, shook his head with a smile. "Blake wasn't kidding when he said you don't have a defined job description—you're everywhere."

"I'm wherever I'm needed. *That's* my job description."

He studied her intently, then shrugged.

"Hey, if you'd rather work than join me on the water, that's your loss."

This laughing whirlwind of a man was making her crazy. Because for just a moment, she wondered if it really *would* be her loss if she didn't go kayaking with him.

She quickly dismissed the thought. Her in a kayak with Nick West? Not happening.

CHAPTER THREE

NICK LEANED BACK in his office chair, turning away from the security feeds to watch Cassie through the open door. She was on the phone with someone, typing furiously and glancing at the schedule on the tablet propped up on the desk by her computer. The woman could seriously multitask. Was she the calm, cool professional he saw right now? Or was she the meek woman who'd flinched when he'd dropped a pile of papers on her desk this morning? Was she the woman who got uptight if there were more than a couple people in a room? Or was she the woman he saw yesterday, giving him a tour of the property with pride and confidence?

He'd checked her employee file—a perk of his job title. The information was pretty thin. She'd been here only a few months. She'd managed an insurance office in Milwaukee for a while but had been unemployed for over a year before moving here six months ago. Not exactly a red flag. She could have been going to school or job hunting or whatever. She'd clearly won Blake Randall's confidence, but she didn't give off a sense of having a lot of confidence in herself. Instead, Cassie seemed all twisted up with anxiety. Unless she was busy. Then she was cool and... controlled. It was as if being productive was her comfort zone.

She hung up the phone, then immediately dialed someone

else. Her back was to him, ramrod straight. Her auburn hair was gathered in a knot at the base of her slender neck. He wondered what she'd look like if she ever let that hair loose. She was dressed in dark trousers and a pale blue sweater. Sensible. Practical. Almost calculatedly so. He grimaced. This was what happened when you spent eight years as a detective—you started profiling everyone you met.

"Margo? It's Cassandra Smith, Mr. Randall's assistant. Did you see the email I sent you last week? I didn't receive a reply and thought perhaps you missed it…"

Nick's eyes narrowed. There was an edge to Cassie's voice he hadn't heard until now. She was a whole new person. Again. He picked up his foam basketball and started bouncing it off the wall by the doorway. He smirked when Cassie stiffened—the fact that she hated his throwing the ball around was half the fun of doing it.

"Yes… Well, if Mr. Randall saw these numbers, he'd definitely be concerned… Right. And if Mr. Randall is concerned, he might be on the next flight to Miami for a conversation… Exactly. The restaurant is consistently selling less alcohol than they're ordering every week. That inventory has to be going somewhere… What's that?… Oh, I see. The bartender had his own family restaurant and was ordering a little extra for himself? I'm assuming he's no longer employed with us?" She was scribbling furiously on a notepad on her desk. "You know, Margo, you have access to the same reports I do, so you may want to start reading them more closely… I'm sure you will. I'm glad we had a chance to talk… Yes, you, too. Have a great weekend."

Nick moved to the doorway while she talked, working her diplomatic magic with the Miami manager. As she hung up, he leaned against the doorjamb and started to clap slowly. Being Cassie, she just about jumped out of her skin, spinning in her chair with a squeak of alarm. He really was going to have to be more careful around her.

"Sorry, I couldn't help but overhear. Those were some good people skills, Cassie. I'm impressed, but since I'm responsible for loss management, I'm also concerned. Do we have a problem in Miami?"

Color returned to her cheeks and her chin lifted. "Not anymore. I saw the discrepancy last week. It was only a case or two here and there, but it's something the hotel manager should have spotted herself. She won't be ignoring any more of the reports I send out."

"And you really weren't going to tell Blake? Or me?" That might be taking her job responsibility a step too far. She stuttered for a moment, then met his gaze with the slightest of smiles, causing his chest to tighten in an odd way.

"It happened before *you* arrived, and I told Blake the minute I saw it."

Nick replayed the conversation in his head. Cassie let Margo believe Blake wasn't aware, but she hadn't actually stated that. Clever girl.

"Bravo, Miss Smith." She shrugged off the compliment, as usual. "Are you still planning on working the rehearsal dinner tonight?"

"Yes. It will probably run like clockwork as usual, but with Blake out of town and one of our managers off this week, Julie doesn't want anyone thinking they can slack off." She checked the time on her phone. "I should probably get down there. Have fun kayaking."

Nick nodded and wished her a good evening, not bothering to tell her he wouldn't be paddling on the water tonight after all. He'd be sitting in the surveillance room with Brad, learning how everything worked in there. Turned out Brad was in IT and also worked security on the weekends.

Three hours later, his head was spinning with all the information Brad was throwing at him. Nick was comfortable with technology, but remembering which control moved the images from the smaller monitors up to the large wall monitors mounted around the room, which control sped up or reversed the feeds, how to copy a feed to the permanent drive rather than the temporary one that saved them for only fourteen days… It was enough to make his head hurt. And to have it rattled off to him by some geeky kid barely out of college didn't help his mood any.

There were digital cameras all over the resort, both in the public areas as well as in all the employee passageways and the kitchen. He'd spotted Cassie repeatedly. She seemed to be everywhere behind the scenes tonight, clipboard in hand, watching all the action. She'd changed into a crisp white shirt and dark slacks to match the rest of the staff. She didn't interact with a lot of people. He saw her speaking with the manager, Julie. Then she'd been with Dario, the head chef, gesturing toward the plates being prepared.

He'd seen that pattern with her before—if she knew and trusted someone, she was relaxed and looked them straight in the eye when she spoke. But if she wasn't comfortable with someone, her body language was completely different. She avoided both eye contact *and* conversation. She kept her body turned at a slight angle instead of facing them directly. Was she just painfully shy, or had something happened in her past to make her this way? Nick leaned back in his chair, chewing on the cap of his pen and scanning the monitors.

He spotted her a little while later, heading across the lobby toward the side door, purse slung over her shoulder. She was heading home. He frowned and checked the time. It was after ten o'clock and she was alone. They had cameras in the lots, but he'd noticed most of them were trained on customer parking, not the employee lot. He stood and shook Brad's hand.

"This has been a great session, man. Thanks. But I think I'll call it a night." He looked around and frowned. "You're on your own tonight?" Brad was a good kid, but he looked like a younger version of Paul Blart, the mall cop. Nick had doubts about Brad's ability to handle the type of situations that could come up when a wedding crowd got to drinking. "You've got my mobile number, right?"

Brad laughed. "I'm not alone. Tim's on vacation, but Bill's out doing the first night check on doors and gates." The team made the rounds to all exterior access points to the buildings three times every night. Nick nodded and left the room, waiting until he got to the hallway before closing his eyes in frustration.

Bill Chesnutt was even older than Ken Taylor had been. The guy was a retired marine, but he'd retired a *long* time ago. So basically they had Paul Blart and Andy Griffith watching over the resort on a Friday night. Perfect. He was going to need to make some changes here, but he didn't want to rock the boat too early. He'd have a sit-down with Blake when he returned and discuss the options—better training, better people or both. He headed out the side door toward the employee parking lot.

Cassie was walking in the next row over from him, head down and looking tired. There were nowhere near enough lights in this damn lot. Nick headed in her direction, making a mental note to talk to the employees about using a buddy system to walk to their cars after dark until he could get more lights out here. This might not be the streets of LA, but there were bad guys everywhere.

Nick walked up behind Cassie, not happy that he was able to get this close without her noticing. She should be more aware of her surroundings. He was only a few feet away and she didn't even know...

In the blink of an eye, Cassie spun and swung her fist at him. He dodged just in time, and something glinted in the light. Her car keys were sticking out between her fingers. That would have left a mark if she'd connected. She was digging in her purse with her other hand.

He barely had time to register what was happening before the pepper spray hit him in the face.

CHAPTER FOUR

"AGH! SON OF a *bitch*! What the hell is wrong with you? God *damn* it, that hurts!"

Cassie watched in horror as Nick West covered the side of his face and doubled over, yelling in pain and letting out a string of curse words.

"Oh, my God. I didn't know it was you!" She stepped forward to help, but her lungs started to burn and she couldn't get a good breath. She started coughing, her chest burning. Still hunched over, Nick grabbed her arm, spinning her around and shoving her away with a hand to her back.

"What are you…?"

"Get away from me!" Nick's growl was rough and loud. "Get away!"

He was angry. He *pushed* her. She immediately fell back on a practiced reaction.

"I'm sorry…"

That wasn't what she was thinking. She was thinking Nick was an idiot to frighten her like that. But before she could take back her apology, coughing overtook her. Tears ran down her face.

"Damn it!" Nick's hand wrapped around her wrist and he dragged her to the grass along the dark edge of the lot. Then he propelled her even farther away from the cars, sending her stumbling. He was bent over, looking up at her with one eye tightly closed, like the Hunchback of Notre Dame. Rage burned in that one open eye. His voice was tightly controlled. Almost calm.

"Stay back. You inhaled some of your own pepper spray. Hell, Cassie..." He dropped to his knees, raising his hands to his face but not touching them to his skin. "Water..."

She dived back into her bag and pulled out a water bottle. She started to hand it to him, then realized he couldn't see her. "Turn your face up toward me, Nick. I'll pour the water."

He tilted his head. "Just the left side..." She poured the water slowly over the side of his face, and he took a deep, ragged breath. She did the same, noticing her lungs didn't feel like they were in spasms any more.

"What were you thinking, sneaking up on me like that? I thought you were kayaking." He didn't answer, just sat on the grass, his head between his knees, both eyes tightly closed. A low, steady groan was the only sound he made. She sat next to him. "I was only defending myself..."

Sun Tzu said it perfectly. *Invincibility lies in defense.*

His whole body went rigid and he raised his head, glaring at her with his right eye. The left side of his face and neck were bright red in the glow of the parking lot light, his left eye tightly closed.

"*Defending* yourself? I could write an entire training manual on what *not* to do from your performance just now." He closed his good eye and grimaced. "Damn, that hurts."

Cassie was caught between sympathy and anger. Anger seemed easier. "A training manual, huh? Since you're doubled over in pain right now, I'd say I did a pretty good job of rendering you harmless."

Before she could blink, Nick's hand snaked out and grabbed her wrist, yanking her almost onto his lap. His face was so close to hers that she could smell the pepper spray on his skin. She was too stunned to scream, but her heart felt like it was going to leap straight out of her chest.

"Do I look *harmless* to you right now, Cassie? If I'd been an attacker, you'd be dead, or worse. I could have forced you into your car and…" He growled to himself and released her with another curse, driving his fist into the ground at his side. "You did *everything* wrong. You let me get too close. You used the keys first when you should have used the spray. The keys-in-the-fingers trick only works when you're in close hand-to-hand combat, which should be your *last* resort. You took so long getting the pepper spray that I would have had your purse away from you before you could reach it."

Nick picked up the water bottle and poured what was left down the side of his face and neck. "You gave me time to turn away, so you didn't completely incapacitate me. And then, instead of running when you had the chance, you stepped forward, right into your own cloud of pepper spray, and nearly incapacitated *yourself*." He turned to focus his good eye on her. "So, yes. A whole training manual. On what *not* to do."

Cassie stared at the dark ground, focused on bringing her pulse under control. Nick had been careful not to hurt her when he'd grabbed her, but he'd still frightened her. On purpose. She'd hate him for it if it weren't for the truth of what he'd said. If he had been some random attacker—if he'd been *Don*—she would have been a victim. Again.

"Why are you armed with pepper spray? Did something happen to you?"

She didn't look up.

"Yes. Something happened."

"Here?"

She shook her head, her body trembling so badly she didn't trust her voice. The only sound was his wheezing breath. He finally cleared his throat.

"Okay. Something happened. Somewhere." His voice was gravelly from the pepper spray, but it was calmer than it had been a few minutes ago. "And you wanted to protect yourself. That's smart. But you need to do it *right*. I'll teach you."

Her head snapped up. He was doing his best to look at her, even though his left eye was still closed.

"What are you talking about?"

"I'll teach you self-defense, Cassie. The kind that actually works."

"Are you talking karate or something? I thought the pepper spray…"

"It's a tool, but you need more than that. If some guy's amped up on drugs, he'll just be temporarily blind and *really* ticked off." He picked up the pepper spray canister from the grass at her side. "This stuff will spray up to ten feet away. You never should have let me get so close before using it."

"I didn't know that."

"Exactly." He grimaced and swore again. "I need to get home and dunk my face in a bowl full of ice water." He stood and reached a hand down to help her up. She hesitated, then took it.

"Are you okay to drive, Nick? Do you want me to…"

"I'm fine. I'm only a couple miles from here, and I have one functioning eye. How about you?"

She was rattled to the core and definitely wouldn't get any sleep tonight, but one of her favorite things about Nora's place was that there were few places for anyone to hide in the wide-open loft. She always parked her car right next to the metal stairs that led to the back entrance. "I'm good. Don't worry about me."

Nick walked slowly to his Jeep, still cradling the side of his face with one hand. She felt bad that he was suffering, but she also felt a tiny spark of pride. Maybe she hadn't fought back successfully, but she'd *fought*. That was something, right?

Nick went into the office for a few hours on Saturday morning, but there was no sign of Cassie. He should have been relieved, considering she about killed him with that damn pepper spray the night before. Instead, he felt a nudge of disappointment, and more than a nudge of concern.

Something happened.

One of the reasons he wasn't a cop anymore was that he'd run out of patience with victims. He looked at Jada's wedding photo on his shelf. No, that wasn't completely true. He'd run out of patience with victims who didn't help themselves. Who willingly *allowed* themselves to be victims. That's why his partner was dead. If Beth Washington hadn't gone back to her husband, Jada would still be alive.

But Cassie had armed herself with pepper spray and she hadn't hesitated to use it. She'd used it *badly*, but she'd used it. It was a good thing she was so bad with the stuff—at least she'd blinded him in only one eye.

He slid his notes from his time with Brad into a manila folder and put it on the corner of his desk to review on Monday. Blake Randall would be back in the office, and Nick's orientation period would come to an end. He looked forward to getting down to business. But first, he needed to finish unpacking and get himself settled in the small house he'd rented on Gallant Lake. He was getting sick of living out of cardboard boxes.

It was weird not seeing Cassie sitting at her desk when he left the office. He wondered if she'd take him up on his offer to teach her self-defense. She didn't need to become a Krav Maga expert to protect herself. But she was so damn jumpy and twitchy about everything. She'd have to lose that spookiness to be effective at self-defense, which was all about outthinking the enemy. Nick frowned. He didn't like the thought of the quiet brunette having enemies. Especially the kind who drove her to have such a quick trigger finger on a canister of pepper spray.

The heavy blue stapler sat on the corner of her desk, just begging to be hidden somewhere. Maybe he should leave her alone, especially with the boss coming back next week. But what was the fun in that? He set the stapler on the windowsill, tucking it behind the curtains that were pulled back to show the view of

Gallant Lake and the surrounding mountains. Maybe he'd get out in the kayak tomorrow if the nice weather held.

But he woke the next morning to the sound of rain pounding on the metal roof. Kayaking was out of the question. He slid out of bed and opened the blinds on the window facing the water. Looked like a good day to do some shopping for the basics he needed to fill his pantry and refrigerator. He liked to cook healthy meals, but this transition week had seen him settling for far too many pizzas and frozen dinners. Time to get back on track. But first, there was an interesting-looking little coffee shop in Gallant Lake that he'd been meaning to try, and this was a hot-coffee sort of morning.

Apparently lots of people felt the same way, because the Gallant Brew was busy. As he stood in line, he studied the local artwork that lined the brick walls. A large bulletin board was filled with fliers about local events—a quilt show at the library, a spring concert at the elementary school, a senior travel group meeting at one of the churches. Slices of a small-town life he had no idea how to navigate.

His rising sense of panic settled when he saw the notice from the Rebel Rockers climbing club. The group was advertising a spring multipitch climb at the Gunks. The famous Shawangunk Ridge was known to be one of the best rock-climbing sites in the country, and a group climb like this would be a great way for him to learn his way around the cliffs. He'd get to know some local climbers, too. He tore off one of the paper strips with a phone number on it. Maybe this wouldn't be such a bad place after all.

There was a collective burst of female laughter from the back of the shop, and one of the voices sounded oddly familiar. There were two women bustling behind the counter, trying to serve the large group ahead of Nick. One was older and tall, with a long braid of pewter-colored hair. The other was petite, with dark hair and a bright smile. She said something over her shoulder toward the hallway that disappeared into the back of the shop. That's where Cassie Smith stood, juggling a large cardboard box in her arms.

The shorter brunette was filling a metal pitcher with frothy steamed milk, her voice rising over the hiss of the high-tech espresso maker. "Just set those mugs in the kitchen, Cass. I had no idea how low we'd gotten. You're a lifesaver!"

"No problem. I'll go get the second box for you." Cassie, dressed in snug jeans and a short pink sweater that teased a bit of skin at her waist, turned away. Hot damn, her auburn hair was swinging free this morning, falling past her shoulders thick and straight. The box struck the corner hard as she turned. Her grip slipped, and she threw a knee up to keep the box from hitting the floor as she tried to regain control.

Nick was there in three long strides, grabbing the box away from her. To his surprise, both women at the counter rounded on him like he'd gone after Cassie with a machete.

"What the hell do you think you're doing?" The older one slammed the cash register shut, ignoring the protest of her customer and heading his way with fury in her eyes. The petite one was less confrontational.

"Sir, you can't be back here…"

"Nick?" When Cassie spoke his name, both women stopped.

"You *know* this guy?" The taller woman looked him up and down, clearly unimpressed with what she saw. "I've never seen him in here before."

"He works at the resort, Aunt Cathy. He's okay." She reached for the box. "I'll take that."

Nick shook his head. "It's heavy. Tell me where you want it."

She opened her mouth as if to argue, then reconsidered, pointing to the kitchen. "Anywhere in there. Thanks." He set the box down on the stainless steel counter in the tiny kitchen, then turned to face her.

"That's too heavy for you to be carrying."

"Apparently not, since I managed to carry it down a long flight of stairs just fine. I didn't steer very well, that's all." She turned away and headed down the hallway, then looked over her shoulder at him in confusion when he followed. "What are you doing?"

"You said there was a second box. I'll get it."

She turned slowly, her right brow rising.

"No. You won't."

Nick shook his head in frustration. "We can stand here and argue about it as long as you'd like, but I *am* going to carry the other box down. If you'd bumped that one into the wall on the stairs, you could have fallen and broken your neck. Do you care anything at all about your own safety?"

"Seriously? I pepper-sprayed you in the face Friday night. I think that shows how much I care about my safety."

"Yeah? You still haven't agreed to my offer to help you learn how to protect yourself. And you're fighting me about carrying a box of coffee mugs when you know damn well I'm right." His voice rose slightly on those last words, and she stepped back. Her voice, on the other hand, dropped so low he barely heard her.

"I'm sorry..." Her brows furrowed as soon as the words came out, as if she hadn't expected them.

"You don't have to be sorry, Cassie. Just be smart. And accept help when it's offered. Come on..." His hand touched her arm and she flinched. What the hell? Was she *afraid* of him? He dropped the "cop voice" Jada always used to give him hell for and raised his hands in innocence. "Hey, I'm trying to be a nice guy here. Leave the door open. Tell your aunt to call the cops if we're not back down here in five minutes. Do whatever you need to do, but I think you know in your heart you're safe with me. And Cassie?" He waited until she made eye contact with him, eyes full of uncertainty. "Bring some comfortable clothes to the office tomorrow. We're going to hit the workout room and you're *going* to learn some self-defense moves."

CHAPTER FIVE

I THINK YOU know in your heart you're safe with me...

It was Thursday, and Cassie couldn't stop rolling Nick's words around in her head. There wasn't a man in the world she considered safe. Maybe Blake Randall, but as her employer, he held an awful lot of power over her. She trusted him, but he wasn't exactly "safe." There was a difference.

She hadn't felt afraid when Nick stepped inside her apartment Sunday morning to take the second box of mugs from where Nora had them stored in the laundry room. She'd felt...uneasy. On edge. His presence, with his loud, confident, king-of-the-world attitude, seemed to suck all the air out of the place. He was true to his word, taking less than five minutes. He'd taken the mugs downstairs, accepted a free to-go cup from Nora as thanks, then left with barely a nod in her direction.

She pulled the office curtain aside and picked up the hidden stapler. It was the second time this week Nick had used that hiding spot. He was slipping, probably distracted now that Blake was back from vacation and grilling him about his plans for this resort as well as setting up a travel schedule to visit the other Randall Resorts International properties during the next quarter.

But Nick hadn't forgotten his promise to teach her self-defense, no matter how many times she tried to tell him it wasn't necessary. On Monday, he'd pointed to his face and said "pepper spray" to remind her of her so-called failure. Today would be their second session, and he'd warned her things were going to get more challenging. On Monday, he'd basically lectured her about judging proximity—when to use pepper spray (six to ten feet), when to use car keys in the fingers (within a foot) and when to go for the crotch kick (only if there's body-to-body contact). He explained the thumbs-to-the-eyeballs trick for if the struggle was up close. She'd objected, doubting she could press on someone's eyeballs, and he said the move was for life-or-death situations. She'd been in that type of situation more than once with Don. Yeah, she'd have gladly put his eyes out if she could have.

She heard the elevator ping down the hall, followed immediately by the sound of male voices echoing loudly in the hallway. Nick was telling a story about some would-be thief they caught nude in a chimney in LA. She braced herself just as the door to the office suite flew open. Blake was in the lead, laughing and giving her a quick nod before heading to his office. Right on his heels were Brad from IT and Tim from security, and bringing up the rear and laughing the loudest was Nick. The onslaught of noisy men set off all of Cassie's alarms, but she'd taken a deep breath before their arrival and managed to flash them a smile. Brad and Tim waved and greeted her before following Blake, but Nick stopped at her desk, a furrow of concern appearing between his brows.

"Everything okay?"

"You mean other than being invaded by what sounded like the entire second fleet? Yeah, I'm fine." She thought she'd managed to hold on to her bright smile, but he clearly didn't buy it.

"Sorry about that. I wasn't thinking."

She wasn't sure what to do with his apology. It wasn't something she had a lot of experience with when it came to men. Before she could come up with a response, Blake stuck his head out of his office door.

"You coming, Nick?" He frowned when he saw Nick leaning over Cassie's desk. "What's going on?"

"I was just apologizing to Cassie for the racket we made. I've gotta grab my file on the lighting I was looking at for the parking lots, and I'll be right in." Nick headed into his office, but Blake stayed put.

"Did our noise really bother you?" he asked.

"No, no. Of course not." Her face warmed.

"Then why was Nick apologizing?"

She busied herself moving papers around on her desk. She didn't want Blake fretting about her.

"I have no idea. Honestly, everything's fine."

Blake watched her for another moment, then shrugged and turned away. Before she could relax, Nick strolled out of his office with a file in his hand. He slowed as he passed her, his voice low and just for her ears.

"Five o'clock in the gym?" Worried that Blake might still be listening, she nodded, not even looking up. Nick reached out and knocked over her stapler with his finger as he passed, causing her to jump.

She reached for the stapler with a roll of her eyes.

"West!" Blake shouted from his office. "Come on, man!"

Nick gave her a playful grin. "Later, slugger."

The door to Blake's office had barely closed when Amanda Randall arrived, tanned and smiling. She set a paper bag on the corner of Cassie's desk.

"I'm betting you haven't had lunch yet, right?"

Cassie reached for the bag eagerly. Amanda was a great cook, which had never been Cassie's strong point. "No, but something tells me I'm going to have lunch now."

Amanda sat in one of the chairs by the window. "Only if you like roast beef sandwiches with cheddar cheese and horseradish sauce. Hey, the girls and I are going to the Chalet tonight for pizza. Wanna join us?" As much as Cassie liked "the girls"— Amanda's cousins Nora, who owned the coffee shop, and Melanie, who owned a clothing boutique in town—she had another commitment tonight that she was oddly reluctant to cancel.

"I can't, but thanks anyway."

Amanda, for all her blond curls, baby blue eyes and bubbly demeanor, was a smart and intuitive woman. "Can't? Or won't? I don't like the thought of you sitting alone in that apartment all the time. Being a hermit isn't good for you."

Being a hermit kept her safe, but she didn't bother reminding her friend of that. Amanda's assumption that she was turning into a recluse, while true, still rankled.

"I actually have plans tonight." She regretted the words as soon as she said them. Now she was going to have to explain something she wasn't sure she even understood.

"I'm sorry… What? You have *plans*? What kind of plans?"

She stalled by taking a bite of the sandwich. "Oh, wow, this is delicious…"

"Yeah, yeah, I know." Amanda took the arm of Cassie's chair and turned it so they faced each other. "Now tell me about these 'plans' of yours."

She glanced at Blake's closed door and lowered her voice. "I'm…meeting with Nick West at five o'clock." She took another bite of the sandwich, watching the speculation in Amanda's eyes.

"Meeting him for…?"

"A training session of sorts." More sandwich. The heck with stalling. The sandwich was really just that good.

Amanda leaned back in her chair, crossing her legs and folding her arms.

"Honey, I have two children. One's a teenager and one's a toddler. They will both tell you that I always sniff out the truth no matter how long it takes, so you may as well spill it."

Cassie set the sandwich down on a napkin, nodding in surrender.

"He's teaching me self-defense."

Cassie's mouth and eyes went round simultaneously.

"Nick West? Nick West, the hot security guy?"

"Shh! He's in Blake's office, for God's sake."

Amanda lowered her voice, but not her astonishment.

"Nick West is teaching you self-defense? As in, really teaching you? One-on-one? Or is this some class he's offering?"

"It's a...private class."

"Holy shit, what happened to you in the week I was gone? You're going to let a hot hunk of man show you self-defense moves? Let him touch you? Learn to throw him down on the floor? Of course, now that I've met the guy, I wouldn't mind throwing him down myself!"

"It's not like that. And you're married. To Nick's boss."

"Hey, just because I'm married to the sexiest man I know doesn't mean I'm *blind.* But I'm more interested in what *you* think. The guy just got here, and you've become such good friends that you're okay engaging in hand-to-hand combat with him? All sweaty, up close and personal? That's not the Cassie I left in Gallant Lake last week." Her smile faded. "Wait, did something happen? Are you doing this because Don did something?"

Cassie was so caught up in the thought of "up close and personal" that she almost didn't answer. And when she did, she once again shared more than she'd intended.

"I pepper-sprayed him."

"Who? *Don?*"

"Of course not! *Nick.* He startled me in the parking lot last Friday night and I hit him with pepper spray. He was somewhat critical of my technique."

Amanda's look of horror quickly slid into one of great amusement. "You pepper-sprayed the new head of security? Here at the resort? That's priceless! Does Blake know?"

"Not from me. And I doubt Nick's bragging about it, since it didn't end well for him."

"So you assaulted the man and he responded by generously offering to give you private self-defense lessons? Why?"

And that was just one of several hundred-thousand-dollar questions, wasn't it? Why was Nick offering to help her? Why had she agreed? And would there really be sweaty, up-close contact in the process? And how exactly did she feel about that?

Nick had been in the resort's third-floor workout room for a full fifteen minutes with no sign of Cassie. Looked like she was going to blow him off. He was half hoping she *would* quit. Offering private lessons was a bad idea on a couple of levels. It was probably considered unprofessional—it showed favoritism, or something. It could be taken the wrong way, for sure. Was it creepy? Forward? She didn't seem any more interested in him than he was in her, though. She was a looker, but he'd never been drawn to meek women.

He moved from the treadmill to the free weights. He should have told her to go take a class or read a book or a dozen other things besides offering to train her personally. After all, while she was at work, his security team would keep her safe. And when she wasn't at work, it was none of his business. If she didn't show up today, he'd urge her to go find a gym somewhere and relieve himself of the responsibility. He'd learned with Jada that getting involved in solving someone else's problems only led to heartache.

There was a movement near the door and he looked up to find Cassie watching him, her eyes dark and unreadable. Her hair was pulled back into her usual ponytail. She wore a baggy gray sweatshirt over black leggings, with a pair of sneakers that looked new. So she'd been paying attention on Monday when he told her those old canvas flats were not going to cut it for actual exercise. That was good. It meant that, despite her skepticism, she was taking this seriously. Which meant there was no good way to get out of teaching her what she needed to know.

He set the weights down quietly, conscious of her aversion to loud noises.

"You're late."

Her cheeks flushed pink. "I had a last-minute call, and then I had to change. I'm sorry..." Her brows furrowed that way they always did when she said those two words. As if they were acid on her lips. Her shoulders straightened. "But I'm here now, so we should get sweaty... I mean...busy."

He laughed at her stammered words. "Sweaty, huh? We can do sweaty if you want, but I think we should take it slow. I want to show you some basics today that you won't need a lot of strength for."

"You're the instructor."

"You know, it wouldn't hurt for you to get sweaty once in a while." Her eyes went big and he laughed again. "I meant you should start some strength training and maybe some running. The stronger you are, the more confident you'll feel, and the more effective you'll be."

She scoffed. "Running? You think I should start *running*? I don't think so."

"If not running, then find something you enjoy that will give you some cardio and strength. Go hiking, or mountain biking, or anything. I'm telling you, Cassie, the more you move, the better you'll understand your body, and the better you'll be at defending yourself. Not to mention it's just healthy to do."

She looked at him for a long moment before shaking her head. "I'm not looking to become some health nut or kickboxer. Let's stick to the plan. Teach me the basics."

"You need to warm up first. Give me fifteen minutes on the elliptical."

"Why?"

"As you said, I'm the instructor. And you're my little grass-hopper, so hop on that machine and show me what you got."

She obeyed, but not happily. "I don't understand what this has to do with self-defense. I'm not going to be able to elliptic away from someone." After only a few minutes, she was puffing for air and grimacing. Her legs were probably already cramping. She was in worse shape than he'd thought. He grabbed a fresh bottle of water from his bag and handed it to her. She came to a stop.

"If you can't make it five minutes on this machine, you aren't going to be able to do diddly against an attacker. You think you can fight a man the size of me or bigger? When you're standing there wheezing at me after doing basically nothing?" He didn't let her reply, grabbing the bottle from her hands and gesturing to her to get moving. "Okay, new plan. You hit this room every morning, and you get on the elliptical and go until you can't go anymore. Eventually, you'll be going thirty minutes or more, and you'll thank me for how great you feel."

"Don't...hold your...breath..."

It was ironic, listening to her talk about breath when she didn't have any. He gave her a wide grin.

"Okay, let's review while you're warming up. I'm an attacker. I'm six feet away and coming at you. What do you do?"

"I...use the...pepper spray..." She huffed out the words between gasps for air.

He shook his head. "Do you have pepper spray in your hands right now?"

She shot him a glare. "No!"

"Then forget it. If the perp is within twenty feet and running at you, you don't have time to dig in your purse for pepper spray. Same with a gun. Unless it's in your hand at that point, it's useless."

"I don't...want a...gun."

He rubbed the left side of his face. "Yeah, you're dangerous enough with pepper spray. I hate to think what you'd have done the other night with a handgun. So what do you do?"

"Scream?"

He shrugged. "Meh. It's not a bad thing, but it's not going to save you unless you're lucky enough to have the dumbest bad guy in the world and he's attacking you in a public place. Try again."

"Hit...him?"

"Where? With what?"

"I don't… Oh, shit… I can't…do this." She stopped moving. "Okay, maybe you're right about my conditioning." A soft sheen of sweat covered her face. "I'd hit him with my fist."

"Yeah?" Nick folded his arms on his chest. "Show me a fist."

She did what so many inexperienced fighters do. She folded her fingers over her thumb and into a fist.

"Do you intend to hit me as hard as you can with that fist? Maybe right on my jaw?"

She looked at her fist, frowning, as if she knew this was a trick question. Finally she nodded, but without conviction.

"Cassie, if you hit me hard with your hand folded like that, you'll not only break your damn thumb, but you won't hurt me at all. Go ahead, get off the elliptical and take a swing in my direction. Punch at my hand." He saw the doubt in her eyes. "I won't let you hurt yourself. I'm just trying to show you how limited your motion is with your hand like that."

She took a swing, hitting the flat of his hand, but he didn't offer any resistance, letting his hand come away.

"Okay. Now make a fist with your thumb *outside* your fingers, like this." He clenched his hand in a fist, releasing it the minute he saw her skin go pale. Shit. She'd seen a man's fist before. He swallowed hard. "Show me."

She did as he asked. He took her hand and moved her thumb, then curled her wrist so her knuckles were forward. "Now hit my hand. And put some oomph behind it. Start with your body low and rise up into the punch."

Her first attempt wasn't half-bad. Her next few were better, as she started to grasp the concept of lowering her center of gravity and propelling upward with her body, not just her small fist. When she actually connected with his hand with enough force to send it snapping back, she flashed him a wide grin.

"I did it!"

"You did. But throwing a punch is going to be your last re- sort. You need to know how to do it, but honestly, unless you connect with the guy's nose, or maybe the center of his chest, you're not going to stop him. He'll return the punch and it'll be lights out for you unless it's an eighty-year-old mugger."

Her eyes narrowed in on him. "So I can't use pepper spray and I can't scream and I can't punch. What do I do, just stand there?"

His curiosity got the best of him.

"What happened to you, Cassie? Were you assaulted? Mugged?"

She stepped back and visibly shrank before his eyes, shoulders dropping, head lowered, gaze fixed on the floor by his feet.

"I don't want to talk about it." His chest tightened at some of the darker possibilities.

"I get that, but it would help me to know what's driving your fear."

She stared at the floor so long and so intently he wouldn't have been surprised if smoke started rising from near his feet. He'd done enough interrogations to know that it was human instinct to fill a silence with words. He *could* wait her out, but she wasn't a perp. He opened his mouth, but she beat him to it, painting a picture he was hoping not to see.

"I was in a parking garage. At night. He came from between two cars. I was checking my phone and he was on me before I knew it." Her voice was monotone, like a robot reciting a programmed recording. "That's all you need to know."

"That's why you're so vigilant now. And jumpy."

Her head snapped up. "I'm not that jumpy."

"Says the woman who threw a stapler at my head and pepper-sprayed me in the face."

A trace of a smile tugged at her mouth.

"Okay. I'm jumpy. And I hate it."

He nodded, considering the best way to come at this problem. The "problem" at hand being Cassie's fear. He'd deal with the problem of his physical reaction to her vulnerability—a trait he generally abhorred in women—when he was alone and could think more clearly.

"Look, if a guy is coming at you with the intent to do you harm, you need to fight. Show him you mean business. Plant your feet wide and solid, like this." He took up a fighter's stance, and she did her best to mimic it. "Get in his face. Make noise. Fight like hell, and fight dirty."

"You said not to scream."

"No, I said it probably wouldn't do any good. But I'm not talking about screaming. I'm talking about *noise*. Aggressive noise. Have you ever watched karate or judo or even tennis?" She nodded. "Did you notice how some players make loud noises as they're swinging? Even if they're just chopping a wooden board? That sound makes them feel more powerful. It's more like a roar than a scream, and you can learn to do that once your confidence gets better."

He stepped up in front of her, hating the way she shrank back, but not reacting to it. She was going to have to get used to this. "When the attacker is up close and personal, look to find a weak spot."

"You mean his balls?"

He barked out a laugh. "No, that's another lesson, when I'm wearing protection. Look at my face. What are my weak spots there?"

She studied him intently, and he did his best not to fidget under her examination. There was something about her gaze that made him energized and restless. Uncomfortable and excited at the same time. The sensation kicked him way outside his comfort zone.

"You told me about the eyes already."

"What else do you see that's vulnerable?"

"Your nose?"

"Right. But here's the key—don't swing at it from the side. Come at it from below, with the heel of your hand slamming up against it. Picture yourself driving his nose right into his skull.

It'll hurt like hell, and it could give you a chance to break free. Like this." He took her hand and pressed it against the base of his own nose. And damned if he didn't have the crazy urge to kiss the palm of her hand. He shook it off and tried to stay focused. "But just like the punch, put your whole body into it. Think of every move as your only shot." She pressed against his nose and he grinned at her. "We won't be practicing that one. At least not on me. Now what else do you see that's vulnerable?"

Her eyes darkened when her gaze fell to his mouth. He did his best to ignore the stirring he felt below his waist. It was a normal response to a pretty woman studying his mouth, right?

"Yes, the mouth can be vulnerable. It's not the best place to start, but lips are tender. Pinch, bite or smack him with your elbow, like this." In slow motion, he swung his elbow out and stopped an inch from her mouth. "If you've got room to swing, use your elbow before you use your fist. It's harder and more likely to do harm without hurting yourself in the process. What else?"

"I don't know. That's about it, right?"

He moved his hands to each side of her face and gently tugged on her ears. Her eyes met his, and it took all his focus to stay on topic. "No one likes having their ears yanked. And if you really latch on and pull, the guy will be screaming. If you're in close contact and your hands are free, don't hesitate to pull on those ears as hard as you can." He released her ears, but his fingers lingered, brushing back her hair and stroking the tender skin of her neck… *What the hell?* He pulled his hands back and stepped away from Cassie. She looked as confused as he felt. But she hadn't stopped him. Interesting. He cleared his throat.

"Yeah…so…that's about it, I guess…for tonight…um…" Nick couldn't believe his own voice. He was babbling. Nick West, tough cop, was *babbling*. And all because he'd touched Cassie's warm, soft skin with the tips of his fingers.

Color flooded her cheeks as she blinked and looked away. "Yes. Of course. That gave me plenty to…um…think about…

Thanks." She turned and grabbed the small canvas bag she'd dropped by the door.

He regained some composure once she turned her back on him. "Hey, don't forget about the elliptical in the morning."

She looked over her shoulder, her hand on the door handle. "Tomorrow's Friday."

"Yeah? And? No excuses, girl." He nodded toward the machine. "You need to make yourself stronger, Cass. Give yourself a fighting chance. You owe yourself that much."

CHAPTER SIX

CASSIE STOOD OUTSIDE the door to the Chalet for a long time. A really long time.

Amanda had been relentless about Cassie getting out more, threatening to drop off a dozen cats at the apartment to complete her transition into a little old crazy cat lady. Amanda knew why Cassie was leery of going out, getting attached to people, exposing herself. But Cassie knew she had a point. When Julie Brown invited her to the weekly gathering of resort employees at the local bar tonight, as she did almost every week, she'd surprised them both by agreeing.

Maybe it was Nick's king-of-the-world attitude rubbing off on her. Her self-defense classes had morphed into strength and agility training over the past few weeks. He'd been horrified by her lack of conditioning and athleticism, which she'd never seen as a problem. But the time he forced… No, that wasn't fair… The time he *encouraged* her to spend on the elliptical had proved his point. She'd had no stamina at all. She absently rubbed her lower back. She was paying the price with a host of sore muscles, but she was also starting to feel a little more confident. A little stronger, both physically and mentally. He was challenging her, and surprisingly, she liked it.

She could hear the band playing country rock, and the hoots

and hollers of the patrons inside. Some of them were her co-workers. Julie. Tim. Brad. Josie from the restaurant. It was the innocent sound of people having a fun Friday night in a small town. Nothing to worry about. But she hadn't thought there was anything to worry about in Milwaukee either, that night she went out to have fun with some coworkers and ended up in intensive care.

It was the anger of that memory that propelled her forward. This was *not* Milwaukee. She steeled herself and stepped inside. She could do this. She had to do this. She had to start living again.

Julie ran over, laughing in a high-pitched voice that suggested she'd already had more than a few drinks. "Cassie! Oh, my God, I'm so glad you came tonight! It's turned into quite a party." Julie waved her arm vaguely in the direction of the U-shaped bar. "It's one of those nights when everyone invited actually showed up, even *you*!"

Cassie recognized most of the people gathered on one side of the bar. Mostly front desk staff. And one tall, dark-haired man at the corner of the bar, watching her with a wry smile over the rim of his beer glass. Nick West. What was he doing here? Trying to prove he was one of the guys? She frowned. That wasn't fair. Maybe he was just trying to make friends in a new town.

Julie followed Cassie's gaze and nudged her shoulder.

"I know, right? The girls have been practically killing each other to take that empty stool next to him, but he said he's saving it for a friend. We're all hoping that friend is as hot as Nick is, without the I'm-your-boss baggage."

"He's not my boss." Cassie said the words to herself, but Julie managed to hear them in the noisy bar. Maybe Julie read lips.

"That's right, you both report to Blake. Are you interested?"

"What?" Cassie forced herself to look away from Nick and met Julie's speculative gaze. "Interested? I'm not interested in any man. Been there. Done that."

Got the scars to show for it...

"One and done, huh? He must have been a doozy." Julie linked her arm through Cassie's. "Come on, let's get us some drinks."

Cassie did her best not to make eye contact with Nick when they walked past, but he made that impossible when he stood and greeted them.

"If you gals are looking for seats, you can have these two." He gestured to the bar stool he'd just vacated and the one beside it.

"I thought you were saving it for someone."

Nick looked directly at Cassie. "You're someone."

Julie looked back and forth between them with a grin. "Okay, then. Thanks!"

Having Nick here set her plans to *slowly* start a social life a little off balance. This was no longer a gathering of employees having fun. This was Nick West, and she was never on her best footing when he was around. For one thing, he made her snarkier than usual.

"Sitting at a bar seems a little tame for you, Mr. West. I'm surprised you're not out climbing a mountain or hunting wild boar with your bare hands."

His right brow arched high, making a direct hit on her heart. "And I'm surprised you're not curled up in a bathrobe with a book of pretty poetry and cup of tea, Miss Smith."

He had no idea how tempting that idea was. "That actually sounds lovely. You might want to try it sometime."

He grinned. "Are you inviting me to a private poetry reading?"

She tried to picture the two of them sitting by the big windows in her loft, reading quietly and glancing at each other warmly as they sipped their tea. Her reaction to the vision was visceral, with her entire body heating and a shiver of some unknown emotion tracing down her spine. She forced herself to laugh lightly but wasn't sure if it sounded genuine at all. This was a game she wasn't used to playing.

"I think there's as much chance of that happening as there is of the two of us going mountain climbing together."

Julie chimed in, looking delighted. "Oh, my God, you two are adorable together!"

She and Nick both looked at her in surprise, speaking in unison.

"We're not together!"

Julie waved her hand dismissively. "Whatever. You're both so serious at work, but here you are being all teasing and flirty and it's... It's cute. That's all."

Nick glanced around, and it burned Cassie to realize he might be wondering if any other employees thought he was being "cute." Probably not a trait the head of security wanted to be known for. And she'd started it all with her sarcastic comment.

"I'm... I'm sorry." She closed her eyes, furious with herself for saying those two words so often. "I should probably..." She started to slide off her seat, but Nick stopped her with a hand on her hip. He moved his hand away as soon as she stopped, but she could still feel the warmth of it.

"No, don't go. And stop with the damn apologizing." His voice dropped for her ears only. "You do that way too much." His gaze locked on hers, and she swallowed hard. Yes, she apologized too much. It was a survival tool she hadn't managed to shake. His eyes softened. He leaned against the bar, his chest only inches from her back, his breath blowing across her neck as he spoke. "What'll you have to drink, ladies?"

Julie held up her glass. "Chardonnay for me, thanks."

Cassie managed to nod and speak without stuttering. "Sounds good. I'll have the same."

Nick caught the bartender's attention and placed the order, chatting with the guy as he filled their glasses. That was Nick. Outgoing. Full of life and laughs. Her total and complete opposite. Their drinks were delivered, and Nick moved on down the bar to talk to Tim. Cassie was relieved. She didn't want to be rude to the guy, but she also didn't want to hang out at a bar with a man who made her body tingle in dangerous ways.

Everyone started to mingle back and forth, and within an hour, there was a cluster of resort employees standing around Julie and her. People were laughing and jostling each other, and some even took to the dance floor when the music started. Cassie couldn't relax completely, but she did her best, laughing along with everyone else at the stories being told. She didn't have any funny stories of her own to share, but no one pressed her. Most gave her a quick look of surprise when they saw her, but no one made a big deal of her first outing with them.

Julie was telling a story about the woman who tried to tell her the rottweiler she had stuffed into her wheeled dog carrier was within the resort's fifteen-pound limit for pets. Cassie excused herself for the ladies' room, located beyond the dance floor and down a darkened hall. The back of her neck prickled as she stepped into the hall, and her hand automatically reached for her bag. Damn it. She'd left the bag, and her pepper spray, on her chair. She pulled her shoulders back and scolded herself for being paranoid. She couldn't live the rest of her days afraid of being around people. As Nick said, there were ways of being smart that would keep her safe without needing weapons or an armed guard. She just had to focus on her surroundings and be prepared. She locked the bathroom door quickly.

She saw the man as soon as she stepped back out into the shadowy hall. He was behind her, near the men's room. Waiting. He smiled when she glanced his way. She was in a small-town bar with friends. It wasn't likely he was an actual threat. But being alone with him in this hall with the music blaring so loudly that no one would hear her scream was not a wise thing. And self-protection was all about acting wisely. Cassie straightened.

Never look like a victim.

Nick had repeated those words a dozen times in the past few weeks. *If you look like a victim, you're a temptation someone might not be able to resist.* It wasn't about dressing or looking a certain way. He was trying to make the point that a distracted, weak-looking woman was exactly what bad guys were looking for. A smart bad guy would think twice about approaching an alert woman with a bold stride and a don't-mess-with-me expression, even if she was faking it. As Sun Tzu said, *all warfare is based on deception.*

She gave a quick, polite grin to let the man know she saw him and turned toward the dance floor, acting far more unconcerned than she felt. Then she felt his hand on her arm. She swallowed her panic and tried to pull away, but he didn't release her.

"I saw you laughing with your friends at the bar. You're pretty. Wanna dance?" His words rolled into each other just enough to tell her he was drunk. As much as her heart was screaming *Danger! Danger!* her brain told her there was no threat to his words. He wasn't out to hurt her. He was a drunk guy on a Friday night looking for a dance. All the same, she curled her hand into a proper fist, just in case. She struggled to come up with an appropriately noncommittal smile.

"Thanks, but no. Now if you'll excuse me…" She tried again to tug her arm away from him, but he wasn't giving up. The booze had clearly given him a shot of confidence in his ability to woo a woman in the bathroom hallway. *Damn it, please give up!*

"Aw, come on, babe. Just one dance. And after that, you can walk away if you want…"

Her spine went rigid with defiance. She was so tired of being ordered around. Of being told what she could and could not do. There was no attempt to smile this time around.

"Actually, I can walk away from you right now, *without* dancing. And that's what I'm going to do." She planted her feet firmly, imagining herself lowering her center of gravity as Nick taught her to do. Then she pressed the heel of her hand against the guy's chest and pushed, pulling her arm free. He stumbled back a step, eyes wide in surprise.

"Okay. Okay. You're one of those independent women. I dig it. But, honey…"

He reached for her, but before she could decide how much pain this drunk deserved to feel, he was gone in a blur of dark color that came from behind her. She heard the thump of the guy's back hitting the wall, and the whoosh of air that escaped him at impact.

"You want to walk out of here under your own power?" Nick West growled the words through clenched teeth as he leaned on his forearm, which was braced against the guy's chest. "If so, I suggest you keep your grabby-ass hands in your pockets and find an exit *now*."

The drunk nodded quickly, and Nick stepped back. The man scooted past Cassie without even glancing in her direction. Leaving Cassie alone in the dark hallway. With Nick. Which suddenly felt far more dangerous than before.

"What do you think you're doing?" She was surprised at the edge of anger to her voice, and Nick seemed to be, too.

"I *think* I'm saving your ass from the drunk dude who just ran off." Nick frowned. "Did he hurt you?"

"No! I didn't need your help, Nick. I had it under control."

"He had you by the arm. Out of sight in a dead-end hallway. I swear to God, woman, you seem determined to put yourself in harm's way…"

"I freed my own damn arm, and he was just a drunk." She lifted her chin. "And now I'm in that lonely hallway with *you*, so what's the difference?"

"The difference is you know *I'm* not going to drag you into one of these closets and hurt you. You didn't know that about him. But you're right—you did free your own arm. Without me." The corner of his mouth quirked up into a crooked grin. "Wonder where you learned that trick?"

He was fishing for compliments. When she didn't answer right away, he rubbed the back of his neck, glancing over his shoulder at the crowded dance floor, where people were stomping along to a line dance. Her sense of fairness finally kicked in.

"Yes, I'm a good little student." She looked around, chagrined to realize she hadn't noticed the other doors in the hall, one labeled "office" and the other labeled for "employees only." The drunk *could* have pulled her into one of those rooms and no one would have known. Except Nick, who'd apparently followed her. Looked out for her. She lost more of her anger. "Now you know why I stay home and read books. I don't have to fight my way to and from the restroom when I'm home by myself."

Nick stepped closer, and her back brushed the wall as she tried to retreat.

"Maybe not, but sitting around alone, doing nothing, is no way to live." He shuddered. "I'd go stir-crazy."

She couldn't help smiling at the thought of always-restless Nick sitting in an easy chair with a book in his hand. "Maybe we both live the lives best suited for us. You charge after adventure, and I read about it."

The timbre of his voice changed, lowering in volume and increasing in intensity.

"Maybe the proper balance is somewhere between our two extremes."

She nodded. "You might be right. Maybe we could help each other out with that."

There was something about this guy that made her blurt out her thoughts before she had a chance to digest them.

"What are you proposing?"

"What? Oh…um…nothing. It was just a random thought. An observation more than an invitation."

She needed to get out of here. She wasn't used to this type of banter with a man, and she wasn't good at it. All this push and pull, advance and retreat, was a mysterious dance she'd never done before. After all, Don always made sure there were no obstacles to her being attracted to him. He'd paved the way and groomed her to rely on him. But Nick didn't do that. Nick kept her guessing, left her wondering if he wanted to be around her or if she was nothing more than a pest. She started to turn away but stopped when Julie walked into the hallway, carrying Cassie's purse.

"There you are! I thought you left and forgot this... Oh..." Julie noticed Nick's presence and her eyes went wide. "What's going on, guys?"

Nick moved a bit farther from Cassie, but his eyes never left hers. "We were just talking about helping each other out with a few things."

Julie looked speculative. "Out *with* or out *of* a few things?"

"Oh, my God, don't be ridiculous!" Cassie felt her cheeks warming. "We just bumped into each other, and now I'm leaving." She grabbed her bag from Julie. Nick took her arm.

"I'll walk you to your car." Of course he would, and it would be a waste of time to argue. Julie winked as they walked past her. Cassie and Nick would probably be gossip fodder at the resort Monday morning.

The employees were still at the bar, laughing and drinking. A few waved at them, and a few more watched with interest. Cassie didn't like people talking. Too much talk was why she'd had to leave Cleveland. That's how Don found her there. That's why her last name was now Smith. Nick nodded good-night to the group, then opened the door and held it for her to go out.

"You can go join the guys, Nick. I'll be..."

He looked down at her and continued to hold the door, his expression saying it all.

"Right. You're going to walk me to my car whether I need it or not."

"Now you're getting it." He followed her across the dark lot, and she tried to define the emotions swirling around inside her. It wasn't fear—she knew what fear felt like. But the jolt of adrenaline wasn't dissimilar. She was on edge. Anticipating, but anticipating what? That Nick would touch her again? Or that he wouldn't?

She resolved that question when she almost walked right past her car. She stopped so quickly that Nick bumped against her back, his hand resting on her waist to steady them both. But she didn't feel steady. He was usually quick to remove his hands from her, ever since that second training session when he let his fingers linger on her neck. But his hand wasn't moving now. In fact, she could almost swear his grip tightened just a little. And damn if she didn't lean into him.

"Cassie..." Nick cleared his throat, his grip loosening but not releasing her. "Isn't this your car?"

"Oh...yes. Sorry." She stepped away, proud of herself for being able to do it calmly and thanking the heavens for the dimly lit lot. He wouldn't be able to see her confusion. She reached in her bag for her keys.

"You aren't going to pepper-spray me again are you?" She welcomed the wry humor in his voice. This was the Nick she knew how to deal with.

"No, you're too close for it to be effective." His brow rose in admiration, and she grinned. "At this range, I'd probably try running first, or maybe throwing something at you and screaming, since we're in a public place." She glanced around, trying to remember her lessons. "If you came any closer..." He stepped toward her, stopping just short of brushing against her chest. He was testing her, and she was ready. "Now it's heel time. I'd stomp on the bridge of your foot with my heel while simultaneously jamming the heel of my hand into the bottom of your nose." She mimicked the moves as she spoke.

Nick gave a short laugh. "You really are a good little student."

Cassie felt an unexpected burst of pride. It had been only a few weeks, but she was stronger. And smarter. She gave him what he was looking for, because he deserved it.

"I've had a good teacher."

"You have. But you also listened and followed through. That'll come in handy when we go rock climbing tomorrow."

Cassie stepped back, bumping into the car. "Excuse me?"

"Wasn't that the deal you suggested? I teach you to have a life, and you try to teach me how to sit still and read a book?"

"No, I wasn't serious…that was just… No. We're not doing that. I am *not* hanging from some cliff by a rope!"

He folded his arms across his chest.

"Fair enough. How about a simple hike up Gallant Mountain? There's a trail. We'll stop before the rock climbing part." His head tilted. "Let's see how all that elliptical work has helped your stamina."

A rough laugh escaped her. "That's a hard *no*. Not happening."

It was as if she hadn't spoken. "Blake has a conference call scheduled with the Barbados resort at two, so I'll pick you up after that. We'll still have enough daylight. It'll get chilly as the sun gets lower, so bring a sweatshirt or jacket. And good walking shoes."

"Did you hear me? Not. Happening."

"It's a lot of walking—wear thick socks or double up so you don't blister."

"Nick! I'm not doing that." What part of *not happening* did he not understand?

He reached behind her to open her car door. "Come on, get in. I want to make sure you get out of here safely. Text me when you're in your apartment."

"I don't have your number…"

He handed her his phone. "Send a text to yourself. Then you'll have it."

She stared at Nick's phone in her hand.

"Yeah, and you'll have mine." A total of four people knew her current mobile number. Amanda. Blake. Her mom. And an assistant district attorney in Milwaukee. Everyone else had the landline number at the apartment.

…I think you know in your heart you're safe with me…

She typed her number in and sent a short text, knowing he'd read it.

Not happening.

She handed the phone back. He read it but didn't react.

"Text me when you're inside, or I'll be driving over to check on you."

"Don't give that number to anyone."

Nick's head snapped up. This was a matter of life and death for her.

"I won't, Cass. You have my word." She thought about all the promises Don broke in the past. But Nick wasn't Don. At least, he didn't seem to be. It was too late to take the number back, so she finally nodded. What was done was done.

She kept her eyes on Nick in the rearview mirror as she drove out of the lot, his expression troubled in the glow of her taillights. He had questions. And she wasn't about to answer them.

CHAPTER SEVEN

NICK HAD NEVER been the type to go after viral social media fame. But the look on Cassie's face when she opened the back door to her apartment Saturday afternoon was so priceless he regretted not capturing it with his phone. She clearly wasn't expecting him, judging from the unicorn leggings and oversize T-shirt she was wearing. Her hair was pulled up into some kind of messy twist on top of her head. Her feet were bare, showing off surprisingly bright blue toenails.

But her expression? That was the prizewinner. Her green-gold eyes were wide, and her mouth formed a perfect, pink-lined O. She seemed frozen there, her hand clutching the edge of the door. Cassie slowly took him in, and once again, her lingering gaze had the power to make his blood heat. She started with his well-worn hiking shoes, then on up to his cargo shorts and rugby shirt before her gaze finally reached his face.

"What are you doing here?"

"Uh… We're going hiking, remember?"

Her head went back and forth emphatically. "What I remember is telling you that I was *not* going hiking. So thanks for stopping, but you're on your own." She started to push the door closed, but Nick's hand shot out to stop it.

"Have you even stepped outside today?" He gestured behind

him to the bright blue May sky and the maples leafing out on the other side of the parking lot. The air was fresh and rain-washed from the showers they'd had that morning. "You haven't, have you? You've been cooped up in this place all damn day." She opened her mouth to protest, but it was obvious he was right. "Come on. Go change, and we'll take a pleasant stroll on the mountainside—nothing challenging. You need to get some sun and exercise, and you'll love the views from up there." She still hesitated, so he offered a trade-off. "Look, you go for a hike with me today, and I promise to give you a day doing whatever you want. Including reading and sipping tea, if you insist."

Her eyes narrowed, but the corner of her mouth betrayed her amusement.

"Whatever I want?"

Nick had the sinking feeling he was getting the losing end of this bargain, but it was too late to back out now.

"Whatever you want." He held back a groan at her obvious pleasure with his concession. "But it's late and it's gonna get cool as the sun gets low, so hurry up."

There was another moment of indecision before Cassie nodded. "Fine. Give me ten minutes. And this had better be a nice 'stroll' because I am not climbing any cliffs. Got it?"

"Yes, ma'am." He remembered how tense she'd been a few weeks ago when he went into her apartment to carry that box of mugs. "I'll wait for you in the Jeep." He tapped his watch. "Ten minutes."

The drive to the trailhead wasn't long, but it sure seemed that way with the silence hanging over the vehicle. Cassie had changed clothes in a flash, but she'd also withdrawn into Nick's least favorite of her personas—the quiet mouse. She was answering his questions about her day in single syllables, staring out the window instead of at him, huddled against the passenger door as if ready to open it at any second and throw herself out of the moving vehicle. He finally had enough and pulled off on the side of the mountain road.

"Tell me what's going on."

Her cheeks flamed, then paled. "Wh-what do you mean?"

"I know I coerced you into joining me on this hike, but the idea is for you to enjoy it. And you are definitely not enjoying yourself right now. Why?"

The color came back to her face and she straightened a little at his brusque question. "You can't just order me to have fun, Nick. I told you last night I didn't want to hike a mountain with you."

"And yet you changed your clothes and hopped into the Jeep with me when I showed up at your door. What's happening? Do you want to go back?"

A slideshow of emotions played across her face. As a cop, he'd always been good at reading people, but this woman defeated him every time. He had no idea what she was feeling, and he had a hunch she didn't know, either. But the primary emotion he picked up from her body language was...fear.

"Are you *afraid* of me?" Her silence spoke volumes. "You have got to be freaking kidding me..."

He slammed the Jeep into gear and did a U-turn. He wasn't kidnapping the woman, for God's sake. He was only trying to help her get out more. Had she really been too intimidated to refuse him? The thought gave him pause. How many times had Jada warned him about his "steamroller" approach when he thought he was right? Was that what he'd done to Cassie? He'd driven only a mile or two back toward town when Cassie sat up straight and spoke.

"Stop, Nick. Turn around. I don't want to go home."

This woman gave him emotional whiplash.

"Are you sure?" She nodded, and he pulled into the next driveway and turned back up the mountain. "Are you going to tell me what the problem is?"

She chewed on her lip for a moment, then turned to face him, her words coming out in a rush.

"I haven't been alone in a car with a man in a long time..."

When her words trailed off, he took his eyes off the winding road just in time to see a single tear spill over. Damn. He hated when women cried. She hadn't told him much of her story since that day in the gym. She'd been attacked in a parking garage. Maybe the guy dragged her into a vehicle? *Shit.*

"When you were attacked…"

"No, not then." Her hands twisted in her lap. "I just haven't been alone in a car with a man driving in a really long time, and it freaked me out more than I thought it would." He turned away to focus on driving, and was thankful when she continued. "I tried to work through it in my head, but I couldn't get past it. I thought I'd be relieved when you turned the car around, but I wasn't. It felt like surrendering, and I don't want to do that."

"You're a fighter." His words were low, almost unintentional, but she heard him and gave a soft snort of laughter.

"You've said that before, but I'm *not*. I'm a mess." She gave a gasp of surprise when he turned off the pavement and started up the steep dirt track. "Where are we going?"

Nick was thankful for the change in subject. "We're going up the mountain. In the Jeep for as far as we can. Unless you'd rather walk?" The truck rocked as it hit a dip on the path. She grabbed the door, but she no longer looked like she wanted to escape. In fact, she was smiling and leaning forward, watching the brush sweep the sides of the truck. She laughed when the wheels spun in the mud from last night's rain, finally catching hold of solid ground and catapulting the vehicle forward.

He had his hands full with the driving, but he soaked in the sound of Cassie's laughter and held it in his heart like the precious thing it was. He couldn't help stealing a glance at her, and her smile had him letting up on the gas pedal and nearly driving into a tree.

It was the first *real* smile he'd seen on her. Oh, he'd seen her smile. The warm-but-professional smile she had for Blake Randall. The conspiratorial smile of friendship she shared with Amanda or Julie. The cool, polished smile she used with employees and visitors. And the involuntary smile of frustrated amusement she occasionally sent his way when he'd been teasing her over something.

But this smile... He glanced over again, and she laughed, one hand on the door and one braced on the dashboard as they climbed the rutted path... *This* smile was really something. It was...uninhibited. Genuine. Uncensored. Unguarded. All of Cassie's protective shields had come down, and he was seeing his new, most favorite version of her ever. He was seeing Cassie unfiltered.

"Is this what they call four-wheeling?"

They reached the small clearing where the path leveled off. A wooden gate with a no-trespassing sign blocked their way. Nick turned off the truck, glad to be able to face her now without putting their lives at risk.

"Not exactly. Four-wheeling is usually done on four-wheelers, but I guess sometimes it's with trucks. And that was actually a pretty decent track to drive up—not exactly off-roading..." Nick stopped abruptly. He was babbling like a nervous schoolboy. And Cassie was still smiling at him. In fact, she may have even giggled—something he wouldn't have thought possible before now.

"That was fun! I'm so glad we turned around!" Yeah, so was he. She looked around at the thick woods surrounding them. "Will you have room to turn here?"

"Eventually, sure. But first, we hike."

She looked at the gate and the posted sign and arched her brow. "You want me to go trespassing with you to take a hike I didn't want to take in the first place? I don't think so."

He grinned at her last-ditch attempt to avoid hiking and opened his door. "It's not trespassing if you have permission from the owner. And Blake Randall told me it's just fine."

Cassie was pretty sure her calf muscles were tearing apart. The burning pain had her wincing as she followed Nick up the steep path. She wondered if she'd ever walk without pain again. A "nice stroll," huh? This was more like climbing Kilimanjaro with no training.

A few weeks on the elliptical were no match for Gallant Mountain. She could ask Nick to stop, but she'd just asked for a break a few minutes ago, and that was the third one. She hadn't missed his amusement or his sigh of impatience when he'd glanced up the trail. She vowed not to stop again. Surely they'd be stopping soon. He'd *promised* her there would be no rock climbing, and she could see a wall of rugged gray getting closer.

Too bad her legs would be destroyed beyond repair by the time they got there.

Nick glanced over his shoulder and slowed. She knew he was already taking this hike much slower than he usually would, so she gave him the brightest smile she could muster.

He frowned. "You okay?"

No, I'm dying. Literally dying.

"I'm fine! Great!"

I'm in agony, and you know it, you bastard.

His brow rose. "Really? You're feeling great?"

How much longer are you going to torture me?

"Sure, great! Absolutely!"

He shook his head, and she was pretty sure he was laughing at her, but she couldn't prove it, since he was climbing up the trail again. She stuck her tongue out at his back and bit back a groan of pain as she followed. If only they'd stopped their little adventure after the truck drive up the mountain. That was fun.

She'd never done anything like it, with the engine growling, the tires searching for traction and the Jeep rocking back and forth like some amusement park ride. She'd been so inside her head when they left the apartment, fighting off her unease at being alone with a man who was literally in control of the vehicle and, therefore, her. But once Nick confronted her silence, and then was willing to take her *home* rather than make her uncomfortable, she'd finally set her fear aside. Nick was right—

it was a gorgeous day and she'd been missing it, sitting inside with her book.

When he'd turned the truck onto the steep dirt road—all rutted and muddy—she was so surprised that all she could do was laugh. Never in a million years had she ever pictured herself bouncing around in a Jeep going up a mountain. And it was... *fun*. She couldn't remember the last time she'd had actual fun doing something. Not that she hadn't had moments of happiness or laughter since leaving Milwaukee, but to *do* something that was fun, instead of just laughing along while someone else did something... Yeah, she hadn't done that in years.

Even this hike, with all its pain—and she was in serious pain—was almost fun in a weird way. She was so far outside her normal comfort zone that she was pretty amazed at herself. And proud. She slowed for a moment, thinking about that last word. She was *proud* of herself. Pride was that odd, unrecognizable sensation she'd felt over the past few weeks as she pushed herself to become stronger. As she started taking responsibility for protecting herself. For standing her ground.

She tried to remember the last time she'd felt proud of herself. High school? She'd always had good grades, but reading and studying had come easy for her, so it wasn't a big challenge. College? Her social awkwardness as an introvert made it hard to fit in with any of the cliques and clubs, but she had worked hard to stay on the dean's list every semester. That was something to be proud of, right?

"Cass? Seriously, are you okay?" Nick was right in front of her now, snapping her out of her thoughts and back into the present. The present where her legs were in flames. She blew out a long, slow breath and tried to keep her face as neutral as possible.

"I'm great, Nick. Don't stop for me."

He gave her a crooked smile. "I didn't stop for you. I stopped because we're here."

She looked around in surprise. They'd reached a small, grassy clearing. To her right, a giant boulder—the size of a city bus—sat at the base of the rocky summit far above. To her left was a view of Gallant Lake that took her breath away.

The mountains around the lake glowed with the bright green of new growth. The clear blue sky above was reflected in the calm waters of the lake, creating a palette that screamed, "Spring!" Cassie walked toward the rocky drop-off, mesmerized by the view. Nick gently stopped her with a hand on her shoulder, releasing her as quickly as he'd touched her.

"After yesterday's rain, let's not chance the slip-factor on this cliff, okay?"

She didn't respond right away, staring at the view. Then she spun to face him.

"We did it! We made it to the top of the mountain! And my legs aren't cramping anymore… Well, not as much, anyway…"

His quick flash of amusement vanished. "Your legs were cramping? Here, drink some water." He reached around and pulled a metal water container out of the small canvas pack he had slung over his shoulder. "You're probably dehydrated. You didn't say you were getting leg cramps—that's nothing to mess around with."

She took the water and drank deep. It was cold and refreshing. Then she handed it back with a wide grin. "Thanks." She gestured toward the view. "This made it worth it. I can't believe I climbed to the top of a mountain!"

He chuckled, his laughter warm and deep. "You didn't 'climb' a mountain. You hiked up a mountain path after I drove halfway up here. And we're not at the top." He looked over his shoulder. "But I can get you a little closer to it. Come on." He took her hand and gave a gentle tug. It felt oddly right to have her hand in his. He led her to the bus-sized boulder and she discovered there was a little path to the side that allowed her, with minimal climbing skills, to scramble to the top of the rock.

"Here," Nick said, tugging her back to the cliff wall. "From back here if you look out, it's like you're standing at the edge of the cliff with nothing below you. Without the risk of falling a few hundred feet down the mountain."

He was right. If she put her back to the rocks, the boulder was wide enough that it hid the grassy opening and trail, showing nothing but the lake and mountains.

"It's like flying." She barely whispered the words, but Nick nodded in agreement.

"That's what it's like when you climb a peak. You're on top of the world, and it feels like no one has ever been there before you."

There was something magical about standing here, sharing this moment with him.

"You've only been here a month—how did you find this amazing little secret up here?"

"It's not exactly a secret. Blake said it's a pretty popular spot for the locals, because it's such an easy walk…" She huffed out a laugh and he grinned. "Easy for the kids who like to climb up here, anyway. They call it the Kissing Rock."

She didn't answer right away. Gallant Lake seemed to inspire a lot of romantic names for places. Amanda called Cassie's apartment a love shack, and now she was standing on the Kissing Rock.

"It's a stone with a view," she said. "What makes it a Kissing Rock?"

Nick shrugged, and the movement caused his arm to rub the length of hers, pointing out how close they were standing. She could step away. But she didn't.

"I guess it's been called that for generations. People came up here with picnic lunches, and maybe the view, um…*inspired* them. Or maybe they came up in the evenings and watched the sun setting, like it's starting to do now, and they were alone at the edge of the world like this…" He looked down at her, his eyes dark and his emotions hidden. Was he pressing more tightly against her? Or was that her leaning in? "And I imagine a young couple might feel their inhibitions disappearing up here. No one would see them. No one would know if they stole a kiss or two."

They were facing each other now. She wasn't sure how that happened, but they'd both turned, so it was mutual. The sun was warm. A soft breeze rustled the young leaves in the trees that lined the view toward the lake. There were birds singing, but it felt like silence. Like a warm, safe cocoon of silence and…safety.

…you know in your heart you're safe with me…

They were so close she could feel the vibration in his chest when he spoke.

"It's a little like Vegas, I guess. What happens on Kissing Rock stays on Kissing Rock."

His hands were resting on her waist. How had that happened? And hers were on his biceps. His strong, hard biceps. This was an afternoon for new sensations. First was fun. Then pride. And now? Now she was feeling something she hadn't felt in…maybe forever. Sure, Don made her want to be with him. He'd paved the way to make it feel inevitable. But she'd never felt this pool of warmth deep in her belly as she flexed her fingers against Nick's arms and saw his nostrils flare in response. She'd never felt the tingle of excitement that had moved her so close her pelvis brushed across the zipper of his shorts, earning a low, strangled sound from him as his grip tightened on her.

He turned, putting her back to the rocks. Blocking the sun. Blocking everything but this new kind of burn. Not one of pain, but one of need. She whispered his name, and he closed his eyes, holding them tightly closed as if having a battle with himself. She said his name again, and he shook his head. His eyes didn't open until he started to speak in a voice filled with gravel and deep with emotion.

"This isn't why I brought you here. I didn't plan this…" He cupped her cheek with his hand. "There are a hundred ways this can go wrong…"

She rested her hand over his on the side of her face. "I can't believe you're the one being timid right now. *You.*" He smiled at that, but he didn't make a move. Oh, God, why wasn't he making a move?

He closed his eyes again, shaking his head slowly. "This is a mistake." He stepped back, moving his hand away from her face and running it through his own hair. "We're coworkers. We hardly know each other. We've both got baggage. You're not..."

A chill ran through her veins. Nick didn't want Cassie. Of course he didn't. He was a cool, confident ladies' man, and she wasn't his type. She was a timid bookworm who jumped and flinched at everything, and big, bold Nick West, hero cop, didn't want someone like her. Nick wanted a fearless woman who swung from cliffs and rode a mountain bike. A woman who didn't need self-defense lessons. She straightened and moved out from between him and the rock face.

"Of course. You're right. I'm sorry." Damn it to hell, there she went, apologizing again. Apologizing for this *mistake*. Apologizing for being who she was.

Nick reached for her, but she tugged free, moving to the spot where they'd climbed up onto this stupid Kissing Rock. The sun was getting lower, and they really should get back to the Jeep and back to reality. The reality where she understood her place and knew her limits. She took hold of a small tree and put her foot on a root that had acted like a ladder rung on the way up here. But her heel couldn't grip that damp, round root the way her toes had earlier. Before she knew it, she was falling, her butt hitting the rock hard and catapulting her forward on her hands and knees on the ground. The fall, and abrupt halt, stunned her into silence. But it had the opposite effect on Nick, who was scrambling down while calling her name and cursing.

"Cassie! Are you okay? Damn it, Cass, say something!" He hit his knees next to her just as she sat back and rubbed the palms of her hands on her jeans, wincing a little. The mud softened her landing, but her wrists were still sore. And her knees. And her butt.

Nick's hands were running down her arms now, and then her back, before running up her neck and holding her face from each side. "Are you hurt?"

"Other than my pride? I don't think so." She gently pushed his hands away, not ready to fall into that temptation trap again. She stood, and he rose with her, one arm around her waist to steady her. The pain in her hip, where she slammed into the rock, made her grimace. "I'm such a klutz. I bet you've never seen your mountain climbing buddies do that move. As you know, my hand-eye coordination is subpar at best..."

"Cass, I once missed a cleat on a rock face and fell twenty feet before the rope caught me. But my harness was too loose and I ended up hanging upside down fifty feet in the air, swinging back and forth like a pendulum, with my ass exposed to the whole world."

She couldn't help a short laugh. "I would have liked to have seen that."

"Oh, you can. My buddy caught it all on his phone, and it briefly went viral on the rock climbing forums." His hand ran down her back, stopping at her hip when she flinched. "Yeah, I thought I saw you bounce off the rock right there. You'll have a hell of a bruise. Do you think it's any more than that?"

She took a few steps. She was sore, but that was probably as much from the climb up as from the fall. "I'm good. We should get back before it starts getting dark." He nodded, but he didn't head for the trail. Instead, he walked straight to her. She put her hands up and he stopped, his chest brushing against hers. "Wh-what are you doing?"

He stared at her hard, then slid his arms around her. She didn't resist when he pulled her up tight to him. "I'm doing what I should have done up on that damn Kissing Rock. Or maybe what I shouldn't have done. I don't know. I only know there's no way in hell I'm leaving this mountain before I've kissed you." Her fingers twisted into his shirt, just to make sure he didn't change his mind again. He didn't move, waiting for her consent.

She tugged on his shirt and lifted her chin.

"Well, what are you waiting for?"

And just like that, his lips were on hers. His kiss was firm and commanding. In control without making her feel overpowered. And skilled. Oh, so skilled. She parted her mouth and his tongue was inside her in a flash. She melted against him, trusting him to hold her upright, and he did, with a low growl of approval. Their mouths moved as one, in a dance as seductive as a tango. He took and she gave, then she rose on her toes and took from him, and his fingers gripped her waist and held her there. Her hands were eager to be part of the game and slid up so she could clutch the back of his head. Their teeth clicked together and apart and together again, and it wasn't enough for her. She wanted more, and she stretched even taller to meet him. To have a moment of control all for herself. As if knowing what she needed, Nick bent his knees, then lifted her up so her head was above his. The kiss never broke, but now she was the one being demanding. She was the one taking over. Her hands cupped his face. He stared up at her with a fire that mirrored hers. Startled, she pulled back.

Nick let her slide slowly down to her feet, his eyes never leaving hers. He kissed her again, but this kiss was different. This wasn't the experienced player using his skills to leave her legless. This was a kiss with more uncertainty in it, as if he was exploring some new territory where he'd never been before. Tender, cautious and slow. He drifted from her lips to her chin, then down her neck and up to the tender skin below her ear, then back to her lips. She was drunk on him. Drunk on Nick West. And she was hopelessly dependent. Craving her next fix before this one even ended.

Then his lips were gone from hers. He'd set her at arm's length from him, staring at her in bewilderment, then turning away.

"Holy shit, Cass." He shook himself as if to shake off whatever spell had come over them both. "What the hell was that?"

"Uh…a kiss?"

"Baby, that was a lot more than just a kiss."

Baby? Cassie did her best to ignore the endearment. It didn't seem as if Nick was using it that way anyhow.

He stared at the ground, then looked out to the lake, and the sun lowering beyond it. He kept his back to her.

"We should get back to the truck before it gets dark. Can you walk?"

What just happened? That kiss had seemed *electric*…until Nick flipped off the switch and pushed her away. But then again, Don always told her she was a boring lover.

"I'm sorry…" Every time she said those words, it burned her. But this time they felt appropriate. Clearly, she'd had a different experience than Nick had. "I'm not very good at that stuff. Kissing. Sex. All of it…none of it…whatever…"

CHAPTER EIGHT

NICK STARED AT Cassie in confusion. What the hell was she apologizing for? She'd just rocked his world with a kiss that would forever raise the bar on any future kisses that came his way. And did she say she wasn't good at *sex*? No way did he believe that. Not after a kiss that had him turning away to hide the erection tenting his shorts. If he didn't get her off this mountain, they'd be joining the decades-long list of couples who'd consummated their relationships on the Kissing Rock. And as much as his body wanted that to happen—*right now*—Nick knew Cassie deserved better. This wasn't where or how he wanted it to happen. *If* it happened. And it probably shouldn't happen. But *damn*...

She turned away, her head hung low. He had to fix this, and fast.

"Cassie, I don't know who the idiot was who told you that you weren't—" he raised his fingers into air quotes "—'good at this,' but he was wrong. Like, *really* wrong. Like, he couldn't have been *more* wrong." He walked toward her. "Did you not feel how great that was?" How could she not have felt that?

Her cheeks flamed. "I did think it was pretty...great. But then you stopped..."

He chuckled softly. "Uh... I had no choice. It was either put some space between us or embarrass myself like some middle school teen. You had me thinking some very impure thoughts, Cass, and if we'd stayed that close, you would have felt just how strong those thoughts were."

Her brows furrowed, then rose in surprise.

"Oh…"

Nick wouldn't have thought it possible, but the color in her cheeks deepened even further.

"Oh!" Her mouth lifted into a slightly proud smile. *Damn straight, girl.* "Oh. I thought…"

"You thought, once again, that you'd done something wrong. That's always your first response, isn't it? Why is that?"

Her smile vanished, and he kicked himself for speaking his thoughts out loud. But instead of avoiding the subject, she looked at him and nodded.

"It's generally my go-to. I… I had a lot of years of someone telling me I was doing everything wrong. Apologizing becomes habit after a while." She ran her fingers through her dark hair, smoothing the ponytail that had been mussed from her fall, and then from their kiss. "And you seemed to be…fighting it. Up there…" She glanced up to the top of the rock. "We were so close, and you started listing all the reasons we shouldn't…"

Nick couldn't help laughing. "That little speech up there? The list of all the reasons kissing you was a mistake? That was me giving myself a verbal cold shower." He ran his hands down her arms and caught her hands. "Being that close to you had my blood rushing to places it had no business rushing to. Not in the middle of the day on the side of a mountain. Rattling off that list cooled me down enough to step away and gather my wits."

He squeezed her hands. "But when you got upset and tumbled down the side of the rock trying to get away from me, I knew 'space' wasn't what I needed. Or at least, it wasn't what I wanted. But if I thought being close to you was a turn-on, *kissing* you was… Well, like I said. That was more than chemistry. That was a whole damn laboratory fire going on."

She held his gaze, and he could see her mind racing and stalling and crashing. Yeah, he should have just kissed her again before she had a chance to overthink things. She swallowed hard.

"But you weren't wrong... It's a mistake. We *do* work together. And we *do* have baggage. And we *don't* know each other that well..."

He let her pull away, sensing her rising panic.

"*Now* who's taking the cold shower?" He grinned, and she did her best not to grin back, but failed. He shook his head. "First— I think we know each other pretty well. I'd like to think we're friends, even. We may not have shared our life stories yet, but that can be remedied over dinner some night. Second—everyone has baggage. That's an empty excuse. And third—yeah, we work together. But I'm not aware of any rules against fraternization at Randall Resorts International. I'm not your boss, and we didn't kiss in the office." He shrugged. "Honestly, so far all we've done is have a stellar kissing session at the Kissing Rock. I'd like to have *another* stellar kissing session with you somewhere else, but that's your call, Cassie."

"I... I'm not good at this..." She held up her hand to stop his objection to the way she always put herself down. "That's not self-pity, Nick. I mean I'm not...experienced...at dating, or relationships, or kissing guys on mountains. I don't know how to navigate what happens next."

"Okay. Executive decision time." He took her hand and tucked it in the crook of his arm. They headed for the trail. "Let's stop worrying and get away from this damn rock. What happens at the rock, stays at the rock and all that." Cassie snorted in laughter. He liked all her laughs, even the snorting ones, so he kept lying to her. "No, really. No one has to know, and our friendship doesn't have to change. On Monday, we'll have a normal day at work, and a normal gym session afterward, like today never happened. And if one of us decides we need to pursue this— whatever this is—we'll discuss it like adults. Deal?"

She glanced his way quickly, careful to also watch where

she was stepping as they went down the trail. He wasn't fooling anyone. Nothing would be the same between them, and the thought made him sad. He'd enjoyed the teasing and fun they'd shared. Watching Cassie gain new confidence and strength as they worked out together. He didn't want to lose that. As tempting as it was to pursue more kisses, or perhaps more than just kissing, he didn't like the thought of anything changing their existing relationship.

"Of course. That makes sense." She was playing along. "Nothing needs to change... Oh!" She stumbled on the trail, but Nick caught her waist and kept her upright, resisting the sudden and unexpected urge to pull her into his arms, bury his hands in her hair and kiss her senseless.

Bad idea... Too complicated...baggage...coworker...

"Exactly. Nothing needs to change. Nothing at all."

"Cassie-girl, where *are* you this morning? Nora called your name three times to tell you your cappuccino is ready."

Cathy set the foam-topped mug in front of Cassie on the window table inside the Gallant Brew. "Is everything okay? You haven't heard from Don...?"

"No, Aunt Cathy. It's not that. I'm just tired. I overdid things a bit yesterday."

That was the understatement of the century. She'd not only agreed to hike Gallant Mountain with Nick West, she'd also *kissed* the man. More than once. And she'd *liked* it. A lot. Definitely overdone.

"What'd you do, honey? Is Blake working you too hard up there at the resort?"

"Uh...no. He's not." Amanda Randall walked in. "Why would you ask that?"

Nora walked over with a plate of ginger cookies and a sly smile. Over the past few weeks, Cassie had given in to Amanda's pestering about becoming a hermit and started joining the cousins and Aunt Cathy for their before-the-Sunday-rush coffee in Nora's shop.

Nora set the cookies on the table and grabbed a chair. "Cassie said she overdid things yesterday and Cathy was worried. But I don't think it was Blake who kept her busy." Nora winked at Cassie, and she felt a sense of dread. "I think Nick West might be the one 'overworking' her these days."

Amanda sat quickly, putting her elbows on the table and her chin in her hands. "*Really?* Do tell, Nora!"

Cathy's eyes narrowed. "Nick West? That guy who was in the shop a few weeks ago and followed you upstairs? Cassie, what's going on?"

Amanda laughed. "I *told* you that apartment was a love shack! Come on, Nora, spill what you know."

"Hey, wait!" The last of the cousins, Melanie Lowery, rushed into the shop, smoothing her hair with her hand and looking flustered. "No spilling anything until I get some espresso and join in. I'm always missing the good stuff!"

Nora sighed and went behind the counter to make Melanie's coffee. "Maybe if you weren't always late to the party, Mel, you wouldn't miss everything."

The tall brunette waved a dismissive hand. "Honey, my fiancé's been on the West Coast for a week. By the time his flight landed, we had a lot of...um...catching up to do, if you get my drift." She took a cookie and sighed as she took a bite. "Oh, I love my gingers."

"Got it, Mel. Sweet ginger cookies. Hot ginger fiancé." Amanda fixed her gaze back on Nora as she rejoined them, delivering Mel's espresso with a flourish. "Spill it, girl."

Nora glanced out toward the empty sidewalk, making sure there were no customers heading their way, then leaned forward, lowering her voice dramatically.

"Well, I just happened to set some trash outside the back door yesterday afternoon to keep it from stinking up the kitchen. I always clean out the fridge and the display on Saturday after-noons to make way for the fresh Sunday baked goods..."

Amanda rolled her eyes. "Yes, yes, we know you're the queen of organization. Get to the good stuff."

"Seriously?" Cassie interrupted, glaring at Amanda. "Is this the 'magic of having girlfriends' you told me I needed?" No one paid any attention, all eyes fixed on Nora.

"Well," Nora said. "Imagine my surprise when I saw Nick sitting in his Jeep out in the parking lot. Before I could set the trash down and wave, I heard footsteps on the back stairs, and there was Cassie—" all four heads swiveled in Cassie's direction "—trotting down the stairs and over to the Jeep and hopping right in. Then they drove off together. On a Saturday afternoon. Almost like a date or something."

Three sets of eyebrows rose, but Cathy was scowling. "Cassie, you don't know this guy. Don't you think it's a little soon to jump right back into a relationship?"

Being the center of attention put Cassie on the defensive. "One kiss doesn't make it a relationship."

Oh, damn her filter-free mouth when she was nervous...

There was a collective gasp of delight from the cousins. Mel-anie rested her hand on Cassie's arm.

"You *kissed* Nick West?"

She bit her lip, upset that she'd blurted that out, but also want-ing the advice of women she trusted and admired. She hadn't lied yesterday when she told Nick she had little experience at this. After college, Don had pretty much been her only rela-tionship, and that was hardly the measuring stick she wanted to use for future ones.

Amanda's voice softened. "Hey, guys, it's a big deal to move on after what Cassie's been through. If she doesn't want to talk about it..."

"Actually, I think I *do* want to talk about it."

"Oh, thank God! Tell us everything!" Amanda's laugh made Cassie smile.

She gave the women a summary of the Nick-and-Cassie story. Their disastrous first meeting when she threw the stapler at him. Pepper-spraying him. Agreeing to let him help her with self-defense and fitness training. The playful teasing they did at work, with him hiding her stapler and her scattering reports across his desk in an untidy array that annoyed him every time. The bar Friday night, where she told him she would *not* go hiking with him. Nick showing up at her door anyway. The hike she thought would kill her. The kiss that nearly did. And finally, her and Nick's agreement to not allow it to change anything. There was silence for a moment when she finished, then Amanda spoke.

"So you think you and Nick might be friends, and you don't want to screw that up."

She thought about that. She looked forward to going to work when Nick was there. She never knew what she'd find on her desk or where her stapler might be. He always dropped some off-the-cuff comment that made her smile. He drove her crazy with that stupid foam basketball. He also did his best to make sure she felt secure, while pushing her to try new things. She'd never had a big brother, but if she had, she had a feeling that's what their relationship would be like.

She nodded at Amanda's guess. "I like Nick. I mean, like him like a friend. A fun coworker. He's a good guy who annoys me to no end, but he's also…"

"He's also someone you want to climb like a tree?" Melanie lifted her coffee mug in a toast. "I think we've all been there, right, ladies?"

The three cousins laughed and agreed, but Cathy wasn't amused.

"Keep it in the friend zone, honey. If you get attached and have to…"

Cassie nodded. The go-bag sitting by her door upstairs was a constant reminder that she could end up running again. Changing her name again. Starting over again. It hadn't been that hard to leave Cleveland, but leaving Gallant Lake? This move was going to hurt if it ever came. And getting involved with Nick West would make it that much more complicated. He didn't strike her as the kind of guy to just let her leave. He'd want to rescue her, and the thought of him going up against someone as flat-out evil as Don made her shudder.

"It's not easy to do." Amanda sighed. "Blake and I were friends, and I worked for him, but after that first kiss... Well, as hard as we tried, the friend zone was toast." Nora and Mel nodded in agreement, dreamy-eyed and smiling.

Cassie finished her coffee, trying to block the memory of yesterday's kisses. Going down that path would only lead to heartbreak.

"Aunt Cathy's right. I can't let this change things. Yesterday was a surprise. And yes—" she rolled her eyes at Amanda's snicker "—it was a nice surprise. It's nice to know I can still feel desire for a man, and that a man might desire me. That I could melt like that..." And there she went, oversharing again. She needed to get better at this girlfriend thing. Nora stood as a group of customers walked in, dressed in their Sunday church clothes.

"I gotta run," Nora said. "But if that man made you 'melt,' you should think twice before passing him up."

CHAPTER NINE

"MAN, THAT CLIMB was turbocharged today, Nick! Was there a race that I didn't know about?" Terrance Hudson took a long drink from his water bottle, then poured some on the edge of his shirt and wiped the sweat from his face. Nick, Terrance and the rest of the Rebel Rockers climbing club were sitting atop the Arrow Wall at the Shawangunk cliffs, known locally as the Gunks. "Shit, man. For someone who's never climbed this sucker, you were on fire. I ain't never seen a guy go up this wall that fast!"

Nick took a swig from his own water, pouring the rest of it over his head. The sun was high and hot today. He nodded to his climbing partner, whom he'd met only a week ago at his first meeting of the Rebel Rockers at the Chalet in Gallant Lake.

"Sorry for the pace. I tend to climb quick. That last part of the climb—what do they call it, Modern Times? That was pretty intense for a 5.8 rating. I just wanted to get it over with and get up here to relax." Also, he was running from the memories of yesterday's kisses with the not-so-shy-after-all Cassandra Smith. But Terrance didn't need to know that.

"Yeah, that last stretch is a challenge, but man, the views, right?" Terrance nodded toward the valley that stretched out hundreds of feet below them. It was impressive, but it had nothing on yesterday's view of Gallant Lake reflected in Cassie's golden eyes right before his lips touched hers. He shook off the memory. So many reasons not to do that again. And so many nerve endings humming in his body, begging for more.

Terrance turned and started chatting with another climber—Sam something—leaving Nick to consider all the options with Cassie. As much as he'd dismissed the coworker issue, he knew how messy workplace flings could be. He'd seen the damage done at the precinct back in LA when two of his fellow detectives had a quick affair. She'd ended it, but the guy didn't want to take no for an answer. Things got so ugly they ended up transferring the woman across town, which never sat right with Nick. She wasn't the one causing problems.

And he and Cassie would probably end up being a quick affair. They had nothing in common, other than driving each other crazy with office pranks. He was still finding new places to hide that blue stapler every morning. He'd even snuck into the ladies' room to set it on the sink in there. And ever since he told her how much he valued organized files, she'd started coming into his office and shuffling his folders or scattering them all over his desk.

But other than the office high jinks, what did they have? Well...hot chemistry, for sure. But besides that, what was there? He was restless and liked to be physically active. He hated sitting around, and that was her favorite thing to do—sit with her tea and a book. As much as she was improving her strength and fighting skills in their gym sessions, she was still jumpy and quick to take on blame. Always apologizing. He tucked his water bottle back in his pack.

She was a victim. He thought about Beth Washington going back to her brute of a husband over and over, until Nick shot the man dead. After Earl Washington had murdered his partner. Beth's refusal to leave the man, to protect herself, had directly led to Jada's death.

The fire of his physical attraction to Cassie started to cool as common sense prevailed. If she was one of those perpetual victims, then she wasn't right for him long-term, and short-term wasn't really an option when they worked in the same damn office. Problem solved. Sharing any more kisses was a no go.

"You ready for the return trip? Got your lines ready?" Terrance stood, his dark skin shining with sweat. He was sure-footed and relaxed, just inches from the cliff edge. Good climbers respected the mountain but were never intimidated by it. Nick stood and checked his gear.

"I'm ready if you are."

"Cool. Let's not race this time, okay? We won't be back here until next month, so try to enjoy it, man."

Nick nodded. His little self-talk had him settled down now where he could focus. From this point forward, he and Cassie were friends, and that kiss was an aberration that wouldn't be happening again.

"Nick, I swear to God, you're driving me crazy! I need my stapler!" Cassie slammed her desk drawer closed. She'd checked her desk twice and Blake's desk once. She'd looked on the coffee counter and the storage cabinets and the empty office by the door. She'd pulled the curtains completely open, and checked under the air-conditioning unit. She'd gone through Nick's office once while he was meeting with Tim in the surveillance room and was ready to toss it again, whether Nick was in there or not. And he was. Smirking at her from his desk chair, twirling his pen innocently.

She stood in the doorway and folded her arms, glaring at him. He'd upped his prank game this week to whole new levels. The stapler, of course. But, with Blake out of town and just the two of them sharing the office suite, he'd gone all out. Her desk phone went missing on Monday, hidden behind the drapes. On Tuesday her tape *and* the stapler *and* her notebook were sitting on Blake's desk. Her wireless keyboard was tucked behind the coffeepot on Wednesday. Yesterday the stapler was *inside* the empty coffeepot. And today, when he knew damn well she had to put together presentation packets for Blake's investor meeting this weekend, the stapler was nowhere to be found.

"Is there a problem?"

"Yes. A big, stupid problem who needs to get a life. Where. Is. My. Stapler?"

He tossed his pen in the air and caught it. That devilish grin made her heart jump. Damn, he was sexy. And annoying, she reminded herself. An annoying friend and coworker who was like a big brother and she wasn't attracted to him at all. Nope. Not one bit. She hadn't been attracted to him yesterday in the gym when he taught her how to use her elbows to break free from being grabbed from behind. Which meant he'd had to grab her over and over again, insisting that she get it right. Nope. Not attracted at all.

He'd been cool as a cucumber all week. He'd brought up the kiss first thing Monday morning, assuring her that it wasn't going to be a problem between them, and they should forget it ever happened. It was nothing more than a Kissing Rock spell that had been broken as soon as they left the mountain. She'd felt a sting of disappointment that he could set it aside so easily after telling her he'd had a hard-on after kissing her, but his actions seemed to support his words. He'd been the same Nick he'd been the weeks before—joking, teasing, playing basketball with the foam ball, teaching her, clowning around with the staff.

It seemed Nick had moved on from their kiss with nothing more to show for it than a renewed enthusiasm for his job. And driving her crazy. He tossed his pen again, almost to the ceiling, and had to lean back to snatch it out of the air when it came down. She bit back a sigh of frustration. He'd wait her out until the offices closed if he had to.

"Where is it, Nick?"

"Where have you looked?"

Her eyes narrowed on him. She was done playing. She

reached for his desk and tried to take his cell phone, but he was too quick for her. He held it over his head and laughed.

"Seriously? You thought you'd outmaneuver a cop?"

"You're not a cop anymore, Nick. You're just the jackass who won't give me my stapler."

A frown flickered across his face. He didn't talk about his days on the LA police force. Amanda told Cassie last week she'd learned the beautiful woman in the wedding gown in the photo behind Nick was his former partner. And that she was dead.

He summoned a fresh smile and shook off whatever he'd been thinking about. "Check the coat closet. You might have to work for it this time."

"Wonderful. As if I'm not already working." She turned and went to the closet. She didn't see it at first. She looked up and saw the edge of the stapler barely peeking over the top shelf. She called over her shoulder as she rolled a desk chair to the closet. "Nice job, Nick. There's only an eighty percent probability this thing will bonk me on the head when I try to get it."

She was just putting her foot on the chair and praying it would stay put when she felt Nick's arm around her waist, pulling her back. "Are you actively trying to kill yourself? You can't stand on a chair with wheels." He sent the chair rolling back to the empty desk. "I'll get it. I didn't think about it hitting you, but you're right…" He stretched and worked the stapler off the shelf with his fingertips, while still holding her waist with his other arm. Her skin was tingling, but he seemed unaffected. "If it was going to happen to anyone, it'd happen to you. Here." He handed her the stapler, then rubbed his knuckles in her hair. Like she was his kid sister. Like she was a puppy. Like he had no desire for her whatsoever. And it ticked her off.

She swatted his hand away. "Here's an idea—stop hiding the damn thing! You're not a twelve-year-old, Nick, and this isn't grade school. What's next? Putting gum in my hair? This is an *office*. You said you wanted to keep things professional between us, so why don't you surprise me and actually *act* professional for once?"

"Whoa...easy!" Nick held up both hands in surrender. "What just happened?"

It was a fair question, but she wasn't in the mood to answer it.

"Nothing. I've just got actual work to do, Nick. And I'm pretty sure you do, too." She brushed past him and went back to sit at her desk. He closed the closet door and studied her, but she refused to make eye contact. She didn't trust her feelings right now, especially with the traitor tears threatening to spill over. What was *wrong* with her? Hadn't she decided that being friends was better than trying to follow up on that kissing business and possibly ruining everything? Wasn't that exactly what she'd agreed to on Monday—pretend the kiss didn't happen? Nick not being attracted to her was the best possible scenario. Besides, apparently the kiss really *had* been just a fluke for him, and that whole "chemistry lab on fire" that made him want a cold shower was a momentary phenomenon that had clearly passed. She was no longer the woman whose kisses made him hot and bothered. She was just a girl he liked to tease, whose hair he liked to noogie.

Nick walked over and sat on the corner of her desk, facing her. "Come on, kiddo, what's going..."

Kiddo?

She was on her feet in a flash.

"I'm not your *kiddo* or your *grasshopper* or anything else." And that was the truth. She wasn't anything else to him. And that was a *good* thing, damn it.

"What the hell is wrong with you today?" He took her arm, but she pulled away. She was losing it. She needed to get away from him before she burst into tears or threw herself into his arms. Either one would be a huge mistake.

"I need to go." She looked at the clock on the wall. "I'm taking an early lunch."

"Early lunch? It's not even eleven..." She glared at him and he stepped back, shaking his head. "Okay! Early lunch. Maybe we can talk this out later."

She nodded mutely, grabbed her purse and headed out the door.

CHAPTER TEN

CASSIE HEADED FOR the lakeside path, hoping to avoid other humans for a while. It felt like something had just snapped inside her back in the office. Something that had been simmering since Saturday when she and Nick kissed up on the mountain that now rose above her, reflected in the water. When he slid his arm around her waist by the closet, everything she'd felt on Gallant Mountain had come rushing back. The heat, the liquid desire, the way his lips felt on hers, the sensation when he lifted her into the air and she'd looked down into his eyes, with the lake beyond him.

How could Nick deny what happened up there? How could he just continue to tease and taunt and touch her as if nothing had changed, when she knew she'd be forever changed? If nothing else, she'd learned she was capable of feeling not just desire, but as if *she* was *desirable*. Not a trophy on a shelf like Don treated her. But a woman who could appeal to a man like Nick West. Could make him want her. And damn it, she *knew* she'd made him want her, even if only for that moment.

To her, the sensation had been new and transformative. But Nick had kissed plenty of women in his life. She'd probably just been one more on a long list of fun little interludes he could easily forget. She slowed her pace, pausing to stare out over the water.

If that was the case, then it wasn't fair to be angry with him. He'd moved on because he'd had practice at moving on. And if he could do it, so could she. It would just take her a little longer. Like forever. She laughed softly to herself. *Stop being melodramatic.*

She was getting stronger. Smarter. Tougher. And Nick was the guy who'd helped her get there. Even when he didn't mean to. Sure, he taught her self-defense. But he also gave her noogies and hurt her feelings and kissed her senseless and hid her damn stapler. It seemed that *everything* Nick did made her stronger. And she couldn't be mad about that. She turned to head back to the resort. All she needed to figure out now was how to explain her little meltdown to Nick so they could continue as…friends. Wise, experienced, worldly friends who kissed one afternoon and were strong enough to move on without causing a ripple in their relationship.

Nick was gone when she walked into the office. Her stapler sat in the center of her desk, next to a vase filled with hydrangeas. They looked suspiciously similar to the blue hydrangeas near the back veranda of the resort. Stolen daffodils had gone out of season. She picked up the note he'd left, in his usual hurried scribble that made it seem the words were ready to dash right off the page.

Your stapler looked sad, so I thought it might like some "borrowed" company. I forgot I have that meeting with the staffing firm in White Plains this afternoon. Let's start fresh tomorrow, and I'll give you a proper apology? —Nick

She smiled. He was a hard man to stay mad at. She'd forgotten all about the meeting in White Plains. They used temporary staff for large events, and Nick was training the company on proper security procedures. He'd be there all afternoon. Maybe it was for the best that they were going to have a little time apart. It would give her a chance to get her mind straight and put Nick firmly in the friend zone again. If he could move on from that kiss, well, then, so could she.

"Hey, Cassie! I'm so glad you're here." Julie came into the office. "Blake called a little while ago, but you and Nick were both gone." Julie gave her a pointed look, and Cassie rushed to set her straight.

"Nick's on his way to a meeting. I took an early lunch." She should have made sure the office was staffed. It wasn't like her to forget such a basic thing as making sure calls were handled. "I'm sorry. I should have let you know I was stepping out. What did Blake need?"

Julie looked flustered. "His flight is delayed, so he won't be here until almost midnight, and the welcome reception for the investors is tonight. Amanda offered to play hostess for dinner, but he wanted us to help her out for a few hours. He figured the group would go party on their own at the bar after that. Can you join us?"

Cassie frowned. A party with a bunch of powerful people she didn't know was not her idea of a good time. But she owed it to her friends and her boss to do her best. Besides this was new, improved Cassie—she was strong enough to do this. She put her hand on Julie's arm.

"I'll run home later and change into something dressy, and I'll be back in time for dinner."

Julie grinned. "You're a champ, Cassie! And after dinner, maybe you and Amanda and I can have a few Friday night cocktails together."

"Yeah, maybe." She had no intention of doing that, but Julie seemed so excited at the idea that Cassie didn't want to burst her bubble. She was sure she'd be so exhausted from pretending to be an extrovert and entertaining important investors over dinner that she'd beg off later with an excuse and head home.

But it ended up being a more relaxing evening than she'd anticipated. The four representatives from the investment firm were older, extremely professional and actually pretty interesting. The one woman in the group, Margaret Ackerman, was a book lover like Cassie, and they ended up discussing their favorite women's fiction while Amanda and Julie talked sports and travel with the three gentlemen. It made for an enjoyable meal. When the dessert plates had been cleared and the investors had gone off to their rooms to rest up for the early round of golf Blake had arranged for them, Cassie found herself with no viable excuse not to join the other women at the bar. After all, that's what girlfriends did, right?

Besides, she was eager to shake off her emotional morning with Nick. As happy as she was with her new plan to follow his example and just be buddies, there was a restlessness humming inside her. Her senses were on high alert, sending images of Nick's intense dark eyes through her mind. She could hear the breeze rustling through the trees up on Gallant Mountain, and the low growl in Nick's chest as he kissed her. She could feel his hands on her waist, lifting her into the air without breaking their kiss. She could smell the pines...

"Can I have another?" She blurted out the words as the bartender, Josie, passed by.

"Easy, girl! You're already on your second Gallant Lake Sunset." Amanda laughed.

Cassie shrugged. "Hey, it's just orange juice, right? And a little honey liqueur?"

Julie held her empty wineglass up to let Josie know she needed a refill. "And vodka. Don't forget the vodka that's in there. But don't worry, I can drive you home later."

Amanda looked at Julie's wineglass. "Isn't it customary for the designated driver to abstain from alcohol? Cass, there's always a room open at Halcyon, and it's right next door." Amanda and Blake lived in an actual castle, built on the lake over a hundred years ago. The place had at least ten bedrooms. But she didn't feel drunk at all. She checked her phone.

"It's only nine thirty, ladies, and this drink isn't that strong. I'll stop at three drinks and be done. Now, Julie, finish telling

us about this old farmhouse you bought." Julie was more than
happy to oblige, describing the adventures she'd already had
with the old house outside town. Cassie sat back and sipped
her drink. This was part of the girlfriend game that she could
get used to. Listening to women laugh and share their joys and
frustrations together. It was much nicer when *she* wasn't the
topic of conversation.

She was halfway through her fourth Sunset by the time the
conversation started to wind down. The drinks were sweet and
tasty and proved very effective at helping her forget all that
earlier confusion about…what's-his-name. They helped her be
better at girl talk, too. She giggled at Julie's stories about the
leaky roof and sagging floors at the old house she'd bought.
She laughed at Amanda's description of her young daughter,
Maddie, throwing a tantrum at preschool because their nap
time was on yoga mats, not "real" beds with lacy canopies like
she had at home.

"That's one of the reasons we wanted her in preschool as
early as possible," Amanda explained. "We're not *intentionally*
spoiling her, but the kid lives in a castle, and Blake and Zach-
ary dote on her every whim."

"And you don't?" Cassie winked at Julie, who was holding
back laughter.

"No! I mean…not on purpose. But you guys, she's so damn
cute. And smart. Way too smart." Amanda yawned. "And that
busy brain likes to wake up early, so I'd better get home. It'll
be midnight by the time Blake gets here from LaGuardia, and
he won't want to get up with her. Cassie, you're coming with
me, right?"

They all stood, but Cassie was the only one who had to reach
out and grab the edge of the bar to steady herself. The room
wasn't exactly spinning, but it wasn't staying still, either.

Julie shook her head. "I tried to tell you mixed drinks will
get you every time. Stick to wine or beer, girl. I'll drive her
home, Amanda. I switched to water a while ago." Amanda

looked skeptical, but Julie closed her eyes and touched her fingers to her nose while standing on one foot. She didn't stop until Amanda gave in.

"Fine! Text me once she's inside, since I don't think *she'll* remember to do it."

Cassie frowned. Her face felt funny, almost like she couldn't quite feel her own mouth moving. "*She* is standing right here between the two of you. I know I had too much to be able to drive, but I'm not exactly wasted." She turned and gave Amanda her most serious look, which, for some reason, made Amanda giggle. "And I *will* remember to text you when I'm home. Mom."

"Yeah, yeah, laugh all you want at the responsible adult trying to keep everyone safe. That's fine. I'm outta here." Amanda gave them each a quick, fierce hug and headed out of the bar. Halcyon was a short walk up the hill, and Cassie saw Bill Chesnutt heading toward the boss's wife to escort her up to their home. She'd be fine.

"I have to get my stuff from the back office," Julie said, "and hit the ladies' room. Meet you by the staircase in five minutes?" Julie side-eyed Cassie as they headed out into the lobby. "Are you going to throw up or anything? Because my car has leather seats, and…"

"I am *not* going to throw up! I'm not drunk. I'm…tipsy. And I'm very much enjoying this rare and precious little buzz, so you buzz on out of here and do whatever." She looked across the lobby. "Maybe I'll go get a cup of tea."

Nick watched the two women from the top of the lobby stairs. He couldn't believe it. Cassie Smith was *drunk*? No, not drunk. *Tipsy.* She called it a "precious little buzz." Cassie was damn cute when she was buzzed.

He'd spent the afternoon in meetings and training sessions, but she'd been on his mind the entire time. She'd been really upset with him that morning. Things had been so good all week, after they agreed to pretend that kiss on Saturday never happened. He might have been a little more of a pest than usual, but he was only trying to show her that nothing was going to be weird or awkward just because they'd slipped up and kissed a few times. By accident. When he'd given her that little noogie today, it was just to emphasize how totally cool they were. But something had set her off, and she'd hissed at him like she'd done that very first day, when she sent the stapler flying at his face. And then she'd...well, he was pretty sure she'd almost... cried. Over *him*. It had bugged him all afternoon.

He tucked his planner under his arm and descended the staircase. The planner was more an excuse than anything else. It was a reason to paddle over to the resort tonight. Via the kayak he was thinking of buying.

The short, sturdy kayak he'd brought from California was designed for white water. And while there was some of that around, especially farther north in the Adirondacks, it wasn't the best for lake paddling. On lakes, the longer kayaks gave a faster, smoother ride. The only problem with this one, which the hardware store owner, Nate Thomas, was selling, was that it was a little *too* long. It was a two-person kayak, and Nick wasn't sure he wanted that, even if the extra seat could come in handy for carrying a cooler or other supplies. But he wasn't planning on paddling out on a three-day trip anywhere. And it wouldn't sit on the Jeep very well if he ever wanted to travel with it. He'd pretty much talked himself out of buying it before he put it in the water.

But the sleek vessel had cut through the water like a hot knife through butter tonight on the journey from his house to the resort, and was stable and easy to handle. He just never expected the trip to end with Cassie giggling and weaving across the lobby in front of him. At eleven o'clock at night. He frowned. How were these two women planning on getting home?

Her hair was pulled back, as usual, but tonight it was held in place with sparkly clips behind her ears. She was wearing a dress instead of her usual slacks and sweater. The dark gold dress, swirling above her knees, was loose and fluttery. The fabric followed her curves when she moved. Her smile was a little crooked, and a lot adorable, as she watched Julie walk away. She headed for the coffee bar—definitely a good idea in her condition—and swayed only a little.

She was so intent on opening her tea bag packet and actually getting the bag *inside* the cup that she jumped when he walked up behind her.

"Pulling an all-nighter, Miss Smith?"

"Nick! What are you doing here? And why are you dressed like..."

She gestured to his attire, which he'd forgotten about. Battered cargo shorts and a well-worn T-shirt from Yosemite. A ball cap sat backward on his head, and he quickly grabbed it off and ran his fingers through his hair, tucking the cap in his back pocket.

"I'm more interested in why you're so dressed up. What was the occasion?"

Her brows furrowed, then she looked down at her dress.

"Oh! This? Uh... Blake's flight was delayed and Amanda needed Julie and me to help entertain some investors who arrived today."

"And how exactly did you entertain them?" Had she been hanging out at the bar with sleazebag bankers all night?

She rolled her eyes. "We had *dinner* with them, Nick. No self-defense moves required. Then we decided we deserved a girls' night out and went to the bar. And I had my first Gallant Lake Sunset. Well..." She smiled and shrugged. "I had my first four Gallant Lake Sunsets."

"You had *four* drinks? And you think you're driving home?"

She turned away from him, finally managing to get the tea bag inside the cup. She filled it with hot water and added her usual three packets of sugar. Her voice turned prim. "That's not really your concern, is it? After all, we're just coworkers.

Just friends. So go on and do whatever it is you're doing, and don't worry about me."

She said "just friends" as if it was an accusation. It was what they'd *both* agreed to Monday morning. Unless maybe she wanted more? That possibility had Nick once again reciting all the reasons they shouldn't. Coworkers. Baggage. And... What was the last one? The memory of how she felt in his arms was short-circuiting his ability to focus. He forced himself to be the responsible one.

"I heard somewhere that friends don't let friends drive drunk, so I have every right to ask how you're getting home."

She heaved a dramatic sigh. "Fine. If you must know, Julie's driving me."

Nick couldn't help laughing. "The same Julie who was drinking with you and Amanda? Where is Amanda, anyway?" The last thing he needed was for the boss's wife to get in trouble under his watch.

"She went home. And before you ask, no, she didn't drive, and yes, Bill walked her to Halcyon. There he is right now." She gestured toward the main entrance and took a sip of her tea.

Bill saw them and headed their way at the same time Julie did.

"What's up, boss? I just walked Mrs..."

"Yeah, I know. Thanks." Nick fixed his gaze on Julie. "Are you in any shape to drive?"

"Sure. I had water for the last round, so I should be good." She pushed her short brown hair behind her ear and gave him a confident smile.

"But the multiple rounds before that were not water, right?"

"Yeah, but it was only wine. I wasn't pounding the cocktails like Little Miss Cassie here. That's why I'm driving her home."

Nick looked at Bill, who sighed and nodded in agreement with the unspoken request. He turned back to Julie. "No, you're not. Even if you feel sober, there's no way you'd pass a Breathalyzer, and Dan doesn't seem like the type of cop to let that slide." Nick had met the local sheriff's deputy, Dan Adams, for lunch last week to discuss security measures at the resort. The guy seemed like a stand-up cop who cared about his community, and the community returned the sentiment. Everyone called him Sheriff Dan. "Julie, Bill's gonna drive you home."

She opened her mouth to object, but thought better of it.

Cassie spoke up. "What about me?"

"I'll get you home." He didn't mention it would be via kayak, but once they got back to his place, he'd put her in the Jeep and drive her to her apartment. Just like any good friend would do.

It was a sign of how much alcohol she'd had that she followed him out the back door of the resort without question. It wasn't until they were halfway down the lawn that she realized where they were headed.

"Wait. This isn't the parking lot. Where are we going?"

"I came here by boat. It'll only take a few minutes to get to my place and the Jeep."

"Oh. Okay. A boat ride sounds fun."

It wasn't until they got to shore and he pointed her in the direction of the long kayak that she balked.

"That's not a boat, it's a canoe!"

"It's not a canoe, it's a kayak."

"It has no motor!"

"*I'm* the motor. Don't worry about it. You sit up front and I'll have us back to my place in no time."

"Will it hold both of us without sinking?"

"It won't sink, trust me."

"But it's pitch-black out there! No one will see us if we drown. Will it tip over?"

"Not if you behave yourself. Come on, slip your shoes off and I'll help you get in."

That effort was a little tricky between her dress and alcohol consumption, but he finally got her settled and pushed off the beach, hopping in behind her. She squealed when the kayak rocked, and made a move to jump out.

"Sit!" He barked out the word, and she froze. "Stay still and trust me, okay?"

She didn't answer, but she did settle back into her seat, tense but curious.

"So you've done this before? Kayaked in the dark?" She hesitated. "With a girl?"

"I've competed in white-water kayak races, and I've kayaked in four different countries. And yes, I have been out on some waters with just the light of the moon to guide me."

She turned so quickly he had to steady the craft with the paddle. "But have you been with a *girl* after dark?"

Was shy little Cassie *flirting* with him right now? He needed to get her tipsy more often.

"I've been with plenty of girls after dark."

"But in a *kayak*?"

"No, sweetie, you're my first."

She did a fist pump that had him resting the paddle in the water again to steady the vessel.

"Yes! I'm your first!" A weird something fluttered in his chest.

"Turn around and sit still, will you? I'm trying to keep this thing upright."

She turned as requested, dropping her hand to run her fingertips through the moonlit water. But she wasn't done being playful.

"Are you really worried you can't keep it upright, Nick?"

He swallowed hard and didn't answer. This woman would have no problem keeping him "upright." He was almost there now. He put a little more effort into paddling, and the kayak started slicing through the water. The light on the back of his rental house was glowing bright. He angled them toward shore.

Cassie sat back, looking up at the moon as her fingers traced in and out of the water. Her voice was low and soft, as if she was talking to herself.

"It's beautiful out here."

Another big swallow for Nick, his eyes never leaving her. "Yes, it is."

She was so quiet the rest of the way that he thought she might be nodding off. The alcohol was probably catching up to her. He wasn't prepared when, as he was nearing the shoreline, she sat up and moved to leave the kayak.

"Oh! We're here! I'll help pull the boat in…"

"No! Cassie!"

She didn't do a bad job of holding her body up and swinging her legs over the kayak before dropping into the water. The problem was, even though they were only fifteen feet offshore, the water was still over four feet deep. Cassie's eyes went wide as she kept going, not hitting bottom until the cold water was up to her chest. She grabbed at the kayak, tilting it wildly. He struggled for a moment to keep it steady, then realized he had no choice but to get wet if he was going to get her safely out of the water without flipping the boat. He emptied his pockets and dived in, grabbing the kayak line with one hand when he came up and Cassie with the other.

"Come on, you goofball. Out of the lake and inside the house."

She was sputtering and starting to shiver.

"I thought you were driving me home?"

"Yeah, well, that was before you decided to take us for a chilly swim. We both need to get warm and dry first." She didn't argue, the night air cold on their wet skin. He pulled the kayak up and onto the lawn, then took her arm and led her inside.

CHAPTER ELEVEN

MOST OF CASSIE'S alcohol-induced glow popped like a bubble when she hit the cold water of Gallant Lake. She'd watched Nick wade several yards offshore at the resort in knee-deep water. When she saw how close to shore they were at his place, she figured she'd be helpful—the level of her helpful ability probably inflated by cocktails—and bring the kayak in. It wasn't as much the cold as it was that moment of terror as she kept going and wondered if she'd ever hit bottom that sobered her up in a hurry. By the time her feet hit bottom, she was soaked up to her breasts, the gold dress clinging to her and turning nearly transparent.

She followed Nick up the steps to the deck behind his cute little rental house. As soon as they were inside, he grabbed a blanket from the back of the sofa and wrapped it tightly around her.

"Hang on and I'll get some towels." He saw her head-to-toe shiver and frowned. "On second thought, maybe you should go take a hot shower to warm up. I've got a shirt you can put on after, and some sweats."

She shook her head sharply. "I can shower at home."

"I know that." He took her shoulders and turned her toward the hall. "But you're cold and wet *now*, and we're not heading to your place right away because I am *also* cold and wet. Go on, and I'll bring you dry things. I'll shower in my room." He gave her a light push toward the bathroom door, reaching in front of her to turn on the light.

And just like that, she was alone in the bathroom. She waited for him to return with dry clothes before peeling off her cold dress, then locked the door and stepped into the shower. The blast of hot water killed any remaining intoxication, but she still felt...something. To be here in his house, naked, even if it was behind a locked door, felt exciting. Which was silly. But she couldn't deny what she felt. It was the same sensation she'd had on the mountain last weekend. It was desire. She moved the washcloth slowly over her skin, closing her eyes and pretending it was Nick's hands she felt. And really... What harm was there in that? She'd been without male company for a long time now, and her own fingers could do only so much. She was ready for more. And maybe a little sexy time with a player like Nick West was the solution. He'd just bragged about how many women he'd been with after dark. Why couldn't she be one of them? And then this itch would be scratched and maybe *then* they could be just friends.

She lost track of time as she let the hot steam seep into her skin. It was after midnight, but she felt wide awake. Maybe she could come up with a plan to keep Nick from taking her home tonight. Eventually she turned off the water and dried off. She slipped into Nick's sweats and shirt, both woefully too big on her, and stepped out of the bathroom. The house was quiet, and she had no sense of where Nick might be. She checked the kitchen and living area first, but it was empty. She headed farther down the hall, finding an empty guest bedroom and then Nick's room.

The only light was from the attached bathroom. Nick was on the bed, as if he'd stretched out there to wait for her. He'd showered, because his hair was rumpled and wet. He was sound asleep, one arm behind his head, the other resting on his bare chest, rising and falling in slow, deep breaths. She shook her head and sighed. So much for her big plans. He'd had a long day, and it had clearly caught up with him. She pulled his blanket up to cover him, but not before admiring his chest, cut with muscle and highlighted with a fine layer of dark hair that trailed down to vanish beneath his shorts. She wanted to reach out and touch him, but she was afraid of waking him, so she covered him and went to stretch out on the sofa to sleep.

Nick woke her two hours later. "Cass, what are you doing? Are you okay?"

"Uh…yeah. I was sleeping. Are *you* okay?"

He ran his fingers through his dark hair, leaving it standing even more on end than it was to start with. "Did I fall asleep while you were showering? Damn, I'm sorry. Why don't you use the spare room and I'll run you home in the morning. Or I can take you now if you want…"

Cassie shrugged off the blanket and stood. She'd been dreaming about Nick and now he was there in front of her. The hum she'd felt before was still moving under her skin. She put her hand on Nick's chest, sad that he'd slipped on a T-shirt before coming to find her. He sucked in a sharp breath.

"What are you doing?"

"What do you think I'm doing?" She moved closer, and his eyes darkened. "Let's face it, Nick. The whole 'just friends' thing isn't going to work if we're both wondering what we'd be like together. That kiss last Saturday promised some things that don't fit in the friend zone."

He set his hand over hers. "Cassie, you've been drinking, and…"

"That was hours ago, and the dunk in the cold lake pretty much took care of it. Any liquor left in my system after that was washed away in the shower. I'm perfectly sober." She was also tired, and steadfastly ignoring that ever-present "be careful" voice in her head. If she woke up too much…if she thought about this too much… She'd never go through with it. She pushed onto her toes and pressed her lips against his. He didn't react at first, but it wasn't long before he let out a low sound and slid his arm around her, pulling her tight as he took over the kiss, pushing his way into her mouth to let her know he was on board with this plan of hers.

"Are you sure?" he asked softly as he left her mouth and trailed kisses along her jawline.

She made a sound of some kind. It wasn't a word, really, but he understood it was her assent. He looked down at her with a crooked smile. "Here or in my bed?"

The sofa had been fine for sleeping, but she wanted something a little more special than a thirty-year-old pine-and-plaid sofa that had clearly been included in the lease. She took his hand and started down the hall with him obediently behind her. She could feel his amused smile, and who could blame him? It was pretty rare for her to take charge of anything, especially sex. After all, with Don...

She stopped so fast in the doorway that Nick brushed up against her, resting his hands on her shoulders. Her bravado was fading fast. If tonight was just an attempt to erase Don's hold on her, it wouldn't be fair to Nick. Could something ever be good if it was done for the wrong reason? Doubts started a whispering campaign in her head. What if it wasn't good at all? What if she couldn't please him?

Her mind was racing and blank all at the same time. This was it. The moment of truth. She focused on the electricity she felt through Nick's fingertips on the bare skin at the base of her neck and took a deep breath, still staring straight ahead.

"Nick, I want this. I really do. It's just that..." Her shoulders sagged as she felt her confidence waning. "I'm not exactly experienced... I mean, I've only been with two men in my whole life." She gave a short laugh. "The first was my college boyfriend, which was hardly memorable. The second was...well... memorable for all the wrong reasons... I'm not very good at this sex stuff. I don't want to disappoint you..."

Before she could continue, Nick kissed the back of her neck, setting her body on fire.

"My beautiful Cassandra..." She tensed at the name. Nick didn't know it wasn't really hers. There was so much he didn't know. He continued to softly kiss her neck and shoulders as he spoke. "I have two important things to say to you. First, nothing that's happened before tonight—before right this instant—matters at all. Second..." Nick's kisses moved up her neck and toward her left ear. Cassie tilted her head to expose more of her skin to his lips as he continued. "Second... We are very definitely *not* having 'sex stuff' tonight. That's what teenagers do the in the back seat of their dad's Buick. If you walk through that door, I am going to give you a night like you've never experienced before."

With that, Nick gently turned Cassie so they were facing each other. He rested his forehead on hers and spoke again, staring straight into her wide eyes. "But Cassie, you're going to have to walk through that door on your own."

She felt every cell in her body singing to her to make the move.

...nothing that's happened before tonight matters at all...

She smiled and turned, lifting her chin and stepping through the doorway with determination. She walked to the center of the room, near the foot of the bed, and turned to face Nick. He was still in the doorway, with his hands resting on each side of the door frame. His coffee-colored hair fell across his forehead. His gaze was intense, his eyes so dark they were nearly black. He looked so damned sexy she thought she'd swoon right then and there.

Cassie didn't flinch from the desire she saw in his eyes. When he stepped into the room, Cassie let out the breath she didn't realize she'd been holding. He walked to her slowly, and she didn't back away. She felt no fear, had no second thoughts. She wanted this.

He folded her into his arms and kissed her. She gave as

good as she got, standing on tiptoe to push against him as their tongues teased and danced together. Nick reached down and lifted the hem of her borrowed sweatshirt. She stepped away to allow him to pull it over her head, shimmying out of the loose sweatpants at the same time.

Maybe she should have felt insecure as she stood naked before him for the first time, but...no. She felt self-assured. She felt beautiful. Nick made her feel beautiful, with his dark stare and the upward curve at the edge of his mouth. He was already making love to her with his eyes, and she reveled in it.

With one smooth motion, he peeled his shirt off over his head. Cassie was more than happy to have another chance to admire his broad shoulders and the sharply defined six-pack. He was one fine specimen of a man.

He lifted her into his arms. She embraced his neck and placed her lips on his. The kiss was full of lust and need. He laid her on top of the sheets, then stepped away to shed his shorts. Nick walked to the bed and placed one knee on the edge of the mattress. He looked into her eyes and she knew he was looking for permission. She granted it with a barely perceptible nod.

She could feel his gaze sweeping across her skin, and it made her blood burn with need. When his eyes reached hers, he fell on her like a starving man falls on an all-you-can-eat buffet.

They were consumed by the heat of their desire. Their hands ran over each other's bodies frantically. Nick's kisses began on her forehead and ran down her neck and chest. He paused along the way to trace her breasts with his lips, as light as a whisper, before he went across her abdomen, then ever lower. Cassie's nervous anticipation of everything that was to come had her writhing in excitement before he even reached his goal. His fingertips were tracing the same trail around her breasts that his lips had just followed. She moaned, her eyes closed as his mouth settled on her most private and sensitive place. She tried to resist letting herself go too soon, but failed. Loudly. He was too damned good at what he was doing, and she fell hard.

Now it was Nick's turn to moan as he continued, ignoring Cassie's pleas for mercy as she continued to move under his onslaught. He stopped only to tear open a condom wrapper grabbed from the nightstand, then he followed his own trail of kisses back up to her lips. Her legs curled around his torso, and she cried out his name when he entered her. She dug her fingernails into his back, causing him to grunt in response. His muscles rippled under her fingers.

They both felt a driving sense of urgency. The sheets wrapped around them as they moved across the bed. At one point, Nick grasped Cassie tightly and rolled so that she was astride him. She braced herself with her arms beside his shoulders. They stopped moving momentarily and she looked down at him. Her hair fell wildly around her face. She felt giddy with power.

Nick smiled up at her. "You seem pleased with yourself, ma'am."

Cassie gave a throaty laugh. "Oh, I am very pleased indeed. I'm even *more* pleased to see that I'm pleasing you."

"Oh, you are definitely doing that, babe."

They smiled slyly at each other as if they were both in on some very special secret. Nick put his hand securely on her back and rolled so that she was lying under him again, without breaking their bond. He kissed her gently and began to press into her at an increasing pace. Cassie felt the room spinning as her body responded yet again. She closed her eyes and arched her back. As she did, Nick slid his arm under her and lifted her lower body up into the air as he rose to his knees. And that was it for her. She cried out and let herself fly.

Nick shouted her name roughly and dropped her back to the bed, setting his teeth on the tender skin at the base of her throat as he drove on to his own release. His face dropped over her shoulder into the pillow beneath her. They lay in that position for several minutes, their deep breaths the only sound in the room.

As Nick's body weight pressed down on Cassie, she finally

had to react. She tapped the front of his shoulder and softly said, "Nick, you have to move."

"No." He muttered it into her hair without flinching. "You destroyed me. I can't move."

"Yeah, well, I can't breathe, so you're going to have to move or listen to me suffocate."

Nick groaned loudly and rolled to lie at her side, with one arm draped over her ribs as he got rid of the condom with the other. Cassie put her hand on her chest and felt the sheen of sweat on her skin. Her heart was pounding.

Nick covered her hand with his. She turned away from him, pressing her back against his chest. He pulled her tight and kissed the base of her neck.

"I'm a shell of a man right now. I knew we had a physical attraction going on, but...damn, girl! That was some wickedly world-class sex."

Cassie smiled in contentment. "I didn't even know there *could* be sex like that, Nick. If this house were on fire right now, I wouldn't have the strength to move, much less stand or run."

Nick laughed softly, his mouth near her ear. "Then we'd burn together, babe, because I can't move, either. Now go to sleep. You're safe in my arms. Just go to sleep..." His voice was fading as he spoke.

When she woke, the digital clock on the side of the bed read 4:28 a.m. She'd rolled over onto her stomach in her sleep, and someone's fingers were lightly tracing up and down her spine. She lifted her head and Nick, propped up on one elbow, smiled down at her softly.

"So," he said, "it wasn't a dream."

Cassie stretched like a cat, turned on her side to face him and returned his smile. "Felt pretty dreamy to me."

He reached out and brushed Cassie's hair behind her ear. "There's only one problem. It left me wanting more."

"Really? I seem to have the same problem..."

Cassie leaned forward and kissed him, sliding her arm around his neck. Without saying another word, they made love again. But this time, it was less frantic, less desperate. They took things slow and easy. There was no crying out of names, only sighs and whispers and soft moans as they caressed each other, exploring each other's bodies with their fingers and lips. Eventually they brought each other to a sweet and tender release that left them both trembling. Cassie fell asleep clasped tightly in Nick's embrace, and she felt more secure and protected than she'd ever felt in her life.

It couldn't last, of course. She'd kept secrets from him. Big ones. They were just two grown-ups scratching an itch and all that.

But Cassie couldn't shake the illogical but powerful conviction that here, in Nick's arms, was exactly where she belonged.

CHAPTER TWELVE

NICK SLIPPED OUT of bed shortly after dawn. Cassie turned and murmured something unintelligible, then settled back to sleep. He watched her for a moment, then walked away. He needed to clear his head.

He thought maybe last night would be a resolution of their "chemistry" issue. But he'd been a fool to think one night with Cassie would ever be enough. He'd seen enough addicts on the street to know that for some, all it took was one time—one hit—and they were hooked. That's how he felt. Just one night with Cassie, and he was toast. Her kiss had ruined him for all other kisses, and making love with her had destroyed him for all other women.

What did it mean, though? Was there any chance in hell of them having a relationship that wouldn't make a mess of both their work life *and* their friendship? Was she even interested in a relationship? Or was last night enough for her? Maybe she'd explored their chemistry and found it wanting. Would that be a good thing? Or would it make the ache he felt in his chest just that much worse?

He took his cup from the coffee maker and gulped half of it, anxious to clear the fog in his head. He glanced around for his phone, then remembered he'd taken it out of his pocket before diving in the lake last night. Hopefully it was still in the kayak. He headed outside, where a gentle mist rolled across the smooth surface of the water.

The phone screen was lit up with messages, and something else was buzzing in the boat. Cassie's purse was still there, and her phone was going off, too. Had something happened at the resort? His phone chimed with an incoming call. Blake Randall. He frowned. *Something* was happening, that's for sure. Blake wouldn't call him this early on a Saturday morning otherwise.

"Blake? What's up?"

"I don't know, man. You tell me."

"I...what?"

Blake let out a sigh. "Just tell me if Cassie's with you, wherever you are."

"I... I'm home." Nick stalled. "Why are you asking about Cassie?"

"Julie said you were giving Cassie a ride home. But she's *not* home. Are you saying she's not with you?" Blake's tone sharpened with concern, and Nick had to come clean.

"She's here."

"Thank Christ." Blake's voice grew faint as he spoke away from the phone. "She's okay. She's with Nick." Amanda's voice was muffled in the background. Blake came back on the phone. "Did something happen? My wife's been texting and calling her all damn night. She was getting ready to call Dan Adams and report her missing. Was she scared to go home or something? She's not running, is she?"

"Running? Running where?" Nick grabbed Cassie's purse and headed back into the house, trying his best to catch up with this conversation.

"From Don. The asshole who almost killed her a couple years ago. Damn. She hasn't told you that yet, has she?" Blake paused. "Wait. If she wasn't scared to go home, then why is she at...?" Another pause. "Aw, hell. Are you two a *thing* now?"

Amanda's voice was much louder now. "I knew it!"

Blake shushed her. "So she's at your place because *why* exactly?"

Nick wasn't used to being grilled by his employer about whom he did or didn't sleep with.

"No offense, Blake, but I don't see how that's your concern. I'm sorry you two were worried, but Cassie's safely asleep and this won't affect our job performance on Monday."

Blake digested that for a minute, then agreed. "Fair enough, but I call BS on the job bit. It'll affect you at work, one way or the other." Amusement crept into his voice. "Just do your best to keep things cool, and don't hurt that woman or you'll have to deal with my wife *and* her cousins. Trust me when I say that won't be pretty."

"O-kay." This was one of those small-town things he'd have to get used to. People knew your business and took sides. In LA, they were too busy to care. Blake's voice dropped.

"Nick, now that my wife is out of the room, let me say one more thing. Cassie and Amanda have some stuff in common from their pasts, and you need to know about it before you go much further. If you're serious about her, you need to talk. If you're not serious about her, well… You're an idiot. She's a hell of a woman."

"Yeah. I know. Thanks."

After the call, Nick sat on the sofa and watched the lake wake up with Saturday action. At this hour, it was primarily local fishermen, drifting or trolling with their lines in the water, occasionally pulling in a fish. A blue heron strolled calmly along the shoreline, watching for minnows.

So Cassie had secrets. As a former cop, it bugged Nick that he didn't know that. Of course, he knew she'd been assaulted in a parking garage, and the incident made her hypervigilant. Maybe that's all Blake had been referring to. But Nick suspected there was a lot more to it than that. It was something Amanda had in common with her, but that information wasn't helpful, since Nick didn't know Amanda's past. Had she been a victim of some crime, too? Was everyone at the resort hiding some dark past, or was it simply overblown small-town drama?

"Good morning." He turned to see Cassie standing near the kitchen. She'd pulled on the sweatshirt he'd given her last night, and it fell off one shoulder to reveal a swath of white skin he suddenly hungered for. Secrets or not, he wanted her again.

"Good morning." He stood and headed into the kitchen to start breakfast. Keeping busy would settle his mind and make the situation less awkward. "Scrambled eggs and sausage okay?"

"Um, sure. Or I could go…"

"Do you want to go?"

She stared at the floor and shrugged. Insecure Cassie had returned. "I'll do whatever you prefer. I don't want to be in your way."

He'd learned that a blunt approach tended to snap Cassie out of this timid persona that always made him angry. Angry *for* her, not with her.

"What I'd prefer is you naked on the sofa while I cook, so I can enjoy the best view in town."

Her mouth dropped open and her face colored. Then she laughed, and he saw the spark of confidence return to her eyes.

"And what about *my* view? What would I get out of this deal?"

"I don't think nudity and frying pans go together very well, so you'll have to wait for your special view."

"Yeah, well—so will you. I'm going to go freshen up and see if my dress is salvageable. I left it hanging in the bathroom. I don't suppose you have any tea?"

"I think there's a box in the cupboard on the end."

Cassie found the green box and smiled. "English Breakfast. My favorite."

"I don't have a teapot."

"Don't need one. I'll run water through the coffee maker without putting a pod in there. That's how I do it at the office."

She dropped the tea bag into a mug, pressing the button with a grin. "I'm very resourceful."

The conversation was neutral. Normal, even. They were just a couple of adults, standing in the kitchen together. He had no shirt. She had no pants. Making breakfast. It was nice.

A sizzle from the stove brought his attention back to cooking, and by the time he looked up again, she was gone. She returned as he was plating the food, wearing a wrinkled, but dry, dark yellow dress. Her hair was pulled back into her usual ponytail. Her skin was radiant. Nick frowned. *Radiant?* Since when did he start using words like that? She took her plate to the small table by the windows. Since he met a woman like Cassandra.

They were almost done eating breakfast before he thought to tell her that Blake had called.

"Oh, God, I was supposed to text Amanda last night! I completely forgot. Where's my purse?" She jumped up from the table.

"Relax. She knows you're here and you're okay." He carried the plates and utensils to the kitchen, nodding at her purse as he passed it.

"Amanda knows I'm *here*? Oh, no. That means they all know..."

"They?"

"The cousins. Amanda, Nora and Mel are basically one unit. What one knows, they all know." She groaned. "I hope Nora didn't tell Aunt Cathy..." She scrolled through her phone, then hurriedly typed a message. It chirped a minute later, and her shoulders relaxed. "Amanda said Cathy doesn't know and she's off today anyway. She also said I have lots of 'splaining to do. Tomorrow's coffee meeting should be fun."

"Coffee meeting?" This was the problem with having a casual breakfast conversation with someone you didn't know all that well. There were too many blanks to fill in. Which reminded him that he had a few blanks he needed filled in sooner rather than later.

"We have coffee early on Sunday at Nora's café, before the after-church crowd starts filling up the place. Amanda insisted I join them, because she thinks I need friends." She frowned, and he had a feeling she'd said more than she'd intended.

"You don't have friends?" Nick finished cleaning the cooking pans and put them away. Cassie shrugged, looking everywhere but at him. "Cass?"

"Well... I'm fairly new to town, and it's not always easy to make new friends. Especially when you're a homebody like me."

"What about your friends in Milwaukee?"

She stiffened. "There weren't many. Not *any* that lasted past me leaving town." She gave him a bright, tense smile. "Like I said, I'm a homebody. Give me tea and a book and I'm happy."

"But you had a job there. Didn't you make friends at work?"

Nick knew how to read body language, and hers was screaming that she didn't want to have this conversation. He moved closer and put his hands on her shoulders, tipping her chin up with his thumbs.

"Hey, it's me. The guy you had wild-and-crazy sex with last night." The corner of her mouth twitched toward a smile, but her eyes were clouded. He bent over and kissed her.

It was supposed to be a quick kiss to jolt her into trusting him, but as soon as his lips touched hers, he forgot all about his motivation. He wanted more. His hands slipped behind her head and he kissed her hard and long. And damn if she didn't kiss him right back, matching him beat for beat. Her fingers buried in his hair, and she pressed her hips against him, creating an instant response. He pushed her against the wall and dropped his hands to cup her behind and hold her against his now-aching body. She hooked a leg around his, as if afraid he'd move away. Not a snowball's chance in hell. He lifted her up and slipped his hand under her dress, quickly moving past the lacy underwear he encountered.

She moaned his name, long and slow and rough, and he slid his mouth down her neck to nip at her throat, all the while moving his fingers inside her. She was grinding against him, and he was ready to lose his mind. It was broad daylight. They'd just had breakfast. He was supposed to be taking her home because everyone was so concerned about them being together. It was a mistake to keep this going. They worked together. They had baggage. She was keeping secrets. The back of her head hit the wall with a thud as she arched her body against him. That cold-shower list of excuses didn't work anymore. He knew what sex with her was like now, and when she shuddered in his arms and cried out as she came for him, he knew where they were going to end up.

"I want you. In my bed. Right now."

She dropped her head to his shoulder and nodded against him. It was all he needed. He scooped her into his arms and carried her down the hall. There was a flurry of clothing hitting the floor. He was so desperate to be inside her that he almost forgot protection. She laughed when he swore at the foil package, which didn't open anywhere near as fast as he needed it to. And finally, *finally*, they were connected and moving as one. It was fast and hard and hot and they both made the same strangled sound of ecstasy when they reached their goal together. He stayed over her, unable to look away from the sight of her hair splayed out on the mattress beneath her like a flame.

She pinched his side. "You gonna stay there all day?"

He bent down and kissed her. "Would you mind if I did?"

Her smile lost some of its light. "Real life is going to catch up with us sooner or later."

He nodded. "Yeah, this was a very nice but unexpected detour on our morning." He reluctantly left her softness and slid off the bed. "I'm going to shower, then I'll take you home. After we talk about what comes next."

CHAPTER THIRTEEN

WHAT COMES NEXT...

Cassie tried to sort out her poor, abused gold dress for the second time that morning, but it was hopeless. Somehow, it had been torn both near the neckline and under one arm. She couldn't blame Nick, because he hadn't undressed her. No, that was her, in a frenzy to get naked, who had torn the most expensive dress she owned. It was bad enough she'd be doing the walk of shame to her apartment in broad daylight, but to do it in a rumpled, water-stained and torn dress? With hopeless bed hair, kiss-swollen lips and a general haze of good-sex vibes in her eyes? Ugh. If the cousins saw her like this, she'd never hear the end of it.

...what comes next...

She glanced at the bedroom window. She could probably escape the upcoming conversation by climbing through it, but she had no idea how to get home from here. Like it or not, she was going to have to talk about "what comes next" with Nick. Sex last night was beyond her dreams. She'd thought she was going to have a night with a guy who kissed her senseless, and then she'd be able to move on. Easy-peasy. Sure, she'd expected it to be good. But being in bed—or against a wall—with Nick was more than good. It was...transformative. There wasn't a chance in hell either one of them would be able to pretend last night, or this morning, didn't happen.

So…what? A relationship? Bad idea. Despite her best efforts to pretend it wasn't the case, her life was a mess. At any moment she might have to pack up and run. If she and Nick were going to be more than just one night—and morning—he needed to know that. He needed to know everything.

She did her best to tame her hair back into a ponytail and found a clean black T-shirt in Nick's dresser. She pulled it over her dress and tied it into a knot at her hip. Not exactly a fashion statement, but it concealed the torn fabric and most of the wrinkles. She grinned at her reflection. If she pulled her ponytail over to the side of her head and teased it a little, she'd look like a flashback to *Flashdance*.

Nick apparently thought the same thing. He gave her a wide smile.

"Nice look. Are you off to the disco later?"

"I did the best I could. Maybe we should wait until after dark to take me home." It was bad enough the cousins knew she'd spent the night with Nick. The whole town would know it if she tried to sneak into her apartment in the center of town in an outfit straight out of the 1980s.

"That's your decision, babe. But first…" He patted the sofa cushion next to him. "We need to talk, Miss Smith."

"That's not my name." Not exactly the way she wanted to start this conversation, but the words just blurted out. Nick leaned forward and frowned.

"Your last name isn't Smith?"

She twisted her fingers together. She was in it now, and Nick deserved to know the truth.

"My last name isn't Smith. It's Zetticci. And my first name isn't Cassandra. It's Cassidy."

"Your name is Cassidy Zetticci. For real." He started to smile, as if he thought she might be pulling his leg. When she didn't respond, he realized it was no joke. "How did you manage to get past the resort's background check?"

"Really? *That's* the first question you have?"

He stared at the floor for a moment, his foot tapping anxiously. "I looked at your employee file." He glanced up and noted her surprise. "I look at *everyone's* files, Cassie. It's my job. You picked the most common surname in America to make yourself harder to find. Who's looking? Don?"

Now it was her turn to be surprised. "How do you know about Don?"

"Well, I didn't hear about him from *you*." He stood and paced by the windows. Carefully avoiding her. "Blake mentioned the name this morning, and it's not that hard to put together. He's the one who assaulted you, right?"

On which occasion?

"Yes."

Nick stopped, his brows furrowed.

"And now he's stalking you?"

"Yes."

"You were in a relationship with him?"

He was in full cop mode now.

"He was my husband."

Blake didn't move, yet Cassie could feel him backing away. His eyes went icy cold. His hands curled into fists, then quickly released. His mouth slid into a disapproving frown.

"You stayed married to a guy who beat you." He was no longer asking questions. He was accusing. And she didn't like it.

"I said he *was* my husband. Past tense."

"Did you leave the first time he hit you?"

"Am I a suspect in some crime here, Officer?"

He rubbed the back of his neck, his jaw sawing back and forth. He turned away, staring out the window toward the lake. She waited, not willing to give him any more information until she knew what he was thinking. Of all the reactions she'd anticipated, anger with *her* hadn't been one of them. He shoved his hands in his pockets and let out a long breath.

"I wasn't ready to hear that you were a victim of domestic violence. I thought it was some stranger..."

"Does it matter?"

"It shouldn't."

"No kidding. But it obviously does." She shook her head. "In the interest of full disclosure, he was a police officer. A patrolman."

Nick turned. "He was a *cop*?"

"Yes, Nick. He was a cop. Believe it or not, cops do bad stuff, too. Or are you going to stand behind your 'blue line' bullshit and deny that?"

They'd completely traded places now. She was the angry one, while Nick seemed chagrined.

"The blue line is a brotherhood, not a blindfold. It doesn't protect criminals."

She scoffed at that, remembering the lost friendships and lack of support from the police in Milwaukee after Don was charged. The roadblocks that were thrown up time and again as the district attorney put the case together. The mishandling of evidence that led to the retrial now pending. While Don remained free.

Nick took a step toward her, and she tensed. He stopped, reaching out to take her hands gently.

"Okay, let me rephrase that. It *shouldn't* be used to protect bad guys. I'm sorry. I... I have some history with domestic abuse victims as a detective. Some bad history." He gave her hand a squeeze and she looked up to meet his gaze.

The coldness was gone. She was once again looking at the man who'd whispered kisses across her ear when he thought she was asleep last night. The man she trusted. The corner of his mouth lifted into a half smile.

"Last week we agreed we both had baggage, Cass. I brushed it off as no big deal. But I'm beginning to suspect the things that led each of us to be in Gallant Lake are a little more connected than we imagined." He lifted her hand and pressed a kiss to her knuckles. "We had a deal that if you went hiking with me, then I was going to owe you a day of sitting quietly. Today's that day. Let's sit and talk."

"Actually, I think you said you owed me a day of doing whatever I wanted, and you're crazy if you think I want to talk about this."

"You can have the rest of the day to boss me around. But right now we need to talk. No assumptions. No grilling for answers. Okay?"

Her voice dropped to almost a whisper. "It makes me feel weak. Vulnerable. Stupid."

"Hey." Nick tipped her chin up with his finger. "I saw from the first moment we met that you were a fighter. Not weak. Not vulnerable. And definitely not stupid. So get those words out of your vocabulary. That's *him* talking, and you need to kick that asshole out of your head. Now I understand why you apologize and doubt yourself all the time, and that needs to stop."

"It's not that easy."

He pressed a soft kiss on her lips, and she welcomed the warmth of it. "Nothing worthwhile ever is."

They settled onto the sofa. She sipped her fresh cup of tea, stalling for time. Nick waited patiently, and she finally had to fill the silence with something. So she started at the beginning.

She told him how she'd always been a shy kid. Her parents had a volatile marriage and an even more volatile divorce. To avoid their arguments as a child, she'd stayed in her room and lost herself in books. She was good with numbers and awkward with people. Don was the opposite—outgoing, with the ability to charm everyone he met, from children to little old ladies.

She was working at an insurance company when Don came in to discuss an accident investigation involving one of their clients. She'd been fascinated by the handsome, blue-eyed blond in uniform. He looked like a Nordic god, and he paid attention to *her*. He was ten years older and had the kind of calm confidence she'd craved. She couldn't believe it when he asked her out for coffee.

He made it easy to want to be with him. He took her mom to the ballet, and he took her dad fishing on Lake Michigan. He was the first thing in years that her parents agreed on—they adored him. He treated Cassie like a princess, and if he was a little controlling, he'd always explain that it was only because he loved her so much and wanted the best for her. And she'd believed him. She'd married him, ignoring the little warning signs leading up to the big day.

"What kind of warning signs?" Nick reached over and took her hand.

"He made *all* the decisions about the wedding. Where. When. What I'd wear. Whom we'd invite—which did *not* include any of my friends from school or my coworkers. He started distancing me from my former life, told me I was 'too mature for that crowd.' He pressured me to be like the other, older police wives. I was so eager for his approval that I threw myself into it, not noticing I was leaving my life behind for his." She took another sip of tea, delaying the words that made her cringe with shame. "We'd been married a year when he hit me for the first time. I had a flat tire one night. A coworker changed it for me, but I was late getting home. Don accused me of lying and told me I must be cheating on him. It was so ridiculous that I laughed, and he slapped me. Hard."

Nick didn't say a word, but his grip tightened on her hand as she told him the rest. About Don's tearful apology. That time, and the next time, and the next time after that. The way he subtly made everything her fault. If only she wouldn't "provoke" him, he wouldn't lose control. The episodes were sporadic at first, and she thought he really meant it every time he said he'd never hurt her again.

But when he was passed over for sergeant, things took a darker turn. It was all her fault, of course. She'd distracted him

tended to be fraught with danger because they were so unpredictable. Did something happen? She reached out to touch his hand, but he flinched and she pulled back, hurt and confused. Never one to stay still for long, Nick got up and started pacing again. He rubbed his neck in agitation, coming to a stop but not making eye contact.

"I should probably get you back to your place." Her heart fell.

"That's all you have to say?"

He finally met her gaze, and she was shocked to see his eyes shining with…tears? She stood, and he blinked away from her as if he knew what she'd seen. This wasn't about her. This reaction of his may have been triggered by her story, but it wasn't about *her*. It was about someone else.

His voice was gruff. "I know I'm being a jackass right now, and I'm sorry. But I need a little time to digest this."

"Was it the woman in the photo? Your partner? Was she abused?"

Cassie knew his partner was dead. Had she been murdered by her spouse?

His mouth hardened. "Jada wasn't abused. She would never have put up with tha…" She did her best not to show how much that hurt.

Nick shook his head. "Shit, I don't mean it like that. I just…" He stared up at the ceiling. "Jada was killed on the job. By a guy who beat his wife."

Cassie sucked in a sharp breath.

…the things that brought each of us to Gallant Lake are a little more connected than we imagined…

"Nick, I'm so sorry."

He gave a short laugh, but there was no humor in it. "I haven't even said those words to you, have I? I didn't tell you how sorry I am for the hell you went through. That's how far in my own head I am right now. Look, I need to process this…"

They stood there for a few minutes, neither of them moving or speaking. He was wound so tight she thought he'd snap. She knew what that felt like. It was her normal. But Nick—this strong man who kept people safe for a living—didn't know how to deal with the fear of losing control. It wasn't until she saw a small shudder go through his body that she knew she had to help him. And she had a crazy idea that might snap him out of his melancholy.

"So the plan is for us to spend today doing what I want to do, right?"

Nick finally took his eyes off the ceiling and looked at her.

"I don't think that's a good idea, Cass. I'm feeling a little… raw…right now. I won't be good company. Let me just take you home, okay?" He walked to the sliding glass doors but froze when she placed her hand on his shoulder. She hated to see him in this kind of pain.

"What I have planned will help you relax. Come on."

He pulled the door open, still not looking back. "I don't think…"

"You don't have to think. You just have to do what I say. That was the deal, and you're a man of your word, right?"

She peeked around his shoulder to glimpse up at his face and saw the quick, reluctant smile.

"I'm a man of my word."

"I thought so. Get moving."

"Where are we going?"

"My place. I have everything we need there."

"Need for *what* exactly?"

She gave him a push to propel him through the door. "You'll see when you get there."

"That's wrong. I told you what we were doing last week."

She laughed. "You told me it was going to be a *stroll*. That was a hell of a lot more than a stroll."

He turned, his gaze heated. "Yeah, it was a lot more than a stroll."

She shoved him again, knowing he was referring to that redhot kiss that ultimately led to them falling into bed together last night. "Go on. You climb rocks to unwind. I'm going to show you how I do it."

CHAPTER FOURTEEN

"YOU EXPECT ME to take a *bubble bath*?"

Nick stared, stupefied. No way in hell was he getting into that tub full of sweet-smelling foam, surrounded by candles. *Candles!*

"You expected me to climb a mountain, so yes, I expect you to take a bubble bath. It's decadent and a lot like being in a sensory-deprivation capsule. The world just falls away, and you can't help but relax." Cassie looked pretty proud of herself.

He never saw this coming. He'd tried to bail on her, but she had a stubborn streak a mile wide, and she was determined this was his Day to Obey. When they got to her place, they'd sat in the living room of her funky little loft above the coffee shop for a while. He didn't think anything of it when she excused herself, figuring she'd gone to change. She *had* changed, into a simple top and jeans, but she'd also created…this.

After she'd dropped that bombshell on him earlier about having a crazy ex-husband who nearly beat her to death, he'd been having a hard time pulling his thoughts into line. The story filled him with rage. Rage that someone had hurt her. Put her on the run. Made her feel like a lesser person.

He already had an endless slideshow running on a loop in his head 24/7 from that night two years ago. Beth Washington admitting she'd let Earl move back into her house. His partner, Jada, who had always wanted children, carrying the Washingtons' baby down the hall to put her to bed. The sound of a shotgun blast.

Now those familiar images were mixed with new ones from his imagination. Cassie being slapped hard across the face. Cassie at the top of a long flight of stairs, fighting for her life. Cassie being brutally attacked in a deserted parking garage. Maybe he did need the distraction of whatever silliness she was going to subject him to. But a bubble bath?

"If you think I'm going into that tub, you don't know me very well."

"I *don't* know you all that well, Nick. But I know you're taking this bath, because you're a man of your word, remember?"

"With the emphasis on *man*. I don't do bubble baths."

She was unimpressed.

He resorted to begging. "Come on, Cass. I don't want to do this. It won't be relaxing, it'll be…embarrassing. Annoying."

She folded her arms and arched a brow high.

"I distinctly remember telling you I did *not* want to go hiking. It was hard, and exhausting, and I was embarrassed when you had to keep stopping for me. I was pretty damn annoyed by the time we got to the top of the trail. And I was in pain."

He grabbed her waist and tugged her close. "Yeah, but look how much fun we had once we got up there. That made it all worth it, didn't it?"

The sound of her light laughter made his chest feel funny. "And who's to say you won't get a nice surprise later today…" She pushed away from him and reached for the door. "*After* you get in that tub." She gave him a wink. "Man of your word, remember?"

He groaned, knowing he'd been outplayed. She flipped off the lights and closed the door behind her, leaving him in the candlelit bathroom. It was a big tub, framed in large marble tiles. She'd told him Nora had remodeled the downstairs bathroom before Cassie moved in.

Cassie's voice called through the door. "I don't hear any splashing in there! Don't think you can bluff me, Nicholas West. I'm going to deliver a glass of wine in a little while, and you'd better be chin-deep in bubbles."

Nick shook his head. May as well get it over with. Besides, the idea of Cassie bringing wine sounded pretty damn good. Maybe he could convince her to join him after all, and restore his manly pride. He shed his clothes and stepped into the not-quite-scalding water. As he settled down into the tub, he tried to remember the last time he took an actual bath, other than soaking in some hotel hot tub. He had to have been a kid, and there were no bubbles involved that he could remember.

What was he supposed to do? Scrub behind his ears? Or just sit here and wait? He felt ridiculous. But Cassie was right—she'd hiked a mountain last weekend when she really didn't want to, and he'd made a deal. He finally leaned back and let himself settle into the water a bit. The warmth felt pretty good on his muscles, tired from a night of lovemaking, and the flickering yellow light of the candles was almost hypnotic. He closed his eyes. That hideous slideshow was still playing in his head, but the images started to shift as he inhaled the perfumed suds.

He saw Jada, but she was at her wedding now, kissing her wife, Shayla, under an arbor of ivory roses. Laughing in the car on a stakeout, teasing him about his "obsession" with healthy eating while she devoured a bacon double cheeseburger. He saw Cassie, but she was trimming the daffodils he'd given her, bending over her desk to inhale their scent and smiling to herself. She'd had no idea he'd been watching her, or she never would have let on how much she liked the stolen goods.

There was a soft tap on the door, and Cassie stepped in. Her eyes lit up when she saw him in the water, chin-deep as ordered. And the hell if he didn't feel relaxed and sated. He didn't even bother trying to deny it.

"I could do without the actual bubbles, but I gotta admit—this feels pretty good."

"Now you know another of my secrets, Nick. I do this a few times a week, just to relax and feel pampered." She handed him a glass of wine, and he was glad to see she'd brought one for herself. That meant she was staying. To her, bubble baths were about feeling pampered. *He* wanted to be the one to make her feel that way. He wanted to be the one who kept her safe and spoiled her rotten and made her forget anything bad that had ever happened to her.

She sat on the corner of the tub, her hair falling loose over one shoulder. The candlelight made her skin glow as if from within. She was the prettiest thing he'd ever seen.

He crooked his finger at her, ignoring the white bubbles that drifted away from the movement.

"Join me."

Her smile was playful. "That defeats the purpose of pampering *yourself*. You're supposed to be relaxing alone."

"And I was doing that...until you walked in. Which makes me think maybe you really want to join me in here before the water gets too cool."

Her mouth opened, then closed again and she stood. "Soak up a little more warmth and relaxation, and I'll see you in the kitchen when you're ready." She moved to walk past him, but he reached out and grabbed her hand. She was the only comfort he craved.

"Don't go, Cass. Being alone with my thoughts is not... It's not relaxing."

She sat again, this time behind his shoulder. "Why don't you tell me about it. Tell me what happened in LA."

"Not much to tell. My partner died because of me."

"I don't believe that." Her answer was quick and sure.

"It's true. I made a bad call, and she paid the price. Jada was shot. Killed. Because of *me*." Her fingers traced patterns through his hair, her words barely a whisper.

"Tell me."

He told her about the night that replayed in his dreams over and over again. When he'd heard uniforms were called to Beth Washington's house earlier that night, he'd felt sick. He and Jada had been there a dozen times in previous years, but, with their encouragement, Beth had dumped her bastard of a husband. Nick and Jada had been there the day Earl moved out, to make sure there wasn't any trouble.

"Let me guess," Cassie said. "She took him back, because he promised he'd change?"

"She seemed like such an intelligent woman, but…" Nick glanced up at Cassie and grimaced. "Sorry, I didn't mean to say you aren't intelligent, but at least you left and didn't go back. I don't understand how someone can go back to a guy who does that. He broke her freakin' arm *twice*, and she still took him back."

Cassie sighed. "I had plenty of opportunities to leave before I finally did it. Abusers are very good at convincing you they'll change. They're the world's best apologizers. They play head games better than anyone else. They make you think *you* were the one who caused it, so if you just behave the way they want, things will be fine. But things never are."

Nick couldn't imagine forgiving someone for beating on him. But he'd heard all the science supporting what Cassie was saying. His head knew she was right, but his heart couldn't get past that night at Beth Washington's. Couldn't get past Jada paying the price.

"Jada and I drove by the house a few hours after the patrol unit responded to the call. The report said a neighbor had complained about a loud argument and crashing sounds next door. Of course, Earl gave them some BS story. He said they'd been watching a movie with the volume way up, and that was what the neighbor heard. His wife and kids backed him up, so the patrol told him to keep the volume down and left."

"But they weren't watching a movie, were they?" Cassie's

fingers stopped moving. She knew what was coming next. Too bad *he* hadn't been smart enough to see it. It was only supposed to be a wellness call at the end of their shift. Jada had already taken her vest off. They'd argued about that constantly—she hated wearing a vest.

"We knocked on the door and Beth answered. I told her we were just checking on things, and she told us the same movie nonsense. But there was something about the look in her eyes. In the eyes of those kids lined up on the sofa. Jada took the youngest girl down to her room, and I asked Beth where her husband was. She said everything was fine. Kept saying we needed to go."

And just like that, Nick was back in that living room again. Nice house. Nice neighborhood. No sign of the horrors that had occurred. No warning of the horror to come. Jada returned from putting the baby to bed, stopping at the end of the hall-way. Nick was lecturing Beth about how they couldn't protect her if she wouldn't protect herself. Beth looked up at him, tears and terror filling her eyes. That moment was his first clue that something was *wrong. Really* wrong. The hair on the back of his neck stood on end when she grabbed his shirt, hissing that Earl had a gun. He'd said he was going to kill them all, and if she couldn't get Nick and Jada to leave, he'd kill them, too.

"I looked up at Jada. We both reached for our weapons. There was a shotgun blast, and Jada…" Cassie stroked his head again. "When she fell, Earl was right there behind her, reloading the shotgun. I shot him in the chest, then grabbed the two kids and Beth and hustled them out the door. Everyone was screaming. I went around to the back door to get the baby from her room. The neighbor took a picture of me running out of the house with the screaming kid in my arms, and the media went nuts, making me out as some kind of hero cop. It was all bullshit." He swallowed hard. "I did everything wrong, and my partner… my friend…died in my arms. Because of me. My colleagues on the force knew it, too. I could see it in their eyes when the story hit the news. I could see it at the funeral. The way they looked at me. The way her wife, Shayla, looked at me. They all knew."

"Nick…" Cassie waited until he turned to look up at her. "Are you sure you weren't just projecting your own guilt into their eyes?"

Cassie watched Nick consider her words. He weighed them, almost gave in to the temptation of believing them, then dismissed them, opting to hang on to his pain.

"Good cops don't let their partners get shot in the back. That was on me."

"That's a lot of weight to carry around." He shrugged, staring at one of the candles that were burning low. She'd almost forgotten where they were. What a bizarre place to be having this conversation. "It's why you left LA."

"I was done being a cop. I didn't have the fire for it anymore. I started blaming the victims for putting themselves…"

Cassie nodded. "You blamed them for putting themselves in danger. For being victims." It certainly explained why he'd reacted so angrily to discovering her ex-husband had assaulted her.

Nick raked his fingers through his hair. "I know it's bad. It's wrong. And it sounds even *worse* when you say it out loud. But the fact is, if Beth hadn't taken Earl back, Jada would still be alive."

"So now you're saying it's Beth's fault that Jada is dead, not yours."

"Don't twist my words. It was *my* fault. I walked us right into the middle of a disaster."

"Did Jada not want to go? Do you think she had any idea what was going to happen when she took the baby and left you alone in the living room?"

"No, of course not."

"Then how is this all *your* fault? You both stopped at the house out of concern, and Jada agreed to it. Neither of you expected to run into a lunatic. Something terrible happened, but I don't see how you made any huge mistake that led to it." She tugged at his hair gently until he looked up at her, his dark eyes troubled with memories of a night too horrible to imagine, much less witness. She leaned forward, resting her forehead on his. "Nick, if you and Jada hadn't stopped that night, that whole family would be dead. Those innocent children would be dead."

He closed his eyes. He didn't *want* to feel better about it. He wanted to hurt.

"Shayla tried to tell me that, but it doesn't help."

"Because you don't want it to?"

He pulled away, looking at the bathtub with a flash of surprise, as if he'd forgotten he was in there. She didn't want to push him any further. They'd both shared a lot, and he was probably feeling as raw and wiped out as she was. She stood and handed him a towel.

"I imagine that water's pretty cold by now. I'll make some grilled cheese sandwiches and warm up some tomato soup, and we'll sit and relax for the rest of the afternoon. That will square us up on the deal we made."

He stared at the towel before reaching for it, avoiding eye contact with her.

"It might be better if I head home."

"And I think it would be better if we both had some food and took some time to recover from all the soul-baring that's gone on today. And since this is *my* day to call the shots, you don't get a vote."

He looked up, one brow arched, his mouth sliding into a devastating grin. And then he stood, glistening wet and completely naked. A small cluster of bubbles slid slowly down his chest, and she watched their journey in fascination. He sounded amused.

"I think I liked you better when you were timid. This bold-and-bossy Cassie makes me think I've created a monster."

Cassie licked her suddenly dry lips. Her mind was empty of

coherent thought. The bubbles were below his ribs now, gliding towards…

"My eyes are up here, babe."

She blinked and looked away from him, which finally freed her tongue. "I know where your eyes are. They're right above your smart-ass mouth. Get dressed and…"

He stepped out of the tub. The combination of hard male body and floral-scented bubbles was frying her brain cells. Nick chuckled.

"Are you sure you want me to get dressed? Or did you mean to say you want me just like this?"

Oh, yes. She wanted him alright. Just like this. Just *exactly* like this. The crooked grin. The mischievous light in his eye. The vulnerability he'd shown earlier. The tenderness when he'd held her in his arms. The strength of those arms, the safety she felt when she was with him. It was all so new.

Nick was her friend. He was her safety net. The man she'd made love to. No—had sex with. No. Made *love* to. The man she was falling for. Freefalling for. She had no right to. She was a fool if she did. But it was too late. He was her everything. And she was falling in love with him.

The realization caught her by such surprise that a nervous giggle bubbled up. She covered her mouth to keep from blurting the words out loud, since this man always left her thoughts in chaos and her mouth with no filter whatsoever. She giggled again as she, for some reason, remembered a Sun Tzu quote from her self-help book.

In the midst of chaos, there is also opportunity…

CHAPTER FIFTEEN

NICK WAS STANDING naked and wet in a bathroom with a woman who was giggling at him.

It wasn't exactly great for his ego, but he tried not to take it personally. She seemed as surprised by it as he was, the way her hand came up and covered those soft lips. The way her eyes went wide. The way her cheeks flushed pink. He cleared his throat loudly.

"So the sight of me standing like this makes you laugh, huh?"

"I'm sorry. I really am. It's been such a...*day*... Hasn't it?" Her hands went wide. "I don't know what we're doing, Nick. I don't know what's happening, or what comes next, or how to..."

"Shh." He put his fingers over her lips this time. "Let's not overthink this, okay? One day at a time seems like a good place to start. Let's take it a day at a time, together, and we'll figure it out as we go."

Her eyes went more gold than green, her brows furrowed. "But shouldn't we have a plan?"

She'd been on the run for a year now, planning for all kinds of contingencies. All sorts of what-ifs, ready to flee in the middle of the night. Letting their relationship simply play out was clearly scaring the daylights out of her. But he needed time to sort through his own feelings, and he couldn't do that while laying out some master plan of how this might work. He decided to distract her.

He kissed her softly, his hand pushing her hair back from her face. She trembled when his lips touched hers. And that was it.

That little tremble was his moment of truth. He was falling for this woman. Not *because* she trembled at his touch. That was just his wake-up call. He was falling for her because she was strong and tough and kind and funny. Because she made him want to be a better man. Made him want to be her protector. Forever. He'd known lots of women. But only one made him think of forever. And it was this woman. Right here. Right now.

"You're naked." She said the words against his mouth, and he felt her smile. He'd gotten her to smile again. And it made him feel like a god. He grinned.

"I am. It's generally the way to bathe, or did I do the bubble bath thing wrong?"

She shook her head. "No. You did it just right, Nick." She was still smiling, but there was something else going on behind those eyes. Something deep. She blinked and straightened. "I'd like to think we can do more than hop in bed every five minutes, though. So let's eat and sit and have that quiet afternoon together, okay?"

He didn't want her thinking they were just bed bunnies. He knew now that he wanted more. He wanted all of her.

"This is your day and I'm at your command." He kissed the tip of her nose. "And I *know* that we can do more than hop in bed every five minutes, Cass. We're more than that."

She looked into his eyes intently. He wasn't sure what she was looking for, but she seemed to find it. She nodded and relaxed against him. Then, remembering his nakedness, she pulled back and gave a nervous giggle. Glancing down, she noted his physical response to their close proximity. It was pretty tough to hide while naked, and he didn't bother trying. The corners of her mouth tipped up. "Who knows? Maybe I'll decide on some bed hopping later."

"Whatever you want, babe."

The rest of the day passed in quiet, peaceful time together. They were both exhausted—emotionally from all the sharing they'd done, and physically from a night full of activity. Nick was shocked at how much he enjoyed settling onto the flowered sofa and having another glass of wine while he watched Cassie read her book in the armchair by the window. She'd explained that the furniture all belonged to her landlady, Nora, who owned the coffee shop downstairs. Much of the main floor of the apartment was open to the beamed ceilings two stories above. There were metal stairs leading to a loft where Cassie slept every night. He wanted to see that loft, but, surprisingly, he wasn't in a rush. It was nice to be here with her, each lost in their own thoughts, but together. And the together part felt really good.

He glanced toward the door and frowned at the duffel bag sitting there. The only dark spot of the afternoon had been when Cassie explained it was her "go-bag," packed and ready to grab if Don ever tracked her down here. Nick wanted to tell her to unpack that thing and forget about leaving, but he could sense the security it gave her to feel...prepared somehow. They'd discuss it some other time, when he'd convince her it was no longer needed, because she had *him* to protect her now. Now and forever.

Damn, that word kept moving through his thoughts. *Forever*. They'd had one night. One night, even one amazing night, couldn't possibly lead to a forever. Could it?

He dozed off for a while, and when he woke, the lake outside the windows was peach colored from the setting sun. Cassie had fallen asleep, too, her book open in her lap, her head back against the corner of the wingback chair. He got up as quietly as he could and took the brightly colored throw from the back of the sofa, wrapping it around her. He figured he'd leave a note and slip out before she woke. They both needed the sleep. But as soon as he straightened, her eyes swept open and she stretched, yawning before smiling up at him.

"Whatcha doin', Nick?"

"I figured it's time for me to head to my own bed. We're both wiped out."

"Stay." It wasn't a question. Just one simple word that could lead to a whole lot of complications.

"Are you sure?"

"I'm sure I don't want to go to bed alone tonight. Do you?"

She had him there. He knew he'd be reaching for her in his dreams.

"No, I don't." He helped her to her feet. "But be sure, Cass. Because one night together is…one night. *Two* nights is a relationship. Even if it's not a long one, it's a relationship. It means something." This already meant something to him, but he wasn't certain where Cassie's head was. If they were doing this thing, they were doing it. All or…nothing? He didn't even want to think about what nothing might feel like.

Luckily, he didn't have to worry about it. Cassie took his hand and led him up the long flight of steps to where a huge iron bed sat, facing the arched windows on the top level of the loft. She turned to face him by that bed, repeating the only word he needed to hear.

"Stay."

Cassie smiled into her tea, staring at her computer screen, struggling to focus on work. She and Nick had settled into a happy routine over the past few weeks. Most of their free time was spent at Nick's house, to avoid the prying eyes of Nora and Aunt Cathy. Nora and the cousins were delighted over their being together. Amanda reminded Cassie that now the apartment really was an indisputable "love shack."

Aunt Cathy, on the other hand, was not delighted. She worried that Cassie was jumping into a serious relationship too soon. That Nick was "smothering" her by being around all the time. Cassie tried to explain that the difference between this and her former marriage was that she *wanted* Nick around. Cathy reminded her that Nick was a cop, just like Don. But that wasn't fair. There were thousands of honorable police officers out there, and Nick was one of them. Cathy had finally agreed to reserve judgment until she had a chance to get to know Nick better. Which would be happening that weekend.

Here at work, things were easier than she'd anticipated. They made a deal to stay focused on the job while at the resort, and, for the most part, it worked. Nick still hid her stapler every damn day, just like always. They continued to have sparring sessions in the gym like always. He continued to *borrow* flowers for her desk. Other than Blake, no one would ever know things had changed. Unless they saw Nick pull Cassie into his office for a lunchtime make-out session.

Blake wasn't exactly enthusiastic about the new office dynamic, but he didn't post any objections, either. Other than a quiet warning that first Monday to keep it professional and to save their personal life for their personal time, he'd stayed quiet.

A foam basketball went whizzing past her head, bouncing off the window and up into the air. She jumped and squeaked in surprise, then turned her chair to see Nick leaning against the door frame to his office, looking very pleased with himself.

She rolled her eyes. "Are you bored?"

"Hey, you're the one who said nothing should change at work. So this is me, not changing." He picked the ball up from the floor and flipped it into the air, catching it behind his back with a flourish. "I thought maybe we'd take the kayak out after dinner tonight, and watch the sunset from the water."

"You really think it's a good idea to put me back in a kayak?"

He bounced the foam ball off her desk, snatching it from midair in front of her face. She did her best not to flinch. He grinned, impressed.

"I don't know. You in a kayak worked out pretty well once before."

She tried to hold back her laughter, but failed. "Fair enough. I'll give it another try, and I'll try to stay inside the boat this time."

And she succeeded. Nick rowed them out toward the center of the lake that night, where they drifted on the calm water and watched the sun slide behind the mountains. Nick had come prepared, with cookies and wine. She teased him about drinking and rowing. But when she insisted on trying to row herself, they ended up going in circles, so she finally conceded and let him take them home. Neither of them got wet, but they still ended up in bed later, wrapping themselves up in each other after making love.

Aunt Cathy arrived for a cookout on Saturday wearing a healthy dose of skepticism. Nick laid on all of his charm, but Cathy was tough. She'd been through a lot of men back in her day, and most of them had been bad apples. But as the afternoon went on, and Nick presented flawless grilled steaks and veggies, sharing stories and treating Cassie like a queen the whole day, Cathy seemed to relax. Cassie thought maybe they'd won her over, so she was blindsided when her aunt leveled a look at Nick across the picnic table.

"So what are you going to do when Cassie has to pack up and leave Gallant Lake?"

There was a beat of silence. Nick looked at Cassie, then back to Cathy. His voice strong and sure.

"That won't happen."

"Really? Don found her once. What's to say he won't find her here?"

"Aunt Cathy..." Cassie didn't want to talk about this today. Especially after getting two hang-up calls this week from a Milwaukee number she didn't recognize. But that could have been anyone. She hadn't mentioned the calls, because talking about them gave them more weight than they probably deserved.

"No, it's okay, Cass." Nick looked her aunt right in the eyes. "I didn't say Don wouldn't find her. But that's not what you asked. You asked about Cassie leaving, and *that's* not going to happen. Because I'm here, and I'll keep her safe."

It wasn't the first time he'd said that this week, and it was beginning to grate on Cassie. She didn't want him thinking he had to protect her all the time. After all, that's why he'd taught her self-defense.

"I'll keep *myself* safe," she said. Nick and Cathy both turned to look at her in surprise. "One way or the other, I'll keep myself safe."

Cathy frowned. "Your go-bag is still packed and ready."

"And it'll stay that way." She cut off Nick's objection. "Until Don's in jail, I need to be ready to go. It's not just me he'll be looking to hurt. He'll go after anyone near me. I'm not saying he will find me. I've been careful. But he has connections. He's smart. And I've got to be ready, just in case."

Nick's jaw worked back and forth.

"Don't you leave me, Cassie. You call me, no matter what, and we'll face it together. Promise me you'll call me before you do anything." He reached out and took her hand. "Promise me, babe."

She hesitated, then nodded. "I promise." He stroked her hand with his fingers, the way he often did when they were sitting together, and they gave each other a warm smile.

Cathy looked back and forth between them.

"Well, I'll be dipped. There really is something going on between you two."

Cassie scrunched her brow. "Uh, yeah. That's why you're here, remember?"

Cathy waved her hand in dismissal. "I don't mean the shacking-up part. I wasn't crazy about you two playing with fire when you were in such a precarious position, honey. But you're not *playing* with the fire. You're already dancing in the flames, aren't you?"

Nick looked as confused as Cassie felt.

"Aunt Cathy, what are you saying?"

Her aunt sat back, pushing her pewter-colored braid over her shoulder. She looked at the two of them, then started to chuckle lowly.

"You don't even know it yet, do you? Okay." She stood, and Nick scrambled to his feet, reaching out to help Cassie extricate herself from the picnic table. Cathy shook her head. "I had my doubts about this, and it could still all go down like the *Titanic*, but one thing I know after today. Whatever's happening here is real. And real lo... I mean, real...well...you deserve a chance to make it. If you want my blessing, you have it. But remember one thing." She fixed one last glare on Nick. "I know where you live now. And if you hurt this girl, I will be paying you a visit. Got that?"

"Yes, ma'am."

After her aunt left, Cassie looked at Nick. "What on earth was she talking about?"

"Damned if I know. She's *your* aunt."

"Ugh. I need a cup of tea. You want anything?" These days, Nick's kitchen was fully stocked with tea, sugar and wine for Cassie, along with her favorite cereal and cookies. He'd teased her about her sweet tooth, but she shut him down fast when he suggested she try baked kale instead of a cookie. She didn't mind getting herself in better shape. She didn't mind the new curves and muscles she was developing, or the stamina she hoped would get her up Gallant Mountain tomorrow with less huffing and puffing than the last time. She didn't even mind cutting her carb intake a *little*. But trade cookies for kale? Nope.

Her phone buzzed in her pocket. She pulled it out, and a shadow fell on her happy afternoon. It was the Milwaukee area code again, but a different number this time. She quickly tucked it back into her shorts. If it was someone she knew, or someone from the DA's office there, they'd leave a message. If it was the random hang-up caller, there wouldn't be any message. Was it Don? One of his pals? But how would they have her number? Maybe it was just a fluke.

"Cass? Who was it?" Nick was frowning at her. "What's wrong?"

"Nothing. Just one of those telemarketing places that got my number somehow."

His forehead creased. "How would they get that number? I thought you said only a few people had it."

She shrugged, heading to the house. "Who knows? Probably on some random list out there. If I don't answer, they'll give up." She hoped. Especially since she knew, deep in her heart, that it was not a random call. It wasn't fair that, at a moment when happiness was finally staking a claim in her life, her past was trying to kick down the door.

The calls didn't stop. She received three more the next week. She answered one of them to see if the caller would speak, but they hung up immediately. The fourth call came the following Sunday, while she and Nick were coming home from the crazy-high cliffs he'd climbed with his buddies, called the Something-Gunks. She'd stayed at the base with a handful of nonclimbers, male and female, who agreed their respective significant others were insane for clambering up the sheer rock face. But when Nick came back down laughing with his pal Terrance a few hours later, he looked energized and happy. As long as he never expected *her* to do anything like that, she was cool with being an observer.

The call came just as Nick was driving down the hill into Gallant Lake. She looked at it, bit back a sigh and moved to put her phone away. But Nick grabbed it from her, glaring at the screen.

"Why didn't you answer? Who is it? Why do they keep calling?"

She bristled at his tone. "Don't use your cop voice with me. You know I don't like it."

His voice softened, but she could see from the set of his chin he was agitated. "Cass, you've been getting these calls for over a week now that I know of." She started to speak, but he cut her off. "And don't give me that telemarketer BS. What area code is that? Milwaukee? Is it Milwaukee? Is it Don?"

She didn't answer. She couldn't, not with him pressuring her like that. Firing off questions that sounded more like accusations. She shrank back in the seat, hating herself for feeling vulnerable right now. With the guy who was supposed to make her feel safe. Nick muttered something under his breath as he pulled into the parking lot behind the apartment. Even in his anger, he'd remembered she wanted to pick up some more clothes. He put the Jeep in Park and sat back against the seat with a sigh.

"I'm sorry. I don't mean to give you the third degree. But I'm worried. I see the expression on your face when those calls come in. The way your whole body goes tense. Something's going on, and you're keeping it a secret for some reason."

"Okay, okay. I've had a few calls from a Milwaukee area code. I don't recognize the numbers, and they're not always the same. They always hang up. Maybe it's just somebody with a wrong number."

"Somebody in *Milwaukee* with a wrong New York number? That's quite a coincidence, don't you think?"

Cassie shrugged. She didn't want to tell him that's how it started in Cleveland, too. Random hang-ups until one night it was Don's voice on the line. Nick thought she was a fighter. He'd given her the tools to take care of herself. She didn't want him thinking she was just another helpless victim.

He didn't ask about the calls again, but he started hovering more than usual over the next few weeks. He was hanging around if she worked late, even after she told him she'd meet him back at the lake house. He jumped to attention every time she looked at her phone, even if she was just checking the time. Maybe she should be more appreciative of his desire to protect her, but instead, she found it annoying. She didn't tell him about either of the two new calls that came in, for fear he'd overreact and start insisting on driving her everywhere like some damn bodyguard.

A few months ago, she'd have given anything to have a big, strong bodyguard. But that was before she learned to protect *herself*. Before Nick pushed her to be stronger, smarter, tougher. And now that she was finally seeing herself that way, he suddenly wasn't.

CHAPTER SIXTEEN

THE FINAL STRAW came when she and Julie went to lunch the following Wednesday at the Chalet to celebrate Julie's birthday. The place was crowded with noisy tourists and locals.

"You're different now," Julie said as she finished up her cheeseburger.

Cassie picked up her taco. "Different in what way?"

"I don't know." Julie studied her for a moment. "You're calmer these days, almost mellow, and it's not just because you're shagging Nick West."

Cassie coughed and sputtered, trying not to scatter taco crumbs everywhere. "What are you talking about? I'm not…"

"Oh, please, everyone in town knows you two are together." Julie waved her hand. "I know you're trying to be discreet at work, but no one can miss those sizzling looks going on between you two. But that's not why you're different. No…" Julie reached over and pinched Cassie's bicep, then nodded. "You're leaner. Stronger. You're not as jumpy and timid. You make eye contact with people. You even *walk* different, with that don't-mess-with-me vibe. It's a good look on you, girl. You came out of your shell."

They moved on to talk about the new proposal Blake was working on, trying to build vacation condos on the water. But

Cassie kept rolling Julie's words around in her head. If other people were noticing how much she'd changed, why couldn't Nick?

When they walked out to Julie's car, Cassie couldn't believe her eyes. Nick's red Jeep was pulling out of the parking lot. She recognized the climbing sticker on the back door. Had he *followed* her? Her eyes narrowed. This wasn't a coincidence any more than the Milwaukee calls were a coincidence. He was following her, just like Don used to. Not for the same reason, of course. But it still ticked her off. She didn't say anything to Julie, but she was fired up when she got back to the resort.

Nick's head snapped up in surprise when she stomped into his office and closed the door sharply behind her. He quickly smiled and came to greet her.

"Hey, babe, what's up? Did you miss me…? Oof! What was *that* for?" He rubbed his upper arm, where she'd punched him. Hard.

"Did I *miss* you? How can I ever miss you when you never let me out of your sight?"

"What…?"

She held her hand up flat in front of his face. "Stop! Don't tell me you weren't at the Chalet just now. You probably know what I ordered, what I drank and what time I went to the ladies' room. I didn't get rid of one stalker just to pick up another!"

"Whoa. I am *not* stalking you, for Christ's sake. I know you're worried about those calls you refuse to talk about, and I want you to feel safe!"

"But isn't that what all the self-defense classes were for?"

"Well, yeah, in case you're alone and in trouble. But you don't have to be alone anymore. You've got me to protect you."

She dropped her head in frustration. He cared about her. In fact, there were times when she saw the spark of something in his eyes that looked a lot like how she felt for him. A lot like love. But she couldn't let this obsession keep going. She met his gaze. His expression was somewhere between amusement and worry. Damn the man for making her feel this way.

"Nick, I love...how much you care." Whew, that was close. This was no time to blurt out that she loved him. "But you have to trust me to handle myself. You've given me the tools. I've got the moves. Let me have a chance to use them."

He rested his hands on her shoulders. "Today was a fluke, I swear. I had to run up to the sports shop in Hunter. I drove by the Chalet, saw your car and remembered you were going to lunch with Julie. I knew there was that mountain biking event in town. I knew you were in there with a bunch of testosterone-loaded adrenaline junkies, so I figured I'd just...make sure..." His words trailed off, and he had the good sense to look embarrassed. "I don't want you to *have* to use those skills I taught you, Cass."

"I'm not saying I want to put myself at risk. But you can't always follow me around. What about when you're gone this fall to visit the other resorts? I'll be alone then, so why can't you let me be alone now?"

Nick scowled in thought, then gave her a begrudging nod. He cupped the side of her face with his hand and leaned in to kiss her.

"Be patient with me, babe. I'll try to do better. It's just... I tend to lose the people I care about... And I don't want to lose you."

Her eyes went to the photo of Jada on the bookcase, and her chest tightened. He was fretting because he cared. She had to remember that.

"Okay. You try to do better—and I mean *really* try. And I'll try to be patient. But you have to understand that having someone watch my every move brings back bad memories. We *both* have baggage, remember?"

Nick tugged her into a warm embrace, and she rested her head on his shoulder. He really was her safe place. They just had to figure out how to keep him from also being what she wanted to run away from.

A soft knock on the door forced them apart. Nick opened it, and Blake walked in, stopping short when he saw Cassie there.

"Oh…uh… Am I interrupting…?"

"No, we're done." Cassie blushed. "I mean, we're done *talking*. Just talking. And now… We're done."

Nick started to laugh. "Quit while you're ahead, Cassie." He pulled her in for a surprising kiss in front of their boss, and whispered into her ear. "I'll see you at home tonight, and you can show me some of those moves you've got."

She knew her face had to be flaming. She didn't answer, but she also couldn't keep a straight face when she passed Blake and went back to her desk, thinking about which self-defense moves would translate best to the bedroom.

Her muscles were still protesting her successful efforts the next day when she joined Nora and Cathy at the Gallant Brew to help them take inventory. The coffee shop was too busy on weekends to do it, so Blake had given her Thursday afternoon off to help her aunt.

"Hey, Cassie, should I start looking for a new tenant upstairs?" Nora winked at her. "You two don't seem to be spending much time there these past few weeks."

Cathy barked out a sharp laugh. "They prefer his place, where no one's watching their comings and goings. You must be moved in there by now, right?"

Cassie waved her clipboard with one of Nora's infamous checklists attached, and stared at the two women in mock exasperation.

"It's a little early for me to be permanently taking up residence there, and I still have clothes and a toothbrush upstairs, so don't evict me yet." She and Nick hadn't formally discussed their living arrangements, but it was true they seemed to be unofficially living together. And last night they'd managed to christen the few rooms they hadn't already made love in, including the shower in the master bath. Yeah, that was fun. She bit back a triumphant grin. "But I did not come here to be quizzed on my love life, ladies. I came here to help with inventory, remember?"

Cathy glanced at the only occupied table in the place and lowered her voice. "Closing time was half an hour ago. They've paid, but they don't seem interested in leaving. Should I say something?"

Cassie looked at the teens sitting near the window. They were involved in an intense discussion, or at least the shaggy-haired boy was. He was leaning forward, his blond hair hiding his face. But his head jerked as he spoke, his shoulders rigid. The girl couldn't be more than sixteen. She didn't do much talking, just nodded, her head down and shoulders rounded. She was closing in on herself, in a protective stance that Cassie recognized immediately. That girl was afraid of him.

"I'll take care of it." Nora and Cathy looked at each other and shrugged.

The girl startled when she saw Cassie approaching, then brushed her dark hair back over her shoulder and looked away. There was a yellowed bruise on her wrist. The boy sat up and looked at Cassie with a contempt she was sadly familiar with. It was like staring into the eyes of a younger Don. And, just like Don, he quickly smoothed a cool smile onto his face to conform with expected polite behavior.

Cassie looked him straight in the eye and returned the thin, insincere smile. "Hi, guys. Is there anything else you two need today? I don't want to chase you away, but we're doing inventory and we'll be shutting down the coffee machines."

The girl rushed to apologize. "I'm so sorry. We're ready to go." She glanced across the table, suddenly uncertain. "Aren't we, Tristan?"

He sat back lazily and shrugged before slowly standing. "I guess so. If we're gonna be thrown out." There was challenge in his eyes, and Cassie didn't blink.

"I'm not throwing you out, but we do need to shut down. We won't be able to serve you."

He jerked his head toward the girl and she leaped to her feet as if he'd tased her. He turned his back and tossed his words over his shoulder as he opened the door.

"Whatever. This place sucks anyway."

The girl hurried to follow, whispering a quick "I'm sorry" as she passed Cassie. They left, and Cassie stood by the door, filled with regret. That girl was in trouble, and Cassie hadn't done anything to help. She went outside to the sidewalk, but they were gone from sight. She'd missed her chance. She rejoined Nora and Cathy.

"Is there any kind of shelter for abused women around here?"

Cathy shook her head. "Not in Gallant Lake. But there's a place over in White Plains, probably half an hour or so away. Why?"

"I was just wondering. It's too bad there's not someplace closer." It would have been nice if she could have at least handed that poor girl a number to call for counseling. She'd have to check out the shelter and learn more about it. Maybe even volunteer. She didn't help that girl, but maybe she could help someone else.

Nora lifted the trash bag out of the bin behind the counter and Cassie reached for it. She needed the distraction.

"I'll take it out, Nora. You two get started counting cups and spoons and whatever else we have to count."

She was barely three steps out of the back door when she heard a frightened cry.

"No, Tris, stop! That hurts!"

The boy's voice was rough and angry. "It oughtta hurt, you stupid cow! I heard you apologize for me to that bitch in there. Don't you *ever* make apologies for me again, you got it?"

It was the kids from the coffee shop. He'd yanked the girl around the corner of the building and pushed her up against the empty bakery two doors down. Cassie dropped the trash bag and headed toward them. He continued to berate the girl, and was raising his arm in the air when Cassie reached them.

He never saw her coming, and let out a yelp when she grabbed his wrist and twisted his arm behind his back before releasing him with a shove that sent him stumbling a few steps.

"What the hell are you doin', you crazy…"

Cassie nodded toward the girl, now wide-eyed and silent. "Go!"

Tristan avoided Cassie's grip, keeping his distance as he glared. "Shut up! Daynette, don't you listen to her!"

Daynette looked between Tristan and Cassie, crying and confused. Cassie kept her voice level.

"Daynette, this isn't the first time he's hurt you, is it? I saw the bruises on your wrist. Let me guess—he always says he'll never do it again, right? And then he does?" Cassie took a step toward her. "And then he makes it your fault, right? Blames *you* for making him mad?" She could see in the girl's eyes that her words were hitting home. "He's never going to change, Daynette. I've been where you are, and I can tell you he's never going to change. Get out while you can."

Tristan sneered. "And who's gonna stop me from chasing after her? *You?*"

Cassie ignored him. "Daynette, do you have someplace safe to go? Is home nearby?" The girl nodded. "Okay. Go there. Talk to someone about this. And stay away from this jerk."

The boy stepped forward. He was thin, but solid, and Cassie knew she'd have her work cut out for her if he got physical.

"Don't you leave, girl. Don't you walk away from me."

Daynette hesitated, then looked at Cassie, searching her eyes for the promise of something better. Cassie nodded toward the street.

"Go."

Tristan moved to grab Daynette when she ran off, but Cassie elbowed him hard in the ribs. He grunted, then jumped away.

"Lady, you are batshit crazy!" He grabbed her arm, and

Cassie could hear Nick's steady voice in her head. *Lower your center of balance. Don't try to outpower him, just go after the pain points.* She didn't try to pull away, surprising him by stepping into his grip, coming close enough to bring her heel down on the top of his arch. He cursed and let go of her arm. Adrenaline was pounding through her veins. She should walk away, but she wanted to push him onto his ass and kick the living daylights out of him right there in the parking lot. Before she could decide between the two options, she was shoved aside.

By *Nick.*

All Nick saw was red. He was driving back to the resort when he saw some punk kid drag a girl around the corner and into the lot behind Cassie's apartment. It took him a minute to turn around and swing back there to make sure the girl was okay. The last thing he expected was to see this guy grab *Cassie* and yank her around. Nick jumped out of the Jeep so fast he wasn't even sure if he'd put it in Park. Cass was fighting back—he saw her stomp on the guy's foot. The kid didn't have time to straighten before Nick grabbed the little piece of garbage and slammed him against the brick wall.

He looked like he was ready to soil his underwear when he got a look at Nick pulling back his fist. He started talking, and fast.

"No, man! You got it all wrong! My girl and I had a little fight, and this lady thought I was going to hurt Daynette, and I was explaining that I'd never do that! We're cool! Everything is cool, man, I swear!"

Cassie pushed past Nick, wagging her finger in the boy's face.

"Liar! You've been using that girl as a punching bag, and that's going to stop. You don't own that girl, and you don't put your hands on her again. Got it?"

"Cassie, damn it, get back! I got this."

"No, Nick, I *had* this before you got here. And why the hell *are* you here?"

The teen struggled, and Nick twisted his shirt up at his throat.

"I'm gonna let you go now, and you're gonna apologize to this lady and walk away. And whoever you were using as a punching bag? You stay the hell away from her. Got it?"

"Yeah, yeah, I got it. I'm sorry, lady." He took off like he was on fire.

Nick turned to Cassie, trying not to think about how many ways this scene could have gone wrong. "Are you okay? What the *hell* were you thinking, going after that guy?"

"Why do you keep insisting on being my knight in shining armor?"

"Most women *want* a knight in shining armor, don't they? Why are you mad at *me*?"

"Because I don't *need* your help, Nick! Wasn't that the whole point?"

"The whole point of *what*?" Nick raked his fingers through his hair.

"Of *us*!" Cassie gestured angrily between them. "I was your little pet project, right?"

"What the hell are you talking about?"

"Come on, Nick. You wanted to be a hero for teaching me a few self-defense moves, and you got a little fun between the sheets on the side. Big man, right?" She stepped back and looked him up and down, hands on her hips, eyes flashing with emotion. "Well, I don't want to be your project anymore, Nick. I'm an independent woman and I can take care of myself!"

Nick's mouth fell open, but he couldn't form any words that he trusted. But Cassie didn't have that problem.

"I've already been with a man who controlled my every move. And *he* tried to tell me it was for my own good, too. But it *wasn't*. It was all for *him*. To make him feel like a big man. And you're doing the same thing. You've got some kind of hero complex…"

Anger rushed through his veins, white-hot. "I am *nothing* like your ex."

"You're *exactly* like him!" She threw her hands in the air. "You're trying to tell me what to do and how to think and where to be…"

"I would never hurt you!" His voice echoed off the brick wall. There was a time when shouting made Cassie flinch and stammer. That time was apparently long gone. Now she stepped right up to him, shaking her finger in *his* face this time.

"You hurt me *today*, by not trusting me!"

Guilt punched him hard in the gut, but he pushed it aside.

"I'm not Don. I'd never put a hand on you."

She blinked, lowering her hand slowly. Maybe she was finally hopping off the hissy-fit train. Her voice steadied, but there was still fury and hurt in every trembling word.

"Fine. You'd never hurt me physically. But the broken bones weren't the worst thing Don did to me, Nick. Stealing my self-worth, sucking away my confidence, changing who I was— *that's* the most serious damage he inflicted. And now you're doing the same thing."

"Cassie…"

She spun away, her shoulders so tight and straight he thought she'd snap. And he'd made her that upset. But how? By wanting to keep her safe? How could that be so wrong?

He scrubbed his hands down his face with a growl, staring at the ground. *Damn it.* She accused him of stealing her self-worth? He'd taught her how to defend herself and stand up for herself. Sucking away her confidence? She'd climbed a fucking mountain with him. Change who she was? He'd made her a better person…

His shoulders dropped. But was it his place to do that? She said he had a hero complex. Jada used to say the same thing. She'd died because of his hero complex. And look what he was doing to Cassie now. Christ, he was such a screwup. He looked up and found her staring at him. And he couldn't help defending himself, because…screwup.

"I thought I was helping. I thought that's what you wanted. I thought you…"

I thought you loved me.

But he couldn't say that out loud, not when she was staring at him with so much anger and hurt. This wasn't the time to tell her he was in love with her. He might be stupid, but he wasn't *that* stupid. He couldn't throw those words out there when there was a very good chance she'd stomp on them and fling them back in his face.

Cassie's arms wrapped tightly around her own body, as if holding herself together. He wanted to be the one to do that. He started to step forward, but she shook her head sharply, stopping him in his tracks.

"Don't. I can't…" She shook her head slowly. "I… I don't trust my feelings right now, Nick. Maybe I'm mixing you and Don up in my head. Maybe I'm lashing out at you because I never had the chance to lash out at him. Or the *courage* to lash out at him. Or maybe you deserve every bit of it because you built me into something you don't seem to like very much."

"That's bullshit, and you know it."

"Is it? You didn't want me to be a victim anymore because you don't like victims. But victims are the ones who need a hero's rescue. So if I'm not a victim anymore, you no longer have a role to play. I don't need you to save me, because you taught me how to save myself. You taught me that I don't need a hero. So where does that leave us?"

His mouth opened, but he had no idea what to say to her convoluted logic. If he *loved* her, it was his job to protect her, right? But then, why had he taught her how to protect herself? His brain was spinning faster than tires on ice, and his frustration boiled up again.

"You've got all the answers, Cassie. You've clearly psychoanalyzed me and come to your own rock-solid conclusion. So why don't *you* tell *me* where it leaves us?"

Her eyes hardened.

"So now the big, bad cop is refusing to take a stand. Who's the victim now?"

He bit back the angry words begging to be said. They'd reached the point in this argument where someone was going to have to walk away before they burned down any hope of repairing the damage already done. His jaw tightened. It galled him to be the one walking. It galled him to quit before a winner was declared. But he could see it in her eyes. She was drunk on her newfound ability to take a stand, and she wasn't going to back down.

He got it. For years, she hadn't landed even a glancing blow on her asshole of an ex. She was going to stand and fight now just to enjoy the adrenaline rush of getting her punches in. But it wasn't in his nature to be someone's punching bag.

They could finish this conversation when they were both more reasonable. He turned for the Jeep, his parting words spoken over his shoulder to the woman he loved.

"I think we're done here."

CHAPTER SEVENTEEN

I THINK WE'RE DONE...

Those words rolled around in Cassie's mind on an endless repeat cycle as she stared into her morning coffee.

We're done.

She hadn't slept at all, tossing and turning until the sheets were in a twisted heap. After Nick left, she'd sent a text to Cathy, saying she had a bad headache and begged off from the inventory. Then she'd quietly gone up to the apartment to assess what just happened.

Done.

She didn't know where all that rage had come from. One moment she'd been standing there, feeling like an Amazon warrior after setting Tristan back on his heels. And the next, it was as if Nick had snatched all of her power away. After teaching her those skills, he'd been furious when she'd used them. And something inside of her had just...snapped.

She brushed a fresh wash of tears from her cheeks. How many tears could a human body produce, anyway? She'd been crying all damn night.

All the hurt and rage of a decade had risen to the surface like lava in a volcano yesterday, and she'd unleashed it on Nick. It was frightening to be so completely out of control, with no ability to hold back words she wasn't even sure she believed. Wasn't sure if they should be aimed at Nick or at Don. Or perhaps even at herself.

The one person who could help her sort it all out, and the only person whose opinion mattered to her, had ended things yesterday. She sniffed back the tears threatening to drown her again.

I think we're done here.

Just like that, after she'd attacked him one too many times, he'd walked away.

We're done.

The man she was in love with, the man she *thought* loved her back, had declared them over. In a way, it may have been best that he'd left, as the argument had been racing toward a flameout. She'd kept throwing his words back at him over and over, until he finally said the one word she didn't have the strength to repeat.

Done.

Had Nick truly given her strength only to resent her for having it? That might not be fair. He came upon the situation with Tristan and Daynette without knowing what had happened. If the first thing he saw was Tristan's hand on Cassie's arm, it wasn't unreasonable for him to assume the worst. He wasn't wrong to want to protect her. But it *felt* wrong. It felt like he didn't want her to step up and be strong, even though that was all he'd been talking about since they met.

Her coffee had turned cold enough to make her grimace when she took a sip. A sad realization pressed down on her. Nick might never be able to see her as anything other than a victim. If she was going to start a new life as a new Cassie, she might have to do it somewhere other than Gallant Lake. Somewhere where no one knew her past. Where people would know only brave, strong Cassie. She glanced at her dusty go-bag by the door. She wouldn't be running away. She wouldn't be hiding. She'd be looking for a place to blossom and grow and be her best self. That would be a good thing. So why did the thought of leaving Gallant Lake, of leaving *Nick*, make her heart hurt?

Another one of those damned Sun Tzu quotes came to mind, and it stung.

Who wishes to fight must first count the cost...

Was losing Nick really a price she was willing to pay?

Her phone started vibrating across the stone counter, making her jump so high she almost fell off the kitchen stool. It wasn't Don, thank God. It was Blake Randall. She glanced at the clock and swore. She was late for work. She looked down at the sweats and cami she was still wearing. Whom was she kidding? She wasn't going to work today. She couldn't possibly face Nick in the office until she had some kind of control over her thoughts. Until she had some sort of plan. Or at least until she stopped crying.

Blake's call was on its third ring before she swiped to answer. "Um…" She had to clear her throat and dislodge the tears. "Hi, Blake."

"Hi, Cass. Did you have a Friday off I'd forgotten about?"

"No. I should have called, sorry. I know I took time yesterday, but I need a personal day. Will that be a problem?"

"Of course not. Well, it's always a problem when I have to take care of my own damn self, but…" He paused, waiting for her to laugh at his little joke, but she didn't have it in her to even try. "Are you okay? Has something happened?"

"Yes. I mean… No, nothing's happened, and yes, I'm fine." She cursed the shaky breath she took and hoped he couldn't hear it. "I just…need a day."

"Just a wild guess—does this *need* have anything to do with the dark bags under Nick's eyes this morning and his general air of stay-away-or-I'll-stab-you?"

Cassie's chest tightened. Nick had been the one to end things, but at least he was paying a price for it right along with her. Was it wrong if that knowledge gave her a small dose of satisfaction?

"Cassie?"

"Oh...um... What?"

"Yeah, that's what I thought." Blake sounded resigned. "Is this going to be a problem?"

Does a broken heart qualify as a "problem"?

"At work? No, of course not. I just need a day, okay?"

"Don't be surprised if you have company shortly." Was Nick on his way over? Why? He'd said they were finished. She started to rise until Blake continued. "Amanda took one look at Nick this morning and managed to deduce everything in about five seconds. She scares the shit out of me when she does that, because she's never wrong. She called Nick a few choice names and flew out of here a few minutes ago. Odds are she's headed your way."

As if scripted, there was a sharp knock at the door.

She opened the door to find Amanda standing with hands on hips. She gave Cassie a quick once-over and stepped in for a sneak-attack hug. Cassie didn't bother pretending she didn't need it right now. She even returned it, and felt Amanda flinch in surprise. They stood in the doorway like that, and Cassie did her best to hold back the tears that threatened yet again. It was Amanda who stepped back first, wiping something from her face before meeting Cassie's gaze.

"How bad is it? Do I have to hire a hit man? Should I make Blake fire him? Banish him to Bali? Tell me and I'll make it happen."

Cassie couldn't stop the laugh that bubbled up. She'd never had a friend who had her back like this. It eased the pain, if only for a moment.

"Bodily harm won't be necessary." Although, to be honest, she had no idea how she'd be able to face Nick at work every day. "Let's face it, this was inevitable. I was never going to be able to trust Nick not to hurt me somehow, and he was never going to be able to see me as anyone other than a victim. It's better for both of us that it happened now instead of..." The words choked her into silence.

Instead of after I told him I loved him.

"That's a load of bull. You two are crazy for each other. And if it makes you feel any better, he looks even worse than you do, so there's no way he's thinking this is a good thing. Come on, pour me some coffee and tell me what happened."

Nick called and texted Cassie a dozen times with no response Friday. Ignoring him was childish, and it irritated him. Sure, the fight was bad, but pulling the silent treatment on him was ridiculous. He sent another text near the end of the workday, basically saying exactly that. Half an hour later, the boss's wife walked into his office and made it clear that he'd be putting himself in mortal danger—from *her*—if he bothered Cassie again for at least the next twenty-four hours.

"I get that you already regret breaking up with her," Amanda said, "and you *should* regret it, but leave her the hell alone for a few days. That kind of hurt doesn't go away with an *I'm sorry*. And as far as I know, you haven't bothered to actually say you were sorry yet." Nick frowned, going over his texts and messages in his mind. He'd apologized. Right? He must have apologized. Or had he just talked about how they "needed to talk" before he started chastising her for not responding? Damn, he was really bad at this relationship business.

Blake appeared in the doorway, an amused smile on his face as he slid his arms around his wife.

"Is there a problem here, honey?"

She twisted her neck to look up at him, then leaned back into his embrace. Nick felt a pinch of pain in his chest at the look of intimacy between them. It was the same type of look he and Cassie had shared more than once.

"Nothing serious, dear. Your idiot of a security chief made an ass of himself and hurt the woman he loves, but he's going to make it better. Right, Nick?"

...you already regret breaking up with her...

"Wait...did you say I *broke up* with her? We had a fight, and it was ugly, but…" He tried to rewind their argument. They both said hurtful things, sure, but not *that*. "Did she tell you I broke up with her?"

It was the first look of hesitation he'd seen in Amanda's blue-eyed glare since she'd spotted his unshaven, disheveled appearance that morning, then looked to Cassie's empty desk and lit into him for obviously being the reason for her absence. She tipped her head to the side, her eyes narrowing again.

"Are you telling me you didn't tell her you two were 'done'—" she lifted her fingers into air quotes "—before you stormed off?"

"I…" Nick's mouth stayed open, but no more words came out. *Had* he said that? No. Well… Yes, he had. But…

"I didn't mean it that way." He knew that sounded bad, and Blake's sharp laugh confirmed it.

"Dude. You told the woman you love that you were done in the middle of a fight, but you 'didn't mean it'?" Now it was Blake's turn to do air quotes. "How does done not mean *done*? There aren't that many ways to interpret the word."

"I meant the *argument* was done. I was done *fighting*. I figured we needed to stop before it got worse, so I declared an end to it." He knew without hearing Amanda and Blake's sharp intake of breath that he sounded like a controlling asshole. Kinda like the guy Cassie had accused him of resembling last night. He scrubbed both hands down his face in aggravation. "Okay. Maybe I was wrong." Amanda's brow lifted sharply. "Okay, I *was* wrong. But damn it, how could she think I'd end us like that?"

Amanda started to answer, but Blake rested his hand on her shoulder.

"Let me field this one." He sat in one of the chairs in front of Nick's desk, pulling his wife onto his lap. He gestured for Nick to take the other chair. "You're in love with a woman that…"

"Okay, why do you two keep throwing the *L* word around

here like it's some foregone conclusion? I've never told you I'm in love with Cassie."

Amanda bristled, but Blake chuckled and held her tight.

"It's okay, babe. I was the same damned way. I refused to admit the truth about my feelings for you. I didn't ever *want* to be in love, so I clearly *couldn't* love you. Don't you remember?"

Her eyes softened and she patted his arm. "We both had a lot of denial going on back then."

Blake nodded. "And that's where Nick is right now. He doesn't *want* to need anyone, so he won't admit he needs that woman more than he needs air to breathe."

Nick straightened. "'He' is sitting right here."

"Yeah, you are. And she's sitting alone in an apartment in town. And you both feel like shit. I've been there, Nick." Blake glanced at his wife. "*We've* been there. You ask how Cassie could believe you'd end it, but the question is—why would she believe you *wouldn't*? Have you told her you love her?"

Nick didn't need to answer that. They all knew he hadn't.

"Okay. Have you thought about her past?"

"I'm the one who taught her self-defense, remember?"

"That's nice. But have you *really* thought about it? How deep it goes?" Blake sat back and sighed. "Look, I knew about Amanda's past, and her issues with trust, once we got involved. We'd talked about it, and everything was cool in my mind. What's done is done, right?" Nick saw the flash of pain that crossed Amanda's face, and Blake must have sensed it, because he pulled her close again. "Then Amanda thought I'd lied to her about something. I hadn't lied, despite all the evidence to the contrary. I *told* her I didn't lie, but her past taught her that men weren't to be trusted. I was so butt-hurt that she wouldn't believe me that I got pissed off and left, basically proving she was right—men couldn't be trusted." Blake shook his head, lost in the memory of what was clearly a bad time for them.

Cassie had accused Nick of having a hero complex. Of refusing to see her as anything but a victim to be rescued. That he wanted to rescue her and simultaneously resented her need for rescue. How twisted up his beliefs were with what happened to Jada. He glanced at her photo on the bookshelf. If Jada were here right now, she'd kick his ass six ways from Sunday for being such a lunkhead.

He frowned. She'd kick his ass for a lot of reasons. And at the top of the list would be the guilt he'd carried around for two years. The way he'd avoided Shayla since the funeral. The anger he'd been carrying toward Beth Washington. The way he ran from LA, trying to flee all those memories. The way he'd projected all of that baggage onto Cassie, when she was already carrying a full load. He stood, but Amanda jumped up before he could bolt out the door.

"Give her some space, Nick. You're both exhausted and hurting right now. Spend a little time thinking about things, and give her time to do the same." She turned to smile at Blake behind her. "Those days we spent apart were brutal, but, looking back, I think we needed that space to decide if we were both willing to change. Tomorrow you'll be thinking more clearly and can come up with a way to win her back."

He looked at Blake. "Is that what you did? You won her back?"

He was hoping for a few pointers, but Blake laughed. "Nope. She beat me to it. Chased me down and basically dared me *not* to be in love with her." He shrugged. "It worked."

Everything in Nick was telling him to run to Cassie, but he resisted. He looked at Jada's photo again. He was no good to Cassie if he couldn't confront his own demons. He slapped Blake on the back and tapped Amanda under the chin with his finger.

"Thanks, you two. I'm still new in the corporate world, but I'm pretty sure this conversation is way above and beyond what's expected from an employer. I appreciate it."

Amanda smiled, but there was a steeliness in her eyes.

"That's great. Just make sure you know what you want. And don't hurt her again, Nick. Or you'll be dealing with me."

Blake laughed again. "Okay, Rocky, let's go. Good luck, man."

Nick went home and sent one last text to Cassie.

I'm SORRY. We're NOT done. Let's talk when you're ready.

He was frustrated, but not all that surprised, when she ignored that text, just like she'd ignored the others. For all he knew, she'd turned her phone off after he'd kept hounding her earlier. Saturday passed without a word, but he didn't text her again, even though he checked his phone at least fifty times.

He poured a glass of whiskey and sat on the deck Saturday night, watching the sun setting over Gallant Lake. The ice cubes were almost melted before he finally picked up the phone and dialed. Shayla's voice was surprised and guarded.

"Hello? Nick?"

"Hi, Shayla." Silence stretched taut while he watched a blue heron walking on the lakeshore, pausing every other step to stare into the water, looking for dinner.

"It really is you. Is something wrong?" He pictured Shayla, her hair long and wild with curls, the way Jada liked it. Shayla was the light and energy to Jada's practical and, yes, controlling ways. Jada had been all business, the consummate professional police officer, while Shayla was the free-spirited dance teacher. They'd both had to compromise their ways to make the marriage work, and they'd done it without a second thought. At least it seemed that way.

"Hello? Look, Nick, if this is a drunk dial, I don't have time for it. I've got a recital tonight at the school…"

"I'm not drunk. I mean… I'm drinking, but it's my first one of the night. Do you have a few minutes?"

He heard her snort of laughter. "If you're gonna *speak*, I got an hour. If you're just crying into your whiskey, I ain't got the time or temperament for it, Nick. I haven't heard from you in more than a year…"

"I'm so sorry, Shayla."

There was a beat of silence. "Sorry for *what*?"

The heron was on the other side of the dock now, frozen on one leg, head tipped to the side as if he was waiting for Nick's answer, too.

"For every damn thing. But mostly for taking Jada from you."

There was a sharp intake of breath on the other end of the call, then he heard a rustle of fabric as if she was sitting down.

"Earl Washington took Jada away from me. From us. I told you at the funeral not to listen to those idiots at the department, didn't I? That you weren't to blame?"

"If I hadn't gone to that house…"

"If you hadn't gone there, Beth Washington and those kids would be dead. Is that why you haven't called before now? Is that why you left LA? Because you think you're responsible for me being a widow?" She paused. "I absolved you of that two years ago."

His short laugh had no humor in it. "It didn't take, Shayla."

"Clearly. Where are you?"

"I'm in the Catskills. I took a security job for a chain of resorts based here."

"Putting that master's degree to work, eh? And today, out of the blue, you sat down with a drink and decided to beg my forgiveness for Jada's death?"

"Pretty much, yeah."

"Why?"

Nick smiled. Shayla had picked up some of Jada's directness in their brief time together.

"Someone… Someone's been pushing me to face my past."

"In other words, you've met a woman who called you on your bullshit?"

The heron struck out, its head diving under the surface of

the water, coming up with a wiggling minnow. Nick chuckled. "You sound just like Jada. Straight to the point."

"That's why you were so good together. You didn't take any shit from each other, and you almost knew what the other one was going to do before they did it. Jada said you two were like one person when you worked together."

Nick thought back to the years he and Jada worked together. Once they'd hashed out their initial power struggle, they really were like a well-oiled machine. They broke up a sex-trafficking ring. They moved a drug gang out of a residential neighborhood so children could feel safe playing on the sidewalks. They solved dozens of murders. Probably hundreds of crimes. As weird as it might sound, they'd had a great time doing it. It just worked.

Until it didn't. Until he saw Jada falling from the blast of Earl's shotgun. Once Nick had everyone out of the house, he'd rushed back in to hold Jada in his arms. The sound of her rattling breaths drowned out the screams of the children and the wail of approaching sirens outside.

"Her last words were about you."

"I know, Nick. You told me. You came to me and repeated every word she said, just like she'd asked you to do." The tremor in her voice betrayed her tears. "Are you sure this isn't a drunk dial?"

He shook his head and took another swig of whiskey.

"You listen to me, Nick West. Jada's death is. Not. Your. Fault. She was a police officer following up on a domestic violence call. That's as unpredictable and dangerous as it gets. She knew that as well as you did. She used to tell me all the time that sometimes bad shit happens, and you can't always control it."

"She didn't have her vest on."

"That's not on you. She hated that vest. We used to argue about it all the time. Jada did whatever the hell Jada wanted, and she wasn't going to be bossed around by you or me or anyone else. The vest was her choice. And as high as the shot was, it may not have saved her anyway. Nick, you gotta let go of the guilt. It's too much to carry."

Cassie had told him basically the same thing. *Too much to carry.* Maybe he needed to start listening to the women in his life. He heard a rustle on the phone... Tissues? Shayla sniffled, then her voice steadied again.

"What if the situation was reversed?"

"What do you mean?"

"What if you were the one killed, and Jada survived? Would you have wanted her to be burdened with guilt over it? Would you want her quitting the force, running away, torturing herself over some made-up idea of being responsible for controlling your actions or the actions of a madman with a gun?"

He didn't answer right away. He couldn't. It was too much truth to take in. If Earl Washington had come in the front door, behind Nick, it would have been *him* shot in the back. And Jada would have been the one watching in horror. He'd trade his life for hers in a heartbeat, but that's not what happened. Earl came in from the back of the house, behind Jada. And there wasn't a damn thing Nick could do to roll back time and change it.

"Nick? What would you want if it was reversed?"

He drained the whiskey, welcoming the sharp burn of it sliding down his throat.

"I'd give anything for it to have been me who died that night. I'd want Jada to be alive, you two to be together, having that baby you dreamed about. But no, I wouldn't want her feeling responsible for me."

"Because...?"

"Because sometimes bad shit happens, and we can't always control it."

Neither of them spoke for a moment, then Shayla sighed.

"I've gotta go get the kids ready for this recital tonight. But Nick, you should know that I'm adopting a little girl. It's what Jada and I always wanted. Tamra's four years old, and I swear to God she's a reincarnation of Jada." Nick smiled at the thought.

"She's all spit and fire and power, and she's gonna take over the world by the time she's ten if I'm not careful. I miss Jada every single damn day, but seeing love in this little girl's eyes keeps Jada with me in a *good* way. I honor her memory by loving someone the way she loved me. You should do the same. Maybe with this woman who's got the brains to tell you to straighten the hell up."

CHAPTER EIGHTEEN

CASSIE SCROLLED THROUGH Nick's messages for the who-knows-how-many-eth time. It was Sunday afternoon, and she hadn't heard from him since Friday night. His final message said they *weren't* done, but it sure felt that way from the silence. On Friday, silence was exactly what she'd wanted. He'd been driving her crazy with all the texts and messages. Just like he'd driven her crazy trying to run her life.

She stared out the window of the apartment—the *love shack*—as cars passed below on Main Street. She wasn't being fair. He said they'd talk when she was ready. He was giving her control. He wasn't intentionally trying to run her life. Or maybe he was. She dropped her head back against the overstuffed chair. The whole thing was such a confusing mess!

On one of their hikes a few weeks ago, Nick had pointed out a small whirlpool in a mountain stream. A maple leaf was swirling around and around in the water, unable to break free. That's what she and Nick were like. Neither could break free from their individual whirlpools.

Whoa. That was deep.

She grinned to herself as she reached for her wineglass. Teatime had ended yesterday when she declared it sadly ineffective. Last night's bubble bath was equally unrewarding, since it only reminded her of Nick standing in a tub full of bubbles. Not productive at all.

Wine was doing a much better job of freeing her mind to drift, as well as dulling the pain when she bumped up against a painful memory. Every kiss. Every moment between the sheets. Against the wall. In the tub. On the sofa. In the Jeep. On the mountain. In the gym. She took a sip of wine. Okay, maybe a gulp of wine. It was more effective than tea, but not effective enough.

She was going to have to go to work tomorrow, and Nick would be there. Nick, who hadn't reached out since Friday. Amanda said he was a mess then. Was he still a mess? Awash in guilt and regret? Anger? Or was he tucking it all inside, as he so loved to do, ignoring the truth? Would he pretend everything was fine, the way they tried to do after their first kiss? Would he confront her and defend his controlling ways?

She frowned. Not fair again. And it had been especially not fair for her to compare him to Don. Those mysterious hang-up calls had put her on edge Friday. Then she saw Tristan and Daynette, and Cassie just flipped. And it felt *good*.

It felt good to help someone instead of being the victim. It felt good to see Tristan back down. Yes, he was just a kid, but she'd been drunk with power at that moment, and she wasn't seeing Tristan anymore. She'd been seeing Don. She'd been imagining making *him* back down. Making *him* stop hurting her. Following her. Stalking her. Frightening her. Having power over her.

And then Nick robbed her of all of that by swooping in to the rescue. And she was so damned angry that he took her power away. Except… He hadn't. Not really. Not on purpose. Don worked at making her powerless. Nick did the exact opposite. He wanted her to be strong. Did she really expect a man, especially an ex-cop, to *not* rush to help if he thought the woman he… Cassie closed her eyes. She was so sure he loved her. Just as sure as she knew she loved him. Of course he'd leaped to the rescue.

And what had she given him in return? All that rage that she'd been holding on to for Don. She'd just spewed it all at Nick. He hadn't deserved it. Yeah, he was overprotective. But he'd watched his best friend die in his arms. He'd convinced himself that Jada's death was his fault. It made sense that he'd react by wanting to protect the people he cared about from any chance of harm.

Cassie stared at her wineglass. Damn, this stuff was making her pretty smart today. Maybe after she had another she'd have the courage to call Nick and tell him to come over so they could work it out. Better tonight than tomorrow in the office, with Blake and Amanda watching them and playing matchmaker.

But that third glass of wine only made her sleepy. Or perhaps it was the fact that she'd hardly slept in two nights that made her fall asleep in the big chair. The apartment was dark when she heard her phone ringing on the counter. By the time she woke up and got to it, the ringing stopped. Her heart jumped. Was it Nick? She didn't recognize the number, but she knew the area code. Milwaukee. She ignored it and checked the time. Almost eleven.

She and Nick would have to figure things out tomorrow after all. It was too late and she was too tired to do it now. Her phone chirped with an incoming text. It was from the same mystery number that had just called. That was new—she hadn't received any texts since leaving Cleveland.

Cute little place you found there.

No. It couldn't be. A dagger of ice hit her heart.

She didn't touch the phone, willing it to stay silent on the counter. It chirped again.

Nice little waterfront tourist town.

Don couldn't have found her. Not now. The comments were vague, though. Maybe he was just fishing for information. She picked up the phone, hoping he was done. Several minutes passed before the final chirp.

Gallant Lake sure looks pretty in the moonlight.

Cassie dropped the phone onto the counter. Don was *here*. In Gallant Lake. He didn't mention her apartment, but if he was in town, it wouldn't take long for him to find her. She glanced at the go-bag by the door. She didn't want to run. But if she didn't, Don would ruin everything. Again. And he might hurt the people she cared about. Aunt Cathy. Nora. Amanda. Blake. A chill swept over her. Don would kill Nick. There wasn't a doubt in her mind of that. There was only one way to keep everyone safe. She grabbed a jacket, leaving her phone in the kitchen. If he was tracking her with it, she had to leave it behind. She'd buy a burner phone and call everyone tomorrow, once she was safe. Once *they* were safe.

She went to the door, picked up the duffel bag and flipped off the lights. It looked like she'd be making that fresh start in a new place after all. But this time she would go there unafraid of the shadows. She wasn't the same person anymore. She'd found her strength. She'd found her heart. She blinked back tears as she locked the door behind her. That heart wouldn't be coming with her, though. Because she'd given that heart away.

Nick knew walking into the office on Monday morning that the day would be tough. Cassie was probably still angry with him. After all, she'd never responded to his final text. Maybe he really *had* ended things, simply by being an idiot. He stood outside his car and gave himself a stern lecture.

He loved her, and he'd do whatever it took to make sure she understood that. He'd earn her love in return if it took him the rest of his days to do it. He'd make sure she knew how much he respected her. How strong he knew she was. How willing he was to let her stand on her own without him hovering around like a bodyguard. Although that last one would be tough. But he'd do it for Cassie. She said he'd taken her strength away, and he needed to give it back.

It wasn't until he started walking toward the resort that he noticed her car wasn't there. He stopped behind her parking spot and frowned. It hadn't occurred to him that she wouldn't show up. Blake would have let him know, wouldn't he? Nick checked the time. His sleepless night had him up and moving earlier than usual. It was barely seven o'clock. She'd be here. And when she arrived, he was going to bring her into his office, close the door and kiss her senseless. Then they'd talk. It was going to be fine.

But three hours later, Cassie still hadn't arrived. Wasn't answering her phone. Wasn't answering *anyone* on her phone. Amanda and Blake were in his office, looking as worried as he was. Amanda called Nora, who said Cassie's car was gone. Blake didn't wait for Nick to ask.

"Go. I'll call Dan Adams and see if he's heard…anything."

He didn't want to think about what the deputy sheriff might have heard. Maybe there'd been an accident. Or maybe she'd had car trouble somewhere. Maybe she was at the auto shop out on the highway. Maybe she'd broken down on the way to work.

"Nick?" Blake was holding the phone, staring at him. He'd been frozen in place as his brain tried to solve the mystery of Cassie's disappearance. Nick gave Blake a quick nod and left.

Cathy and Nora were already in the apartment when he arrived. The police-detective part of his brain was annoyed that people were traipsing around, possibly destroying evidence of what happened. Where Cassie went. But then Nora motioned to the phone sitting on the kitchen island.

"We didn't touch anything, Nick. I knew you'd want to see everything the way we found it. She left her phone. And…she took her bag."

He spun to look by the door. Her go-bag was gone.

"That doesn't make sense." He refused to believe she'd go without a goodbye to anyone. To him. "That was her panic bag. Why would she take that instead of packing her stuff and talking to someone?"

Cathy folded her arms. "You *know* why."

Thinking she was referring to Friday's argument, he held his hands up in innocence. "It was just an argument. We'd have worked it out. She wouldn't have run away because of a fight."

Cathy's eyes narrowed. "I wasn't talking about any argument, but I'd definitely like to hear more about that. I was talking about that crazy ex-husband of hers."

"He's in Milwaukee," Nick said.

"Is he?" Cathy walked over to the phone.

"He's on probation. A restraining order…"

"And those always work, right?" She twirled the phone and slid it across to him. "Her pass code is 1111."

Nick grimaced. "Original."

"It's her birthday."

"It's four ones. Not a very secure passcode."

Nora threw her hands in the air. "Oh, my God. Stop debating cybersecurity and unlock the phone!"

It opened to Cassie's text screen. It was a number he didn't recognize, and the words chilled him to the marrow of his bones.

Gallant Lake looks nice in the moonlight.

Innocent words on their own, but on Cassie's phone, from a Milwaukee area code, they dripped with danger.

Don had found Cassie somehow. And he'd managed to convince her he was in Gallant Lake. And she *left*. Nick walked to the windows and looked down to the street. If someone *had* been out there watching, she would have been an obvious and vulnerable target fleeing in the middle of the night. Although she'd certainly give Don a better fight now than a few months ago.

But something didn't feel right. His instincts told him Don was still in Milwaukee. That the bastard was playing head games with Cassie for his own amusement. He could have an accomplice, of course, but that didn't feel right, either. Don was in it for the game. He wouldn't want someone else to have the fun. Abusive husbands didn't hire out their dirty work. Like Earl Washington, they wanted their victory all to themselves.

Cathy walked up beside him. "She said if she ever had to use the bag, she'd buy a throwaway phone the next day and call to let us know she was okay."

"She promised she wouldn't leave without me."

"I know, Nick, but we don't know what happened. All we can do now is wait."

He nodded mutely. Waiting wasn't his thing. But he had no idea where she'd go. Farther east? North to Canada? Catch a flight to the West Coast? None of that felt right. And she would have left in the middle of the night, so how far could she have gone? As a detective, he'd always trusted his gut. And his gut was telling him she wasn't far away. He turned and strode to the door.

"I'm going to drive around and see what I can find."

Cathy's hand rested over her heart. "What you can find? You think Don…?"

Nick shook his head, but it was Amanda who answered, walking through the door with her phone in her hand and looking ticked off.

"Don's not in New York," she said. "I just talked to the sheriff. He called and talked to Don's probation officer in Milwaukee. The probation officer went to Don's place with the police. He was at home. They found three burner phones he was making calls from. The idiot had them sitting right there next to his chair, along with a bottle of scotch. They're charging him with violating his probation, among other things."

"So Cassie's not in danger? Thank God." Cathy sat at the kitchen island. "Maybe my heart can start beating again."

Cassie might be safe from Don, but she didn't *know* that. She was on the run.

He headed for the door. "I've got to find her."

Amanda turned to walk with him. "I'll pick up Blake and we'll head west if you want to go east."

Nora walked over and gave Nick's hand a squeeze. "I have to get back down to the shop, but my husband, Asher, knows the area really well. I'll have him head north toward Hunter. We'll find her, Nick."

Nick hadn't prayed in a very long time, but he did his best to plead his case with whoever might be listening as he drove out of Gallant Lake. He was desperate for some clue of where she might be. He passed the mountain road that led to the walking trail up Gallant Mountain. It didn't make sense that she'd hike up the mountain alone at night. But he couldn't ignore the nagging thought that he'd find her there. After driving less than a mile farther down the highway, he pulled a U-turn and headed up the winding road. He turned onto the rutted track that led to the base of the Kissing Rock trail.

His head told him her little car probably wouldn't have made it up here, but his heart told him he was getting closer to her. Sure enough, when he pulled into the clearing by the gate, her compact car was there, covered with mud. It was empty. He smiled and looked up the trail. She was on Gallant Mountain.

He took his phone out of his pocket as he grabbed his small pack from the back seat, texting Blake. No sense in everyone else searching. Even if he didn't have eyes on her yet, he knew Cassie was here.

Got her.

As he went through the gate, he thought of her going up the trail in the dark. It was a decent path, but steep, and through dense woods. She might be here, but was she okay? He'd just picked up his pace when Blake's response came.

i'll let the others know. Amanda says make sure you KEEP her this time.

Nick shook his head. He deserved whatever Amanda threw at him. And whatever Cassie threw at him once he found her. He'd been an idiot, and he'd almost lost her. But that would never happen again. He tapped a quick reply as he hurried up the trail.

Tell her to count on it.

CHAPTER NINETEEN

CASSIE HAD WATCHED the sunrise from the top of the Kissing Rock. Actually, she watched the effects of the sunrise, since it came up behind her. It cast the shadow of Gallant Mountain on the lake and the smaller mountain on the opposite side, but that shadow receded slowly as the sun climbed higher. Pretty soon she'd be warmed by its light, and she wouldn't mind that one bit.

In her panic, she'd left everything in the car before climbing up here in the silver predawn light, including the go-bag with her jacket in it. It was amazing she'd made it here in one piece, but someone must have been watching over her as she did her best to remember the trail and not walk smack into a tree.

She stretched her legs in front of her. There was water and granola bars in the bag, too. The bag that was in her car. She really should have thought this through a little bit better. She didn't dare go back, in case Don somehow found the car. Highly improbable, but even if he *did*, he'd have no idea where she'd gone. Unlike Nick, Don *hated* the outdoors. She'd left the apartment in such a mad blur of panic after Don's texts. Then heartbreak took over as she drove out of Gallant Lake and away from Nick. She couldn't leave him. She couldn't bring herself to *go* to him, either. She'd said some awful things to him. His last text said they *weren't* done, but... What if they were?

Her flight out of town had been horrible. The road out of Gallant Lake led past the resort and the large estate called Halcyon, both on the lake. She'd slowed by the resort, filled with regret that she wasn't going to be able to say goodbye. At two in the morning, the lake had been black as ink beyond it. She didn't want to wake Blake and Amanda at that hour. What would she say?

Hello, I'm an idiot who chased off the only man I've ever loved and I don't know how to fix it. I thought I was tougher now, but I freaked out when my ex tried to scare me. So clearly I'm not tough. I'm just stupid and I don't know what to do... Help!

She could imagine the expression on their faces if she woke them up with that little pity party in the middle of the night. Amanda would do her best to make her feel better, but...no.

Cassie was so afraid Don would find her that she panicked every time she saw headlights. She'd finally turned off the main highway and started on the twisting mountain roads. It wasn't long before she was hopelessly lost, with no cell phone to call for help. By some miracle, she'd recognized the road Nick used to get to the Kissing Rock trail. She slowed until she found the opening in the trees to the dirt road leading up the mountain. Up to the place where she and Nick had kissed for the first time. Where they'd made love under the stars just last week. Where she'd felt like she was on top of the world. Invincible. If there was any place on this earth where she could figure out what to do next, this was it. And Don would never find her here.

The first hint that she wasn't alone made her pulse jump. She heard footsteps. Rustling branches. Was it Don? Maybe a hiker? A bear? She glanced up the rock wall behind her. She had no idea how to climb it, but if a bear strolled out of those trees, she might just give it a try. She scooted across the rock, wishing there was more cover, and knowing if she stood she'd be even more visible. She caught a glimpse of blue in the trees. Not a bear.

Nick stepped out from the shadows and stopped, looking straight at her as if he wasn't the least bit surprised to see her. She rolled her eyes at herself—duh, he'd seen her car, of course. But how had he known where to look? And what was that expression on his face? Anger? Relief?

"Do you mind having company up there?"

She shook her head, straightening against the cliff again. "Not if that company is you."

He climbed that little path up the side of the rock like it was nothing. He hesitated, then sat next to her, with his legs out in front of him like hers were. He looked out at the lake. Not at her. Her heart fluttered in her chest. They sat like that for several minutes before he spoke, his voice like honey and electricity in her veins.

"Don was never in Gallant Lake."

"I got texts. He knew where I was."

"I saw the texts. He knew about Gallant Lake, but he's not here."

She turned to him in surprise. "You opened my phone? How?"

"Seriously?" He gave her the first glimmer of a smile. "Your password is 1111. It wasn't that hard. He's not here, Cass. He's in Milwaukee. They arrested him there this morning and found the phones he's been using. You're safe."

She didn't answer. All that panic. For nothing. She was overwhelmed with exhaustion.

Nick nudged her shoulder with his. It was an innocent move, but the contact instantly had her nerves on end. His eyes met hers.

"That was pretty smart, hiding up here. But it doesn't surprise me. You're a pretty smart lady. You can take care of yourself." He grew more solemn. "You've always been able to take care of yourself, Cassie. You never needed me. Not now. Not before."

She let those words settle in. She hadn't realized how much she needed to hear them. She thought she could dismiss their argument and forgive everything. But forgiving wasn't the same as forgetting. It meant a lot to know he'd *heard* her on Friday.

"Thank you for saying that. I'm sorry about what I…"

He put his finger to her lips. "You were right. About everything. I mean, yeah, you twisted me up a little too closely with Don, but I get it." His words came out in a rush. "I was all tangled up with my guilt over Jada and the anger I hadn't dealt with… And then I fell in love with you and it scared the daylights out of me. The stronger my feelings got, the more I kept thinking that I couldn't lose someone *else* like that. I couldn't stand having you out of my sight, and I smothered you. I know that now. I see how it could make you think I was doing it for all the wrong reasons…"

Cassie moved his finger aside so she could speak.

"Say that again."

His brows rose.

"All of it?"

"The only part that matters." She needed to be sure she'd heard him right. He looked at the ground for a second, rewinding his rambling speech. Then his mouth curled into a smile, his eyes deepening to the color of hot, black coffee. He cupped her face with his hand and leaned in, repeating the words against her lips before he kissed her.

"I fell in love with you."

She sighed and let him kiss her. Let him pull her onto his lap and tip her back and kiss her until she was dizzy. When he lifted his head, she was clinging to his shoulders. Then she released her hold, fell back and grinned up at him as she stretched her arms out wide. It felt as if she was dangling over the edge of the mountain, with the lake glistening blue beyond them. Nick was bemused.

"Whatcha doin', slugger?"

"I'm letting you take care of me, Nick." She glanced up at him before gazing back out at the dizzying upside-down view. "I *am* able to take care of myself. And I *will* take care of myself. But it's okay to lean on the arms of the man I love and trust him to keep me safe."

Nick pulled her upright so fast she gasped, resting her hands on his arms.

"Say that again." His voice was thick with emotion.

Their smiles mirrored each other.

"All of it?"

"Just the part that matters."

"I love you, Nick. And I trust you." He kissed her again, scattering her thoughts until all she felt were his lips and his hands sliding under her shirt and up her back.

"God, Cassie, I love you so much. Don't ever leave me again. You promised you wouldn't."

She pulled away, pinched with guilt at the pain she saw in his eyes.

"I'm so sorry. I didn't know where we stood after that horrid fight. I was afraid I'd blown everything. When I saw that kid grab his girlfriend and threaten to hit her I…kinda lost it. The mistake was that I lost it with *you*." She gave him a quick kiss. "I got a little carried away with my newfound independence and daring-do, and it went to my head. Then the text came through last night and…"

He placed his lips on her forehead and stayed there, as if reveling in the moment, before he answered.

"I went all caveman on you. I took your victory away. I get it. But from now on…"

She snuggled into his arms and finished the sentence. "From now on, you and I will talk things through and trust each other. I'll trust you to take care of me without making me feel helpless…"

"And I'll trust you to make the right decisions for yourself, even if they aren't the decisions *I'd* make." He kissed her. "I'll trust you to love me, even when I'm an overprotective husband."

"*Husband?* Did I miss a question somewhere?"

"The question won't come until there's a ring in my hand, but trust me, it's coming."

"O-kay. Then I'll trust you to love me, even when I'm a stubbornly independent wife."

"Sounds like we may be having a few…um…fun discussions down the road."

"Maybe. But as long as we remember the love-and-trust part, I think we'll be okay." She cupped his face with her hands. "You were wrong earlier, Nick. You said I didn't need you, but I do. I need you as much as I need the air I'm breathing. When those 'fun' discussions come up in the future, and I'm sure they will, we have to remember that need. That promise to love and trust."

He pulled her close. "We'll write it into our vows." He grinned. "I'm sorry, that sounded bossy, didn't it? I *suggest* we put it into our vows. Only if you agree, of course."

She chuckled against his chest. "I think that's a very good 'suggestion.' And now to a more important question…"

He looked down at her, one brow raised, waiting.

"Do you have food in that pack of yours? Because I am starving!"

Nick laughed and reached for the pack while cradling her in his other arm.

"You know I do. And water, too."

"I can always count on you, Nick."

With a quick twist, he laid her back on the rock and rested on top of her, his hand running down her side and around to her buttocks, pulling her up against him.

"Yeah, you can always count on me, babe. Don't ever forget that."

She knew what he was thinking, and frankly, she was thinking the same thing.

"What if someone hikes up to the Kissing Rock this morning?"

"On a Monday? Highly unlikely. I think we're safe." He kissed her. "Well, I don't know if *safe* is the right word. I never feel safe with you, because you make me crazy." He kissed her again. "I love you, Cassidy Zetticci. And I'll never stop loving you. You still hungry?"

"Oh, I'm hungry, alright. Hungry for you. I love you, Nick West."

"Don't ever stop loving me, Cass. It'll break me."

"I couldn't stop loving you if I tried. Always."

He kissed her.

"And forever."

* * * * *

Miss Prim's Greek Island Fling

Michelle Douglas

Forever

Glamorous and heartfelt love stories.

Michelle Douglas has been writing for Harlequin since 2007 and believes she has the best job in the world. She lives in a leafy suburb of Newcastle on Australia's east coast with her own romantic hero, a house full of dust and books and an eclectic collection of '60s and '70s vinyl. She loves to hear from readers and can be contacted via her website, michelle-douglas.com.

Books by Michelle Douglas

The Vineyards of Calanetti

Reunited by a Baby Secret

The Wild Ones

Her Irresistible Protector
The Rebel and the Heiress

The Redemption of Rico D'Angelo
Road Trip with the Eligible Bachelor
Snowbound Surprise for the Billionaire
The Millionaire and the Maid
A Deal to Mend Their Marriage
An Unlikely Bride for the Billionaire
The Spanish Tycoon's Takeover
Sarah and the Secret Sheikh
A Baby in His In-Tray
The Million Pound Marriage Deal

Visit the Author Profile page
at millsandboon.com.au for more titles.

Dear Reader,

I have a deep and abiding love for the beach, and I'm ridiculously lucky as I have a whole host of gorgeous beaches that are just a short drive from where I live. I find few things more relaxing than bobbing about in the ocean after a hard (?) day's writing. The scent of the sea and the sound of the waves put me straight into my happy place.

So when I toyed with the idea of setting a book on an idyllic Greek island my muse gave a resounding cheer...and that's how the fictional island of Kyanós was born. I promptly fell in love with Kyanós, and over the course of the story so do Audra and Finn. It's fun watching these seeming opposites learn to relax and unwind and find the courage to follow their hearts' desires—and, seriously, where better to do that than on a Greek island, right?

Writing this story made me so absolutely happy. Research included eating baklava and playing old ABBA albums, which were the perfect complements. So I can certainly suggest those during the reading of the book. :) I hope the story puts a smile on your face, too.

Happy reading!

Michelle x

To Pam, who is always happy to share a bottle of
red and to talk into the wee hours of the night.

Praise for
Michelle Douglas

"Captivatingly sweet...! Great characters, a
heartwarming story line and just a whole lot of
feel-good reading!"

—*Goodreads* on *The Spanish Tycoon's Takeover*

CHAPTER ONE

IT WAS THE sound of shattering glass that woke her.

Audra shot bolt upright in bed, heart pounding, praying that the sound had been a part of one of her frequent nightmares, but knowing deep down in her bones—in all the places where she knew such things were real—that it wasn't.

A thump followed. Something heavy being dropped to the floor. And then a low, jeering voice. The sound of cupboard doors opening and closing.

She'd locked all the doors and windows downstairs! She'd been hyper-vigilant about such things ever since she'd arrived two days ago. She glanced at her bedroom window, at the curtain moving slowly on a draught of warm night air, and called herself a fool for leaving it open. Anyone could have climbed up onto the first-floor balcony and gained entry.

Slipping out of bed, she grabbed her phone and held it pressed hard against her chest as she crept out into the hallway. As the only person in residence in Rupert's Greek villa, she'd seen no reason to close her bedroom door, which at least meant she didn't have to contend with the sound of it creaking open now.

She'd chosen the bedroom at the top of the stairs and from this vantage point she could see a shadow bounce in and out of view from the downstairs living room. She heard Rupert's liquor cabinet being opened and the sound of a glass bottle being set down. Thieves were stealing her brother's much-loved single malt whisky?

Someone downstairs muttered something in... French?

She didn't catch what was said.

Someone answered back in Greek.

She strained her ears, but could catch no other words. So... there were two of them? She refused to contemplate what would happen if they found her here—a lone woman. Swallowing down a hard knot of fear, she made her way silently down the hallway, away from the stairs, to the farthest room along—the master bedroom. The door made the softest of snicks as she eased it closed. In the moonlight she made out the walk-in wardrobe on the other side of the room and headed straight for it, closing that door behind her, fighting to breathe through the panic that weighed her chest down.

She dialled the emergency number. 'Please help me,' she whispered in Greek. 'Please. There are intruders in my house.' She gave her name. She gave the address. The operator promised that someone was on the way and would be there in minutes. She spoke in reassuringly calm tones. She asked Audra where in the house she was, and if there was anywhere she could hide. She told Audra to stay on the line and that helped too.

'I'm hiding in the walk-in wardrobe in the master bedroom.' And that was when it hit her. She was all but locked in a closet. *Again.* It made no difference that this time she'd locked her-self in. Panic clawed at her throat as she recalled the suffocating darkness and the way her body had started to cramp after hours spent confined in her tiny hall closet. When Thomas had not only locked her in, but had left and she hadn't known if he would ever return to let her out again. And if he didn't return, how long would it take for anyone to find her? How long before someone raised the alarm? She'd spent hours in a terrified limbo—after screaming herself hoarse for help—where she'd had to fight for every breath. 'I can't stay here.'

'The police are almost there,' the operator assured her.

She closed her eyes. This wasn't her horridly cramped hall closet, but a spacious walk-in robe. It didn't smell of damp leather and fuggy cold. This smelled of…the sea. And she could stretch out her full length and not touch the other wall if she wanted to. Anger, cold and comforting, streaked through her then. Her eyes flew open. She would *not* be a victim again. Oh, she wasn't going to march downstairs and confront those two villains ransacking her brother's house, but she wasn't going to stay here, a cornered quaking mess either.

Her free hand clenched to a fist. *Think!* If she were a thief, what would she steal?

Electrical equipment—televisions, stereos and computers. Which were all downstairs. She grimaced. Except for the television on the wall in the master bedroom.

She'd bet they'd look for jewellery too. And where was the most likely place to find that? The master bedroom.

She needed to find a better hiding place—one that had an escape route if needed.

And she needed a weapon. Just in case. She didn't rate her chances against two burly men, but she could leave some bruises if they did try to attack her. She reminded herself that the police would be here soon.

For the first time since arriving in this island idyll, Audra cursed the isolation of Rupert's villa. It was the last property on a peninsula surrounded by azure seas. The glorious sea views, the scent of the ocean and gardens, the sound of lapping water combined with the humming of bees and the chattering of the birds had started to ease the burning in her soul. No media, no one hassling her for an interview, no flashing cameras whenever she strode outside her front door. The privacy had seemed like a godsend.

Until now.

Using the torch app on her phone, she scanned the wardrobe for something she could use to defend herself. Her fingers closed about a lacrosse stick. It must've been years since Rupert had played, and she had no idea what he was still doing with a stick now, but at the moment she didn't care.

Cracking open the wardrobe door, she listened for a full minute before edging across the room to the glass sliding door of the balcony. She winced at the click that seemed to echo throughout the room with a *come-and-find-me* din when she unlocked it, but thanked Rupert's maintenance man when it slid open on its tracks as silent as the moon. She paused and listened again for another full minute before easing outside and closing the door behind her. Hugging the shadows of the wall, she moved to the end of the balcony and inserted herself between two giant pot plants. The only way anyone would see her was if they came right out onto the balcony and moved in this direction. She gripped the lacrosse stick so tightly her fingers started to ache.

She closed her eyes and tried to get her breathing under control. The thieves would have no reason to come out onto the balcony. There was nothing to steal out here. And she doubted they'd be interested in admiring the view, regardless of how spectacular it might be. The tight band around her chest eased a fraction.

The flashing lights from the police car that tore into the driveway a moment later eased the tightness even further. She counted as four armed men piled out of the vehicle and headed straight inside. She heard shouts downstairs.

But still she didn't move.

After a moment she lifted the phone to her ear. 'Is it…is it safe to come out yet?' she whispered.

'One of the men has been apprehended. The officers are searching for the second man.' There was a pause. 'The man they have in custody claims he's on his own.'

She'd definitely heard French *and* Greek.

'He also says he's known to your brother.'

'Known?' She choked back a snort. 'I can assure you that my brother doesn't associate with people who break into houses.'

'He says his name is Finn Sullivan.'

Audra closed her eyes. *Scrap that.* Her brother knew *one* person who broke into houses, and his name was Finn Sullivan.

Finn swore in French, and then in Greek for good measure, when he knocked the crystal tumbler from the bench to the kitchen tiles below, making a God-awful racket that reverberated through his head. It served him right for not switching on a light, but he knew Rupert's house as well as he knew his own, and he'd wanted to try to keep the headache stretching behind his eyes from building into a full-blown migraine.

Blowing out a breath, he dropped his rucksack to the floor and, muttering first in French and then in Greek, clicked on a light and retrieved the dustpan and brush to clean up the mess. For pity's sake. Not only hadn't Rupert's last house guest washed, dried and put away the tumbler—leaving it for him to break—but they hadn't taken out the garbage either! Whenever he stayed, Finn always made sure to leave the place exactly as he found it—spotlessly clean and tidy. He hated to think of his friend being taken advantage of.

Helping himself to a glass of Rupert's excellent whisky, Finn lowered himself into an armchair in the living room, more winded than he cared to admit. The cast had come off his arm yesterday and it ached like the blazes now. As did his entire left side and his left knee. Take it easy, the doctor had ordered. But he'd been taking it easy for eight long weeks. And Nice had started to feel like a prison.

Rupert had given him a key to this place a couple of years ago, and had told him to treat it as his own. He'd ring Rupert tomorrow to let him know he was here. He glanced at the clock on the wall. Two thirty-seven a.m. was too late…or early…to call anyone. He rested his head back and closed his eyes, and tried to will the pain coursing through his body away.

He woke with a start to flashing lights, and it took him a moment to realise they weren't due to a migraine. He blinked, but the armed policemen—two of them and each with a gun trained on him—didn't disappear. The clock said two forty-eight.

He raised his hands in the universal gesture of non-aggression. 'My name is Finn Sullivan,' he said in Greek. 'I am a friend of Rupert Russel, the owner of this villa.'

'Where is your accomplice?'

'Accomplice?' He stood then, stung by the fuss and suspicion. 'What accomplice?'

He wished he'd remained seated when he found himself tackled to the floor, pain bursting like red-hot needles all the way down his left side, magnifying the blue-black ache that made him want to roar.

He clamped the howls of pain behind his teeth and nodded towards his backpack as an officer rough-handled him to his feet after handcuffing him. 'My identification is in there.'

His words seemed to have no effect. One of the officers spoke into a phone. He was frogmarched into the grand foyer. Both policemen looked upwards expectantly, so he did too.

'Audra!'

Flanked by two more police officers, she pulled to a dead halt halfway down the stairs, her eyes widening—those too cool and very clear blue eyes. 'Finn?' Delicate nostrils flared. 'What on earth are you doing here?'

The glass on the sink, the litter in the kitchen bin made sudden sense. '*You* called the police?'

'Of course I called the police!'

'Of all the idiotic, overdramatic reactions! How daft can you get?' He all but yelled the words at her, his physical pain needing an outlet. 'Why the hell would you overreact like that?'

'Daft? Daft!' Her voice rose as she flew down the stairs. 'And what do you call breaking and entering my brother's villa at two thirty in the morning?'

It was probably closer to three by now. He didn't say that out loud. 'I didn't break in. I have a key.'

He saw then that she clutched a lacrosse stick. She looked as if she wouldn't mind cracking him over the head with it. With a force of effort he pulled in a breath. A woman alone in a deserted house...the sound of breaking glass... And after everything she'd been through recently...

He bit back a curse. He'd genuinely frightened her.

The pain in his head intensified. 'I'm sorry, Squirt.' The old nickname dropped from his lips. 'If I'd known you were here I'd have rung to let you know I was coming. In the meantime, can you tell these guys who I am and call them off?'

'Where's your friend?'

His shoulder ached like the blazes. He wanted to yell at her to get the police to release him. He bit the angry torrent back. Knowing Audra, she'd make him suffer as long as she could if he yelled at her again.

And he *was* genuinely sorry he'd frightened her.

'I came alone.'

'But I heard two voices—one French, one Greek.'

He shook his head. 'You heard one voice and two languages.' He demonstrated his earlier cussing fit, though he toned it down to make it more palatable for mixed company.

For a moment the knuckles on her right hand whitened where it gripped the lacrosse stick, and then relaxed. She told the police officers in perfect Greek how sorry she was to have raised a false alarm, promised to bake them homemade lemon drizzle cakes and begged them very nicely to let him go as he was an old friend of her brother's. He wasn't sure why, but it made him grind his teeth.

He groaned his relief when he was uncuffed, rubbing his wrists rather than his shoulder, though he was damned if he knew why. Except he didn't want any of them to know how much he hurt. He was sick to death of his injuries.

A part of him would be damned too before it let Audra see him as anything but hearty and hale. Her pity would...

He pressed his lips together. He didn't know. All he knew was that he didn't want to become an object of it.

Standing side by side in the circular drive, they waved the police off. He followed her inside, wincing when she slammed the door shut behind them. The fire in her eyes hadn't subsided. 'You want to yell at me some more?'

He'd love to. It was what he and Audra did—they sniped at each other. They had ever since she'd been a gangly pre-teen. But he hurt too much to snipe properly. It was taking all his strength to control the nausea curdling his stomach. He glanced at her from beneath his shaggy fringe. Besides, it was no fun sniping at someone with the kind of shadows under their eyes that Audra had.

He eased back to survey her properly. She was too pale and too thin. He wasn't used to seeing her vulnerable and frightened.

Frighteningly efficient? *Yes.*

Unsmiling? *Yes.*

Openly disapproving of his lifestyle choices? *Double yes.*

But pale, vulnerable and afraid? *No.*

'That bastard really did a number on you, didn't he, Squirt?'

Her head reared back and he could've bitten his tongue out. 'Not quite as big a number as that mountain did on you, from all reports.'

She glanced pointedly at his shoulder and with a start he realised he'd been massaging it. He waved her words away. 'A temporary setback.'

She pushed out her chin. 'Ditto.'

The fire had receded from her eyes and this time it was he who had to suffer beneath their merciless ice-blue scrutiny. And that was when he realised that all she wore was a pair of thin cotton pyjama bottoms and a singlet top that moulded itself to her form. His tongue stuck to the roof of his mouth.

The problem with Audra was that she was *exactly* the kind of woman he went after. If he had a type it was the buttoned-up, repressed librarian type, and normally Audra embodied that to a tee. But at the moment she was about as far from that as you could get. She was all blonde sleep-tousled temptation and his skin prickled with an awareness that was both familiar and unfamiliar.

He had to remind himself that a guy didn't mess with his best friend's sister.

'Did the police hurt you?'

'Absolutely not.' He was admitting nothing.

She cocked an eyebrow. 'Finn, it's obvious you're in pain.'

He shrugged and then wished he hadn't when pain blazed through his shoulder. 'The cast only came off yesterday.'

Her gaze moved to his left arm. 'And instead of resting it, no doubt as your doctors suggested, you jumped on the first plane for Athens, caught the last ferry to Kyanós, grabbed a late dinner in the village and trekked the eight kilometres to the villa.'

'Bingo.' He'd relished the fresh air and the freedom. For the first two kilometres.

'While carrying a rucksack.'

Eight weeks ago he'd have been able to carry twice the weight for ten kilometres without breaking a sweat.

She picked up his glass of half-finished Scotch and strode into the kitchen. As she reached up into a kitchen cupboard her singlet hiked up to expose a band of perfect pale skin that had his gut clenching. She pulled out a packet of aspirin and sent it flying in a perfect arc towards him—he barely needed to move to catch it. And then she lifted his glass to her lips and drained it and stars burst behind his eyelids. It was the sexiest thing he'd ever seen.

She filled it with tap water and set it in front of him. 'Take two.'

He did as she ordered because it was easier than arguing with her. And because he hurt all over and it seemed too much trouble to find the heavy-duty painkillers his doctor had prescribed for him and which were currently rolling around in the bottom of his backpack somewhere.

'Which room do you usually use?'

'The one at the top of the stairs.'

'You're out of luck, buddy.' She stuck out a hip, and he gulped down more water. 'That's the one I'm using.'

He feigned outrage. 'But that one has the best view!' Which was a lie. All the upstairs bedrooms had spectacular views.

She smirked. 'I know. First in and all that.'

He choked down a laugh. That was one of the things he'd always liked about Audra. She'd play along with him…all in the name of one-upmanship, of course.

'Right, which bedroom do you want? There are another three upstairs to choose from.' She strode around and lifted his bag. She grunted and had to use both hands. 'Yeah, right—light as a feather.'

He glanced at her arms. While the rucksack wasn't exactly light, it wasn't that heavy. She'd never been a weakling. She'd lost condition. He tried to recall the last time he'd seen her.

'Earth to Finn.'

He started. 'I'll take the one on the ground floor.' The one behind the kitchen. The only bedroom in the house that didn't have a sea view. The bedroom furthest away from Audra's. They wouldn't even have to share a bathroom if he stayed down here. Which would be for the best.

He glanced at that singlet top and nodded. *Definitely* for the best.

Especially when her eyes softened with spring-rain warmth. 'Damn, Finn. Do you still hurt that much?'

He realised then that she thought he didn't want to tackle the stairs.

'I—' He pulled in a breath. He *didn't* want to tackle the stairs. He'd overdone it today. He didn't want her to keep looking at him like that either, though. 'It's nothing a good night's sleep won't fix.'

Without another word, she strode to the room behind the kitchen and lifted his bag up onto the desk in there. So he wouldn't have to lift it himself later. Her thoughtfulness touched him. She could be prickly, and she could be mouthy, but she'd never been unkind.

Which was the reason, if he ever ran into Thomas Farquhar, he'd wring the mongrel's neck.

'Do you need anything else?'

The beds in Rupert's villa were always made up. He employed a cleaner to come in once a week so that the Russel siblings or any close friends could land here and fall into bed with a minimum of fuss. But even if the bed hadn't been made pride would've forbidden him from asking her to make it...or to help him make it.

He fell into a chair and slanted her a grin—cocky, assured and full of teasing to hide his pain as he pulled his hiking boots off. 'Well, now, Squirt...' He lifted a foot in her direction. 'I could use some help getting my socks off. And then maybe my jeans.'

As anticipated, her eyes went wide and her cheeks went pink. Without another word, she whirled around and strode from the room.

At that precise moment his phone started to ring. He glanced at the caller ID and grimaced. 'Rupert, mate. Sorry about—'

The phone was summarily taken from him and Finn blinked when Audra lifted it to her ear. Up this close she smelled of coconut and peaches. His mouth watered. Dinner suddenly seemed like hours ago.

'Rupe, Finn looks like death. He needs to rest. He'll call you in the morning and you can give him an ear-bashing then.' She turned the phone off before handing it back to him. 'Goodnight, Finn.'

She was halfway through the kitchen before he managed to call back a goodnight of his own. He stood in the doorway and waited until he heard her ascending the stairs before closing his door and dialling Rupert's number.

'Before you launch into a tirade and tell me what an idiot I am, let me apologise. I'm calling myself far worse names than you ever will. I'd have not scared Audra for the world. I was going to call you in the morning to let you know I was here.' He'd had no notion Audra would be here. It was a little early in the season for any of the Russels to head for the island.

Rupert's long sigh came down the phone, and it made Finn's gut churn. 'What are you doing in Kyanós?' his friend finally asked. 'I thought you were in Nice.'

'The, uh, cast came off yesterday.'

'And you couldn't blow off steam on the French Riviera?'

He scrubbed a hand down his face. 'There's a woman I'm trying to avoid and—'

'You don't need to say any more. I get the picture.'

Actually, Rupert was wrong. This time. It wasn't a romantic liaison he'd tired of and was fleeing. But he kept his mouth shut. He deserved Rupert's derision. 'If you want me to leave, I'll clear out at first light.'

His heart gave a sick kick at the long pause on the other end of the phone. Rupert was considering it! Rupert was the one person who'd shown faith in him when everyone else had written him off, and now—

'Of course I don't want you to leave.'

He closed his eyes and let out a long, slow breath.

'But...'

His eyes crashed open. His heart started to thud. 'But?'

'Don't go letting Audra fall in love with you. She's fragile at the moment, Finn...vulnerable.'

He stiffened. 'Whoa, Rupe! I've no designs on your little sister.'

'She's *exactly* your type.'

'Except she's your sister.' He made a decision then and there to leave in the morning. He didn't want Rupert worrying about this. It was completely unnecessary. He needed to lie low for a few weeks and Kyanós had seemed like the perfect solution, but not at the expense of either Rupert's or Audra's peace of mind.

'That said, I'm glad you're there.'

Finn stilled.

'I'm worried about her being on her own. I've been trying to juggle my timetable, but the earliest I can get away is in a fortnight.'

Finn pursed his lips. 'You want me to keep an eye on her?'

Again there was a long pause. 'She needs a bit of fun. She needs to let her hair down.'

'This *is* Audra we're talking about.' She was the most buttoned-up person he knew.

'You're good at fun.'

His lips twisted. He ought to be. He'd spent a lifetime perfecting it. 'You want me to make sure she has a proper holiday?'

'Minus the holiday romance. Women *like* you, Finn...they fall for you.'

'Pot and kettle,' he grunted back. 'But you're worrying for nothing. Audra has more sense than that.' She had *always* disapproved of him and what she saw as his irresponsible and daredevil lifestyle.

What had happened eight weeks ago proved her point. What if the next time he did kill himself? The thought made his mouth dry and his gut churn. His body was recovering but his mind... There were days when he was a maelstrom of confusion, questioning the choices he was making. He gritted his teeth. It'd pass. After such a close brush with mortality it had to be normal to question one's life. Needless to say, he wasn't bringing anyone into that mess at the moment, especially not one who was his best friend's little sister.

'If she had more sense she'd have not fallen for Farquhar.'

Finn's hands fisted. 'Tell me the guy is toast.'

'I'm working on it.'

Good.

'I've tried to shield her from the worst of the media furore, but...'

'But she has eyes in her head. She can read the headlines for herself.' And those headlines had been everywhere. It'd been smart of Rupert to pack Audra off to the island.

'Exactly.' Rupert paused again. 'None of the Russels have any sense when it comes to love. If we did, Audra wouldn't have been taken in like she was.'

And she was paying for it now. He recalled her pallor, the dark circles beneath her eyes...the effort it'd taken her to lift his backpack. He could help with some of that—get her out into the sun, challenge her to swimming contests...and maybe even get her to run with him. He could make sure she ate three square meals a day.

'If I'd had more sense I'd have not fallen for Brooke Manning.'

'Everyone makes a bad romantic decision at least once in their lives, Rupe.'

He realised he sounded as if he were downplaying what had happened to his friend, and he didn't want to do that. Rupert hadn't looked at women in the same way after Brooke. Finn wasn't sure what had happened between them. He'd been certain they were heading for matrimony, babies and white picket fences. But it had all imploded, and Rupert hadn't been the same since. 'But you're right—not everyone gets their heart shredded.' He rubbed a hand across his chest. 'Has Farquhar shredded her heart?'

'I don't know.'

Even if he hadn't, he'd stolen company secrets from the Russel Corporation while posing as her attentive and very loving boyfriend. That wasn't something a woman like Audra would be able to shrug off as just a bad experience.

Poor Squirt.

He only realised he'd said that out loud when Rupert said with a voice as dry as a good single malt, 'Take a look, Finn. I think you'll find Squirt is all grown up.'

He didn't need to look. The less looking he did, the better. A girl like Audra deserved more than what a guy like him could give her—things like stability, peace of mind, and someone she could depend on.

'It'd be great if you could take her mind off things—make her laugh and have some fun. I just don't want her falling for you. She's bruised and battered enough.'

'You've nothing to worry about on that score, Rupe, I promise you. I've no intention of hurting Audra. Ever.'

'She's special, Finn.'

That made him smile. 'All of the Russel siblings are special.'

'She's more selfless than the rest of us put together.'

Finn blinked. 'That's a big call.'

'It's the truth.'

He hauled in a breath and let it out slowly. 'I'll see what I can do.'

'Thanks, Finn, I knew I could count on you.'

Audra pressed her ringing phone to her ear at exactly eight twenty-three the next morning. She knew the exact time because she was wondering when Finn would emerge. She'd started clock-watching—a sure sign of worry. Not that she had any intention of letting Rupert know she was worried. 'Hey, Rupe.'

He called to check on her every couple of days, which only fed her guilt. Last night's false alarm sent an extra surge of guilt slugging through her now. 'Sorry about last night's fuss. I take it the police rang to let you know what happened.'

'They did. And you've nothing to apologise for. Wasn't your fault. In fact, I'm proud of the way you handled the situation.'

He was? Her shoulders went back.

'Not everyone would've thought that quickly on their feet. You did good.'

'Thanks, I… I'm relieved it was just Finn.' She flashed to the lines of strain that had bracketed Finn's mouth last night. 'Do you know how long he plans to stay?'

'No idea. Do you mind him being there? I can ask him to leave.'

'No, no—don't do that.' She already owed Rupert and the rest of her family too much. She didn't want to cause any further fuss. 'He wasn't looking too crash hot last night. I think he needs to take it easy for a bit.'

'You could be right, Squirt, and I hate to ask this of you...'

'Ask away.' She marvelled how her brother's *Squirt* could sound so different from Finn's. When Finn called her Squirt it made her tingle all over.

'No, forget about it. It doesn't matter. You've enough on your plate.'

She had nothing on her plate at the moment and they both knew it. 'Tell me what you were going to say,' she ordered in her best boardroom voice. 'I insist. You know you'll get no peace now until you do.'

His low chuckle was her reward. Good. She wanted him to stop worrying about her.

'Okay, it's just... I'm a bit worried about him.'

She sat back. 'About Finn?' It made a change from Rupert worrying about her.

'He's never had to take it easy in his life. Going slow is an alien concept to him.'

He could say that again.

'He nearly died up there on that mountain.'

Her heart clenched. 'Died? I mean, I knew he'd banged himself up pretty bad, but... I had no idea.'

'Typical Finn, he's tried to downplay it. While the medical team could patch the broken arm and ribs easily enough, along with the dislocated shoulder and wrenched knee, his ruptured spleen and the internal bleeding nearly did him in.'

She closed her eyes and swallowed. 'You want me to make sure he takes it easy while he's here?'

'That's probably an impossible task.'

'Nothing's impossible,' she said with a confidence she had no right to. After all her brother's support these last few weeks—

his lack of blame—she could certainly do this one thing for him. 'Consider it done.'

'And, Audra...?'

'Yes?'

'Don't go falling in love with him.'

She shot to her feet, her back ramrod straight. 'I make one mistake and—'

'This has nothing to do with what happened with Farquhar. It's just that women seem to like Finn. *A lot*. They fall at his feet in embarrassing numbers.'

She snorted and took her seat again. 'That's because he's pretty.' She preferred a man with a bit more substance.

You thought Thomas had substance.

She pushed the thought away.

'He's in Kyanós partly because he's trying to avoid some woman in Nice.'

Good to know.

'If he hurts you, Squirt, I'll no longer consider him a friend.'

She straightened from her slouch, air whistling between her teeth. Rupert and Finn were best friends, and had been ever since they'd attended their international boarding school in Geneva as fresh-faced twelve-year-olds.

She made herself swallow. 'I've no intention of doing anything so daft.' She'd never do anything to ruin her brother's most important friendship.

'Finn has a brilliant mind, he's built a successful company and is an amazing guy, but...'

'But what?' She frowned, when her brother remained silent. 'What are you worried about?'

'His past holds him back.'

By *his past* she guessed he meant Finn's parents' high-octane lifestyle, followed by their untimely deaths. It had to have had an impact on Finn, had to have left scars and wounds that would never heal.

'I worry he could end up like his father.'

She had to swallow the bile that rose through her.

'I'm not sure he'll ever settle down.'

She'd worked that much out for herself. And she wasn't a masochist. Men like Finn were pretty to look at, but you didn't build a life around them.

Women had flings with men like Finn…and she suspected they enjoyed every moment of them. A squirrel of curiosity wriggled through her, but she ruthlessly cut it off. One disastrous romantic liaison was enough for the year. She wasn't adding another one to the tally. She suppressed a shudder. The very thought made her want to crawl back into bed and pull the covers over her head.

She forced her spine to straighten. She had no intention of falling for Finn, but she could get him to slow down for a bit—just for a week or two, right?

CHAPTER TWO

'YOU HAD BREAKFAST YET, Squirt?'

Audra almost jumped out of her skin at the deep male voice
and the hard-muscled body that materialised directly in front of
her. She bit back a yelp and pressed a hand to her heart. After
sitting here waiting for him to emerge, she couldn't believe
she'd been taken off guard.

He chuckled. 'You never used to be jumpy.'

Yeah, well, that was before Thomas Farquhar had locked
her in a cupboard. The laughter in his warm brown eyes faded
as they narrowed. Not that she had any intention of telling him
that. She didn't want his pity. 'Broken sleep never leaves me at
my best,' she said in as tart a voice as she could muster. Which
was, admittedly, pretty tart.

He just grinned. 'I find it depends on the reasons for the broken sleep.' And then he sent her a broad wink.

She rolled her eyes. 'Glass shattering and having to call the
police doesn't fall into the fun category, Finn.'

'Do you want me to apologise again? Do the full grovel?'
He waggled his eyebrows. 'I'm very good at a comprehensive
grovel.'

'No, thank you.' She pressed her lips together. She bet he
was good at a lot of things.

She realised she still held her phone. She recalled the conversation she'd just had with Rupert and set it to the table, heat flushing through her cheeks.

Finn glanced at her and at the phone before cracking eggs into the waiting frying pan. 'So... Rupe rang to warn you off, huh?'

Her jaw dropped. How on earth...? *Ah.* 'He rang you too.'

'You want a couple of these?' He lifted an egg in her direction.

'No...thank you,' she added as a belated afterthought. It struck her that she always found it hard to remember her manners around Finn.

'Technically, I called him.' The frying pan spat and sizzled. 'But he seems to think I have some magic ability to make women swoon at my feet, whereby I pick them off at my leisure and have my wicked way with them before discarding them as is my wont.'

She frowned. Had she imagined the bitterness behind the lightness?

'He read me the Riot Act where you're concerned.' He sent her a mock serious look. 'So, Squirt, while I know it'll be hard for you to contain your disappointment, I'm afraid I'm not allowed to let a single one of my love rays loose in your direction.'

She couldn't help it, his nonsense made her laugh.

With an answering grin, he set a plate of eggs and toast in front of her and slid into the seat opposite.

'But I said I didn't want any.'

Her stomach rumbled, making a liar of her. Rather than tease her, though, he shrugged. 'Sorry, I must've misheard.'

Finn never misheard anything, but the smell of butter on toast made her mouth water. She picked up her knife and fork. It'd be wasteful not to eat it. 'Did Rupert order you to feed me up?' she grumbled.

He shook his head, and shaggy hair—damp from the shower—fell into his eyes and curled about his neck and some pulse inside her flared to life before she brutally strangled it.

'Nope. Rupe's only dictum was to keep my love rays well and truly away from his little sister. All uttered in his most stern of tones.'

She did her best not to choke on her toast and eggs. 'Doesn't Rupert know me at all?' She tossed the words back at him with what she hoped was a matching carelessness.

'See? That's what I told him. I said, Audra's too smart to fall for a guy like me.'

Fall for? Absolutely not. Sleep with…?

What on earth…? She frowned and forced the thought away. She didn't think of Finn in those terms.

Really?

She rolled her shoulders. So what if she'd always thought him too good-looking for his own good? That didn't mean anything. In idle moments she might find herself thinking he'd be an exciting lover. If she were the kind of person who did flings with devil-may-care men. But she wasn't. And *that* didn't mean anything either.

'So…?'

She glanced up at the question in his voice.

'How long have you been down here?'

'Two days.'

'And how long are you here for?'

She didn't really know. 'A fortnight, maybe. I've taken some annual leave.'

He sent her a sharp glance from beneath brows so perfectly shaped they made her the tiniest bit jealous. 'If you took all the leave accrued by you, I bet you could stay here until the middle of next year.'

Which would be heaven—absolute heaven.

'What about you? How long are you staying?'

'I was thinking a week or two. Do some training…get some condition back.'

He was going to overdo it. Well, not on her watch!

'But if my being here is intruding on your privacy, I can shoot off to my uncle's place.'

'No need for that. It'll be nice to have some company.'

His eyes narrowed and she realised she'd overplayed her hand. It wasn't her usual sentiment where Finn was concerned. Normally she acted utterly disdainful and scornful. They sparred. They didn't buddy up.

She lifted her fork and pointed it at him. 'As long as you stop calling me Squirt, stop blathering nonsense about love rays… and cook me breakfast every day.'

He laughed and she let out a slow breath.

'You've got yourself a deal… *Audra.*'

Her name slid off his tongue like warm honey and it was all she could do not to groan. She set her knife and fork down and pushed her plate away.

'I had no idea you didn't like being called Squirt.'

She didn't. Not really.

He stared at her for a moment. 'Don't hold Rupert's protectiveness against him.'

She blinked. 'I don't.' And then grimaced. 'Well, not much. I know I'm lucky to have him…and Cora and Justin.' It was a shame that Finn didn't have a brother or sister. He did have Rupert, though, and the two men were as close as brothers.

'He's a romantic.'

That made her glance up. 'Rupert?'

'Absolutely.'

He nodded and it made his hair do that fall-in-his-eyes thing again and she didn't know why, but it made her stomach clench.

'On the outside he acts as hard as nails, but on the inside…'

'He's a big marshmallow,' she finished.

'He'd go to the ends of the earth for someone he loved.'

That was true. She nodded.

'See? A romantic.'

She'd never thought about it in those terms.

His phone on the table buzzed. She didn't mean to look, but

she saw the name Trixie flash up on the screen before Finn reached over and switched it off. *Okay.*

'So...' He dusted off his hands as if ready to take on the world. 'What were you planning to do while you were here?'

Dear God. *Think of nice, easy, relaxing things.* 'Um... I was going to lie on the beach and catch some rays—' *not love rays* '—float about in the sea for a bit.'

'Sounds good.'

Except he wouldn't be content with lying around and floating, would he? He'd probably challenge himself to fifty laps out to the buoy and back every day. 'Read a book.'

His lip curled. 'Read a book?'

She tried not to wince at the scorn that threaded through his voice.

'You come to one of the most beautiful places on earth to *read a book*?'

She tried to stop her shoulders from inching up to her ears. 'I like reading, and do you know how long it's been since I read a book for pleasure?'

'How long?'

'Over a year,' she mumbled.

He spread his hands. 'If you like to read, why don't you do more of it?'

Because she'd been working too hard. Because she'd let Thomas distract and manipulate her.

'And what else?'

She searched her mind. 'I don't cook.'

He glanced at their now empty plates and one corner of his mouth hooked up. 'So I've noticed.'

'But I want to learn to cook...um...croissants.'

His brow furrowed. 'Why?'

Because they took a long time to make, didn't they? The pastry needed lots of rolling out, didn't it? Which meant, if she could trick him into helping her, he'd be safe from harm while he was rolling out pastry. 'Because I love them.' That was true enough. 'But I've had to be strict with myself.'

'Strict, how?'

'I've made a decision—in the interests of both my waistline and my heart health—that I'm only allowed to eat croissants that I make myself.'

He leaned back and let loose with a long low whistle. 'Wow, Squ— Audra! You really know how to let your hair down and party, huh?'

No one in all her life had ever accused her of being a party animal.

'A holiday with reading and baking at the top of your list.'

His expression left her in no doubt what he thought about that. 'This is supposed to be a holiday—some R & R,' she shot back, stung. 'I'm all go, go, go at work, but here I want time out.'

'Boring,' he sing-songed.

'Relaxing,' she countered.

'You've left the recreation part out of your R & R equation. I mean, look at you. You even look…'

She had to clamp her hands around the seat of her chair to stop from leaping out of it. 'Boring?' she said through gritted teeth.

'Buttoned-up. Tense. The opposite of relaxed.'

'It's the effect you and your love rays always seem to have on me.'

He tsk-tsked and shook his head. 'We're not supposed to mention the love rays, remember?'

Could she scream yet?

'I mean, look at your hair. You have it pulled back *in a bun*.'

She touched a hand to her hair. 'What's wrong with that?'

'A bun is for the boardroom, not the beach.'

She hated wearing her hair down and have it tickle her face.

'Well, speaking of hair, you might want to visit a hairdresser yourself when you're next in the village,' she shot back.

'But I visited my hairdresser only last week.' He sent her a grin full of wickedness and sin. 'The delectable Monique assured me this look is all the rage at the moment.'

He had a hairdresser called Monique…who was delectable? She managed to roll her eyes. 'The *too-long-for-the-boardroom-just-right-for-the-beach* look?'

'Precisely. She said the same about the stubble.'

She'd been doing her best not to notice that stubble. She was trying to keep the words *dead sexy* from forming in her brain.

'What do you think?' He ran a hand across his jawline, preening. It should've made him look ridiculous. Especially as he was hamming it up and trying to look ridiculous. But she found herself having to jam down on the temptation to reach across and brush her palm across it to see if it was as soft and springy as it looked.

She mentally slapped herself. 'I think it looks…scruffy.' In the best possible way. 'But it probably provides good protection against the sun, which is wise in these climes.'

He simply threw his head back and laughed, not taking the slightest offence. The strain that had deepened the lines around his eyes last night had eased. And when he rose to take their dishes to the sink he moved with an easy fluidity that belied his recent injuries.

He almost died up there on that mountain.

She went cold all over.

'Audra?'

She glanced up to find him staring at her, concern in his eyes. She shook herself. 'What's your definition of a good holiday, then?'

'Here on the island?'

He'd started to wash the dishes so she rose to dry them. 'Uh-huh, here on the island.'

'Water sports,' he said with relish.

'What kind of water sports?' Swimming and kayaking were gentle enough, but—

'On the other side of the island is the most perfect cove for windsurfing and sailing.'

But...but he could hurt himself.

'Throw in some water-skiing and hang-gliding and I'd call that just about the perfect holiday.'

He could kill himself! Lord, try explaining *that* to Rupert. 'No way.'

He glanced at her. 'When did you become such a scaredy-cat, Audra Russel?'

She realised he thought her 'No way' had been in relation to herself, which was just as well because if he realised she'd meant it for him he'd immediately go out and throw himself off the first cliff he came across simply to spite her.

And while it might be satisfying to say I told you so if he did come to grief, she had a feeling that satisfaction would be severely tempered if the words were uttered in a hospital ward... or worse.

'Why don't you let your hair down for once, take a risk? You might even find it's fun.'

She bit back a sigh. Maybe that was what she was afraid of. One risk could lead to another, and before she knew it she could've turned her whole life upside down. And she wasn't talking sex with her brother's best friend here either. Which—*obviously*—wasn't going to happen. She was talking about her job and her whole life. It seemed smarter to keep a tight rein on all her risk-taking impulses. She was sensible, stable and a rock to all her family. That was *who* she was. She repeated the words over and over like a mantra until she'd fixed them firmly in her mind again.

She racked her brain to think of a way to control Finn's risk-taking impulses too. 'There's absolutely nothing wrong with some lazy R & R, Finn Sullivan.' She used his full name in the same way he'd used hers. 'You should try it some time.'

His eyes suddenly gleamed. 'I'll make a deal with you. I'll try your kind of holiday R & R if you'll try mine?'

She bit her lip, her pulse quickening. This could be the perfect solution. 'So you'd be prepared to laze around here with a book if I…if I try windsurfing and stuff?'

'Yep. Quid pro quo.'

'Meaning?'

'One day we do whatever you choose. The next day we do whatever I choose.'

She turned to hang up the tea towel so he couldn't see the self-satisfied smile that stretched across her face. For at least half of his stay she'd be able to keep him out of trouble. As for the other half…she could temper his pace—be so inept he'd have to slow down to let her keep up or have to spend so much time teaching her that there'd been no time for him to be off risking his own neck. *Perfect.*

She swung back. 'Despite what you say, I'm not a scaredy-cat.'

'And despite what you think, I'm not hyperactive.'

Finn held his breath as he watched Audra weigh up his suggestion. She was actually considering it. Which was surprising. He'd expected her to tell him to take a flying leap and stalk off to read her book.

But she was actually considering his suggestion and he didn't know why. He thought he'd need to tease and rile her more, bring her latent competitive streak to the fore, where she'd accept his challenge simply to save face. Still, he *had* tossed out the bait of her proving that her way was better than his. Women were always trying to change him. Maybe Audra found that idea attractive too?

In the next moment he shook his head. That'd only be the case if she were interested in him as a romantic prospect. And she'd made it clear that wasn't the case.

Thank God.

He eyed that tight little bun and swallowed.

'I'll agree to your challenge…'

He tried to hide his surprise. She would? He hadn't even needed to press her.

'On two conditions.'

Ha! He knew it couldn't be that easy. 'Which are?'

'I get to go first.'

He made a low sweeping bow. 'Of course—ladies first, that always went without saying.' It was a minor concession and, given how much he still hurt, one he didn't mind making. They could pick up the pace tomorrow.

'And the challenge doesn't start until tomorrow.'

He opened his mouth to protest, but she forged on. 'We need to go shopping. There's hardly any food in the place. And I'm not wasting my choice of activities on practicalities like grocery shopping, thank you very much.'

'We could get groceries delivered.'

'But it'd be nice to check out the produce at the local market. Rupert likes to support the local businesses.'

And while she was here she'd consider herself Rupert's representative. And it was true—what she did here would reflect on her brother. The Russels had become a bit of a fixture in Kyanós life over the last few years.

'I also want to have a deliciously long browse in the bookstore. And you'll need to select a book too, you know?'

Oh, joy of joys. He was going to make her run two miles for that.

'And...' she shrugged '...consider it a fact-finding mission—we can research what the island has to offer and put an itinerary together.'

Was she really going to let him choose half of her holiday activities for the next week or two? *Excellent.* By the time he was through with her, she'd have colour in her cheeks, skin on her bones—not to mention some muscle tone and a spring in her step. 'You've got yourself a deal...on one condition.'

Her eyebrows lifted.

'That you lose the bun.' He couldn't think straight around that bun. Whenever he glanced at it, he was seized by an unholy impulse to release it. It distracted him beyond anything.

Without another word, she reached up to pull the pins from her bun, and a soft cloud of fair hair fell down around her shoulders. Her eyes narrowed and she thrust out her chin. 'Better?'

It took an effort of will to keep a frown from his face. A tight band clamped around his chest.

'Is it *beachy* enough for you?'

'A hundred per cent better,' he managed, fighting the urge to reach out and touch a strand, just to see if it was as silky and soft as it looked.

She smirked and pulled it back into a ponytail. 'There, the bun is gone.'

But the ponytail didn't ease the tightness growing in his chest, not to mention other places either. It bounced with a perky insolence that had him aching to reach out and give it a gentle tug. For pity's sake, it was just hair!

She stilled, and then her hands went to her hips. 'Are you feeling okay, Finn?'

He shook himself. 'Of course I am. Why?'

'You gave in to my conditions without a fight. That's not like you. Normally you'd bicker with me and angle for more.'

Damn! He had to remember how quick she was, and keep his wits about him.

'If you want a few more days before embarking on our challenge, that's fine with me. I mean, you only just got the cast off your arm.'

He clenched his jaw so hard it started to ache.

'I understand you beat yourself up pretty bad on that mountain.'

She paused as if waiting for him to confirm that, but he had no intention of talking about his accident.

She shrugged. 'And you looked pretty rough last night so...'

'So...what?'

'So if you needed a couple of days to regroup...'

Anger directed solely at himself pooled in his stomach. 'The accident was two month ago, *Squirt.*' He called her Squirt deliberately, to set her teeth on edge. 'I'm perfectly fine.'

She shrugged. 'Whatever you say.' But she didn't look convinced. 'I'm leaving for the village in half an hour if you want to come along. But if you want to stay here and do push-ups and run ten miles on the beach then I'm more than happy to select a book for you.'

'Not a chance.' He shuddered to think what she would make him read as a penance. 'I'll be ready in twenty.'

'Suit yourself.' She moved towards the foyer and the stairs. And the whole time her ponytail swayed in jaunty mockery. She turned when she reached the foyer's archway. 'Finn?'

He hoped to God she hadn't caught him staring. 'What?'

'The name's Audra, not Squirt. That was the deal. Three strikes and you're out. That's Strike One.'

She'd kick him out if he... He stared after her and found himself grinning. She wasn't going to let him push her around and he admired her for it.

'I'll drive,' Finn said, thirty minutes later.

'I have the car keys,' Audra countered, sliding into the driver's seat of the hybrid Rupert kept on the island for running back and forth to the village.

To be perfectly honest, he didn't care who drove. He just didn't want Audra to think him frail or in need of babying. Besides, it was only ten minutes into the village.

One advantage of being passenger, though, was the unencumbered opportunity to admire the views, and out here on the peninsula the views were spectacular. Olive trees interspersed with the odd cypress and ironwood tree ranged down the slopes, along with small scrubby shrubs bursting with flowers—some white and some pink. And beyond it all was the unbelievable, almost magical blue of the Aegean Sea. The air from the open windows was warm and dry, fragrant with salt and rosemary, and something inside him started to unhitch. He rested his head back and breathed it all in.

'Glorious, isn't it?'

He glanced across at her profile. She didn't drive as if she needed to be anywhere in a hurry. Her fingers held the steering wheel in a loose, relaxed grip, and the skin around her eyes and mouth was smooth and unblemished. The last time he'd seen her she'd been in a rush, her knuckles white around her briefcase and her eyes narrowed—no doubt her mind focussed on the million things on her to-do list.

She glanced across. 'What?'

'I was just thinking how island life suits you.'

Her brows shot up, and she fixed her attention on the road in front again, her lips twitching. 'Wow, you must really hate my bun.'

No, he loved that bun.

Not that he had any intention of telling her that.

She flicked him with another of her cool glances. 'Do you know anyone that this island life wouldn't suit?'

'Me…in the long term. I'd go stir-crazy after a while.' He wasn't interested in holidaying his whole life away.

What are you interested in doing with the rest of your life, then?

He swallowed and shoved the question away, not ready to face the turmoil it induced, focussed his attention back on Audra.

'And probably you too,' he continued. 'Seems to me you don't like being away from the office for too long.'

Something in her tensed, though her fingers still remained loose and easy on the wheel. He wanted to turn more fully towards her and study her to find out exactly what had changed, but she'd challenge such a stare, and he couldn't think of an excuse that wouldn't put her on the defensive. Getting her to relax and have fun was the remit, not making her tense and edgy. His mention of work had probably just been an unwelcome reminder of Farquhar.

And it was clear she wanted to talk about Farquhar as much as he wanted to talk about his accident.

He cleared his throat. 'But in terms of a short break, I don't think anything can beat this island.'

'Funnily enough, that's one argument you won't get from me.'

He didn't know why, but her words made him laugh.

They descended into the village and her sigh of appreciation burrowed into his chest. 'It's such a pretty harbour.'

She steered the car down the narrow street to the parking area in front of the harbour wall. They sat for a moment to admire the scene spread before them. An old-fashioned ferry chugged out of the cove, taking passengers on the two-hour ride to the mainland. Yachts with brightly coloured sails bobbed on their moorings. The local golden stone of the harbour wall provided the perfect foil for the deep blue of the water. To their left houses in the same golden stone, some of them plastered brilliant white, marched up the hillside, the bright blue of their doors and shutters making the place look deliciously Mediterranean.

Audra finally pushed out of the car and he followed. She pulled her hair free of its band simply to capture it again, including the strand that had worked its way loose, and retied it. 'I was just going to amble along the main shopping strip for a bit.'

She gestured towards the cheerful curve of shops that lined the harbour, the bunting from their awnings fluttering in the breeze. Barrels of gaily coloured flowers stood along the strip at intervals. If there was a more idyllic place on earth, he was yet to find it.

'Sounds good to me.' While she was ambling she'd be getting a dose of sun and fresh air. 'Do you mind if I tag along?'

He asked because he'd called her Squirt earlier to deliberately rub her up the wrong way and he regretted it now.

Cool blue eyes surveyed him and he couldn't read them at all. 'I mean to take my time. I won't be rushed. I do enough rushing in my real life and...'

Her words trailed off and he realised she thought he meant to whisk her through the shopping at speed and...and what? Get to the things he wanted to do? What kind of selfish brute did she think he was? 'I'm in no rush.'

'I was going to browse the markets and shops...maybe get some lunch, before buying whatever groceries we needed before heading back.'

'Sounds like an excellent plan.'

The faintest of frowns marred the perfect skin of her forehead. 'It does?'

Something vulnerable passed across her features, but it was gone in a flash. From out of nowhere Rupert's words came back to him: *'She's more selfless than the rest of us put together.'* The Russel family came from a privileged background, but they took the associated social responsibility of that position seriously. Each of them had highly honed social consciences. But it struck him then that Audra put her family's needs before her own. Who put her needs first?

'Audra, a lazy amble along the harbour, while feeling the sun on my face and breathing in the sea air, sounds pretty darn perfect to me.'

She smiled then—a real smile—and it kicked him in the gut because it was so beautiful. And because he realised he'd so very rarely seen her smile like that.

Why?

He took her arm and led her across the street, releasing her the moment they reached the other side. She still smelled of coconut and peaches, and it made him want to lick her.

Dangerous.

Not to mention totally inappropriate.

He tried to find his equilibrium again, and for once wished he could blame his sense of vertigo, the feeling of the ground shifting beneath his feet, on his recent injuries. Audra had always been able to needle him and then make him laugh, but he had no intention of letting her get under his skin. Not in *that* way. He'd been out of circulation too long, that was all. He'd be fine again once he'd regained his strength and put the accident behind him.

'It's always so cheerful down here,' she said, pausing beside one of the flower-filled barrels, and dragging a deep breath into her lungs.

He glanced down at the flowers to avoid noticing the way her chest lifted, and touched his fingers to a bright pink petal. 'These are...nice.'

'I love petunias,' she said. She touched a scarlet blossom. 'And these geraniums and begonias look beautiful.'

He reached for a delicate spray of tiny white flowers at the same time that she did, and their fingers brushed against each other. It was the briefest of contacts, but it sent electricity charging up his arm and had him sucking in a breath. For one utterly unbalancing moment he thought she meant to repeat the gesture.

'That's alyssum,' she said, pulling her hand away.

He moistened his lips. 'I had no idea you liked gardening.'

She stared at him for a moment and he watched her snap back into herself like a rubber band that had been stretched and then released. But opposite to that because the stretching had seemed to relax her while the snapping back had her all tense again.

'Don't worry, Finn. I'm not going to make you garden while you're here.'

Something sad and hungry, though, lurked in the backs of her eyes, and he didn't understand it at all. He opened his mouth to ask her about it, but closed it again. He didn't get involved with complicated emotions or sensitive issues. He avoided them like the plague. Get her to laugh, get her to loosen up. That was his remit. Nothing more. But that didn't stop the memory of that sad and hungry expression from playing over and over in his mind.

CHAPTER THREE

AUDRA WHEELED AWAY from Finn and the barrel of flowers to survey the length of the village street, and tried to slow the racing of her pulse…to quell the temptation that swept through her like the breeze tugging at her hair. But the sound of the waves splashing against the seawall and the sparkles of light on the water as the sun danced off its surface only fed the yearning and the restlessness.

She couldn't believe that the idea—the temptation—had even occurred to her. She and Finn? The idea was laughable.

For pity's sake, she'd had one romantic disaster this year. Did she really want to follow that up with another?

Absolutely not.

She dragged a trembling hand across her eyes. She must be more shaken by Thomas and his betrayal than she'd realised. She needed to focus on herself and her family, and to make things right again. That was what this break here on Kyanós was all about—that and avoiding the media storm that had surrounded her in Geneva. The one thing she didn't want to do was to make things worse.

The building at the end of the row of shops drew her gaze. Its white walls and blue shutters gleamed in the sun like the quintessential advertisement for a Greek holiday. The For Sale sign made her swallow. She resolutely dragged her gaze away, but the gaily coloured planter pots dotted along the thoroughfare caught her gaze again and that didn't help either. But…

A sigh welled inside her. But if she ever owned a shop, she'd have a tub—or maybe two tubs—of flowers like these outside its door.

You're never going to own a shop.

She made herself straighten. No, she was never going to own a shop. And the sooner she got over it, the better.

The lengthening silence between her and Finn grew more and more fraught.

See what happens when you don't keep a lid on the nonsense? You become tempted to do ridiculous things.

Well, she could annihilate that in one fell swoop.

'If I ever owned a shop, I'd want flowers outside its door too, just like these ones.' And she waited for the raucous laughter to scald her dream with the scorn it deserved.

Rather than laughter a warm chuckle greeted her, a chuckle filled with…affection? 'You used to talk about opening a shop when you were a little girl.'

And everyone had laughed at her—teased her for not wanting to be something more glamorous like an astronaut or ballerina.

Poor poppet, she mocked herself.

'What did you want to be when you were little?'

'A fireman…a knife-thrower at the circus…an explorer…and I went through a phase of wanting to be in a glam-rock band. It was the costumes,' he added when she swung to stare at him. 'I loved the costumes.'

She couldn't help but laugh. 'I'm sure you'd look fetching in purple satin, platform boots and silver glitter.'

He snorted.

'You know what the next challenge is going to be, don't you? The very next fancy dress party you attend, you have to go as a glam rocker.'

'You know there'll be a counter challenge to that?'

'There always is.' And whatever it was, she wouldn't mind honouring it. She'd pay good money to see Finn dressed up like that.

One corner of his mouth had hooked up in a cocky grin, his eyes danced with devilment, and his hair did that 'slide across his forehead perilously close to his eyes' thing and her stomach clenched. Hard. She forced her gaze away, reminded herself who he was. And what he was. 'Well, it might not come with fancy costumes, but playboy adventurer captures the spirit of your childhood aspirations.'

He slanted a glance down at her, the laughter in his eyes turning dark and mocking, though she didn't know if it was directed at her or himself. 'Wow,' he drawled. 'Written off in one simple phrase. You've become a master of the backhanded compliment. Though some might call it character assassination.'

It was her turn to snort. 'While you've perfected drama queen.' But she found herself biting her lip as she stared unseeing at the nearby shop fronts as they walked along. Had she been too hard, too…*dismissive* just then? 'I'm not discounting the fact that you make a lot of money for charity.'

The car races, the mountaineering expeditions, the base jumps were all for terribly worthy causes.

'And yet she can't hide her disapproval at my reckless and irresponsible lifestyle,' he told the sky.

It wasn't disapproval, but envy. Not that she had any intention of telling him so. All right, there was some disapproval too. She didn't understand why he had to risk his neck for charity. There were other ways to fundraise, right? Risking his neck just seemed…stupid.

But whatever else Finn was, she'd never accuse him of being stupid.

She was also officially tired of this conversation. She halted outside the bookshop. 'Our first stop.'

She waited for him to protest but all he did was gesture for her to precede him. 'After you.'

With a big breath she entered, and crossed her fingers and hoped none of the shopkeepers or villagers would mention her recent troubles when they saw her today. She just wanted to forget all about that for a while.

They moved to different sections of the store—him to Non-Fiction, while she started towards Popular Fiction, stopping along the way to pore over the quaint merchandise that lined the front of the shop—cards and pens, bookmarks in every shape and size, some made from paper while others were made from bits of crocheted string with coloured beads dangling from their tails. A large selection of journals and notebooks greeted her too, followed by bookends and paperweights—everything a booklover could need. How she loved this stuff! On her way out she'd buy a gorgeous notebook. Oh, and bookmarks—one for each book she bought.

She lost herself to browsing the row upon row of books then; most were in Greek but some were in English too. She didn't know for how long she scanned titles, admired covers and read back-cover blurbs, but she slowly became aware of Finn watching her from where he sat on one of the low stools that were placed intermittently about the shop for customers' convenience. She surprised a look of affection on his face, and it made her feel bad for sniping at him earlier and dismissing him as a playboy adventurer.

He grinned. 'You look like you're having fun.'

'I am.' This slow browsing, the measured contemplation of the delights offered up on these shelves—the sheer *unrushedness* of it all—filled something inside her. She glanced at his hands, his lap, the floor at his feet. 'You don't have a book yet.'

He nodded at the stack she held. 'Are you getting all of those?'

'I'm getting the French cookbook.' She'd need a recipe for croissants. 'And three of these.'

He took the cookbook from her, and then she handed him two women's fiction titles and a cosy mystery, before putting the others back where they belonged.

'What would you choose for me?' His lip curled as he reached forward to flick a disparaging finger at a blockbuster novel from a big-name writer. 'Something like that?'

'That's a historical saga with lots of period detail. I'd have not thought it was your cup of tea at all.' She suspected the pace would be a bit slow for his taste. 'The object of the exercise isn't to make you suffer.'

Amber eyes darker than the whisky he liked but just as intoxicating swung to her and she saw the surprise in their depths. She recalled the affection she'd surprised in his face a moment ago and swallowed. Had she become a complete and utter shrew somewhere over the last year or two? 'I know that our modus operandi is to tease each other and…and to try to best each other—all in fun, of course.'

He inclined his head. 'Of course.'

'But I want to show you that quieter pursuits can be pleasurable too. If I were choosing a book for you I'd get you—' she strode along to the humour section '—this.' She pulled out a book by a popular comedian that she knew he liked.

He blinked and took it.

She set off down the next row of shelves. 'And to be on the safe side I'd get you this as well…or this.' She pulled out two recent non-fiction releases. One a biography of a well-known sportsman, and the other on World War Two.

He nodded towards the second one and she added it to the growing pile of books in his arms.

She started back the way they'd come. 'If I were on my own I'd get you this one as a joke.' She held up a self-help book with the title *Twelve Rules for Life: An Antidote to Chaos*.

'Put it back.'

The laughter in his voice added a spring to her step. She slotted it back into place. 'I'd get you a wildcard too.'

'A wildcard?'

'A book on spec—something you might not like, but could prove to be something you'd love.'

He pursed his lips for a moment and then nodded. 'I want a wildcard.'

Excellent. But what? She thought back over what he'd said earlier—about wanting to be a fireman, a knife-thrower, an explorer. She returned to the fiction shelves. She'd bet her house on the fact he'd love tales featuring heroic underdogs. She pulled a novel from the shelf—the first book in a fantasy trilogy from an acclaimed writer.

'That's…that's a doorstop!'

'Yes or no?'

He blew out a breath. 'What the hell, add it to the pile.'

She did, and then retrieved her own books from his arms. 'I'm not letting you buy my books.'

'Why not?'

'I like to buy my own books. And I've thrust three books onto you that you may never open.'

He stretched his neck, first one way and then the other. 'Can I buy you lunch?'

'As a thank you for being your bookstore personal shopper? Absolutely. But let's make it a late lunch. I'm still full from breakfast.'

She stopped to select her bookmarks, and added two notebooks to her purchases. Finn chose a bookmark of his own, and then seized a satchel in butter-soft black leather. 'Perfect.'

Perfect for what? She glanced at the selection of leather satchels and calico book bags and bit her lip. Maybe—

With a laugh, Finn propelled her towards the counter. 'Save them for your next visit.'

They paid and while Audra exchanged greetings with Sibyl, the bookshop proprietor, he put all their purchases into the satchel and slung it over his shoulder. 'Where to next?'

She stared at that bag. It'd make his shoulder ache if he wasn't careful. But then she realised it was on his right shoulder, not his left, and let out a breath. 'Wherever the mood takes us,' she said as they moved towards the door.

She paused to read the community announcement board and an advertisement for art classes jumped out at her. Oh, that'd be fun and...

She shook her head. R & R was all very well, but she had to keep herself contained to the beach and her books. Anything else... Well, anything else was just too hard. And she was too tired.

Finn trailed a finger across the flyer. 'Interested?'

She shook her head and led him outside.

He frowned at her. 'But—'

'Ooh, these look like fun.' She shot across to the boutique next door and was grateful when he let himself be distracted.

They flicked through a rack of discounted clothing that stood in blatant invitation out the front. Finn bought a pair of swimming trunks, so she added a sarong to her growing list of purchases. They browsed the markets. Finn bought a pair of silver cufflinks in the shape of fat little aeroplanes. 'My uncle will love these.' He pointed to an oddly shaped silver pendant on a string of black leather. 'That'd look great on you.' So she bought that too. They helped each other choose sunhats.

It felt decadent to be spending like this, not that any of her purchases were particularly pricey. But she so rarely let herself off the leash that she blithely ignored the voice of puritan sternness that tried to reel her in. What was more, it gave her the chance to exchange proper greetings with the villagers she'd known for years now.

Her worries she'd be grilled about Thomas and her reputed broken heart and the upcoming court case dissolved within ten minutes. As always, the people of Kyanós embraced her as if she were one of their own. And she loved them for it. The Russel family had been coming for holidays here for nearly ten years now. Kyanós felt like a home away from home.

'Hungry yet?'

'Famished!' She glanced at her watch and did a double take

when she saw it was nearly two o'clock. 'We haven't done the bakery, the butcher, the delicatessen or the wine merchant yet.'

'We have time.'

She lifted her face to the sun and closed her eyes to relish it even more. 'We do.'

They chose a restaurant that had a terrace overlooking the harbour and ordered a shared platter of warm olives, cured meats and local cheeses accompanied with bread warm from the oven and a cold crisp carafe of *retsina*. While they ate they browsed their book purchases.

Audra surreptitiously watched Finn as he sampled the opening page of the fantasy novel…and then the next page…and the one after that.

He glanced up and caught her staring. He hesitated and then shrugged. 'You know, this might be halfway decent.'

She refrained from saying I told you so. 'Good.'

'If I hadn't seen you choose me those first two books I'd have not given this one a chance. I'd have written it off as a joke like the self-help book. And as I suspect I'll enjoy both these other books…'

If he stayed still long enough to read them.

He frowned.

She folded her arms. 'Why does that make you frown?'

'I'm wishing I'd known about this book when I was laid up in hospital with nothing to do.'

The shadows in his eyes told her how stir-crazy he'd gone. 'What did you do to pass the time?'

'Crosswords. And I watched lots of movies.'

'And chafed.'

'Pretty much.'

'I almost sent you a book, but I thought…'

'You thought I'd misinterpret the gesture? Think you were rubbing salt into the wound?'

Something like that.

He smiled. 'I appreciated the puzzle books.' And then he

scowled. 'I didn't appreciate the grapes, though. Grapes are for invalids.'

She stiffened. 'It was supposed to be an entire basket of fruit!' Not just grapes.

'Whatever. I'd have preferred a bottle of tequila. I gave the fruit to the nurses.'

But his eyes danced as he feigned indignation and it was hard to contain a grin. 'I'll keep that in mind for next time.'

He gave a visible shudder and she grimaced in sympathy. 'Don't have a next time.' She raised her glass. 'To no more accidents and a full and speedy recovery.'

'I'll drink to that.'

He lifted his glass to hers and then sipped it with an abandoned enjoyment she envied. 'Who knew you'd be such fun to shop with?'

The words shot out of her impulsively, and she found herself speared on the end of a keen-edged glance. 'You thought I'd chafe?'

'A bit,' she conceded. 'I mean, Rupert and Justin will put up with it when Cora or I want to window-shop, but they don't enjoy it.'

'I wouldn't want to do it every day.'

Neither would she.

'But today has been fun.' He stared at her for a beat too long. 'It was a revelation watching you in the bookstore.'

She swallowed. Revelation, how?

'It's been a long time since I saw you enjoy yourself so much, Squirt, and—' He shot back in his seat. 'Audra! I meant to say Audra. Don't make that Strike Two. I...'

He gazed at her helplessly and she forgave him instantly. He hadn't said it to needle her the way he had with his earlier *Squirt*. She shook herself. 'Sorry, what were you saying? I was miles away.'

He smiled his thanks, but then leaned across the table towards her, and that smile and his closeness made her breath catch. 'You should do things you enjoy more often, Miss Conscientiousness.'

Hmm, she'd preferred Squirt.

'There's more to life than boardrooms and spreadsheets.'

'That's what holidays are for,' she agreed. The boardrooms and spreadsheets would be waiting for her at the end of it, though, and the thought made her feel tired to the soles of her feet.

CHAPTER FOUR

AUDRA GLANCED ACROSS at Finn, who looked utterly content lying on his towel on the sand of this ridiculously beautiful curve of beach, reading his book. It seemed ironic, then, that she couldn't lose herself in her own book.

She blamed it on the half-remembered dreams that'd given her a restless night. Scraps had been playing through her mind all morning—sexy times moving to the surreal and the scary; Finn's and Thomas's faces merging and then separating—leaving her feeling restless and strung tight.

One of those sexy-time moments played through her mind again now and she bit her lip against the warmth that wanted to spread through her. The fact that this beach was so ridiculously private didn't help. She didn't want the words *private* and *Finn*—or *sexy times*—to appear in the same thought with such tempting symmetry. It was *crazy*. She'd always done her best to not look at Finn in *that* way. And she had no intention of letting her guard down now.

This whole preoccupation was just a…a way for her subconscious to avoid focussing on what needed to be dealt with. Which was to regather her resources and refocus her determination to be of service at the Russel Corporation, to be a valuable team member rather than a liability.

'What was that sigh for?'

She blinked to find Finn's beautiful brown eyes surveying her. And they were beautiful—the colour of cinnamon and golden syrup and ginger beer, and fringed with long dark lashes. She didn't know how lashes could look decadent and sinful, but Finn's did.

'You're supposed to be relaxing—enjoying the sun and the sea…your book.'

'I am.'

'Liar.'

He rolled to his side to face her more fully, and she shrugged. 'I had a restless night.' She stifled a yawn. 'That's all.'

'When one works as hard as you do, it can be difficult to switch off.'

'Old habits,' she murmured, reaching for her T-shirt and pulling it over her head and then tying her sarong about her waist, feeling ridiculously naked in her modest one-piece.

Which was crazy because she and Finn and the rest of her family had been on this beach countless times together, and in briefer swimsuits than what either of them were wearing now. 'I don't want to get too much sun all at once,' she said by way of explanation, although Finn hadn't indicated by so much as a blink of his gorgeous eyelashes that he'd wanted or needed one. She glanced at him. 'You've been incapacitated for a couple of months and yet I'm paler than you.'

'Yeah, but my incapacitation meant spending a lot of time on the rooftop terrace of my apartment on the French Riviera, so…not exactly doing it tough.'

Fair point.

'You ever tried meditation?'

'You're talking to me, Audra, remember?'

His slow grin raised all the tiny hairs on her arms. 'Lie on your back in a comfortable position and close your eyes.'

'Finn…' She could barely keep the whine out of her voice. 'Meditation makes me feel like a failure.' And there was more than enough of that in her life at the moment as it was, thank you very much. 'I know you're supposed to *clear your mind*, but…it's impossible!'

'Would you be so critical and hard on someone else? Cut yourself some slack.' He rolled onto his back. 'Work on quietening your mind rather than clearing it. When a thought appears, as it will, simply acknowledge it before focussing on your breathing again.'

He closed his eyes and waited. With another sigh, Audra rolled onto her back and settled her hat over her face. It was spring and the sun wasn't fierce, but she wasn't taking any chances. 'Okay,' she grumbled. 'I'm ready. What am I supposed to do?'

Finn led her through a guided meditation where she counted breaths, where she tensed and then relaxed different muscle groups. The deep timbre of his voice, unhurried and undemanding, soothed her in a way she'd have never guessed possible. Her mind wandered, as he'd said it would, but she brought her attention back to his voice and her breathing each time, and by the time he finished she felt weightless and light.

She heard no movement from him, so she stayed exactly where she was—on a cloud of euphoric relaxation.

And promptly fell asleep.

Finn didn't move until Audra's deep rhythmic breaths informed him that she was asleep. Not a light and sweet little nap, but fully and deeply asleep.

He rolled onto his tummy and rested his chin on his arms. When had she forgotten how to relax? He'd spent a large portion of every Christmas vacation from the age of twelve onwards with the Russel family.

She'd been a sweet, sparky little kid, fiercely determined to keep up with her older siblings and not be left behind. As a teenager she'd been curious, engaged…and a bit more of a dreamer than the others, not as driven in a particular direction as they'd been either. But then he'd figured that'd made her more of an all-rounder.

When had she lost her zest, her joy for life? During her final years of school? At university? He swallowed. When her mother had died?

Karen Russel had died suddenly of a cerebral aneurysm ten years ago. It'd shattered the entire family. Audra had only been seventeen.

Was it then that Audra had exchanged her joy in life for...? For what? To become a workaholic managing the charitable arm of her family's corporation? In her grief, had she turned away from the things that had given her joy? Had it become a habit?

He recalled the odd defiance in her eyes when she'd spoken about owning a shop—the way she'd mocked the idea...and the way the mockery and defiance had been at odds. He turned to stare at her. 'Hell, sweetheart,' he whispered. 'What are you doing to yourself?'

She slept for an hour, and Finn was careful to pretend not to notice when she woke, even though his every sense was honed to her every movement. He kept his nose buried in his book and feigned oblivion, which wasn't that hard because the book was pretty gripping.

'Hey,' she said in sleepy greeting.

'Hey, yourself, you lazy slob.' Only then did he allow himself to turn towards her. 'I didn't know napping was included on the agenda today.'

'If I remember correctly, the order for the day was lazing about in the sun on the beach, reading books and a bit of swimming.' She flicked out a finger. 'My nap included lying on the beach *and*—' she flicked out a second finger '—lazing in the sun. So I'm following the remit to the letter, thank you very much.'

The rest had brightened her eyes. And when she stretched her arms back over her head, he noted that her shoulders had lost their hard edge. He noted other things—things that would have Rupert taking a swing at him if he knew—so he did his best to remove those from his mind.

In one fluid motion, she rose. 'I'm going in for a dip.'

That sounded like an excellent plan. He definitely needed to cool off. Her glance flicked to the scar of his splenectomy when he rose too, and it took an effort to not turn away and hide it from her gaze.

And then she untied her sarong and pulled her T-shirt over her head and it was all he could do to think straight at all.

She nodded at the scar. 'Does it still hurt?'

He touched the indentations and shook his head. 'It didn't really hurt much after it was done either.' At her raised eyebrows he winked. 'Wish I could say the same about the broken ribs.'

She huffed out a laugh, and he was grateful when she moved towards the water's edge without asking any further questions about his accident. Its aftershocks continued to reverberate through him, leaving him at a loss. He didn't know how much longer he'd have to put up with it. He didn't know how much longer he *could* put up with it.

The cold dread that had invaded the pit of his stomach in the moments after his fall invaded him again now, and he broke out in an icy sweat. He'd known in that moment—his skis flying one way and the rest of him going another—that he'd hurt himself badly. He'd understood in a way he never had before that he could die; he had realised he might not make it off the mountain alive.

And every instinct he'd had had screamed a protest against that fate. He hadn't wanted to die, not yet. There were things he wanted—*yearned*—to do. If he'd had breath to spare he'd have begged the medical team to save him. But there'd been no breath to spare, and he'd started spiralling in and out of consciousness.

When he'd awoken from surgery...the relief and gratitude... there were no words to describe it. But for the life of him, now that he was all but recovered, he couldn't remember the things he'd so yearned to do—the reasons why staying alive had seemed so urgent.

All of it had left him with an utter lack of enthusiasm for any of the previous high-octane sports that had once sung to his soul. Had he lost his nerve? He didn't think so. He didn't feel afraid. He just—

A jet of water hit him full in the face and shook him immediately out of his thoughts. 'Lighten up, Finn. I'd have not mentioned the scar if I'd known it'd make you so grim. Don't worry. I'm sure the girls will still fall at your feet with the same old regularity. The odd scar will probably add to your mystique.'

She thought he was brooding for reasons of...*vanity*?

She laughed outright at whatever she saw in his face. 'You're going to pay for that,' he promised, scooping water up in his hands.

They were both soaked at the end of their water fight. Audra simply laughed and called him a bully when he picked her up and threw her into the sea.

He let go of her quick smart, though, because she was an armful of delicious woman...and he couldn't go there. Not with her. 'Race you out to the buoy.'

'Not a chance.' She caressed the surface of the water with an unconscious sensuality that had his gut clenching. 'I'm feeling too Zen after that meditation. And, if you'll kindly remember, there's no racing on today's agenda, thank you very much.'

'Wait until tomorrow.'

She stuck her nose in the air. 'Please don't disturb me while I'm living in the moment.'

With a laugh, he turned and swam out to the buoy. He didn't rush, but simply relished the way his body slid through the water, relished how good it felt to be rid of the cast. He did five laps there and back before his left arm started up a dull ache... and before he could resist finding out what Audra was up to.

He glanced across at where she floated on her back, her face lifted to the sky. He couldn't tell from here whether she had her eyes open or closed. She looked relaxed—now. And while *now* she might also be all grown up, during their water fight she'd laughed and squealed as she had when a girl.

He had a feeling, though, that when her short holiday was over all that tension would descend on her again, pulling her tight. Because…?

Because she wasn't doing the things that gave her joy, wasn't living the life that she should be living. And he had a growing conviction that this wasn't a new development, but an old one he'd never picked up on before. He had no idea how to broach the topic either. She could be undeniably prickly, and she valued her privacy. *Just like you do.* She'd tell him to take a flying leap and mind his own business. And that'd be that.

Walk away. He didn't do encouraging confidences. He didn't do complicated. And it didn't matter which way he looked at it—Audra had always been complicated. Fun and laughter, those were his forte.

He glided through the water towards her until he was just a couple of feet away. 'Boo.'

He didn't shout the word, just said it in a normal tone, but she started so violently he immediately felt sick to his gut. She spun around, the colour leaching from her face, and he wanted to kick himself—hard. 'Damn, Audra, I didn't mean to scare the living daylights out of you.'

She never used to startle this easily. What the hell had happened to change that?

None of the scenarios that played in his mind gave him the slightest bit of comfort.

'Glad I didn't grab you round the waist to tug you under, which had been my first thought.' He said it to try to lighten the moment. When they were kids they all used to dunk each other mercilessly.

If possible she went even paler. And then she ducked under the water, resurfacing a moment later to slick her hair back from her face. 'Note to self,' she said with remarkable self-possession, though he noted the way her hands shook. 'Don't practise meditation in the sea when Finn is around.'

He wanted to apologise again, but it'd be making too big a deal out of it and he instinctively knew that would make her defensive.

'I might head in.' She started a lazy breaststroke back towards the shore. 'How many laps did you do?'

'Just a couple.' Had she been watching him?

'How does the arm feel?'

He bit back a snap response. *It's fine. And can we just forget about my accident already?* She didn't deserve that. She had to know he didn't like talking about his injuries, but if this was the punishment she'd chosen for his ill-timed *Boo* then he'd take it like a man. 'Dishearteningly weak.'

Her gaze softened. 'You'll get your fitness back, Finn. Just don't push it too hard in these early days.'

He'd had every intention of getting to Kyanós and then swimming and running every day without mercy until he'd proven to himself that he was as fit as he'd been prior to his accident. And yet he found himself more than content at the moment to keep pace beside her. He rolled his shoulders. He'd only been here a couple of days. That old fire would return to his belly soon enough.

He pounced on the cooler bag as soon as he'd towelled off. 'I'm famished.'

He tossed her a peach, which she juggled, nearly dropped and finally caught. He grinned and bit into a second peach. The fragrant flesh and sweet juice hitting the back of his throat tasted better than anything he'd eaten in the last eight weeks. He groaned his pleasure, closing his eyes to savour it all the more. When he opened his eyes again, he found her staring at him as if she'd never seen him before.

Hell, no! Don't look at me like that, Audra.

Like a woman who looked at a man and considered his... um...finer points. It made his skin go hot and tight. It made him want to reach out, slide a hand behind the back of her head and pull her close and—

He glanced out to sea, his pulse racing. He wanted to put colour back into her cheeks, but not like that. The two of them were like oil and water. If he did something stupid now, it'd impact on his relationship with her entire family, and the Russels and his uncle Ned were the only family he had.

He dragged in a gulp of air. Given his current state of mind, he had to be hyper-vigilant that he didn't mess all this up. He had a history of bringing trouble to the doors of those he cared about—Rupert all those years ago, and now Joachim. Rupert was right—Audra had been through enough. He had no intention of bringing more trouble down on her head.

He forced his stance to remain relaxed. 'Wanna go for a run?'

'A run?' She snapped away and then stared at him as if he'd lost his mind. Which was better. Much *much* better. 'Do you not know me at all?'

He shrugged. 'It was worth a shot.'

'No running, no rushing, no racing.' She ticked the items off her fingers. 'Those are the rules for today. I'm going to explore the rock pools.'

He followed because he couldn't help it. Because a question burned through him and he knew he'd explode if he didn't ask it.

They explored in silence for ten or fifteen minutes. 'Audra?' He worked hard to keep his voice casual.

'Hmm?'

'What the hell did that bastard Farquhar do to you?'

She froze, and then very slowly turned. 'Wow, excellent tactic, Sullivan. Don't get your way over going for a run so hit a girl with an awkward question instead.'

A question he noted she hadn't answered. He rolled with it. 'I work with what I've got.'

Her hands went to her waist. She wore her T-shirt again but not her sarong, and her legs... Her legs went on and on...and on. Where had she been hiding them? 'Who's this woman in Nice you're trying to avoid?'

Oho! So Rupert had told her about that. 'You answer my question, and I'll answer any question you want.'

Her brows rose. '*Any* question?'

'Any time you want to ask it.'

CHAPTER FIVE

ANY TIME SHE wanted to ask it?

That meant... Audra's mind raced. That meant if Finn were running hell for leather, doing laps as if training for a triathlon, risking his neck as if there were no tomorrow, then...then she could ask a question and he'd have to stop and answer her?

Oh, she'd try other stalling tactics first. She wasn't wasting a perfectly good question if she could get him to slow down in other ways, but...

She tried to stop her internal glee from showing. 'You have yourself a deal.'

Finn readjusted his stance. 'So what's the story with Farquhar? The bit that didn't make the papers.'

She hiked herself up to sit on a large rock, its top worn smooth, but its sides pitted with the effects of wind and sand. It was warm beneath her hands and thighs.

He settled himself beside her. 'Is it hard to talk about?'

She sent him what she hoped was a wry glance. 'It's never fun to own up to being a fool...or to having made such a big mistake.'

'Audra—'

She waved him silent. 'I'm surprised you don't know the story.' She'd have thought Rupert would've filled him in.

'I know what was in the paper but not, I suspect, the whole story.'

Dear Rupert. He'd kept his word.

Oddly, though, she didn't mind Finn knowing the story in its entirety. While they might've been friendly adversaries all these years, he was practically family. He'd have her best interests at heart, just as she did his.

'Right.' She slapped her hands to her thighs and he glanced down at them. His face went oddly tight and he immediately stared out to sea. A pulse started up in her throat and her heart danced an irregular pattern in her chest.

Stop it. Don't think of Finn in that way.

But...he's hot.

And he thinks you're hot.

Nonsense! He's just... He just found it hard to not flirt with every woman in his orbit.

She forced herself to bring Thomas's face to mind and the pulse-jerking and heart-hammering came to a screeching halt. 'So the part that everyone knows—' the part that had made the papers '—is that Thomas Farquhar and I had been dating for over seven months.'

Wary brown eyes met hers and he gave a nod. 'What made you fall for him?'

She shrugged. 'He seemed so...*nice*. He went out of his way to spend time with me, and do nice things for me. It was just... nice,' she finished lamely. He'd been so earnest about all the things she was earnest about. He'd made her feel as if she were doing exactly what she ought to be doing with her life. She'd fallen for all of that intoxicating attention and validation hook, line and sinker.

'But it's clear now that he was only dating me to steal company secrets.' A fact the entire world now knew thanks to the tabloids. She shrivelled up a little more inside every time she thought about it.

The Russel Corporation, established by her Swiss grandfather sixty years ago, had originally been founded on a watchmaking dynasty but was now made up of a variety of concerns, including a large charitable arm. Her father was the CEO, though Rupert had been groomed to take over and, to all intents and purposes, was running the day-to-day operations of the corporation.

Her siblings were champions of social justice, each in their own way, just as her parents and grandparents had been in their younger days. Their humanitarian activities were administered by the Russel Corporation, and, as one of the corporation's chief operation managers, Audra had the role of overseeing a variety of projects—from hiring the expertise needed on different jobs and organising the delivery of necessary equipment and goods, to wrangling with various licences and permissions that needed to be secured, and filling in endless government grant forms. And in her spare time she fundraised. It was hectic, high-powered and high-stakes.

For the last five years her sister, Cora, a scientist, had been working on developing a new breakthrough vaccine for the Ebola virus. While such a vaccine would help untold sufferers of the illness, it also had the potential to make pharmaceutical companies vast sums of money.

She tried to slow the churning of her stomach. 'Thomas was after Cora's formulae and research. We know now that he was working for a rival pharmaceutical company. We suspect he deliberately targeted me, and that our meeting at a fundraising dinner wasn't accidental.'

From the corner of her eye she saw Finn nod. She couldn't look at him. Instead she twisted her hands together in her lap and watched the progress of a small crab as it moved from one rock pool to another. 'He obviously worked out my computer password. There were times when we were in bed, when I thought he was asleep, and I'd grab my laptop to log in quickly just to check on something.'

She watched in fascination as his hand clenched and then

unclenched. 'You'd have had to have more than one password to get anywhere near Cora's data.'

'Oh, I have multiple passwords. I have one for my laptop, different ones for my desktop computers at home and work. There's the password for my Russel Corporation account. And each of the projects has its own password.' There'd been industrial espionage attempts before. She'd been briefed on internet and computer security. 'But it appears he'd had covert cameras placed around my apartment.'

'How...?'

How did he get access? 'I gave him a key.' She kept her voice flat and unemotional. She'd given an industrial spy unhampered access to her flat—what an idiot! 'I can tell you now, though, that all those romantic dinners he made for us—' his pretext for needing a key '—have taken on an entirely different complexion.' It'd seemed mean-spirited not to give him a key at the time, especially as he'd given her one to his flat.

He swore. 'Did he have cameras in the bedroom?'

'No.' He'd not sunk that low. But it didn't leave her feeling any less violated. 'But...but he must've seen me do some stupid, ugly, unfeminine things on those cameras. And I know it's nothing on the grand scale, but...it *irks* me!'

'What kind of things?'

She slashed a hand through the air. 'Oh, I don't know. Like picking my teeth or hiking my knickers out from uncomfortable places, or... Have you ever seen a woman put on a pair of brand-new sixty-denier opaque tights?'

He shook his head.

'Well, it's not sexy. It looks ludicrous and contortionist and it probably looks hilarious and... And I feel like enough of a laughing stock without him having footage of that too.'

A strong arm came about her shoulder and pulled her in close. Just for a moment she let herself sink against him to soak up the warmth and the comfort. 'He played me to perfection,' she whispered. 'I didn't suspect a damn thing. I thought—' She faltered. 'I thought he liked me.'

His arm tightened about her. 'He was a damn fool. The man has to be a certifiable idiot to choose money over you, sweetheart.'

He pressed his lips to her hair and she felt an unaccountable urge to cry.

She didn't want to cry!

'Stop it.' She pushed him away and leapt down from the rock. 'Don't be nice to me. My stupidity nearly cost Cora all of the hard work she's put in for the last five years.'

'But it didn't.'

No, it hadn't. And it was hard to work up an outraged stomp in flip-flops, and with the Aegean spread before her in twinkling blue perfection and the sun shining down as if the world was full of good things. The files Thomas had stolen were old, and, while to an outsider the formulae and hypotheses looked impressive, the work was neither new nor ground-breaking. Audra didn't have access to the information Thomas had been so anxious to get his hands on for the simple fact that she didn't need it. The results of Cora's research had nothing to do with Audra's role at work.

But Thomas didn't know that yet. And there was a court case pending. 'So...' She squinted into the sun at him. 'Rupert told you that much, huh?'

'I didn't know about the hidden cameras, but as for the rest...' He nodded.

'You know that's all classified, right?'

He nodded again. 'What hasn't Rupert told me?' He dragged in a breath, his hands clenching. 'Did Farquhar break your heart?'

She huffed out a laugh. 'Which of those questions do you want me to answer first?' When he didn't answer, she moved back to lean against the rock. 'I'll answer the second first because that'll move us on nicely to the first.' She winced at the bitterness that laced her *nicely*. 'No, he didn't break my heart. In fact I was starting to feel smothered by him so I…uh…'

'You…?'

'I told him I wanted to break up.'

He stared at her for a long moment. The muscles in his jaw tensed. 'What did he do?'

She swallowed. 'He pushed me into the hall closet and locked me in.'

He swore and the ferocity of his curse made her blink. He landed beside her, his expression black.

'I… I think he panicked when I demanded my key back. So he locked me in, stole my computer and high-tailed it out of there.'

'How long were you in there?'

'All night.' And it'd been the longest night of her life.

'How…?'

He clenched his fists so hard he started to shake. In a weird way his outrage helped.

'How did you get out?'

'He made the mistake of using my access code to get into the office early the next morning. Very early when he didn't think anyone else would be around. But Rupert, who had jet lag, had decided to put in a few hours. He saw the light on in my office, and came to drag me off to breakfast.' She shrugged. 'He found Thomas rifling through my filing cabinets instead. The first thing he did was to call Security. The second was to call my home phone and then my mobile. Neither of which I could answer. He has a key to my flat, so…'

'So he raced over and let you out.'

'Yep.'

She'd never been happier to see her older brother in her life. Her lips twisted. 'It was only then, though, that I learned of the extent of Thomas's double-dealing. And all I wanted to do was crawl back in the closet and hide from the world.'

'Sweetheart—'

She waved him quiet again. 'I know all the things you're going to say, Finn, but don't. Rupert's already said them. *None of this is my fault. Anyone can be taken in by a conman... Blah-blah-blah.*'

She moved to the edge of the rock shelf and stared out at the sea, but its beauty couldn't soothe her. She'd been taken in by a man whose interest and undivided attention had turned her head—a man who'd seemed not only interested but invested in hearing about her hopes and dreams...and supporting her in those dreams. She hadn't felt the focus of somebody's world like that since her mother had died.

She folded her arms, gripped her elbows tight. But it'd all been a lie, and in her hunger for that attention she'd let her guard down. It'd had the potential to cause untold damage to Cora's career, not to mention the Russel Corporation's reputation. She'd been such an idiot!

And to add insult to injury she'd spent the best part of six weeks trying to talk herself out of breaking up with him because he'd seemed so darn perfect.

Idiot! Idiot! Idiot!

'So now you feel like a gullible fool who's let the family down, and you look at every new person you meet through the tainted lens of suspicion—wondering if they can be trusted or if they're just out for whatever they can get.'

Exactly. She wanted to dive into the sea and power through the water until she was too tired to think about any of this any more. It was a decent swim from here back to the beach, but one that was within her powers. Only...if she did that Finn would follow and five laps out to the buoy and back was enough for him for one day.

She swung around to meet his gaze. 'That sounds like the voice of experience.'

He shrugged and moved to stand beside her, his lips tightening as he viewed the horizon. 'It's how I'd feel in your shoes.'

'Except you'd never be so stupid.' She turned and started to pick her way back along the rock pools towards the beach.

'I've done stupider things with far less cause.'

He had? She turned to find him staring at her with eyes as turbulent as the Aegean in a storm. She didn't press him, but filed the information away. She might ask him about that some day.

'And even Rupert isn't mistake free. Getting his heart broken by Brooke Manning didn't show a great deal of foresight.'

'He was young,' she immediately defended. 'And we all thought she was as into him as he was into her.'

He raised an eyebrow, and she lifted her hands. 'Okay, okay. I know. It's just… Rupert's mistake didn't hurt anyone but himself. My mistake had the potential to ruin Cora's life's work to date and impact on the entire Russel Corporation, and—'

Warm hands descended to her shoulders. 'But it didn't. Stop focussing on what could have happened and deal with what actually did happen. And the positives that can be found there.'

'Positives?' she spluttered.

'Sure.'

'Oh, I can't wait to hear this. C'mon, wise guy, name me one positive.'

He rubbed his chin. 'Well, for starters, you'd worked out Farquhar was a jerk and had kicked his sorry butt to the kerb.'

Not exactly true. She'd just been feeling suffocated, and hadn't been able to hide from that fact any more.

'And don't forget that's been caught on camera too.'

She stared up at him. And a slow smile built through her. 'Oh, my God.'

He cocked an eyebrow.

'He argued about us breaking up. He wanted me to reconsider and give him another chance.'

'Not an unusual reaction.'

'I told him we could still see each other as friends.'

Finn clutched his chest as if he'd been shot through the heart. 'Ouch!'

'And then he ranted and paced for a bit, and when he had his back to me a few times I, uh, rolled my eyes and...'

'And?'

'Checked my watch because there was a programme on television I was hoping to catch.'

He barked out a laugh.

'And this is embarrassing, for him, so I shouldn't tell it.'

'Yes, you should. You *really* should.'

'Well, he cried. Obviously they were crocodile tears, but I wasn't to know that at the time. I went to fetch the box of tissues, and while my back was to him I pulled this horrible kind of "God help me" face at the wall.'

She gave him a demonstration and he bent at the waist and roared. 'Crocodile tears or not, that's going to leave his ego in shreds. I'm sorry, sweetheart, but getting caught picking your nose suddenly doesn't seem like such a bad thing.'

'I do *not* pick my nose.' She stuck that particular appendage in the air. But Finn was right. She found she didn't care quite so much if Thomas had seen her pigging out on chocolate or dancing to pop music in her knickers. Now whenever she thought about any of those things she'd recall her hilarious grimace—probably straight at some hidden camera—and would feel partially vindicated.

She swung to Finn. 'Thank you.'

'You're welcome.'

They reached the beach and shook sand off their towels, started the five-minute climb back up the hill to the villa. 'Audra?'

'Hmm?'

'I'm sorry I scared you when I arrived the other night. I'm sorry I scared you with my *boo* out there.' He waved towards the water.

She shrugged. 'You didn't mean to.'

'No, I didn't mean to.'

And his voice told her he'd be careful it wouldn't happen again. Rather than being irked at being treated with kid gloves, she felt strangely cared for.

'I guess I owe you an answer now to your question about the woman in Nice who I'm avoiding.'

'No, thank you very much. I mean, you *do* owe me an answer to a question—that was the deal. But I'm not wasting it getting the skinny on some love affair gone wrong.'

He didn't say anything for a long moment. 'What's your question, then?'

'I don't know yet. When I do know I'll ask it.' And then he'd have to stop whatever he was doing and take a timeout to answer it. *Perfect.*

Finn studied Audra across the breakfast table the next morning. Actually, their breakfast table had become the picnic table that sat on the stone terrace outside, where they could drink in the glorious view. She'd turned down the bacon and eggs, choosing cereal instead. He made a mental note to buy croissants the next time they were in the village.

'What are you staring at, Finn?'

He wanted to make sure she was eating enough. But he knew exactly how well that'd go down if he admitted as much. 'I'm just trying to decide if that puny body of yours is up to today's challenge, Russel.'

A spark lit the ice-blue depths of her eyes, but then she shook her head as if realising he was trying to goad her into some kind of reaction. 'This puny body is up for a whole lot more lazing on a beach and a little bobbing about in the sea.'

'Nice try, sweetheart.'

She rolled her eyes. 'What horrors do you have planned?'

'You'll see.' He was determined that by the time she left the island she'd feel fitter, healthier and more empowered than she had when she'd arrived.

She harrumphed and slouched over her muesli, but her gaze wandered out towards the light gleaming on the water and it made her lips lift and her eyes dance. Being here—taking a break—had already been good for her.

But he wanted her to have fun too. A workout this morning followed by play this afternoon. That seemed like a decent balance.

'You want us to what?'

An hour later Audra stared at him with such undisguised horror it was all he could do not to laugh. If he laughed, though, it'd rile her and he didn't want her riled. Unless it was the only way to win her cooperation.

'I want us to jog the length of the beach.'

Her mouth opened and closed. 'But...why? How can this be fun?'

'Exercise improves my mood.' It always had. As a teenager it'd also been a way to exorcise his demons. Now it just helped to keep him fit and strong. He *liked* feeling fit and strong.

He waited for her to make some crack about being in favour of anything that improved his mood. Instead she planted her hands on her hips and stared at him. She wore a silky caftan thing over her swimsuit and the action made it ride higher on her thighs. He tried not to notice.

'Your mood has been fine since you've been here. Apart from your foul temper when you first arrived.'

'You mean when the police had me in handcuffs?'

She nodded.

'I'd like to see how silver-tongued you'd be in that situation!'

She smirked and he realised she'd got the rise out of him that she'd wanted, and he silently cursed himself. He fell for it every single time.

'But apart from that blip your mood has been fine.'

She was right. It had been. Which was strange because he'd been an absolute bear in Nice. He'd been a bear since the accident.

He shook that thought off. 'And we want to keep it that way.'

'But—' she gestured '—that has to be nearly a mile.'

'Yep.' He stared at her downturned mouth, imagined *again* that mongrel Farquhar shoving her in a cupboard, and wanted to smash something. He didn't want to bully her. If she really hated the idea… 'Is there any medical reason why you shouldn't run?'

She eyed him over the top of her sunglasses. 'No. You?'

'None. Running ten miles is out of the question, but one mile at a gentle pace will be fine.' He'd checked with his doctors.

'I haven't run since I was a kid. I work in an office…sit behind a desk all day. I'm not sure I can run that far.'

He realised then that her resistance came from a sense of inadequacy.

'I mean, even banged up you're probably super fit and—'

'We'll take it slow. And if you can't jog all the way, we'll walk the last part of it.'

'And you won't get grumpy at me for holding you back?'

'I promise.'

'No snark?'

He snorted. 'I'm not promising that.'

That spark flashed in her eyes again. 'Slow, you said?'

'Slow,' he promised.

She hauled in a breath. 'Well, here goes nothing…'

He started them slowly as promised. It felt good to be running again, even if it was at half his usual pace. Audra started a bit awkwardly, a trifle stiffly, as if the action were unfamiliar, but within two minutes she'd found a steady rhythm and he couldn't help but admire her poise and balance.

That damn ponytail, though, threatened his balance every time he glanced her way, bobbing with a cheeky nonchalance that made things inside him clench up…made him lose his tempo and stray from his course and have to check himself and readjust his line.

At the five-minute mark she was covered in a fine sheen of perspiration, and he suddenly flashed to a forbidden image of what she might look like during an athletic session of lovemaking. He stumbled and broke out into a cold sweat.

Audra seemed to lose her rhythm then too. Her elbows came in tight at her sides…she started to grimace…

And then her hands lifted to her breasts and he nearly fell over. She pulled to a halt and he did too. He glanced at her hands. She reefed them back to her sides and shot him a dark glare. 'Look, you didn't warn me that this is what we'd be doing before we hit the beach.'

Because he hadn't wanted her sniping at him the entire time they descended the hill.

'But they created exercise gear for a reason, you know? If I'm going to jog I need to wear a sports bra.'

He stared at her, not comprehending.

'It hurts to run without one,' she said through gritted teeth.

He blinked. *Hell.* He hadn't thought about that. She wasn't exactly big-breasted, but she was curvy where it mattered and…

'And while we're at it,' she ground out, 'I'd prefer to wear jogging shoes than run barefoot. This is darn hard on the ankles.' Her hands went to her hips. 'For heaven's sake, Finn, you have to give a girl some warning so she can prepare the appropriate outfit.'

He felt like an idiot. 'Well, let's just walk the rest of the way.'

It was hell walking beside her. Every breath he took was scented with peaches and coconut. And from the corner of his eye he couldn't help but track the perky progress of her ponytail. In his mind's eye all he could see was the way she'd cupped her breasts, to help take their weight while running, and things inside him twisted and grew hot.

When they reached the tall cliff at the beach's far end, Audra slapped a hand to it in a 'we made it' gesture. 'My mood doesn't feel improved.'

She sounded peeved, which made him want to laugh. But those lips...that ponytail... He needed a timeout, a little distance. *Now.*

She straightened and gave him the once-over. 'You're not even sweating the tiniest little bit!'

Not where she could see, at least. For which he gave thanks. But he needed to get waist-deep in water soon before she saw the effect she was having on him.

He gestured back the way they'd come. 'We're going to swim back.' Cold water suddenly seemed like an excellent plan.

Her face fell. 'Why didn't you say so before? I don't want to get my caftan wet. I could've left it behind.'

He was glad she hadn't. The less on show where she was concerned, the better.

'It'll take no time at all to dry off at the other end.'

'It's not designed to be swum in. It'll fall off my shoulder and probably get tangled in my legs.'

He clenched his jaw tight. *Not* an image he needed in his mind.

'I won't be able to swim properly.'

He couldn't utter a damn word.

Her chin shot up. 'You think I'm trying to wriggle my way out, don't you? You think I'm just making up excuses.'

It was probably wiser to let her misinterpret his silence than tell her the truth.

'Well, fine, I'll show you!'

She pulled the caftan over her head and tossed it to him. He did his best not to notice the flare of her hips, the long length of her legs, or the gentle swell of her breasts.

'I'll swim while you keep my caftan dry, cabana boy.'

Her, in the water way over there? Him, on the beach way over here? Worked for him.

'But when we reach the other end it's nothing but lazing on the beach and reading books till lunchtime.'

'Deal.' He was looking forward to another session with his book.

He kept pace with her on the shore, just in case she got a cramp or into some kind of trouble. She alternated freestyle with breaststroke and backstroke. And the slow easy pace suited him. It helped him find his equilibrium again. It gave him the time to remind himself in detail of all the ways he owed Rupert.

He nodded. He owed Rupert big-time—and that meant Audra was off limits and out of bounds. It might be different if Finn were looking to settle down, but settling down and Finn were barely on terms of acquaintance. And while he might feel as if he were at a crossroads in his life, that didn't mean anything. The after-effects of his accident would disappear soon enough. When they did, life would return to normal. He'd be looking for his next adrenaline rush and…and he'd be content again.

'Jetskiing?'

Audra stared at him with… Well, it wasn't horror at least. Consternation maybe? 'We had a laze on the beach, read our books, had a slow leisurely lunch…and now it's time for some fun.'

She rolled her bottom lip between her teeth. 'But aren't jets-kis like motorbikes? And motorbikes are dangerous.'

He shook his head. 'Unlike a motorbike, it doesn't hurt if you fall off a jetski.' At least, not at the speeds they'd be going. 'They're only dangerous if we don't use them right…if we're stupid.'

'But we're going to be smart and use them right?'

He nodded. 'We're even going to have a lesson first.' He could teach her all she needed to know, but he'd come to the conclusion it might be *wiser* to not be so hands-on where Audra was concerned.

She stared at the jetskiers who were currently buzzing about on the bay. 'A lesson?' She pursed her lips. 'And…and it doesn't look as if it involves an awful lot of strength or stamina,' she said, almost to herself. And then she started and jutted her chin. 'Call me a wimp if you want, but I have a feeling I'm going to be sore enough tomorrow as it is.'

'If you are, the best remedy will be a run along the beach followed by another swim.'

She tossed her head. 'In your dreams, cabana boy.'

He grinned. It was good to see her old spark return. 'This is for fun, Audra, and no other reason. Just fun.'

He saw something in her mind still and then click. 'I guess I haven't been doing a whole lot of that recently.'

She could say that again.

'Okay, well…where do we sign up?'

There were seven of them who took the lesson, and while Finn expected to chafe during the hour-long session, he didn't. It was too much fun watching Audra and her cheeky ponytail as she concentrated on learning how to manoeuvre her jetski. They had a further hour to putter around the bay afterwards to test out her new-found skills. He didn't go racing off on his own. He didn't want her trying to copy him and coming to grief. They'd practised what to do in case of capsizing, but he didn't want them to have to put it into practice. Besides, her laughter and the way her eyes sparkled were too much fun to miss out on.

'Oh, my God!' She practically danced on the dock when they returned their jetskis. 'That was the best fun ever. I'm definitely doing that again. Soon!'

He tried to stop staring at her, tried to drag his gaze from admiring the shape of her lips, the length of her legs, the bounce of her hair. An evening spent alone with her in Rupert's enormous villa rose in his mind, making him sweat. 'Beer?' Hanging out in a crowd for as long as they could suddenly struck him as a sound strategy.

'Yes, please.'

They strode along the wooden dock and he glanced at her

from the corner of his eye. The transformation from two days ago was amazing. She looked full of energy and so...*alive*.

He scrubbed both hands back through his hair. Why *was* she hell-bent on keeping herself on such a tight leash? Why didn't she let her hair down once in a while? Why...?

The questions pounded at him. He pressed both hands to the crown of his head in an effort to tamp them down, to counter the impulse to ask her outright. The thing was, even if he did break his protocol on asking personal questions and getting dragged into complicated emotional dilemmas, there was no guarantee Audra would confide in him. She'd never seen him as that kind of guy.

What if she needs to talk? What if she has no one else to confide in?

He wanted to swear.

He wanted to run.

He also wanted to see her filled with vitality and enthusiasm and joy, as she was now.

They ordered beers from a beachside bar and sat at a table in the shade of a jasmine vine to drink them.

'Today has been a really good day, Finn. Thank you.'

Audra wasn't like the women he dated. If she needed someone to confide in, he could be there for her, couldn't he? He took a long pull on his beer. 'Even the running?'

'Ugh, no, the running was awful.' She sipped her drink. 'I can't see I'm ever going to enjoy that, even with the right gear. Though I didn't mind the swimming. There's bound to be a local gym at home that has a pool.'

She was going to keep up the exercise when she returned home? Excellent.

He leaned back, a plan solidifying in his gut. 'You haven't asked your question yet.'

'I already told you—I don't want to hear about your woman in Nice. If you want to brag or grumble about her go right ahead. But I'm not wasting a perfectly good question on it.'

He wondered if he should just tell her about Trixie, but dismissed the idea. Trixie had no idea where he was. She wouldn't be able to cause any trouble here for him, for Joachim or for Audra. And he wanted to keep the smile, the sense of exhilaration, on Audra's face.

He stretched back, practically daring Audra to ask him a question. 'Isn't there anything personal you want to ask me?'

CHAPTER SIX

DID FINN HAVE any clue how utterly mouth-wateringly gorgeous he looked stretched out like that, as if for her express delectation? Audra knew he didn't mean anything by it. Flirting was as natural to him as breathing. If he thought for a moment she'd taken him seriously, he'd backtrack so fast it'd almost be funny.

Almost.

And she wasn't an idiot. Yet she couldn't get out of her mind the idea of striding around the table and—

No, not striding, *sashaying* around the table to plant herself in his lap, gently because she couldn't forget his injuries, and running her hand across the stubble of his jaw before drawing his lips down to hers.

Her mouth went dry and her heart pounded so hard she felt winded…dizzy. Maybe she was an idiot after all.

It was the romance of this idyllic Greek island combined with the euphoria of having whizzed across the water on a jetski. It'd left her feeling wild and reckless. She folded her hands together in her lap. She didn't do wild and reckless. If she went down that path it'd lead to things she couldn't undo. She'd let her family down enough as it was.

Finn folded himself up to hunch over his beer. 'Scrap that.

Don't ask your question. I don't like the look on your face. You went from curiously speculative to prim and disapproving.'

She stiffened. 'Prim?'

'Prim,' he repeated, not budging.

'I am *not* prim.'

'Sweetheart, nobody does prim like you.'

His laugh set her teeth on edge. She forced herself to settle back in her chair and to at least appear relaxed. 'I see what you're doing.'

'What am I doing?'

'Reverse psychology. Tell me not to ask a question in the hope I'll do the exact opposite.'

'Is it working?'

'Why are you so fixated on me asking you my owed question?'

A slow grin hooked up one side of his mouth and looking at it was like staring into the sun. She couldn't look away.

'Is that your question?'

Strive for casual.

'Don't be ridiculous.' If Rupert hadn't put the darn notion in her head—*Don't fall for Finn*—she wouldn't be wondering what it'd be like to kiss him.

She sipped her beer. As long as speculation didn't become anything more. She did what she could to ignore the ache that rose through her; to ignore the way her mouth dried and her stomach lurched.

She wasn't starting something with Finn. Even if he proved willing—which he wouldn't in a million years—there was too much at stake to risk it, and not enough to be won. She was *determined* there wouldn't be any more black marks against her name this year. There wouldn't be any more *ever* if she could help it.

If only she could stop thinking about him...*inappropriately*!

For heaven's sake, she was the one in her family who kept things steady, regulated, trouble-free. If there were choppy waters, she was the one who smoothed them. She didn't go rocking the boat and causing drama. That wasn't who she was. She ground her teeth together. And she wasn't going to change now.

She stared out at the harbour and gulped her beer. This was what happened when she let her hair down and indulged in a bit of impulsive wildness. It was so hard to get her wayward self back under wraps.

Finn might call her prim, but she preferred the terms self-controlled and disciplined. She needed to get things back on a normal grounding with him again, but when she went to open her mouth, he spoke first. 'I guess it's a throwback to the old game of Truth or Dare. I'm not up for too much daredevilry at the moment, but your question—the truth part of the game—is a different form of dangerousness.'

He stared up at the sky, lips pursed, and just like that he was familiar Finn again—family friend. Their session of jetskiing must've seemed pretty tame to him. He'd kept himself reined in for her sake, had focussed on her enjoyment rather than his own. Which meant that dark thread of restlessness would be pulsing through him now, goading him into taking unnecessary risks. She needed to dispel it if she could, to prevent him from doing something daft and dangerous.

'The truth can be ugly, Finn. Admitting the truth can be unwelcome and…' she settled for the word he'd used '…dangerous.'

Liquid brown eyes locked with hers as he drank his beer. He set his glass down on the table and wiped the back of his hand across his mouth. 'I know.'

'And yet you still want me to ask you a possibly dangerous question?'

'I'm game if you are.'

Was there a particular question he wanted her to ask? He stared at her and waited. She moistened her lips again and asked the question that had been rattling around in her mind ever since Rupert's phone call. 'Why do you avoid long-term romantic commitment?'

He blinked. '*That's* what you want to know?'

She shrugged. 'I'm curious. You've never once brought a date to a Russel family dinner. The rest of us have, multiple times. I want to know how you got to avoid the youthful mistakes the rest of us made. Besides…'

'What?'

'When Rupe was warning me off, he made some comment about you not being long-term material. Now we're going to ignore the fact that Rupert obviously thinks women only want long-term relationships when we all know that's simply not true. He obviously doesn't want to think of his little sister in those terms, bless him. But it made me think there's a story there. Hence, my question.'

He nodded, but he didn't speak.

She glanced at his now empty glass. 'If you want another beer, I'm happy to drive us home.'

He called the waiter over and ordered a lime and soda. She did the same. He speared her with a glare. 'I don't need Dutch courage to tell you the truth.'

'And yet that doesn't hide the fact that you don't want to talk about it.' Whatever *it* was. She shrugged and drained the rest of her beer too. 'That's okay, you can simply fob me off with an "I just haven't met the right girl yet" and be done with it.'

'But that would be lying, and lying is against the rules.'

'Ah, so you have met the right girl?' Was it Trixie who'd texted him?

He wagged a finger at her, and just for a moment his eyes danced, shifting the darkness her question had triggered. 'That's an altogether different question. If you'd rather I answer that one…?'

It made her laugh. 'I'll stick with my original question, thank you very much.'

The waiter brought their drinks and Finn took the straw from his glass and set it on the table. His eyes turned sombre again. 'You know the circumstances surrounding my father's death?'

'He died in a caving accident when you were eight.'

'He liked extreme sports. He was an adrenaline junkie. I seem to have inherited that trait.'

She frowned and sat back.

His eyes narrowed. 'What?'

She took a sip of her drink, wondering at his sharp tone. 'Can one inherit risk-taking the same way they can brown eyes and tawny hair?'

'Intelligence is inherited, isn't it? And a bad temper and... Why?'

He glared and she wished she'd kept her mouth shut. 'Just wondering,' she murmured.

'No, you weren't.'

Fine. She huffed out a breath. 'I always thought your adventuring was a way of keeping your father's memory alive, a way to pay homage to him.'

He blinked.

She tried to gauge the impact her words had on him. 'There isn't any judgement attached to that statement, Finn. I'm not suggesting it's either good or bad.'

He shook himself, but she noted the belligerent thrust to his jaw. 'Does it matter whether my risk-taking is inherited or not?'

'Of course it does. If it's some gene you inherently possess then that means it's always going to be a part of you, a...a natural urge like eating and sleeping. If it's the latter then one day you can simply decide you've paid enough homage. One means you can't change, the other means you can.'

He shoved his chair back, physically moving further away from her, his eyes flashing. She raised her hands. 'But that's not for me to decide. Your call. Like I said, no judgement here. It was just, umm...idle speculation.' She tried not to wince as she said it.

The space between them pulsed with Finn's…outrage? Shock? Disorientation? Audra wasn't sure, but she wanted to get them back on an even keel again. 'What does this have to do with avoiding romantic commitment?'

He gave a low laugh and stretched his legs out in front of him. 'You warned me this could be dangerous.'

It had certainly sent a sick wave of adrenaline coursing through her. 'We don't have to continue with this conversation if you don't want to.'

He skewered her with a glance. 'You don't want to know?'

She ran a finger through the condensation on her glass. He was being honest with her. He deserved the same in return. 'I want to know.'

'Then the rules demand that you get your answer.'

Was he laughing at her?

He grew serious again. 'My father's death was very difficult for my mother.'

Jeremy Sullivan had been an Australian sportsman who for a brief moment had held the world record for the men's four-hundred-metre butterfly. Claudette Dupont, Finn's mother, had been working at the French embassy in Canberra. They'd met, fallen in love and had moved to Europe where Jeremy had pursued a life of adventure and daring. Both of Finn's grandfathers came from old money. They, along with the lucrative sponsorship deals Jeremy received, had funded his and Claudette's lifestyle.

And from the outside it had been an enviable lifestyle—jetting around the world from one extreme sporting event to another—Jeremy taking part in whatever event was on offer while Claudette cheered him from the sidelines. And there'd apparently been everything from cliff diving to ice climbing, bobsledding to waterfall kayaking, and more.

But it had ended in tragedy with the caving accident that had claimed Jeremy's life. Audra dragged in a breath. 'She was too young to be a widow.' And Finn had been too young to be left fatherless.

'She gave up everything to follow him on his adventures—her job, a stable network of friends…a home. She was an only child and there weren't many close relatives apart from her parents.'

Audra wondered how she'd cope in that same situation. 'She had you.'

He shook his head. 'I wasn't enough.'

The pain in his eyes raked through her chest, thickened her throat. 'What happened?' She knew his mother had died, but nobody ever spoke of it.

'She just…faded away. She developed a lot of mystery illnesses—spent a lot of time in hospital. When she was home she spent a lot of time in bed.'

'That's when your uncle Ned came to look after you?' His father's brother was still a big part of Finn's life. He'd relocated to Europe to be with Finn and Claudette.

'He moved in and looked after the both of us. I was eleven when my mother died, and the official verdict was an accidental overdose of painkillers.' He met her gaze. 'Nobody thought she did it deliberately.'

That was something at least. But it was so sad. Such a waste.

'My uncle's verdict was that she'd died of a broken heart.'

Audra's verdict was that Claudette Sullivan had let her son down. Badly. But she kept that to herself. Her heart ached for the little boy she'd left behind and for all the loss he'd suffered.

'Ned blamed my father.'

Wow. 'It must've been hard for Ned,' she offered. 'I don't know what I'd do if I lost one of my siblings. And to then watch as your mother became sicker… He must've felt helpless.'

'He claimed my father should never have married if he wasn't going to settle down to raise a family properly.'

Finn's face had become wooden and she tried not to wince.

'Families aren't one-size-fits-all entities. They don't come in pretty cookie-cutter shapes.'

He remained silent. She moistened her lips. 'What happened after your mother died?'

He straightened in his chair and took a long gulp of lime and soda. 'That's when Ned boarded me at the international school in Geneva. It was full of noisy, rowdy boys and activities specifically designed to keep us busy and out of mischief.'

It was an effort, but she laughed as he'd meant her to. 'I've heard stories about some of the mischief you got up to. I think they need to redesign some of those activities.'

He grinned. 'It was full of life. Ned came to every open day, took me somewhere every weekend we had leave. I didn't feel abandoned.'

Not by Ned, no. But what about his mother? She swallowed. 'And you met Rupert there.'

His grin widened. 'And soon after found myself adopted by the entire Russel clan.'

'For your sins.' She smiled back, but none of it eased the throb in her heart.

'I always found myself drawn to the riskier pastimes the school offered...and that only grew as I got older. There's nothing like the thrill of paragliding down a mountain or surfing thirty-foot waves.'

'Or throwing oneself off a ski jump with gay abandon,' she added wryly, referencing his recent accident.

'Accidents happen.'

But in the pastimes Finn pursued, such accidents could have fatal consequences. Didn't that bother him? 'Did Ned never try and clip your wings or divert your interests elsewhere?' He'd lost a brother. He wouldn't have wanted to lose a nephew as well.

'He's too smart for that. He knew it wouldn't work, not once he realised how determined I was. Before I was of age, when I still needed a guardian's signature, he just made sure I had the very best training available in whatever activity had taken my fancy before he'd sign the permission forms.'

'It must've taken an enormous amount of courage on his behalf.'

'Perhaps. But he'd seen the effect my grandfather's refusals and vetoes had had on my father. He said it resulted in my father taking too many unnecessary chances. In his own way, Ned did his best to keep me safe.'

She nodded.

'The way I live my life, the risks I take, they're not conducive to family life, Audra. When I turned eighteen I promised my uncle to never take an unnecessary risk—to make sure I was always fully trained to perform whatever task I was attempting.'

Thinking about the risks he took made her temples ache.

'I made a promise to myself at the same time.' His eyes burned into hers. 'I swore I'd never become involved in a long-term relationship until I'd given up extreme sports. It's not fair to put any woman through what my father put my mother through.'

It was evident he thought hell had a better chance of freezing over than him ever giving up extreme sports. She eyed him for a moment. 'Have you ever been tempted to break that contract with yourself?'

'I don't break my promises.'

It wasn't an answer. It was also an oblique reminder of the promise he'd made to Rupert. As if that were something she was likely to forget.

'But wouldn't you like a long-term relationship some day? Can't you ever see a time when you'd give up extreme sports?'

His eyes suddenly gleamed. 'Those are altogether separate questions. I believe I've answered your original one.'

Dammit! He had to know that only whetted her appetite for more.

None of your business.

It really wasn't, but then wasn't that the beauty, the temptation, of this game of 'truth or dare' questions—the danger?

Finn wanted to laugh at the quickened curiosity, the look of pique, in Audra's face. He shouldn't play this game. He should leave it all well enough alone, but...

He leaned towards her. 'I'll make a tit-for-tat deal with you.'

Ice-blue eyes shouldn't leave a path of fire on his skin, but beneath her gaze he started to burn. She cocked her head to one side. 'You mean a question-for-question, quid pro quo bargain?'

'Yep.'

She leaned in and searched his face as if trying to decipher his agenda. He did his best to keep his face clear. Finally she eased back and he could breathe again.

'You must be *really* bored.'

He wasn't bored. Her company didn't bore him. It never had. He didn't want to examine that thought too closely, though. He didn't want to admit it out loud either. 'Life has been...quieter of late than usual.'

'And you're finding that a challenge?'

He had in Nice, but now...not really. Which didn't make sense.

Can you inherit a risk-taking gene? He shied away from that question, from the deeper implications that lay beneath its surface. So what if some of his former pursuits had lost their glitter? That didn't mean anything.

He set his jaw. 'Let's call it a new experience.'

Her lips pressed together into a prim line he wanted to mess up. He'd like to kiss those lips until they were plump and swollen and— *Hell!*

'Are you up for my question challenge?' He made his voice deliberately mocking in a way he knew would gall her.

'I don't know. I'll think about it.'

He kinked an eyebrow, deliberately trying to inflame her competitive spirit. 'What are you afraid of?'

She pushed her sunglasses further up her nose and readjusted her sunhat. 'Funny, isn't it, how every question now seems to take on a double edge?'

He didn't pursue it. In all honesty letting sleeping dogs lie would probably be for the best.

Really?

He thrust out his jaw. And if not, then there was more than one way to find out what was troubling her. He just needed to turn his mind to it. Find another way.

Finn laughed when Audra pulled the two trays of croissants from the oven. Those tiny hard-looking lumps were supposed to be croissants? Her face, comical in its indignation, made him laugh harder.

'How can you laugh about this? We spent hours on these and…and *this* is our reward?'

'French pastry has a reputation for being notoriously difficult, hasn't it?' He poked a finger at the nearest hard lump and it disintegrated to ash beneath his touch. 'Wow, I think we just took French cooking to a new all-time low.'

'But…but you're half French! That should've given us a head start.'

'And you're half Australian but I don't see any particular evidence of that making you handy with either a cricket bat or a barbecue.'

Like Finn's father, Audra's mother had been Australian. Audra merely glowered at him, slammed the cookbook back to the bench top and studied its instructions once again. He hoped she wasn't going to put him through the torture of working so closely beside her in the kitchen again. There'd been too much accidental brushing of arms, too much…heat. Try as he might, he couldn't blame it all on the oven. Even over the smell of flour, yeast and milk, the scent of peaches and coconut had pounded at him, making him hungry.

But not for food.

He opened a cupboard and took out a plate, unwrapped the bakery bag he'd stowed in the pantry earlier and placed half a dozen croissants onto it. He slid the plate towards Audra.

She took a croissant without looking, bit into it and then pointed at the cookbook. 'Here's where we went wrong. We—'

She broke off to stare at the croissant in her hand, and then at the plate. 'If you dare tell me here are some croissants you prepared earlier, I'll—'

'Here are some croissants I *bought* at the village bakery earlier.'

'When earlier?'

'Dawn. Before you were up.'

The croissant hurtled back to the plate and her hands slammed to her hips. He backed up a step. 'I wasn't casting aspersions on your croissant-making abilities. But I wanted a back-up plan because…because I wanted to eat croissants.' Because she'd seemed so set on them.

Her glare didn't abate. 'What else have you been doing at the crack of dawn each morning?'

He shook his head, at a loss. 'Nothing, why?'

'Have you been running into the village and back every morning?'

He frowned. 'I took the car.' Anyway, he wasn't up to running that distance yet. And he hadn't felt like walking. Every day he felt a little stronger, but… It hadn't occurred to him to run into the village. Or to run anywhere for that matter. Except with her on the beach, when it was his turn to choose their daily activities. Only then he didn't make her jog anyway. They usually walked the length of the beach and then swam back.

'Or…or throwing yourself off cliffs or…or kite surfing or—'

He crowded in close then, his own temper rising, and it made her eyes widen…and darken. 'That wouldn't be in the spirit of the deal we made, would it?'

She visibly swallowed. 'Absolutely not.'

'And I'm a man of my word.'

Her gaze momentarily lowered to his lips before lifting again. 'You're also a self-professed adrenaline junkie.'

Except the adrenaline flooding his body at the moment had nothing to do with extreme sports. It had to do with the perfect shape of Audra's mouth and the burning need to know what she'd taste like. Would she taste of peaches and coconut? Coffee and croissant? Salty or sweet? His skin tightened, stretching itself across his frame in torturous tautness.

Her breathing grew shallow and a light flared to life in her eyes and he knew she'd recognised his hunger, his need, but she didn't move away, didn't retreat. Instead her gaze roved across his face and lingered for a beat too long on his mouth, and her lips parted with an answering hunger.

'A man of his word?' she murmured, swaying towards him.

Her words penetrated the fog surrounding his brain. *What are you doing? You can't kiss her!*

He snapped away, his breathing harsh. Silence echoed off the walls for three heart-rending beats and then he heard her fussing around behind him…dumping the failed croissants in the bin, rinsing the oven trays. 'Thank you for buying backup croissants, Finn.'

He closed his eyes and counted to three, before turning around. He found her surveying him, her tone nonchalant and untroubled—as if she hadn't been about to reach up on her tiptoes and kiss him. He'd seen the temptation in her eyes, but somehow she'd bundled up her needs and desires and hidden them behind a prim wall of control and restraint. It had his back molars grinding together.

He didn't know how he knew, but this was all related—her tight rein on her desires and needs, her refusal to let her hair down and have fun, the dogged determination to repress it all because...?

He had no idea! He had no answer for why she didn't simply reach out and take what she wanted from life.

She bit into her croissant and it was all he could do then not to groan.

'I have a "truth or dare" question for you, Finn.'

He tried to match her coolness and composure. 'So you've decided to take me up on the quid pro quo bargain?'

She nodded and stuck out a hip. If he'd been wearing a tie he'd have had to loosen it. 'If you're still game,' she purred.

In normal circumstances her snark would've had him fighting a grin. But nothing about today and this kitchen and Audra felt the least bit normal. Or the least bit familiar. 'Ask your question.'

She eyed him for a moment, her eyes stormy. 'Don't you want something more out of life?'

'More?' He felt his eyes narrow. 'Like what?'

'I mean, you flit from adventure to adventure, but...' That beautiful brow of hers creased. 'Don't you want something more worthwhile, more...*lasting*?'

His lips twisted. A man showed no interest in settling down—

'I'm not talking about marriage and babies!' she snapped as if reading his mind. 'I'm talking about doing something good with your life, making a mark, leaving a legacy.'

Her innate and too familiar disapproval stung him in ways it never had before. Normally he'd have laughed it off, but...

He found himself leaning towards her. He had to fight the urge to loom. He wasn't Thomas-blasted-Farquhar. He didn't go in for physical intimidation. 'Do you seriously think I *just* live off my trust fund while I go trekking through the Amazon and train for the London marathon, and—'

'Look, I know you raise a lot of money for charity, but there doesn't seem to be any rhyme or reason to your methods—no proper organisation. You simply bounce from one thing to the next.'

'And what about my design company?'

Her hands went to her hips. 'You don't seem to spend a lot of time in the office.'

His mouth worked. 'You think I treat my company like a…a toy?'

'Well, don't you? I mean, you never talk about it!'

'You never ask me about it!'

She blinked. 'From where I'm standing—'

'With all the other workaholics,' he shot back.

'It simply looks as if you're skiving off from the day job to have exciting adventures. Obviously that's your prerogative, as you're the boss, but—'

He raised his arms. 'Okay, we're going to play a game.'

She stared at him. Her eyes throbbed, and he knew that some of this anger came from what had almost happened between them—the physical frustration and emotional confusion. He wanted to lean across and pull her into his arms and hug her until they both felt better. But he had a feeling that solution would simply lead to more danger.

Her chin lifted. 'And what about my question?'

'By the end of the game you'll have your answer. I promise.' And in the process he meant to challenge her to explore the dreams she seemed so doggedly determined to bury.

Her eyes narrowed and she folded her arms. 'What does this game involve?'

'Sitting in the garden with a plate of croissants and my computer.'

She raised her eyebrows. 'Sitting?'

'And eating…and talking.'

She unfolded her arms. 'Fine. That I can do.'

What was it his uncle used to say? *There's more than one way to crack an egg.* He might never discover the reasons Audra held herself back, but the one thing he could do was whet her appetite for the options life held, give her the push she perhaps needed to reach for her dreams. After all, temptation and adventure were his forte. He frowned as he went to retrieve his laptop. At least, they had been once. And he'd find his fire for them again soon enough.

And he couldn't forget that once he'd answered her question, he'd have one of his own in the kitty. He might never use it—she was right, these questions could be dangerous—but it'd be there waiting just in case.

CHAPTER SEVEN

AUDRA BLINKED WHEN Finn handed her a large notepad and a set of pencils. She opened her mouth to ask what they were for, but when he sat opposite and opened his laptop she figured she'd find out soon enough.

For the moment she was simply content to stare at him and wonder what that stubble would feel like against her palms and admire the breadth of his shoulders and—

No, no. *No!*

For the moment she was content to…to congratulate herself for keeping Finn quiet for another day. And she'd…*admire the view.* The brilliant blue of the sea contrasted with the soft blue of the sky, making her appreciate all the different hues on display. A yacht with a pink and blue sail had anchored just offshore and she imagined a honeymooning couple rowing into one of the many deserted coves that lay along this side of the island, and enjoying…

Her mind flashed with forbidden images, and she shook herself. *Enjoying a picnic.*

'Audra?'

She glanced up to find Finn staring at her, one eyebrow raised. She envied that. She'd always wanted to do it. She tried it now, and he laughed. 'What are you doing?'

'I love the "one eyebrow raised" thing. It looks great and you do it really well. I've always wanted to do it, but...' She tried again and he convulsed. Laughter was good. She needed to dispel the fraught atmosphere that had developed between them in the kitchen. She needed to forget about kissing him. He'd been looking grim and serious in odd moments these last few days too...sad, after telling her about the promise he'd made to himself when he'd turned eighteen.

She didn't want him sad. In the past she'd often wanted to get the better of him, but she didn't want that now either. She just wanted to see him fit and healthy. Happy. And she wanted to see him the way she used to see him—as Rupert's best friend. If she focussed hard enough, she could get that back, right?

She gave a mock sigh. 'That's not the effect I was aiming for.'

'There's a trick.'

She leaned towards him. 'Really?'

He nodded.

'Will you tell it to me?'

'If you'll tell me what you were thinking about when you were staring out to sea.' He gestured behind him at the view. 'You were a million miles away.'

Heat flushed her cheeks. She wasn't going to tell him about her imaginary honeymoon couple, but... 'It's so beautiful here. *So* beautiful. It does something to me—fills me up...makes me feel more...'

He frowned. 'More what?'

She lifted her hands only to let them drop again. 'I'm not sure how to explain it. It just makes me feel more...myself.'

He sat back as if her words had punched the air from his lungs. 'If that's true then you should move here.'

'Impossible.' Her laugh, even to her own ears, sounded strained.

'Nothing's impossible.'

She couldn't transplant her work here. She didn't even want to try. It'd simply suck the colour and life from this place for her anyway, so she shook her head. 'It's just a timely reminder that I should be taking my holidays more often.' She had a ridiculous amount of leave accrued. She had a ridiculous amount of money saved too. Maybe even enough for a deposit on a little cottage in the village? And then, maybe, she could own her own bit of paradise—a bit that was just hers.

And maybe having that would help counter the grey monotony her life in Geneva held for her.

Finn stared at her as if he wanted to argue the point further. No more. Some pipe dreams made her chest ache, and not in a good way. 'Fair's fair. Share your eyebrow-raising tip.'

So he walked her through it. 'But you'll need to practise. You can do an internet search if you want to.'

Really? Who'd have thought?

He rubbed his hands together. 'Now we're going to play my game.'

'And the name of the game...?'

'Designing Audra's favourite...'

'Holiday cottage?' she supplied helpfully.

His grin widened and he clapped his hands. 'Designing Audra's favourite shop.'

Her heart started to pound.

'How old were you when you decided shopkeeping sang to your soul?'

She made herself laugh because it was quite clearly what he intended. 'I don't know. I guess I must've been about six.' And then eleven...fifteen...seventeen. But her owning a shop—it was a crazy idea. It was so *indulgent*.

But this was just a game. Her heart thumped. It wouldn't hurt to play along for an hour or so. Finn obviously wanted to show off some hidden talent he had and who was she to rain on his parade? The lines of strain around his eyes had eased and the grooves bracketing his mouth no longer bit into his flesh so deeply. Each day had him moving more easily and fluidly. Coming here had been good for him. Taking it easy was good for him. She wanted all that goodness to continue in the same vein.

She made herself sit up straighter. 'Right, the name of the game is Designing Audra's Dream Shop.'

He grinned and it sent a breathless kind of energy zinging through her.

'We're going to let our minds go wild. The sky's the limit. Got it?'

'Got it.'

He held her gaze. 'I mean it. The point of the game is to not be held back by practicalities or mundane humdrummery. That comes later. For this specific point in time we're aiming for best of the best, top of the pops, no compromises, just pure unadulterated dream vision.'

She had a feeling she should make some sort of effort to check the enthusiasm suddenly firing through her veins, but Finn's enthusiasm was infectious. And she was in the Greek islands on holiday. She was allowed to play. She nodded once, hard. 'Right.'

'First question...' his fingers were poised over the keyboard of his computer '...and experience tells me that the first answer that pops into your mind is usually the right one.'

'Okay, hit me with Question One.'

'Where is your ideal location for your shop?'

'Here on Kyanós...in the village's main street, overlooking the harbour. There's a place down there that's for sale and...' she hesitated '...it has a nice view.'

His fingers flew over the keyboard. 'What does your ideal shop sell?'

'Beautiful things,' she answered without hesitation.

'Specifics, please.'

So she described in detail the beautiful things she'd love to sell in her dream shop. 'Handicrafts made by local artisans—things like jade pendants and elegant bracelets, beautiful scented candles and colourful scarves.' She pulled in a breath. 'Wooden boxes ornamented with beaten silver, silver boxes ornamented with coloured beads.' She described gorgeous leather handbags, scented soaps and journals made from handcrafted paper.

She rested her chin on her hands and let her mind drift into her dream shop—a pastime she'd refused to indulge in for... well, years now. 'There'd be beautiful prints for sale on the walls. There'd be wind chimes and pretty vases...glassware.'

She pulled back, suddenly self-conscious, heat bursting across her cheeks. 'Is that...uh...specific enough?'

'It's perfect.'

He kept tap-tapping away, staring at the computer screen rather than at her, and the heat slowly faded from her face. He looked utterly engrossed and she wondered if he'd worn the same expression when he'd set off on his ill-fated ski jump.

He glanced at her and she could feel herself colour again at being caught out staring. Luckily, he didn't seem to notice. He just started shooting questions at her again. How big was her shop? Was it square or rectangle? Where did she want to locate the point of sale? What colour scheme would she choose? What shelving arrangements and display options did she have in mind?

Her head started to whirl at the sheer number of questions, but she found she could answer them all without dithering or wavering, even when she didn't have the correct terminology for what she was trying to describe. Finn had a knack for asking her things and then reframing her answers in a way that captured exactly what she meant. She wasn't sure how he did it.

'Okay, you need to give me about fifteen minutes.'

'I'll get us some drinks.' She made up a fruit and cheese platter to supplement their lunch of croissants, added some dried fruits and nuts before taking the tray outside.

Finn rose and took the tray from her. 'Sit. I'll show you what I've done.'

She did as he bid. He turned the computer to face her.

She gasped. She couldn't help it. She pulled the computer towards her. She couldn't help that either. If she could've she'd have stepped right inside his computer because staring out at her from the screen was the interior of the shop she'd dreamed about ever since she was a little girl—a dream she'd perfected as she'd grown older and her tastes had changed. 'How...?' She could barely push the word past the lump in her throat. 'How did you do this?'

'Design software.'

He went to press a button, but she batted his hand away. 'Don't touch a thing! This is *perfect*.' It was amazing. The interior of her fantasy shop lived and breathed there on the screen like a dream come true and it made everything inside her throb and come alive.

'Not perfect.' He placed a slice of feta on a cracker and passed it across to her. 'It'd take me another couple of days to refine it for true perfection. But it gives a pretty good indication of your vision.'

It did. And she wanted this vision. She wanted it so bad it tasted like raspberries on her tongue. Instead of raspberries she bit into feta, which was pretty delicious too.

'If you push the arrow key there're another two pictures of your shop's interior from different angles.'

She popped the rest of the cracker into her mouth and pressed the arrow key...and marvelled anew at the additional two pictures that appeared—one from the back of the shop, and one from behind the sales counter, both of which afforded a glorious view of a harbour. There was a tub of colourful flowers just outside the door and her eyes filled. She reached out and touched them. 'You remembered.'

'I did.'

She pored over every single detail in the pictures. She could barely look away from the screen, but she had to. This dream could never be hers. She dragged in a breath, gathered her resources to meet Finn's gaze and to pretend that this hadn't been anything more than a game, an interesting exercise, when her gaze caught on the logo in the bottom right corner of the screen. The breath left her lungs in a rush. She knew that logo!

Her gaze speared to his. '*You're* Aspiration Designs?'

'Along with my two partners.'

He nodded a confirmation and she couldn't read the expression in his eyes. 'How did I not know about this?'

He shrugged. 'It's not a secret.'

'But…your company was called Sullivan Brand Consultants.'

'Until I merged with my partners.'

She forced her mind back to the family dinners and the few other times in recent years that she'd seen Finn, and tried to recall a conversation—any conversation—about him expanding his company or going into partnership. There'd been some vague rumblings about some changes, but…she'd not paid a whole lot of attention. She wanted to hide her face in her hands. Had she really been so uninterested…so set in her picture of who Finn was?

She moistened her lips. Aspiration Designs was a boutique design business in high demand. 'You created the foyer designs for the new global business centre in Geneva.'

He lifted a shoulder in a silent shrug.

Those designs had won awards.

She closed the lid of the laptop, sagging in her seat. 'I've had you pegged all wrong. For all these years you haven't been flitting from one daredevil adventure to another. You've been—' she gestured to the computer '—making people's dreams come true.'

'I don't make people's dreams come true. They make their

own dreams come true through sheer hard work and dedication. I just show them what their dream can look like.'

In the same way he'd burned the vision of her dream shop onto her brain.

'And another thing—' he handed her another cracker laden with cheese '—Aspirations isn't a one-man band. My partners are in charge of the day-to-day running. Also, I've built an amazing design team and one of my super-powers is delegation. Which means I can go flitting off on any adventure that takes my fancy, almost at a moment's notice.'

She didn't believe that for a moment. She bet he timed his adventures to fit in with his work demands.

'And in hindsight it's probably not all that surprising that you don't know about my company. How often have we seen each other in the last four or five years? Just a handful of times.'

He had a point. 'Christmas…and occasionally when you're in Geneva I'll catch you when you're seeing Rupert.' But that was often for just a quick drink. They were on the periphery of each other's lives, not inside them.

'And when you do see me you always ask me what my latest adventure has been and where I'm off to next.'

Her stomach churned. Never once had she asked him about his work. She hadn't thought he did much. Instead, she'd vicariously lived adventure and excitement through him. But the same disapproval she directed at herself—to keep herself in check—she'd also aimed at him. How unfair was that!

She'd taken a secret delight in his exploits while maintaining a sense of moral superiority by dismissing them as trivial. She swallowed. 'I owe you an apology. I'm really sorry, Finn. I've been a pompous ass.'

He blinked. 'Garbage. You just didn't know.'

She hadn't wanted to know. She'd wanted to dismiss him as an irresponsible lightweight. Her mouth dried. And in thinking of him as a self-indulgent pleasure-seeker it had been easier to battle the attraction she'd always felt simmering beneath the surface of her consciousness for him.

God! That couldn't be true.

Couldn't it?

She didn't know what to do with such an epiphany, so she forced a smile to uncooperative lips. 'You have your adventures *and* you do good and interesting work. Finn...' she spread her hands '...you're living the dream.'

He laughed but it didn't reach his eyes. She recalled what he'd told her—about the promise he'd made to himself when he'd come of age—and a protest rose through her. 'I think you're wrong, Finn—both you and Ned. I think you *can* have a long-term relationship *and* still enjoy the extreme sports you love.' The words blurted out of her with no rhyme or reason. Finn's head snapped back. She winced and gulped and wished she could call them back.

'Talk about a change of topic.' He eased away, eyed her for a moment. 'Wrong how?'

She shouldn't have started this. But now that she had... She forced herself to straighten. 'I just don't think you can define your own circumstances based on what happened to your parents. And I'm far from convinced Ned should blame your father for everything that happened afterwards.' She raised her hands in a conciliatory gesture. 'I know! I know! He has your best interests at heart. And, look, I love your uncle Ned.' He came to their Christmas dinners and had become as much a part of the extended family as Finn had. 'But surely it's up to you and your prospective life partner to decide what kind of marriage will work for you.'

'But my mother—'

Frustration shot through her. 'Not every woman deals with tragedy in the same way your mother did!'

'Whoa!' He stared at her.

Heck!

'Sorry. Gosh, I...' She bit her lip.

What had she been thinking?

'Sorry,' she said again, swallowing. 'That came out harsher than I meant it to—*way* harsher. I just meant, people react to tragedy in different ways. People react to broken hearts in different ways. I'm not trying to trivialise it; I'm not saying it's easy. It's just...not everyone falls into a decline. If you live by those kinds of rules then—'

He leaned towards her and she almost lost her train of thought. 'Um, then...it follows that *you'd* better never marry a woman who's into extreme sports or...or has a dangerous job because if she dies then you wouldn't be able to survive it.'

His jaw dropped.

'And from the look on your face, it's clear you don't think of yourself as that kind of person.'

He didn't.

Finn stared at Audra, not sure why his heart pounded so hard, or why something chained inside him wanted to suddenly break free.

She retied her ponytail, not quite meeting his eyes. 'I mean, not everyone wants to marry and that's fine. Not everyone wants to have kids, and that's fine too. Maybe you're one of those people.'

'But?'

She bit her bottom lip and when she finally released it, it was plump from where she'd worried at it. She shrugged. 'But maybe you're not.'

'You think I want to marry and have kids?'

Blue eyes met his, and they had him clenching up in strange ways. 'I have no idea.' She leaned towards him the tiniest fraction. 'Wouldn't you eventually like to have children?'

'I don't know.' He'd never allowed himself to think about it before. 'You?'

'I'd love to be a mother one day.'

'Would you marry someone obsessed with extreme sports?'

'I wouldn't marry someone obsessed with anything, thank you very much. I don't want my life partner spending all his leisure time away from me—whether it's for rock climbing, stamp collecting or golf. I'd want him to want to spend time with me.'

Any guy lucky enough to catch Audra's eye would be a fool not to spend time with her. *Lots* of time. As much as he could.

'I don't want *all* of his leisure time, though.' She glared as if Finn had accused her of exactly that. 'There are girlfriends to catch up with over coffee and cake...or cocktails. And books to read.'

Speaking of books, he hoped she had reading down on today's agenda. He wouldn't mind getting back to his book. 'But you'd be okay with him doing some rock climbing, hang-gliding or golf?'

'As long as he doesn't expect me to take up the sport too. I mean, me dangling from a thin rope off a sheer cliff or hurtling off a sheer cliff in a glorified paper plane—what could possibly go wrong?'

A bark of laughter shot out of him. 'We're going to assume that this hypothetical life partner of yours would insist on you getting full training before attempting anything dangerous.'

She wrinkled her nose. 'Doesn't change the fact I'm not the slightest bit interested in rock climbing, hang-gliding or golf. I wouldn't want to go out with someone who wanted to change me.'

He sagged back on the wooden bench, air leaving his lungs. 'Which is why you wouldn't change him.' It didn't mean she wouldn't worry when her partner embarked on some risky activity, but she'd accept them for who they were. She'd want them to be happy.

Things inside him clenched up again. So what if laps around a racetrack had started to feel just plain boring—round and round in endless monotonous laps? *Yawn.* And so what if he couldn't remember why he'd thought hurtling off that ski jump had been a good idea. It didn't mean he wanted to change his entire lifestyle. It didn't mean anything. Yet...

He'd never let himself think about the possibility of having children before. He moistened suddenly dry lips. He wasn't sure he should start now either.

And yet he couldn't let the matter drop. 'Do you think about having children a lot?'

Her brow wrinkled. 'Where are you going with this? It's not like I'm obsessed or anything. It's not like it's constantly on my mind. But I am twenty-seven. Ideally, if I were going to start a family, I'd want that to happen in the next ten years. And I wouldn't want to get married and launch immediately into parenthood. I'd want to enjoy married life for a bit first.'

She frowned then. 'What?' he demanded, curious to see inside this world of hers—unsure if it attracted or repelled him.

'I was just thinking about this hypothetical partner you've landed me with. I hope he understands that things change when babies come along.'

Obviously, but...um. 'How?'

She selected a brazil nut before holding the bowl out to him. 'Suddenly you have way less time for yourself. Cocktail nights with the girls become fewer and farther between.'

He took a handful of nuts. 'As do opportunities to throw yourself off a cliff, I suppose?'

'Exactly.'

Except having Finn hadn't slowed his father down. And his mother certainly hadn't insisted on having a stable home base. She'd simply towed Finn and his nanny along with them wherever they went. And when he was old enough, she hired tutors to homeschool him.

And everything inside him rebelled at blaming his parents for that.

'A baby's needs have to be taken into consideration and—'

She broke off when she glanced into his face. 'I'm not criticising your parents, Finn. I'm not saying they did it wrong or anything. I'm describing how *I'd* want to do it. Each couple works out what's best for them.'

'But you'd want to be hands-on. I have a feeling that nannies and boarding schools and in-home tutors aren't your idea of good parenting. You'd want a house in the suburbs, to host Christmas dinner—'

'It doesn't have to be in the burbs. It could be an apartment in the city or a house overlooking a Greek beach. And if I can afford a nanny I'll have one of those too, thank you very much. I'd want to keep working.'

His parents had chosen to not work. At all.

'But when I get home from work, I'd want to have my family around me. That's all.' Their eyes locked. 'It's not how my parents did it...and I'm not saying I hated boarding school, because I didn't. I know how lucky I've been. I'm not saying my way is better than anybody else's. I'm just saying that's the way that'd make *me* happy.'

She'd just described everything he'd wanted when he was a child, and it made the secret places inside him ache. It also brought something into stark relief. She knew what would make her happy in her personal life—she knew the kind of home life and family that she wanted, and it was clear she wasn't going to settle for less. So why was she settling for less in her work life?

The question hovered on his tongue. He had a 'truth or dare' question owing to him, but something held him back, warned him the time wasn't right. Audra was looking more relaxed with each day they spent here. Her appetite had returned, as had the colour in her cheeks. But he recalled the expression in her eyes when he'd first turned his computer around to show her that shop, and things inside him knotted up. It was too new, and too fragile. She needed more time to pore over those pictures…to dream. He wanted her hunger to build until she could deny it no longer.

He loaded two crackers with cheese and handed her one, before lifting the lid of his computer. 'I'll email those designs through to you.'

'Oh, um…thank you. That'll be fun.'

Fun? Those walls had just gone back up in her eyes. That strange restraint pulled back into place around her. He didn't understand it, but he wasn't going to let her file those pictures away in a place where she could forget about them. He'd use Rupert's office later to print hard copies off as well. She might ignore her email, but she'd find the physical copies much harder to ignore.

'What's on the agenda for the rest of the day?'

She sent him a cat-that-got-the-cream grin. 'Nothing. Absolutely nothing.'

Excellent. 'Books on the beach?'

'You're getting the hang of this, Sullivan.' She rose and collected what was left of the food, and started back towards the house. 'Careful,' she shot over her shoulder, 'you might just find yourself enjoying it.'

He was enjoying it. He just wasn't sure what that meant.

He shook himself. It didn't mean anything, other than relief at being out of hospital and not being confined to quarters. He'd be an ingrate—not to mention made of marble—not to enjoy all this glorious Greek sun and scenery.

And whatever else he was, he wasn't made of marble. With Audra proving so intriguing, this enforced slower pace suited him fine for the moment. Once he got to the bottom of her strange restraint his restlessness would return. And then he'd be eager to embark on his next adventure—in need of a shot of pure adrenaline.

His hunger for adventure would return and consume him,

and all strange conversations about children would be forgotten. He rose; his hands clenched. This was about Audra, not him.

Audra stared at the ticket Finn had handed her and then at the large barn-like structure in front of them. She stared down at the paper in her hand again. 'You...you enrolled us in an art class?'

If Finn had been waiting for her to jump up and down in excitement and delight, he'd have been disappointed.

Which meant... Yeah, he was disappointed.

How had he got this wrong? 'When you saw the flyer in the bookshop window you looked...'

'I looked what?'

Her eyes turned wary with that same damn restraint that was there when she talked about her shop. Frustration rattled through him. Why did she do that?

'Looked what?' she demanded.

'Interested,' he shot back.

Wistful, full of yearning...hungry.

'I can't draw.'

'Which is why it says *"Beginners"*—' he pointed '—right here.'

She blew out a breath.

'What's more I think you were interested, but for some reason it intimidated you, so you chickened out.'

Her chin shot up, but her cheeks had reddened. 'I just didn't think it'd be your cup of tea.'

'You didn't think lying on a beach reading a book would float my boat either, but that didn't stop you. And I've submitted with grace. I haven't made a single complaint about your agendas. Unlike you with mine.'

'Oh!' She took a step back. 'You make me sound mean-spirited.'

She *wasn't* mean-spirited. But she *was* the most frustrating woman on earth!

'I'm sorry, Finn. Truly.' She seemed to gird her loins. 'You've chosen this specifically with me in mind. And I'm touched. Especially as I know you'd rather be off paragliding or aqua boarding or something.'

He ran a finger around the collar of his T-shirt. That wasn't one hundred per cent true. It wasn't even ten per cent true. Not that he had any intention of saying so. 'But?' he countered, refusing to let her off the hook. 'You don't want to do it?'

'It's not that.'

He folded his arms. 'Then what is it?'

'Forget it. You just took me by surprise, is all.' She snapped away from him. 'Let's just go in and enjoy the class and—'

He reached out and curled his hand around hers and her words stuttered to a halt. 'Audra?' He raised an eyebrow and waited.

Her chin shot up again. 'You won't understand.'

'Try me.'

A storm raged in her eyes. He watched it in fascination. 'Do you ever have rebellious impulses, Finn?'

He raised both eyebrows. 'My entire life is one big rebellion, surely?'

'Nonsense! You're living your life exactly as you think your parents would want you to.'

She snatched her hand back and he felt suddenly cast adrift. 'You've not rebelled any more than I have.'

That wasn't true, but... He glanced at the studio behind her. 'Art class is a rebellion?'

'In a way.'

'How?'

She folded her arms and stared up at the sky. He had a feeling she was counting to ten. 'Look, I can see the sense in taking a break, in having a holiday. Lying on a beach and soaking up some Vitamin D, getting some gentle exercise via a little swimming and walking, reading a book—I see the sense in those things. They lead to a rested body and mind.'

'How is an art class different from any of those things?'

'It just is! It feels…self-indulgent. It's doing something for the sake of doing it, rather than because it's good for you or…or…'

'What about fun?'

She stared at him. 'What's *fun* got to do with it?'

He couldn't believe what he was hearing. 'Evidently nothing.' Was she really that afraid of letting her hair down?

'When I start doing one thing just for the sake of it—*for fun*,' she spat, 'I'll start doing others.'

He lifted his arms and let them drop. 'And the problem with that would be…?'

Her eyes widened as if he were talking crazy talk and a hard, heavy ball dropped into the pit of his stomach. It was all he could do not to bare his teeth and growl.

'I knew you wouldn't understand.'

'I'll tell you what I understand. That you're the most uptight, repressed person I have *ever* met.'

'Repressed?' Her mouth opened and closed. 'I— What are you doing?'

He'd seized her hand again and was towing her towards a copse of Aleppo pine and carob trees. 'What's that?' He flung an arm out at the vista spread below them.

She glared. 'The Aegean. It's beautiful.'

'And that?' He pointed upwards.

She followed his gaze. Frowned and shrugged, evidently not following where he was going with this. 'The…sky?'

'The sun,' he snapped out. 'And it's shining in full force in case you hadn't noticed. And where are we?'

She swallowed. 'On a Greek island.'

He crowded her in against a tree, his arms going either side of her to block her in. 'If there was ever a time to let your hair down and rebel against your prim and proper strictures, Audra, now's the time to do it.'

She stared up at him with wide eyes, and he relished the moment—her stupefaction…her bewilderment…her undeniable hunger when her gaze lowered to his lips. This moment had seemed inevitable from when she'd appeared on the stairs a week ago to peer at him with those icy blue eyes, surveyed him in handcuffs, and told him it served him right.

His heart thudded against his ribs, he relished the adrenaline that surged through his body, before he swooped down to capture her lips in a kiss designed to shake up her safe little world. And he poured all his wildness and adventurous temptation into it in a devil-may-care invitation to dance.

CHAPTER EIGHT

THE ASSAULT ON Audra's senses the moment Finn's lips touched hers was devastating. She hadn't realised she could feel a kiss in so many ways, that its impact would spread through her in ever-widening circles that went deeper and deeper.

Finn's warmth beat at her like the warmth of the sun after a dip in the sea. It melted things that had been frozen for a very long time.

His scent mingled with the warm tang of the trees and sun-kissed grasses, and with just the tiniest hint of salt on the air it was exactly what a holiday should smell like. It dared her to play, it tempted her to reckless fun…and…and to a youthful joy she'd never allowed herself to feel before.

And she was powerless to resist. She had no defences against a kiss like this. It didn't feel as if defences were necessary. A kiss like this…it should be embraced and relished…welcomed.

Finn had been angry with her, but he didn't kiss angry. He kissed her as though he couldn't help it—as though he'd been fighting a losing battle and had finally flung himself whole-heartedly into surrender. It was *intoxicating*.

Totally heady and wholly seductive.

She lifted her hands, but didn't know what to do with them

so rested them on his shoulders, but they moved, restless, to the heated skin of his neck, and the skin-on-skin contact sent electricity coursing through both of them. He shuddered, she gasped…tongues tangled.

And then his arms were around her, hauling her against his body, her arms were around his neck as she plastered herself to him, and she stopped thinking as desire and the moment consumed her.

It was the raucous cry of a rose-ringed parakeet that penetrated her senses—and the need for air that had them easing apart. She stared into his face and wondered if her lips looked as well kissed as his, and if her eyes were just as dazed.

And then he swore, and a sick feeling crawled through the pit of her stomach. He let her go so fast she had to brace herself against the trunk of the tree behind her. She ached in places both familiar and unfamiliar and…and despite the myriad emotions chasing across his face—and none of them were positive—she wished with all her might that they were somewhere private, and that she were back in his arms so those aches could be assuaged.

And to hell with the consequences.

'I shouldn't have done that,' he bit out. 'I'm sorry.'

'I don't want an apology.'

The words left her without forethought, and with a brutal honesty that made her cringe. But they both knew what she *did* want couldn't happen. Every instinct she had told her he was hanging by a thread. His chest rose and fell as if he'd been running. The pulse at the base of his throat pounded like a mad thing. He wanted her with the same savage fury that she wanted him. And everything inside her urged her to snap his thread of control, and the consequences be damned.

It was *crazy*! Her hands clenched. She couldn't go on making romantic mistakes like this. Oh, he was nothing like Thomas. He'd never lie to her or betray her, but…but if she had an affair with Finn, it'd hurt her family. They'd see her as just another in a long line of Finn's *women*. It wasn't fair, but it was the reality all the same. She wouldn't hurt her family for the world; especially after all they'd been through with Thomas. She couldn't let them down so badly.

If she and Finn started something, when it ended—and that was the inevitable trajectory to all of Finn's relationships—he'd have lost her family's good opinion. They'd shun him. She knew how much that'd hurt him, and she'd do anything to prevent that from happening too.

And yet if he kissed her again she'd be lost.

'I'm not the person I thought I was,' she blurted out.

He frowned. 'What do you mean?'

Anger came to her rescue then. 'You wanted me to lose control. You succeeded in making that happen.' She moved in close until the heat from their bodies mingled again. 'And now you want me to just what…? Put it all back under wraps? To forget about it? What kind of game are you playing, Finn?'

The pulse in his jaw jumped and jerked. 'I just wanted you to loosen up a bit. Live in the moment instead of overthinking and over-analysing everything and…'

She slammed her hands to her hips. 'And?' She wasn't sure what she wanted from him—what she wanted him to admit—but it was more than this. That kiss had changed *everything*. But she wasn't even sure what that meant. Or what to do about it.

'And I'm an idiot! It was a stupid thing to do.' His eyes snapped fire as if *he* were angry with *her*. 'I do flings, Audra. Nothing more.' Panic lit his face. 'But I don't do them with Rupert's little sister.'

The car keys sailed through the air. She caught them automatically.

'I'll see you back at the villa.'

She watched as he stormed down the hill. He was running scared. From her? From fear of destroying his friendship with Rupert? Or was it something else…like thoughts of babies and marriage?

Was that what he thought she wanted from him?

Her stomach did a crazy twirl and she had to sit on a nearby rock to catch her breath. She'd be crazy to pin those kinds of hopes on him. And while she might be crazy with lust, she hadn't lost her mind completely.

She touched her fingers to her lips. *Oh, my, but the man could kiss.*

Audra glanced up from her spot on the sofa when Finn finally came in. She'd had dinner a couple of hours ago. She'd started to wonder if Finn meant to stay out all night.

And then she hadn't wanted to follow that thought any further, hadn't wanted to know where he might be and with whom...and what they might be doing.

He halted when he saw her. The light from the doorway framed him in exquisite detail—outlining the broad width of his shoulders and the lean strength of his thighs. Every lusty, heady impulse that had fired through her body when they'd kissed earlier fired back to life now, making her itch and yearn.

'I want to tell you something.'

He moved into the room, his face set and the lines bracketing his mouth deep. She searched him for signs of exhaustion, over-exertion, a limp, as he moved towards an armchair, but his body, while held tight, seemed hale and whole. Whatever else he'd done—or hadn't done—today, he clearly hadn't aggravated his recent injuries.

She let out a breath she hadn't even known she'd been holding. 'Okay.' She closed her book and set her feet to the floor. Here it came—the 'it's not you it's me' speech, the 'I care about you, but...' justifications. She tried to stop her lips from twisting. She'd toyed with a lot of scenarios since their kiss...and this was one of them. She had no enthusiasm for it. Perhaps it served her right for losing her head so completely earlier. A penance. She bit back a sigh. 'What do you want to tell me?'

'I want to explain why it's so important to me that I don't break Rupert's trust.'

That was easy. 'He's your best friend.' He cared more for Rupert than he did for her. It made perfect sense, so she couldn't explain why the knowledge chafed at her.

'I want you to understand how much I actually owe him.'

'How you *owe* him?' Would it be rude to get up, wish him goodnight and go to bed?'

Of course it'd be rude.

Not as rude as sashaying over to where he sat, planting herself in his lap, and kissing him.

She tried to close her mind to the pictures that exploded behind her eyelids. How many times did she have to tell herself that he was off limits?

'I haven't told another living soul about this and I suspect Rupert hasn't either.'

Her eyes sprang open. 'Okay. I'm listening.'

His eyes throbbed, but he stared at the wall behind her rather than at her directly. It made her chest clench. 'Finn?'

His nostrils flared. 'I went off the rails for a while when we were at school. I don't know if you know that or not.'

She shook her head.

'I was seventeen—full of hormones and angry at the world. I took to drinking and smoking and…and partying hard.'

With girls? She said nothing.

'I was caught breaking curfew twice…and one of those times I was drunk.'

She winced. 'That wouldn't have gone down well. Your boarding school was pretty strict.'

'With an excellent reputation to uphold. I was told in no uncertain terms that one more strike and I was out.'

She waited. 'So…? Rupert helped you clean up your act?'

'Audra, Audra, Audra.' His lips twisted into a mockery of a smile. 'You should know better than that.'

Her stomach started to churn, though she wasn't sure why. 'You kept pushing against the boundaries and testing the limits.'

He nodded.

'And were you caught?'

'Contraband was found in my possession.'

'What kind of contraband?'

'The type that should've had me automatically expelled.'

She opened her mouth and then closed it. It might be better not to know. 'But you weren't expelled.' Or had he been and somehow it'd all been kept a secret?

'No.'

The word dropped from him, heavy and dull, and all of the fine hairs on her arms lifted. 'How...?'

'Remember the Fallonfield Prize?'

She snorted. 'How could I not? Rupert was supposed to have been the third generation of Russel men to win that prize. I swear to God it was the gravest disappointment of both my father's and grandfather's lives when he didn't.'

Nobody had been able to understand it, because Rupert had been top of his class, and that, combined with his extra-curricular community service activities and demonstrated leadership skills...

Her throat suddenly felt dry. 'He was on track to win it.'

Finn nodded.

Audra couldn't look away. The Fallonfield Prize was a prestigious award that opened doors. It practically guaranteed the winner a place at their university of choice, and it included a year-long mentorship with a business leader and feted humanitarian. As a result of winning the prize, her grandfather had gone to Chile for a year. Her father had gone to South Africa, which was where he'd met Audra's mother, who'd been doing aid work there. The Russel family's legacy of social justice and responsibility continued to this very day. Rupert had planned to go to Nicaragua.

'What happened?' she whispered, even though she could see the answer clear and plain for herself.

'Rupert took the blame. He said the stuff belonged to him, and that he'd stowed it among my things for safekeeping—so his parents wouldn't see it when they'd come for a recent visit.'

She moistened her lips. 'He had to know it'd cost him the scholarship.'

Finn nodded. He'd turned pale in the telling of the story and her heart burned for him. He'd lost his father when he was far too young, and then he'd watched his mother die. Who could blame him for being angry?

But… 'I'm amazed you—' She snapped her mouth closed. *Shut up!*

His lips twisted. 'You're amazed I let him take the rap?'

She swallowed and didn't say a word.

'I wasn't going to. When I'd found out what he'd done I started for the head's office to set him straight.'

'What happened?'

'Your brother punched me.'

'Rupert…' Her jaw dropped. Rupert had punched Finn?

'We had a set-to like I've never had before or since.'

She wanted to close her eyes.

'We were both bloody and bruised by the end of it, and when I was finally in a state to listen he grabbed me by the throat and told me I couldn't disappoint my uncle or your parents by getting myself kicked out of school—that I owed it to everyone and that I'd be a hundred different kinds of a weasel if I let you all down. He told me I wasn't leaving him there to cope with the fallout on his own. He told me I wasn't abandoning him to a life of stolid respectability. And…'

'And?' she whispered.

'And I started to cry like a goddamn baby.'

Her heart thumped and her chest ached.

'I'd felt so alone until that moment, and Rupert hugged me and called me his brother.'

Audra tried to check the tears that burned her eyes.

'He gave me a second chance. And make no mistake, if he hadn't won me that second chance I'd probably be dead now.'

Even through the haze of her tears, the ferocity of his gaze pierced her.

'He made me feel a part of something—a family, a community—where what I did mattered. And that made me turn my life around, made me realise that what I did had an impact on the people around me, that it mattered to somebody...that what I did with my life mattered.'

'Of course it matters.' He just hadn't been able to see that then.

'So I let him take the rap for me, knowing what it would cost him.'

She nodded, swiped her fingers beneath her eyes. 'I'm glad he did what he did. I'm glad you let him do it.' She understood now how much he must feel he owed Rupert.

'So when Rupert asks me to...to take care with his little sister, I listen.'

She stilled. Her heart gave a sick thump.

'I promised him that I wouldn't mess with you and your emotions. And I mean to keep my word.'

She stiffened. Nobody—not Rupert, not Finn—had any right to make such decisions on her behalf.

His eyes flashed. 'You owe me a "truth or dare" question.'

She blinked, taken off guard by the snap and crackle of his voice, by the way his lips had thinned. 'Fine. Ask your question.'

'Knowing what you know now, would you choose to destroy my friendship with Rupert for a quick roll in the hay, Squirt?'

He knew he was being deliberately crude and deliberately brutal, but he had to create some serious distance between him and Audra before he did something he'd regret for the rest of his life.

She rose, as regal as a queen, her face cold and her eyes chips of ice. 'I'd never do anything to hurt your friendship with Rupert. Whether I'd heard that story or not.'

And yet they'd both been tempted to earlier.

'So, Finn, you don't need to worry your pretty little head over that any longer.'

He had to grind his teeth together at her deliberately patronising tone.

She spun away. 'I'm going to bed.'

She turned in the doorway. 'Also, the name is Audra—not Squirt. Strike Two.'

With that she swept from the room. Finn fell back into his chair and dragged both hands through his hair. He should never have kissed her. He hadn't known that a kiss could rock the very foundations of his world in the way his kiss with Audra had. Talk about pride coming before a fall. The gods punished hubris, didn't they? He'd really thought he could kiss her and remain unmarked...unmoved...untouched.

The idea seemed laughable now.

He'd wanted to fling her out of herself and force her to act on impulse. He hadn't known he'd lose control. He hadn't known that kiss would fling him out of himself...and then return him as a virtual stranger.

If it'd been any other woman, he'd have not been able to resist following that kiss through to its natural conclusion, the consequences be damned. His mouth dried. Whatever else they were, he knew those consequences would've been significant. Maybe he and Audra had dodged a bullet.

Or maybe they'd—

Maybe nothing! He didn't do long term. He didn't do family and babies. He did fun and adventure and he kept things uncomplicated and simple. Because that was the foundation his life had been built on. It was innate, inborn...intrinsic to who he was. There were some things in this world you couldn't change. Leopards couldn't change their spots and Finn Sullivan couldn't change his freewheeling ways.

Finn heard Audra moving about in the kitchen the next morning, but he couldn't look up from the final pages of his book.

He read the final page...closed the cover.

Damn!

He stormed out into the kitchen and slammed the book to the counter. The split second after he'd done it, he winced and waited for her to jump out of her skin—waited for his stomach to curdle with self-loathing. He was such an idiot. He should've taken more care, but she simply looked at him, one eyebrow almost raised.

He nodded. 'Keep practising, it's almost there.'

She ignored that to glance at the book. 'Finished?'

He pointed at her and then slammed his finger to the book. 'That was a dirty, rotten, low-down trick. It's not finished!'

'My understanding is that particular story arc concludes.'

'Yeah, but I don't know if he gets his kingdom back. I don't know if she saves the world and defeats the bad guy. And...and I don't know if they end up together!'

Both her eyebrows rose.

'You...you tricked me!'

She leaned across and pointed. 'It says it's a trilogy here... And it says that it's Book One here. I wasn't keeping anything from you.'

Hot damn. So it did. He just... He hadn't paid any attention to the stuff on the cover. He rocked back on his heels, hands on hips. 'Didn't see that,' he murmured. 'And I really want to know how it ends.'

'And you feel cheated because you have to read another two books to find that out?'

Actually, the idea should appal him. But... 'I, uh...just guess I'm impatient to know how it all works out.'

'That's easily fixed. The bookshop in the village has the other two books in stock.'

He shoved his hands into his back pockets. 'Sorry, I shouldn't have gone off like that. Just didn't know what I was signing up for when I started the book.'

'God, Finn!' She took a plate of sliced fruit to the table and sat. 'That's taking commitment phobia to a whole new level.'

He indicated her plate. 'I'm supposed to do breakfast. That was part of the deal.'

'Part of the deal was calling me Audra too.'

She lifted a piece of melon to her lips. He tried to keep his face smooth, tried to keep his pulse under control as her mouth closed about the succulent fruit. 'So...what's on the agenda today?'

She ate another slice of melon before meeting his gaze. 'I want a Finn-free day.'

He fought the automatic urge to protest. An urge he knew was crazy because a day spent not in each other's company would probably be a wise move. 'Okay.'

'I bags the beach this morning.'

It took all his strength to stop from pointing out it was a long beach with room enough for both of them.

'Why don't you take the car and go buy your books, and then go do something you'd consider fun?'

Lying on a beach, swimming and reading a book, those things were fun. He rolled his shoulders. So were jetskiing and waterskiing and stuff. 'Okay.' He thrust out his jaw. 'Sounds great.'

She rose and rinsed her plate. 'And you'll have the house to yourself this evening.'

Her words jolted him up to his full height. 'Why?'

'Because I'm going into the village for a meal, and maybe some dancing. *Not* that it's any of your business.'

She wanted to go dancing? 'I'll take you out if that's what you want.'

'No, thank you, Finn.'

'But—'

Her eyes sparked. 'I don't want to go out to dinner or dancing with you.'

'Why not?' The words shot out of him and he immediately wished them back.

She folded her arms and peered down her nose at him. 'Do you really want me to answer that?'

He raised his hands and shook his head, but the anger in her eyes had his mind racing. 'You're annoyed with me. Because I kissed you?' Or because he wouldn't kiss her again?

Stop thinking about kissing her.

'Oh, I'm livid with you.'

He swallowed.

'And with Rupert.'

He stiffened. 'What's Rupert done? He's not even here.'

'And with myself.' She folded her arms, her expression more bewildered than angry now. 'You really don't see it, do you?'

See what?

'Between you, you and Rupert decided what was in my best interests. And—' the furrow in her brow deepened '—I let you. I went along with it instead of pointing out how patronising and controlling it was.' She lifted her chin. 'I'm a grown-up who has the right to make her own choices and decisions, be they wise or unwise. I'm not a child. I don't need looking after, and I do *not* have to consult with either of you if I want to kiss someone or…or start a relationship. And that's why I'm going into the village this evening on my own without an escort—to remind myself that I'm an adult.'

She swept up her beach bag and her sunhat and stalked out of the door.

I do not *have to consult…if I want to kiss someone…*

Was she planning on kissing someone tonight? But…but she couldn't.

Why not?

Scowling, he slammed the frying pan on a hot plate, turned it up to high before throwing in a couple of rashers of bacon. He cracked in two eggs as well. Oops—fine, he'd have scrambled eggs. He ground his teeth together. He *loved* scrambled eggs.

He gathered up the litter to throw into the bin, pushed open the lid...and then stilled. Setting the litter down on the counter again, he pulled out three A4 sheets of paper from the bottom of the bin, wiped off the fruit skins and let forth a very rude word. These were his designs for Audra's shop. He glared out of the glass sliding doors, but Audra had disappeared from view. 'That's not going to work, Princess.'

He pulled the frying pan from the heat, went to his room to grab his laptop and then strode into Rupert's office, heading straight for the printer.

He placed one set of printouts on the coffee table. The next set he placed on the tiny hall table outside her bedroom door. The third set he put in a kitchen drawer. The next time she reached for the plastic wrap, they'd greet her. The rest he kept in a pile in his bedroom to replace any of the ones she threw away.

'You're not taking the car?'

Audra didn't deign to answer him.

He glanced at his watch. 'Six thirty is a bit early for dinner, isn't it?'

She still didn't answer him. She simply peered at her reflection in the foyer mirror, and slicked on another coat of ruby-red lipstick. Utter perfection. She wore a sundress that made his mouth water too—the bodice hugged her curves, showing off a delectable expanse of golden skin at her shoulders and throat while the skirt fell in a floaty swirl of aqua and scarlet to swish about her calves. His heart pounded.

Don't think about messing up that lipstick.

He shoved his hands into his pockets. 'Why aren't you taking the car?'

She finally turned. 'Because I plan to have a couple of drinks. And I don't drink and drive.'

'But how will you get home?'

She raised an eyebrow.

He raised one back at her. 'You've almost got that down pat.'

She waved a hand in front of her face. 'Stop it, Finn.'

'What? It was a compliment and—'

'Stop it with the twenty questions. I know what time I want to eat. I know how to get home at the end of an evening out. Or—' she smiled, but it didn't reach eyes that flashed and sparked '—how to get home the morning after an evening out if that's the way the evening rocks.'

She...she might not be coming home? But—

And then she was gone in a swirl of perfume and red and aqua skirt as the village taxi pulled up in the driveway and tooted its horn.

Finn spent the evening pacing. Audra might be a grown woman, but she'd had fire in her eyes as she'd left. He knew she was angry with him and Rupert, but what if that anger led her to do something stupid...something she'd later regret? What the hell would he tell Rupert if something happened to her?

He lasted until nine p.m. Jumping in the car, it felt like a relief to finally be doing something, to be setting off after her. Not that he knew what he was going to do once he did find her.

She was in the first place he looked—Petra's Taverna. The music pouring from its open windows and doors was lively and cheerful. Tables spilled onto the courtyard outside and down to a tiny beach. Finn chose a table on the edge of the scene in the shadows of a cypress with an excellent view, via two enormous windows, inside the taverna.

Audra drew his eyes like a magnet. She sat on a stool framed in one of the windows and threw her head back at something her companion said, though Finn's view of her companion was blocked. She nodded and her companion came into view—a handsome young local—as they moved to the dance floor.

Beneath the table, Finn's hands clenched. When a waiter came he ordered a lemon squash. Someone had to keep their wits about them this evening! As the night wore on, Finn's scowl only grew and it deterred anyone who might've been tempted from coming across and trying to engage him in conversation.

And the more morose he grew, the merrier the tabloid inside became. As if those two things were related.

Audra was the life of the party. He lost track of the number of dance partners she had. She laughed and talked with just about every person in the taverna. She alternated glasses of white wine with big glasses of soda water. She snacked on olives and crisps and even played a hand of cards. She charmed everyone. And everything charmed her. He frowned. He'd not realised before how popular she was here in Kyanós. His frown deepened. It struck him that she was more alive here than he could ever remember seeing her.

And at a little after midnight, and after many pecks on cheeks were exchanged, she caught the taxi—presumably back to the villa—on her own.

He sat there feeling like an idiot. She'd had an evening out—had let her hair down and had some fun. She hadn't drunk too much. She hadn't flirted outrageously and hadn't needed to fight off inappropriate advances. She hadn't done anything foolish or reckless or ill-considered. She hadn't needed him to come to her rescue.

I'm a grown-up who has the right to make her own choices.

And what was he? Not just a fool, but some kind of creep—a sneak spying on a woman because he'd been feeling left out and unnecessary. And as far as Audra was concerned, he *was* unnecessary. *Completely* unnecessary. She didn't need him.

He could try to dress it up any way he liked—that he'd been

worried about her, that he wanted to make sure she stayed safe—but what he'd done was spy on her and invade her privacy.

Why the hell had he done that? What right did he think he had?

Earlier she'd accused him and Rupert of being patronising and controlling, and she was right.

She deserved better from him. Much better.

CHAPTER NINE

WHEN AUDRA REACHED in the fridge for the milk for her morning coffee and found yet another set of printouts—in a plastic sleeve, no less, that would presumably protect them from moisture and condensation—it was all she could do not to scream.

She and Finn had spent the last three days avoiding each other. She'd tried telling herself that suited her just fine, but...

It *should* suit her just fine. She had the beach to herself in the mornings, while Finn took the car and presumably headed into the village. And then he had the beach in the afternoons while she commandeered the car. In terms of avoiding each other, it worked *perfectly*. It was just...

She blew out a breath. She wished avoidance tactics weren't necessary. She wished they could go back to laughing and having fun and teasing each other as they had before that stupid kiss.

And before she'd got all indignant about Rupert's overprotectiveness, and galled that Finn had unquestioningly fallen into line with it...and angry with herself for not having challenged it earlier. Where once her brother's protectiveness had made her feel cared for, now it left her feeling as if she was a family liability who needed safeguarding against her own foolishness.

Because of Thomas?

Or because if she could no longer hold tight to the label of being responsible and stable then…then what could she hold onto?

Stop it! Of course she was still responsible and stable. Thomas had been a mistake, and everyone was entitled to one mistake, right? Just as long as she didn't compound that by doing something stupid with Finn; just as long as she maintained a sense of responsibility and calm and balance, and remembered who *he* was and remembered who *she* was.

Sloshing milk into her coffee, she went to throw the printouts in the bin when her gaze snagged on some subtle changes to the pictures. Curiosity warred with self-denial. Curiosity won. Grabbing a croissant—Finn always made sure there was a fresh supply—she slipped outside to the picnic table to pore over the designs of this achingly and heart-wrenchingly beautiful shop.

Letting her hair down and doing things she wanted to do just for the sake of it—for fun—hadn't helped the burning in her soul whenever she was confronted with these pictures. They were snapshots of a life she could never have. And with each fresh reminder—and for some reason Finn seemed hell-bent on reminding her—that burn scorched itself into her deeper and deeper.

She bit into the croissant, she sipped coffee, but she tasted nothing.

Ever since Finn had kissed her she'd…*wanted*.

She'd *wanted* to kiss him again. She wanted *more*. She'd not known that a kiss could fill you with such a physical need. That it could make you crave so hard. She was twenty-seven years old. She'd thought she knew about attraction. She'd had good sex before. But that kiss had blown her preconceptions out of the stratosphere. And it had left her floundering. Because there was no way on God's green earth that she and Finn could go *there*. She didn't doubt that in the short term it'd be incredible, but ultimately it'd be destructive. She wasn't going to be responsible for that kind of pain—for wounding friendships and devastating family ties and connections.

She couldn't do that to Rupert.

She wouldn't do that to Finn.

But the kiss had left her wanting *more* from life too. And she didn't know how to make that restlessness and sense of dissatisfaction go away.

So she'd tried a different strategy in the hope it would help. Instead of reining in all her emotions and desires, she'd let a few of them loose. Finn was right: if there was ever a time to rebel it was now when she was on holiday. She'd hoped a mini-rebellion would help her deal with her attraction for Finn. She'd hoped it would help her deal with the dreary thought of returning home to her job.

She'd gone dancing. It'd been fun.

She'd taken an art class and had learned about form and perspective. Her drawing had been terrible, but moving a pencil across paper had soothed her. The focus of next week's class was going to be composition. Her shoulders sagged. Except she wouldn't be here next week.

She'd even gone jetskiing again. It'd felt great to be zipping across the water. But no sooner had she returned the jetski than her restlessness had returned.

She pressed her hands to her face and then pulled them back through her hair. She'd hoped those things would help ease the ache in her soul, but they hadn't. They'd only fed it. It had been a mistake to come here.

And she wished to God Finn had never kissed her!

'Morning, Audra.'

As if her thoughts had conjured him, Finn appeared. His wide grin and the loose easy way he settled on the seat opposite with a bowl of cereal balanced in one hand inflamed her, though she couldn't have said why. She flicked the offending printouts towards him. 'Why are you leaving these all over the house?'

He ate a spoonful of cereal before gesturing to them. 'Do you like the changes I've made?'

'I—'

'Market research suggests that locating the point of sale over here provides for "a more comfortable retail experience"—' he made quotation marks in the air with one hand '—for the customer.'

She had to physically refrain from reaching across and shaking him. Drawing in a breath, she tried to channel responsible, calm balance. 'Why does any of this matter?'

'Because it needs to be perfect.'

Her chest clenched. Her eyes burned. Balance fled. 'Why?'

He shrugged and ate more cereal. 'Because that's what I do. I create designs as near perfect as possible.'

Didn't he know what these pictures and the constant reminders were doing to her?

He pulled the sheets from their plastic sleeve. 'What do you think about this shelving arrangement? It's neither better nor more functional than the ones you've already chosen, but apparently this design is all the range in Scandinavia at the moment, so I thought I'd throw it into the mix just to see what you thought?'

She couldn't help it; she had to look. The sleek lines were lovely, but these didn't fit in with the overall feel she was trying to achieve at all.

You're not trying to achieve an overall feel, remember? Pipe dream!

With a growl she slapped the picture facedown.

'No?' He raised one eyebrow—perfectly—which set her teeth even further on edge. 'Fair enough.'

'Enough already,' she countered through gritted teeth. 'Stop plastering these designs all over the house. I've had enough. I can see you do good work—excellent work. I'm sorry I misjudged you, but I believe I've already apologised. I'll apologise again if you need me to. But stop with the pictures. *Please.*'

He abandoned his breakfast to lean back and stare at her. She couldn't help wondering what he saw—a repressed woman he'd like to muss up?

It was what she wanted to believe. If it were true it'd provide her with a form of protection. But it wasn't true. She knew that kiss had shaken him as much as it'd shaken her. It was why he'd avoided her for these last few days as assiduously as she had him.

'I'll stop with the pictures of the shop if you answer one question for me.'

'Oh, here we go again.' She glared. She didn't raise an eyebrow. She needed more practice before she tried that again. She folded her arms instead. 'Ask your question.'

He leaned towards her. The perfect shape of his mouth had a sigh rising up through her. 'Why are you working as an operations manager instead of opening up your dream shop here on this island and living a life that makes you happy?'

She flinched. His words were like an axe to her soul. How did he know? When Rupert, Cora and Justin had no idea? When she'd been so careful that none of them should know?

He held up the printouts and shook them at her. 'Your face when you described this shop, Audra... You came alive. It was...'

Her heart thumped so hard she could barely breathe.

'Magnificent,' he finally decided. 'And catching.'

She blinked. 'Catching...how?'

'Contagious! Your enthusiasm was contagious. I've not felt that enthusiastic about anything—'

He broke off with a frown. '—for a long time,' he finished. He stared at each of the three pictures. 'I want you to have this shop. I want you to have this life. I don't understand why you're punishing yourself.'

Her head reared back. 'I'm not punishing myself.'

'I'm sorry, Princess, but that's not what it looks like from where I'm sitting.'

'I do worthy work!' She shot to her feet, unable to sit for the agitation roiling through her. 'The work the Russel Corporation does is important.' She strode across to the bluff to stare out at the turquoise water spread below.

'I'm not disputing that.' His voice came from just behind her. 'But…so what?'

She spun to face him. 'How can you say that? Look at the amazing things Rupert, Cora and Justin are doing.'

His jaw dropped. 'This is about sibling rivalry? Come on, Audra, you're twenty-seven years old. I know you always wanted to keep up with the others when you were younger, but—' He scanned her face, rocked back on his heels. 'It's not about sibling rivalry.'

'No,' she said. It was about sibling loyalty. *Family* loyalty.

He remained silent, just…waiting.

She pressed her fingers to her temples for a moment before letting her arms drop back to her sides. 'When our mother died it felt like the end of the world.'

He reached out and closed his hand around hers and she suddenly felt less alone, less…diminished. She gripped his hand and stared doggedly out to sea. She couldn't look at him. If she looked at him she might cry. 'She was the lynchpin that kept all our worlds turning. The crazy thing was I never realised that until she was gone.' She hauled in a breath. 'And the work she did at the Russel Corporation was crucial.'

Karen Russel had been the administrator of the Russel Corporation's charity arm, and Audra's father had valued her in that role without reservation. Humanitarian endeavours formed a key component of the corporation's mission statement and it wasn't one he was comfortable trusting to anyone outside the family.

'But her influence was so much wider than that.' She blinked against the sting in her eyes. 'She worked out a strategy for Rupert to evolve into the role of CEO; she researched laboratories that would attract the most funding and would therefore provide Cora with the most promising opportunities. If she'd lived long enough she'd have found excellent funding for Justin's efforts in South-East Asia.' Justin was implementing a dental-health programme to the impoverished populations in Cambodia. He had ambitions to take his programme to all communities in need throughout South-East Asia.

She felt him turn towards her. 'Instead you found those funding opportunities for him. You should be proud of yourself.'

No sooner were the words out of his mouth than he stilled. She couldn't look at him. He swore softly. 'Audra—'

'When our mother died, I'd never seen the rest of my family so devastated.' She shook her hand free. 'I wanted to make things better for them. You should've seen my father's relief when I said I'd take over my mother's role in the corporation after I'd finished university. Justin floundered towards the end of his last year of study. He had exams coming up but started panicking about the licences and paperwork he needed to file to work in Cambodia, and finding contacts there. The laboratory Cora worked for wanted sponsorship from business and expected her to approach the family corporation. And Rupert... well, he missed the others so having me around to boss helped.'

She'd stepped into the breach because Karen was no longer there to do it. And someone had to. It'd broken her heart to see her siblings hurting so badly.

Finn had turned grey. He braced his hands on his knees, and she couldn't explain why, but she had to swallow the lump that did everything it could to lodge in her throat. 'You've been what they've all needed you to be.'

'I'm not a martyr, Finn. I *love* my family. I'm proud I've been able to help.' Helping them had helped her to heal. It'd given her a focus, when her world had felt as if it were spinning out of control.

He straightened, his eyes dark. 'She wouldn't want this for you.'

'You don't know that.' She lifted her chin. 'I think she'd be proud of me.'

He chewed on his bottom lip, his brows lowering over his eyes. 'Have you noticed how each of you have coped with your mother's death in different ways?'

She blinked.

'Rupert became super-protective of you all.'

Rupert had always been protective, but... She nodded. He'd become excessively so since their mother's death.

'Cora threw herself into study. She wanted to top every class she took.'

Cora had found solace in her science textbooks.

'Justin started living more in the moment.'

She hadn't thought about it in those terms, but she supposed he had.

One corner of Finn's mouth lifted. 'Which means he leaves things to the last minute and relies on his little sister to help make them right.'

Her lips lifted too.

'While you, Princess...' He sobered. 'You've tried to fill the hole your mother has left behind.'

She shook her head. 'Only the practical day-to-day stuff.' Nobody could fill the emotional hole she'd left behind.

'Your siblings have a genuine passion for what they do, though. They're following their dreams.'

And in a small way she'd been able to facilitate that. She didn't regret that for a moment.

'You won't be letting your mother down if you follow your own dreams and open a shop here on Kyanós.'

'That's not what it feels like.' She watched a seabird circle and then dive into the water below. 'If I leave the Russel Corporation it'll feel as if I'm betraying them all.'

'You'll be the only who feels that way.'

The certainty in his tone had her swinging to him.

He lifted his hands to his head, before dropping them back to his sides. 'Audra, they're all doing work they love!'

'Good!' She stared at his fists and then into his face. He was getting really het-up about this. 'I want them to love what they do.'

'Then why don't you extend yourself that same courtesy?'

He bellowed the words, and her mouth opened and closed but no sound came out. He made it sound so easy. But it wasn't! She loved being there for her brothers and sister. She loved that she could help them.

'How would you feel if you discovered Rupert or Cora or Justin were doing their jobs just to keep you feeling comfortable and emotionally secure?'

Oh, that'd be awful! It'd—

She took a step away from him, swallowed. Her every muscle scrunched up tight. That scenario, it wasn't synonymous with hers.

Why not?

She pressed her hands to her cheeks, trying to cool them. Her siblings were each brilliant in their own way—fiercely intelligent, politically savvy and driven. She wasn't. Her dreams were so ordinary in comparison, so lacking in ambition. A part of her had always been afraid that her family would think she wasn't measuring up to her potential.

Her heart started to pound. Had she been using her role in the family corporation as an excuse to hide behind? Stretching her own wings required taking risks, and those risks frightened her.

'I hate to say this, Princess, but when you get right down to brass tacks you're just a glorified administrator, a pen-pusher, and anyone can do the job that you do.'

* * *

'Why don't you tell me what you really think, Finn?'

The stricken expression in Audra's eyes pierced straight through the centre of him. He didn't want to hurt her. But telling her what he really thought was wiser than doing what he really wanted to do, which was kiss her.

He had to remind himself again of all the reasons kissing her was a bad idea.

He pulled in a breath. He didn't want to hurt her. He wanted to see her happy. He wanted to see her happy the way she'd been happy when describing her shop…when she'd been learning to ride a jetski…and when she'd been dancing. Did she truly think those things were frivolous and self-indulgent?

He tapped a fist against his lips as he stared out at the glorious view spread in front of them. The morning sun tinged everything gold, not so much as a breeze ruffled the air and it made the water look otherworldly still, and soft, like silk and mercury.

He pulled his hand back to his side. *Right.* 'It's my day.'

From the corner of his eye he saw her turn towards him. 'Pardon?'

'To choose our activities. It's my day.'

She folded her arms and stuck out a hip. She was going to tell him to go to blazes—that she was spending the day *on her own*. She opened her mouth, but he rushed on before she could speak. 'There's something I want to show you.'

She snapped her mouth shut, but her gaze slid over him as if it couldn't help it, and the way she swallowed and spun seawards again, her lips parted as if to draw much-needed air into her lungs, had his skin drawing tight. She was right. It'd be much wiser to continue to avoid each other.

But…

But he might never get this opportunity again. He wanted to prove to her that she had a right to be happy, to urge her to take that chance.

'The yacht with the pink and blue sail is back.'

She pointed but he didn't bother looking. 'Please,' he said quietly.

She met his gaze, her eyes searching his, before she blew out a breath and shrugged. 'Okay. Fine.'

'Dress code is casual and comfortable. We're not hiking for miles or doing anything gruelling. I just… I've been exploring and I think I've found some things that will interest you.'

'Sunhat and sandals…?'

'Perfect. How soon can you be ready?'

One slim shoulder lifted. 'Half an hour.'

'Excellent.' He gathered up his breakfast things and headed back towards the house before he did something stupid like kiss her.

Their first port of call was Angelo's workshop. Angelo was a carpenter who lived on the far side of the village. He made and sold furniture from his renovated garage. Most of the pieces he made were too large for Audra's hypothetical shop—chest of drawers, tables and chairs, bedheads and bookcases—but there were some smaller items Finn knew she'd like, like the pretty trinket boxes and old-fashioned writing desks that were designed to sit on one's lap.

As he'd guessed, Audra was enchanted. She ran a finger along a pair of bookends. 'The workmanship is exquisite.'

Finn nodded. 'He says that each individual piece of wood that he works with tells him what it wants to be.'

'You've spoken to him?'

'Finn!' Angelo rushed into the garage. 'I thought that was your car out front. Come, you and Audra must have coffee with the family. Maria has just made *baklava*.'

'Angelo!' Audra gestured around the room. 'I didn't know you made such beautiful things.'

Finn stared at her. 'You know Angelo?'

'Of course! His brother Petros is Rupert's gardener. And Maria used to work in the bakery.'

They stayed an hour.

Next Finn took Audra to Anastasia's studio, which sat solitary on a windswept hill. He rolled his eyes. 'Now you're going to tell me you know Anastasia.'

She shook her head. 'I've not had that pleasure.'

Anastasia took Audra for a tour of her photography studio while Finn trailed along behind. If the expression on Audra's face was anything to go by, Anastasia's photographs transfixed her. They'd transfixed him too. It was all he could do to drag her back to the car when the tour was finished.

Then it was back into the village to visit Eleni's workshop, where she demonstrated how she made not only scented soap from products sourced locally, but a range of skincare and cosmetic products as well. Audra lifted a set of soaps in a tulle drawstring bag, the satin ribbon entwined with lavender and some other herbs Finn couldn't identify. 'These are packaged so prettily I can't resist.' She bought some candles too.

They visited a further two tradespeople—a leather worker who made wallets and purses, belts and ornately worked book jackets, and a jeweller. Audra came away with gifts for her entire family.

'Hungry?' he asked as he started the car. He'd walked this hill over the last three days, searching for distraction, but today, for the sake of efficiency, he'd driven.

'Starved.'

They headed back down the hill to the harbour, and ate a late lunch of *marida* and *spanakorizo* at a taverna that had become a favourite. They dined beneath a bougainvillea-covered pergola and watched as the water lapped onto the pebbled beach just a few metres away.

Audra broke the silence first. 'Anastasia's work should hang in galleries. It's amazing. Her photographs reveal a Greece so different from the tourist brochures.'

'She's seventy. She does everything the old way. She doesn't even have the internet.'

She nodded and sipped her wine, before setting her wine glass down with a click. 'I'd love for Isolde, one of my friends from school—she's an interior decorator and stager, furnishes houses and apartments so they look their absolute best for selling—to see some of Angelo's bigger pieces. She'd go into raptures over them.' She started to rise. 'We need to go back and take some photos so I can send her—'

'My *loukoumades* haven't come yet.' He waved her back to her seat. 'There's time. We can go back tomorrow.' He topped up her wine. 'What about Eleni's pretty smelly things? They'd look great in a shop.'

Audra shook her head and then nodded, as if holding a conversation with herself. 'I should put her in touch with Cora's old lab partner, Elise. Remember her? She moved into the cosmetic industry. Last I heard she was making a big push for eco-friendly products. I bet she'd love Eleni's recipes.'

She was still putting everyone else's needs before her own. The *loukoumades* came and a preoccupied Audra helped him eat them. While her attention was elsewhere, he couldn't help but feast his eyes on her. She'd put on a little weight over the last eleven days. She had colour in her cheeks and her eyes sparked with interest and vitality. An ache grew inside him until he could barely breathe.

He tried to shake it off. Under his breath he called himself every bad name he could think of. Did he really find the allure of the forbidden so hard to resist?

He clenched his jaw. He *would* resist. He'd cut off his right hand rather than let Rupert down. He'd cut off his entire arm rather than ever hurt Audra.

But when she came alive like this, he couldn't look away.

She slapped her hands lightly to the table. 'I wonder how the villagers would feel about an annual festival.'

'What kind of festival?'

'One that showcases the local arts and crafts scene, plus all the fresh produce available here—the cured meats, the cheeses, the olive oils and…and…'

'The *loukoumades*?'

'Definitely the *loukoumades*!'

She laughed. She hadn't laughed, not with him, since he'd kissed her…and the loss of that earlier intimacy had been an ache in his soul.

The thought that he might be able to recapture their earlier ease made his heart beat faster.

'What?' she said, touching her face, and he realised he was staring.

He forced himself backwards in his seat. 'You're amazing, you know that?'

Her eyes widened. 'Me?'

'Absolutely. Can't you see how well you'd fit in here, and what a difference you could make? You've connections, energy and vision…passion.'

She visibly swallowed at that last word, and he had to force his gaze from the line of her throat. He couldn't let it linger there or he'd be lost.

Her face clouded over. 'I can't just walk away from the Russel Corporation.'

'Why not?' He paused and then nodded. 'Okay, you can't leave *just like that.*' He snapped his fingers. 'You'd have to hang around long enough to train up your replacement…or recruit a replacement.'

He could see her overdeveloped sense of duty begin to overshadow her excitement at the possibilities life held for her. He refused to let it win. 'Can you imagine how much your mother would've enjoyed the festival you just described?'

Her eyes filled.

'I remember how much she used to enjoy the local market days on Corfu, back when the family used to holiday there…

when we were all children,' he said. Karen Russel had been driven and focussed, but she'd relished her downtime too.

'I know. I just...' Audra glanced skywards and blinked hard. 'I'd just want her to be proud of me.'

Something twisted in Finn's chest. Karen had died at a crucial stage in Audra's life—when Audra had been on the brink of adulthood. She'd been tentatively working her way towards a path that would give her life purpose and meaning, and searching for approval and support from the woman she'd looked up to. Her siblings had all had that encouragement and validation, but it'd been cruelly taken from Audra. No wonder she'd lost her way. 'Princess, I can't see how she could be anything else.'

Blue eyes, swimming with uncertainty and remembered grief, met his.

'Audra, you're kind and you work hard. You love your family and are there for them whenever they need you. She valued those things. And I think she'd thank you from the bottom of her heart for stepping into the breach when she was gone and doing all the things that needed doing.'

A single tear spilled onto her cheek, and he had to blink hard himself.

'The thing is,' he forced himself to continue, 'nobody needs you to do those things any more. And I'd lay everything on the bet that your mother would have loved the shop you described to me. Look at the way she lived her life—with passion and with zeal. She'd want you to do the same.'

Audra swiped her fingers beneath her eyes and pulled in a giant breath. 'Can...can we walk for a bit?'

They walked along the harbour and Audra hooked her arm through his. The accidental brushing of their bodies as they walked was a sweet torture that made him prickle and itch and want, but she'd done it without thinking or forethought—as if she needed to be somehow grounded while her mind galloped at a million miles an hour. So he left it there and didn't pull away, and fought against the growing need that pounded through him.

She eventually released him to sit on the low harbour wall, and he immediately wanted to drag her hand back into the crook of his arm and press his hand over it to keep it there.

'So,' she started. 'You're saying it wouldn't be selfish of me to move here and open my shop?'

'That's exactly what I'm saying. I know you can't see it, but you don't have a selfish bone in your body.'

Sceptical eyes lifted to meet his. 'You really don't think I'd be letting my family down if I did that?'

'Absolutely not. I think they'd be delighted for you.' He fell down beside her. 'But don't take my word for it. Ask them.'

She pondered his words and then frowned. 'Do you honestly think I could fit in and become a permanent part of the community here on Kyanós?'

He did, but… 'Don't you?' Because at the end of the day it wasn't about what he thought. It was what she thought and believed that mattered.

'I want to believe it,' she whispered, 'because I want so badly for it to be true. I'm afraid that's colouring my judgement.'

He remained silent.

'I don't have half the talents of the artisans we visited today.' She drummed her fingers against her thigh. 'But I do have pretty good admin and organisational skills. I know how to run a business. I have my savings.'

She pressed her hands to her stomach. 'And it'd be so exciting to showcase local arts and crafts in my shop—nobody else is doing that so I'd not be going into competition with another business on the island. I'd be careful not to stock anything that was in direct competition with the bookshop or the clothing boutiques. And I could bring in some gorgeous bits and bobs that aren't available here.'

Her face started to glow. 'And if everyone else here thought it was a good idea, it'd be really fun to help organise a festival. All my friends would come. And maybe my family could take time off from their busy schedules.'

She leapt to her feet, paced up and down in front of him. 'I could do this.'

'You could. But the question is...'

She halted and leaned towards him. 'What's the question?'

He rested back on his hands. 'The question is, are you going to?'

Fire streaked through her eyes, making them sparkle more brilliantly than the water in the harbour. 'Uh-huh.' She thrust out her chin, and then a grin as wide as the sky itself spread across her face. And Finn felt as if he were scudding along on an air current, sailing through the sky on some euphoric cloud of warmth and possibility.

'I'm going to do it.'

She did a little dance on the spot. She grinned at him as if she didn't know what else to do. And then she leaned forward and, resting her hands on his shoulders, kissed him. Her lips touched his, just for a moment. It was a kiss of elation and excitement—a kiss of thanks, a kiss between friends. And it was pure and magical, and it shifted the axis of Finn's world.

She eased away, her lips parted, her breath coming fast and her eyes dazed, the shock in her face no doubt reflecting the shock in his. She snatched her hands away, smoothed them down the sides of her skirt and it was as if the moment had never been.

Except he had a feeling it was branded on his brain for all time. Such a small contact shouldn't leave such an indelible impression.

'Thank you, Finn.'

He shook himself. 'I didn't do anything.'

She raised an eyebrow and then shook her head and collapsed back down beside him on the sea wall. 'Don't say anything. I know it needs more practice. And you did do something—

something big. You helped me see things differently. You gave me the nudge I needed and...' She turned and met his gaze, her smile full of excitement. 'I'm going to change my life. I'm going to turn it upside down. And I can't wait.'

Something strange and at odds like satisfaction and loss settled in the pit of his stomach, warring with each other for pre-eminence. He stoutly ignored it to grin back and clap his hands. 'Right! This calls for champagne.'

CHAPTER TEN

AUDRA WOKE EARLY, and the moment her eyes opened she found herself grinning. She drummed her heels against the mattress with a silent squeal as her mind sparked and shimmered with plans and purpose.

She threw on some clothes and her running shoes, before picking her way down to the beach and starting to run.

To run.

Unlike the previous three mornings—when she and Finn had been avoiding each other—she didn't time herself. She ran because she had an excess of energy and it seemed a good idea to get rid of some of it. The decisions she was about to make would impact the rest of her life and, while joy and excitement might be driving her, she needed to make decisions based on sound business logic. She wanted this dream to last forever—not just until her money ran out and she'd bankrupted herself.

She reached the sheer wall of cliff at the beach's far end and leaned against it, bracing her hands on her knees, her breath coming hard and fast. Who'd have thought she could run all this way? She let out a whoop. Who knew running could feel so *freeing*?

She pulled off her shoes and socks and ambled back along

the shoreline, relishing the wash of cool water against her toes as she made her way back towards the villa.

When she walked in, Finn glanced up from where he slouched against the breakfast bar, mug of coffee clasped in one hand. His eyes widened as they roved over her. He straightened. 'Have you been for a run?'

Heat mounted her cheeks. 'I, uh…'

One side of his mouth hooked up in that grin, and her blood started to pound harder than when she'd been running. 'That's not a "truth or dare" question, Audra. A simple yes or no will suffice.'

She dropped her shoes to the floor and helped herself to coffee. 'You got me kind of curious when you wanted us to run that day.' He'd made her feel like a lazy slob, but she didn't say that out loud because she didn't want him to feel bad about that. Not after everything he'd done for her yesterday. 'Made me wonder if I *could* run the length of the beach.'

'I bet you rocked it in.'

His faith warmed her. 'Not *rocked* it in,' she confessed, planting herself at the table. 'But I did it. And it gets a bit easier every day.'

He moved to sit opposite. 'You've been for more than one run? How many?'

She rolled her shoulders. 'Only four.'

'And you don't hate it?'

'It's not like my new favourite thing or anything.' But she didn't *hate* it. Sometimes it felt good to be pounding along the sand. It made her feel…powerful. 'I like having done it. It makes me feel suitably virtuous.'

He laughed and pointed to a spot above her head. 'That's one very shiny halo.'

He leaned back and drained his coffee. 'Who'd have thought it? You find you don't hate running, and I find I don't hate lying on a beach reading a book.'

He hadn't seemed restless for any of his usual hard and fast sports. She opened her mouth to ask him about it, but closed it again. She didn't want to put ideas into his head.

He rose. 'I had a couple of new thoughts about some designs for your shop. Wanna see them after breakfast?'

That caught her attention. 'Yes, please!'

An hour later she sat at the outdoor picnic table with Finn, soaking up the sun, the views and the incredible designs he kept creating. 'These are amazing.' She pulled his laptop closer towards her. 'You've gone into so much detail.'

'You gave me good material to work with.'

She flicked through the images he'd created, loving everything that she saw. 'You said—that first day when you showed me what you did—that the first step was the "dreaming big with no holds barred" step.'

He nodded.

She pulled in a breath. 'What's the next step?'

'Ah.' His lips twisted. 'The next step consists of the far less sexy concept of compromise.'

'Compromise?'

He pointed towards his computer. 'These are the dream, but what are the exact physical dimensions of your shop going to be? We won't know that until you find premises and either buy them or sign a lease. So these designs would have to be modified to fit in with that.'

Right.

'You'll also need to take into account any building works that may need doing on these new premises. And if so, what kind of council approvals you might need. Does the building have any covenants in place prohibiting certain work?'

Okay.

'What's your budget for kitting out your shop? See this shelving system here? It costs twice as much as that one. Is it worth twice as much to you? If it's not, which other shelving system do you settle on?'

'So…fitting the dream to the reality?'

'Exactly. Deciding on the nitty-gritty detail.'

He swung the computer back his way, his fingers flying across the keyboard, his brow furrowed in concentration and his lips pursed. As she stared at him something inside Audra's chest cracked open and she felt herself falling and falling and falling. Not 'scream and grab onto something' falling, but flying falling.

Like anything was possible falling.

Like falling in love falling.

Her heart stopped. The air in front of her eyes shimmered. Finn? She'd...she'd fallen in love with Finn? Her heart gave a giant kick and started beating in triple time. She swallowed. No, no, that was nonsense. She wasn't stupid enough to fall for Finn. He didn't do serious. He treated women as toys. He was a playboy!

And yet... He *did* do serious because they'd had several very serious discussions while they'd been here. She'd discovered depths to him she'd never known. He wasn't just an adrenaline junkie, but a talented designer and canny businessman. The playboy thing... Well, he hadn't been out carousing every night. And he hadn't treated her like a toy. Even when she'd wanted him to. So it was more than possible that she had him pegged all wrong about that too.

In the next moment she shook her head. Rupert had warned her against Finn, and Rupert would know.

But...

She didn't want to kill the hope trickling through her. Was it really so stupid?

'Okay, here's a budget version of your shop.'

Finn turned the laptop back towards her. She forced herself to focus on his designs rather than the chaos of her mind. And immediately lost herself in the world he'd created.

'What do you think?'

'This is still beautiful.'

He grinned and her heart kicked against the walls of her

chest. She brushed her fingers across the picture of the barrel of flowers standing by the front door. 'You have such a talent for this. Don't you miss it when you're off adventuring?'

Very slowly he reached across and closed the lid of his laptop. 'That's a "truth or dare" question, Audra. And the answer is yes.'

Her heart stuttered. So did her breath.

'I've been fighting it. Not wanting to acknowledge it.'

'Why not?'

'Because I want to be more than a boring, driven businessman.'

'That's not boring!' She pointed to his computer. 'That…it shows what an artist you are.'

Hooded eyes met hers. 'I lead this exciting life—living the dream. It should be enough.'

But she could see that it wasn't. 'Dreams can change,' she whispered.

He stared down at his hands. 'I've had a lot of time to think over the last fortnight…and our discussions have made me realise a few things.'

Her mouth went dry. In a part of her that she refused to acknowledge, she wanted him to tell her that he loved her and wanted to build a life and family with her. 'Like?' she whispered.

'Like how much the way I live my life has to do with my parents.'

'In what way?' She held her breath and waited to see if he would answer.

He shrugged, but she sensed the emotion beneath the casual gesture. 'I hated not having a home base when I was growing up. I hated the way we were constantly on the move. I hated that I didn't have any friends my own age. But when my parents died…' He dragged a hand down his face. 'I'd have done anything to have them back. But at the same time—' the breath he drew in was ragged '—I didn't want to give up the life Uncle Ned had created for me. I liked that life a hundred times better.'

Her heart squeezed at the darkness swirling in his eyes—the remembered grief and pain, the confusion and strange sense of relief. She understood how all those things could bewilder and baffle a person, making it impossible to see things clearly.

'And that made me feel guilty. So I've tried to mould my life on a balance between the kind of life they lived and the kind of life Ned lived. I wanted to make them all proud. Similar to the way you wanted to make your mother proud, I guess. I thought I could have the best of both worlds and be happy.'

'But you're not happy.'

He wanted it to be enough. She could see that. But the simple fact was it wasn't. And him wishing otherwise wouldn't change that fact.

She swallowed. 'Have you ever loved a song so much that you played it over and over and over, but eventually you play it too much and you wreck it somehow? And then you don't want to listen to it any more, and when you do unexpectedly hear it somewhere it doesn't give you the same thrill it once did?'

Hooded eyes lifted. 'I know what you mean.'

'Well, maybe that's what you've done with all of your adrenaline-junkie sports. Maybe you're all adrenalined out and now you need to find a new song that sings to your soul.'

He stared at her, scepticism alive in his eyes. 'This is more than that. This is the entire way I live my life. Walking away from it feels as if I'm criticising the choices my parents made.'

'I don't see it as a criticism. You're just...just forging your own path.'

He shrugged, but the darkness in his eyes belied the casual gesture. 'The thing is I can no longer hide from the fact that racing down a black ski run no longer gives me the thrill it once did, or that performing endless laps in a sports car is anything other than monotonous, and that trekking to base camp at Everest is just damned cold and uncomfortable.'

But she could see it left him feeling like a bad person—an ingrate.

He speared her with a glance. 'I can't hassle and lecture you about living your dreams and then hide from it when it applies to my own life. That'd make me a hypocrite on top of everything else.'

Her heart burned. She wanted to help him the way he'd helped her—give him the same clarity. 'How old was your father when he died?'

'Thirty-five.'

'So only a couple of years older than you are now?' She gave what she hoped was an expressive shrug. 'Who knows what he might've chosen to do if he'd lived longer?'

'Give up extreme sports, my father?' Finn snorted. 'You can't be serious.'

'Is it any crazier than me opening a shop?'

He smiled. 'That's not crazy. It's what you have a passion for. It's *exciting.*'

Her heart chugged with so much love she had to lower her gaze in case he saw it shining there. 'We can never know what the future might've held for your father, but he could've had a mid-life crisis and decided to go back to Australia and...and start a hobby farm.'

A bark of laughter shot out of him.

'I know a lot of people have criticised the way your parents lived, wrote them off as irresponsible and frivolous.' And she guessed she was one of them. 'But they didn't hurt anyone living like they did; they paid their bills. They were...free spirits. And free spirits, Finn, would tell you to follow your heart and do the things that make you happy. And to not care what other people think.'

His head snapped up.

'If they were true free spirits they'd include themselves amongst those whose opinions didn't matter.'

She watched his mind race. 'What are you going to do?' she asked when she couldn't hold the question back any longer.

He shook his head. 'I've no idea.'

She swallowed. He needed time to work it out.

When his gaze returned to hers, though, it was full of warmth and…and something she couldn't quite define. Affection… laughter…wonder? 'It's been a hell of a holiday, Audra.'

Her name sounded like gold on his tongue. All she could do was nod.

A warm breeze ruffled her hair, loose tendrils tickling her cheek. She pulled it back into a tighter ponytail, trying to gather up all the loose strands. For some reason her actions made Finn smile. 'I'm going to get it cut,' she announced, not realising her intention until the words had left her.

His eyebrows shot up.

'Short. *Really* short. A pixie cut, perhaps. I hate it dangling about my face. I always have.'

'So how come you haven't cut it before now?'

She had no idea. 'Just stuck in the old ways of doing things, I guess. Walking a line I thought I should and presenting the image I thought I should, and not deviating from it. But now…'

'Now?'

'Now anything seems possible.' Even her and Finn didn't seem outside the realms of possibility. He cared for her, she knew that much. And look at everything they'd shared this last fortnight. Look how much he'd done for her. Look how much of an impact they'd had on each other. It had to mean something, right?

'I'm going to ask Anna in the village if she'll cut it for me.'

'When?'

'Maybe…maybe this afternoon.' If she could get an appointment.

He stared at her for a long moment and she had to fight the urge to fidget. 'What?'

'I did something.'

There was something in his tone—something uncertain, and a little defiant, and…a bit embarrassed, maybe? She didn't know what it meant. 'What did you do?'

He scratched a hand through his hair, his gaze skidding away. 'It might be best if I simply show you.'

'Okay. Now?'

He nodded.

'Where are we going? What's the dress code?'

'Into the village.' His gaze wandered over her and it left her burning and achy, prickly and full of need. 'And what you're wearing is just fine.'

They stopped at the hairdresser's first, because Finn insisted. When Anna said she could cut Audra's hair immediately Finn accepted the appointment on her behalf before she could say anything. Audra surveyed him, bemused and not a little curious.

'It'll give me some time to get set up properly,' he explained when he caught her stare.

She shook her head. 'I've no idea what you're talking about.'

'I know.' He leaned forward and pressed a kiss to her brow. 'All will be revealed soon. I'll be back in an hour.'

He was gone before the fresh, heady scent of him had invaded her senses, before she could grab him by the collar of his shirt and kiss him properly. Dear God, what did she do with her feelings for him? She had no idea! Should she try to bury them… or did she dare hope that, given time, he could return them?

Don't do anything rash.

She swallowed and nodded. She couldn't afford to make another mistake. She and Thomas had only broken up six weeks ago. This could be a rebound thing. Except… She'd not been in love with Thomas. She'd wanted to be, but she could see now it'd been nothing but a pale imitation—a combination of loneliness and feeling flattered by his attentions. She pressed her hands to her stomach as it started to churn.

Don't forget Rupert warned you against falling in love with Finn.

Yeah, but Rupert was overprotective and—

'Audra, would you like to take a seat?'

Audra shook herself, and tried to quiet her mind as she gave herself over to Anna's ministrations.

As promised, Finn returned an hour later. Audra's hair had been cut, shampooed and blow-dried and it felt...*wonderful*! She loved what Anna had done—short at the back and sides but still thick and tousled on top. She ran her fingers through it, and the excitement she'd woken with this morning vibrated through her again now.

She and Anna were sharing a cup of tea and gossip when Finn returned, and the way his eyes widened when he saw her, the light that flared in his eyes, and the low whistle that left his lips, did the strangest things to her insides.

'It looks...' He gestured. 'I mean, you look...' He swallowed. 'It's great. You look great.'

Something inside her started to soar. He wanted her. He tried to hide it, but he wanted her in the same way she wanted him. It wasn't enough. But it was something, right? She could build on that, and... Her heart dipped. Except their holiday was almost over and there was so little time left—

He frowned. 'You're not regretting it, are you?'

She tried to clear her face. 'No! I love it.' She touched a self-conscious hand to her new do. 'It feels so liberating.' She did what she could to put her disturbing thoughts from her mind. 'Now put me out of my misery and show me whatever it is you've done. I'm dying here, Finn!'

'Come on, then.' He grinned and took her arm, but dropped it the moment they were outside. She knew why—because the pull between them was so intense.

What if she were to seduce him? Maybe…

That could be a really bad idea.

Or an inspired one.

Her heart picked up speed. She had to force herself to focus on where they were going.

Finn led her along the village's main street. She made herself glance into the windows of the fashion boutiques with their colourful displays, dragged in an appreciative breath as they passed the bakery that sold those decadent croissants. She slowed when they reached the bookshop, but with a low laugh Finn urged her past it.

At the end of the row stood the beautiful whitewashed building with freshly painted shutters the colour of a blue summer day that had silently sat at the centre of herÁ dreams. The moment she'd seen the For Sale sign when she'd clambered off the ferry a fortnight ago, she'd wanted to buy it. Her heart pounded. This place was…*perfect*.

'I remember you saying there was a place for sale in the village that would be the ideal location for your shop, and I guessed this was the place you meant.'

She spun to him, her eyes wide.

'So I asked around and found it belongs to the Veros family.'

'The Veros family who own the deli?'

'One and the same. I asked if we could have a look inside.' He brandished a key. 'And they said yes.'

Excitement gathered beneath her breastbone until she thought she might burst.

'Shall we?'

'Yes, please!'

He unlocked the door. 'Do you want the shutters open?' He gestured to the shutters at the front window. She could barely speak so she simply nodded. She wanted to see the interior bathed in the blues and golds of the late morning light. 'You go on ahead, then, while I open them.'

Pressing one hand to her chest, she reached out with the

other to push the door open. Her heart beat hard against her palm. Could this be the place where she could make her dreams come true? Was this the place where she could start the rest of her life? She tried to rein in her excitement. This was the next step—making the dream fit the reality. She needed to keep her feet on the ground.

Inside it was dim and shadowy. She closed her eyes and made a wish, and when she opened her eyes again, light burst through the spotlessly clear front window as Finn flung the shutters back. Her heart stuttered. The world tilted on its axis. She had to reach out and brace herself against a wall to stop from falling.

Her heart soared...stopped...pounded.

She couldn't make sense of what she was seeing, but in front of her the designs Finn had created for her shop had taken shape and form in this magical place. She squished her eyes shut, but when she opened them again nothing had changed.

She spun around to find Finn wrestling a tub of colourful flowers into place just outside the front door. Her eyes filled. He'd done all of this for her?

He came inside then and grinned, but she saw the uncertainty behind the smile. 'What do you think?'

'I think this is amazing! How on earth did you manage to do this in such a short space of time?'

One shoulder lifted. 'I asked Angelo to whip up a couple of simple display arrangements—don't look too closely because they're not finished.'

'But...but there's stock on the shelves!'

'I borrowed some bits and pieces from Angelo, Eleni, Kostas and Christina. They were more than happy to help me out when I told them what it was for. You're very well thought of in these parts. They consider you one of their own, you know?'

It was how she'd always felt here.

'So you'll see it gets a little more rough and ready the further inside we go.'

He took her arm and led her deeper into the shop and she saw that he'd tacked pictures of all the things she meant to sell on temporary shelves. It brought her dream to magical life, however—helped her see how it could all look in reality. The layout and design, the colours and the light flooding in, the view of the harbour, it was all so very, *very* perfect. 'I love it.'

'Wait until you see upstairs.' Reaching for her hand, he towed her to the back of the shop. 'There's a kitchenette and bathroom through here and storeroom there.' He swung a door open and clicked on the light, barely giving her time to glance inside before leading her up a narrow set of stairs to a lovely apartment with a cosy living room, compact but adequate kitchen, and two bedrooms. The living room and the master bedroom, which was tucked beneath the eaves on the third floor, had exceptional views of the harbour. It was all *utterly* perfect.

'I can't believe you did this!'

'So you like it?'

'I couldn't love it any better.'

His grin was full of delight and...affection.

Her mind raced. He was attracted to her, and he cared for her. He'd done all of this for her. It had to *mean* something.

'I made enquiries and the price they're asking seems reasonable.'

He named a price that made her gulp, but was within her means. She pulled in a breath. 'I'm going to get a building inspection done and...and then put in an offer.'

He spun back to her. 'You mean it?'

She nodded. She wanted to throw herself at him and hug him. But if she did that it'd make his guard go back up. And before that happened she needed to work through the mass of confusion and turbulence racing through her mind.

She followed him back down the stairs silently. His gaze narrowed when they reached the ground floor. 'Is everything okay?'

'My mind is racing at a hundred miles a minute. I'm feeling a little overwhelmed.'

His eyes gentled. 'That's understandable.'

She gestured around. 'Why did you do this for me, Finn? I'm not complaining. I love it. But...it must've taken a lot of effort on your part.'

'I just want you to have your dream, Princess. You deserve it.'

She stared at him, wishing she could read his mind. 'You've spent a lot of time thinking about my future, and I'm grateful. But don't you think you should've been spending that time focussing on some new directions for yourself?'

His gaze dropped. He straightened a nearby shelf, wiped dust from another. 'I've been giving some thought to that too.'

The admission made her blink. He had?

'Kyanós, it seems, encourages soul-searching.' He shoved his hands into the back pockets of his cargo shorts and eyed her for a long moment. 'I've been toying with a plan. I don't know. It could be a stupid idea.' He pulled his hands free, his fingers opening and closing at his sides. 'Do you want to see?'

Fear and hope warred in her chest. All she could do was nod.

'Come on, then. We'll return the key and then I'll show you.'

The car bounced along an unsealed road that was little more than a gravel track. Audra glanced at the forest of olive and pine trees that lined both sides. She'd thought he'd meant to take them back to the villa. 'I've not been on this road before.'

'I've spent some time exploring the island's hidden places these last few days.'

Along with exploring all the ways she could make her dream a reality. He'd been busy.

'It brings us out on the bluff at the other end of the beach from Rupert's place.'

The view when they emerged into a clearing five minutes later stole her breath. Finn parked and cut the engine. She pushed out of the car and just stared.

He shoved his hands into his pockets, keeping the car between them. 'It's a pretty amazing view.'

Understatement much? 'I'm not sure I've ever seen a more spectacular view. This is…*amazing*.' Water surrounded the headland on three sides. From this height she could only make out a tiny strip of beach to her left and then Rupert's villa gleaming in amongst its pines in the distance.

Directly out in front was the Aegean reflecting the most glorious shade of blue that beguiled like a siren's call, the horizon tinted a fiery gold, the outlines of other islands in the distance adding depth and interest. It'd be a spectacular sight when the sun set.

To her right the land fell in gentle undulations, golden grasses rippling down to a small but perfectly formed beach. A third of the way down was a collection of run-down outbuildings.

'This plot—thirty acres in total—is for sale.' He pointed to the outbuildings. 'The farmer who owns it used those to store olives from his groves…and goats, among other things apparently. They haven't been used for almost fifteen years. The moment I clapped eyes on them I knew exactly how to go about transforming them into an amazing house.'

It was the perfect site for a home—sheltered and sunny, and with that beautiful view. Audra swallowed. 'That sounds lovely.'

'I even came up with a name for the house—the Villa Óneira.'

Óneira was the Greek word for dreams. The House of Dreams. He…he wanted to live here on Kyanós? Her heart leapt. *That* had to mean something.

She tried to keep her voice casual. 'What would you do with the rest of the plot?' Because no matter how hard she tried, she couldn't see Finn as an olive farmer or a goat herder.

He gestured to the crest of the headland. 'Do you remember once asking me what activities I couldn't live without?'

She'd been thinking of the rally-car racing, the rock climbing, the skydiving. 'What's the answer?'

'Hang-gliding.'

She blinked. 'Hang-gliding?'

'It's the best feeling in the world. Sailing above it all on air currents—weightless, free...exhilarating.'

Her heart burned as she stared at him. He looked so *alive*.

'That was a great question to ask, Audra, because it made me think hard about my life.'

It had?

'And when I stumbled upon this plot of land and saw that headland, I knew what I could do here.'

She found it suddenly hard to breathe.

'I've been fighting it and telling myself it's a stupid pipe dream.' He swung to her, his face more animated than she'd ever seen it. 'But after our talk this morning, maybe it's not so daft after all.'

'What do you want to do?'

'I want to open a hang-gliding school. I'm a fully qualified instructor.'

He was?

'And I've had a lot of experience.'

He had?

'The school would only run in the summer.' He shrugged. 'For the rest of the time I'd like to focus on the work I do for Aspiration Designs. But I want to work off the grid.' He flung out an arm. 'And here seems as good a place to do it as any. Kyanós has a great community vibe, and I'd love to become a part of it.'

He stopped then as if embarrassed, shoved his hands in his pockets and scuffed a tussock of grass with the toe of his sneaker.

She stared at him. His dream... It was lovely. Beautiful. 'Your plan sounds glorious, Finn.'

He glanced up. 'But?'

She shook her head. 'No buts. It's just... I remember you saying island life wouldn't suit you.'

'I was wrong. Being on a permanent holiday wouldn't suit me. But being in an office all day wouldn't suit me either. I'd want to leave the day-to-day running of Aspirations to my partners—they're better at that than me. Design is my forte. But the thought of sharing my love of hang-gliding with others and teaching them how to do it safely in this amazing place answers a different need.'

'Wow.' She couldn't contain a grin. 'Looks like we're going to be neighbours.'

He grinned back and it nearly dazzled her. 'Looks like it. Who'd have thought?'

This had to mean something—something big! Even if he wasn't aware of it yet.

He tossed the car keys in the air and caught them. 'Hungry?'

'Starved.'

CHAPTER ELEVEN

'Looks like your sailboat is coming in again, Audra.'

They were eating a late lunch of crusty bread, cheese and olives, and Audra's mind was buzzing with Finn's plans for the future. If they were both going to be living on Kyanós, then…

Her heart pounded. It was possible that things could happen. Romantic things. She knew he hadn't considered settling down, falling in love—marrying and babies. Not yet. But who knew how that might change once he settled into a new life here? Given time, who knew what he might choose to do?

She tried to control the racing of her pulse. She had no intention of rushing him. *She* was in no rush. She meant to enjoy their friendship, and to relish the changes she was making in her life. And—she swallowed—they would wait and see what happened.

He'd risen to survey the beach below. She moved to stand beside him, and was greeted with the now familiar pink and blue sail. 'It looks like they're coming ashore.'

Heat burned her cheeks when she recalled her earlier musings about the honeymooners who might be on board. She hoped they weren't planning to have hot sex on her beach. Not that it was *hers* per se, but… She turned her back on the view, careful not to look at Finn. 'Do you want any more of these olives or cheese?'

He swung back and planted himself at the table again. 'Don't take the olives! They're the best I've ever eaten.'

She tried to laugh, rather than sigh, at the way he savoured one.

He helped himself to another slice of a Greek hard cheese called *kefalotiri*. 'Whose turn is it to choose the activities for the day?'

She helped herself to a tiny bunch of grapes. 'I've no idea.' She'd lost count. Besides, the day was half over.

'Then I vote that a long lazy lunch is the order of the day.'

She laughed for real this time. 'It's already been long and lazy.'

'We could make it longer and lazier.'

Sounded good to her.

'We could open a bottle of wine…grab our books…'

Okay, it sounded perfect. 'Count me in.'

'We could head down to the beach if you want…'

She shook her head. 'Let the visitors enjoy it in privacy. I'm stuffed too full of good food to swim.'

He grinned. 'I'll grab the wine.'

'I'll grab our books.'

But before either of them could move, the sound of voices and crackling undergrowth had them looking towards the track. Audra blinked when Rupert, accompanied by a woman she didn't know, emerged.

A smile swept through her—he should've let them know he was coming! Before she could leap up, however, Finn's low, savage curse had her senses immediately going on high alert. She glanced at him, and her stomach nosedived at the expression on his face.

Finn rose.

Rupert and the woman halted when they saw him. The air

grew thick with a tension Audra didn't understand. Nobody spoke.

She forced herself to stand too. 'What's going on, Finn?'

He glanced down at her and she recognised regret and guilt swirling in his eyes, and something else she couldn't decipher. 'I really should've told you about that woman in Nice I'd been trying to avoid. I'm sorry, Princess.'

Audra stared at the woman standing beside Rupert—a tall, leggy brunette whose eyes were hidden behind a large pair of sunglasses—and her mouth went dry. That gorgeous woman was Finn's latest girlfriend? Her stomach shrivelled to the size of a small hard pebble. *Why* had Rupert brought her to the island? She recalled his warnings about Finn and closed her eyes.

'Trust me!'

Her eyes flew open at Finn's words. She wasn't sure if they were a command or a plea.

His eyes burned into hers. 'I promise I will not allow anything she does to hurt you.'

What on earth…?

'You're going to make damn sure of it,' Rupert snarled, striding forwards. He kissed her cheek with a clipped, 'Squirt.' But the glare he shot Finn filled her stomach with foreboding. And it turned Finn grey. 'Audra, this is Trixie McGraw.'

The woman held out her hand. Audra shook it. Trixie? She *hated* that name. It took all her strength to stop her lips from twisting.

'What Rupert has left out of his introduction,' Finn drawled, 'is that Ms McGraw here is an investigative journalist. *Not* an ex-girlfriend, *not* an ex-lover.'

She wasn't…

She was a journalist!

Audra swung to Rupert, aghast. 'You've brought the press to the island?'

Rupert opened his mouth, but Finn cut in. 'She's not here for you, Audra. She wants to interview me.'

'Why?'

If possible, Finn turned even greyer and she wanted to take his hand and offer him whatever silent support she could, but Rupert watched them both with such intensity she didn't want to do anything he could misinterpret. She didn't want to do anything that would damage their friendship.

'My recent accident—the ski-jump disaster—it happened on a resort owned by a friend, Joachim Firrelli. Trixie here was Joachim's girlfriend before they had an ugly bust-up. She's now trying to prove that his facilities are substandard—that he's to blame for my accident. Except I'm not interested in being a pawn in her little game of revenge.'

'It doesn't sound *little* to me. It sounds bitter and a lot twisted.'

Trixie didn't bat so much as an eyelid. Rupert's mouth tightened.

'As I've repeatedly told Ms McGraw, the accident was nobody's fault but my own. I lost concentration. End of story. And I'm not going to let a friend of mine pay the price for my own recklessness.'

His guilt made sudden and sickening sense. He felt guilty that his actions could cause trouble for his friend. And he felt guilty that he'd unwittingly attracted a member of the press to the island when she was doing all that she could to avoid them. *Oh, Finn.*

Finn had crossed his arms and his mouth was set. Her heart pounded, torn between two competing impulses. One was the nausea-inducing reminder that Finn wasn't the kind of man to settle down with just one woman and that to love him would leave her with nothing but a broken heart.

The other…well, it continued to hope. After all, he'd wasted no time in telling her who this Trixie McGraw was, and what she wanted from him. He hadn't wanted her to think this woman was a girlfriend or lover, and that had to mean something, right?

She glared at Rupert. 'Why on earth…? Did you *know* this woman was on a witch hunt?'

Rupert's hands fisted. He turned to Trixie. 'Is what Finn said true?'

One shoulder lifted. 'Pretty much. Except for the "witch hunt" part.'

The woman had the most beautiful speaking voice Audra had ever heard.

'Your sister seems to think I'm motivated by revenge, though I can assure you that is not the case. I believe it's in the public interest to know when the safety standards on a prominent ski resort have deteriorated.'

It was all Audra could do not to snort. 'I can't believe you've brought the media to the island.' Not when he'd done everything he could to protect her from the attention of the press before she'd arrived here.

'I didn't *bring* her. She was already here. I received an email from her yesterday. That's why I'm here now. I left Geneva this morning. I'm not this woman's friend.'

She took a moment to digest that.

So... None of them wanted to talk to this woman?

The press had made her life hell back in Geneva. She wasn't going to let that happen again here on the island. She wasn't going to let them turn Finn and his friend Joachim into their next victims either. She folded her arms. 'Rupert, you have a choice to make.'

He blinked. 'What choice?'

She met his gaze. It was sombre and focussed. 'This is your house. You can invite whomever you want. But you either choose me or you choose her, because one of us has to leave. And if you do choose her, there will be repercussions. There won't be any family dinners in the foreseeable future, and you can kiss a family Christmas goodbye.'

Rupert's nostrils flared.

'Audra,' Finn started, but she waved him quiet.

'I don't trust her, Rupe, but I do trust Finn.' Something in Rupert's eyes darkened and it made her blink. *Wow.* He didn't?

When had that happened? She swallowed. 'And you trust me, so—'

'Forgive me, Ms Russel,' the beautiful voice inserted. 'I understand your current aversion to the press given the circus surrounding your relationship with Thomas Farquhar but I'm not here to discuss that. Your privacy is assured.'

Maybe, but Finn's wasn't. She ignored her. 'I want her off this property. Choose, Rupert.'

'It's no competition, Squirt. You'd win in a heartbeat. But I need your help with something first. We won't go inside the house, I promise. But bear with me here. This will take ten minutes. Less. If you still want Trixie to leave after that, I'll escort her off the premises.'

It didn't seem too much to ask. And in the face of Rupert's sheer reasonableness she found her outrage diminishing. 'Ten minutes.' She pulled out her phone and set a timer.

Rupert motioned to Trixie and she pulled a large A4 manila envelope from her backpack and placed it on the table. Rupert gestured for her and Finn to take a look at the contents. His glance, when it clashed with Finn's, was full of barely contained violence that made Finn's gaze narrow and his shoulders stiffen. Wasting no further time, she reached inside the envelope and pulled out...photographs.

She inhaled sharply, and her heart plummeted. Pictures of her and Finn.

The first captured the moment yesterday when she'd leant forward and in the excitement of the moment had kissed Finn. The next showed the moment after when they'd stared at each other—yearning and heat palpable in both their faces. She could feel the heat of need rising through her again now. She flipped to the next one. It was of her and Finn drinking champagne in a harbourside tavern afterwards. They were both smiling and laughing. And she couldn't help it, her lips curved upwards again now. This dreadful woman had captured one of the happiest moments of Audra's life.

'This is what you do?' she asked the other woman. 'You spy on people?'

Trixie, probably wisely, remained silent.

She glanced at Rupert. 'You're upset about this? I know you warned Finn off, but *I* kissed *him*, not the other way around. I took him off guard. He didn't stand a chance.' Behind her Finn snorted. 'Besides, it was a friendly kiss…a thank-you kiss. And it lasted for less than two seconds.'

Without a word, Rupert leaned across and pulled that photo away to reveal the one beneath. She stared at it and everything inside her clenched up tight. It was of her and Finn outside the art studio that day, and they were… She fought the urge to fan her face. They were oblivious to everything. They were wrapped so tightly in each other's arms it was impossible to tell where one began and the other ended. It had, quite simply, been the best kiss of her life.

She lifted her head and shrugged. 'I'm not sure she got my best side.'

Nobody laughed.

'Trixie has informed me that unless she gets an interview with Finn, she'll sell these photos to the tabloids.' Rupert speared Finn with a glare that made all the hairs on her arms lift. 'Finn *will* give her that interview and make sure *you* aren't subjected to any more grubby media attention.'

A fortnight ago she might've agreed with Rupert, but now… She drew in a breath, then lifted her chin. 'I'm not ashamed of these photos.'

'It's okay, Princess. I don't mind. I don't have anything incriminating to tell our fair crusader here, so an interview won't take long at all.'

She wanted to stamp her feet in her sudden frustration. 'No, you're not hearing me. *I'm not ashamed of these photographs.*'

He met her gaze, stilled, and then rocked back on his heels. 'I—'

She held up a hand and shook her head. Pursing his lips, he

stared at her for what seemed like forever, and then eventually nodded, and she knew he was allowing her to choose how they'd progress from here. She swung back to Rupert and Trixie. 'In fact, I'm so *not* ashamed of these photographs, if Ms McGraw doesn't mind, I'm going to keep them.'

'I have the digital files saved in several different locations. Your keeping that set won't prevent them from being made public.'

'I didn't doubt that for a moment.' Audra's phone buzzed. 'Time's up, Rupert.'

'You still want her to leave?'

'Absolutely! I'd much rather these pictures appear in the papers than any more gratuitous speculation about me and Thomas.' The situation with Thomas had left her feeling like a fool, not to mention helpless and a victim. The pictures of her and Finn, however... Well, they didn't.

'Besides, we all know how the press can twist innocent words to suit their own purposes. It sounds to me as if Joachim doesn't deserve to become the next target in a media scandal that has no substance.'

'You're mistaken. There's substance,' Trixie said.

'Then go find your evidence elsewhere, because you're not going to hit the jackpot here,' Audra shot back.

Rupert's eyes flashed as he turned to Finn. 'So you refuse to do the honourable thing?'

Rupert's words felt like a knife to his chest. Finn refused to let his head drop. 'I'm going to do whatever Audra wants us to do.' He'd known how disempowered Farquhar had left her feeling. He wasn't going to let Trixie McGraw make her feel the exact same way. *He* wasn't going to make her feel that same way.

He'd sensed that the photographs had both amused and empowered her, though he wasn't sure why. She'd been amazing to watch as she'd dealt with the situation—strong and capable, invulnerable. He wasn't raining on her parade now.

Rupert's hands clenched. 'You promised you wouldn't mess with her!'

Finn braced himself for the impact of Rupert's fist against his jaw, but Audra inserted herself between them. 'Not in front of Lois Lane here, please, Rupe.' She pointed back down the path. 'I believe you mentioned something about escorting her from the premises.'

A muscle in Rupert's jaw worked. 'You sure about this?'

'Positive.'

Trixie shook her head. 'You're making a mistake.'

'And you're scum,' Audra shot back.

Amazingly, Trixie laughed. As Rupert led her to the top of the path, she said, 'I like your sister.'

'I'm afraid she doesn't return the favour. I'll meet you back on the boat later.'

Without another word, Trixie started back down to the beach. She waved to them all when she reached the bottom.

'I think we should take this inside,' Audra said, when Rupert turned to stare at Finn.

Finn's heart slugged like a sick thing in his chest. He'd kissed Audra, and Rupert's sense of betrayal speared into him in a thousand points of pain.

Rupert hadn't been joking when he'd said he'd no longer consider Finn a friend if Finn messed about with Audra. Finn had to brace his hands against his knees at the sense of loss that pounded through him. He'd destroyed the most important friendship of his life. This was his fault, no one else's. The blame was all his. He forced himself to straighten. 'I think we'll do less damage out here, Audra.'

'The two of you are *not* fighting.'

He met the other man's gaze head-on. 'I'm not going to fight, Princess.' But if Rupert wanted to pound him into the middle of next week, he'd let him. Rupert's eyes narrowed and Finn saw that he'd taken his meaning.

'*Rupe,*' Audra warned.

Rupert made for the house. 'You're not worth the bruised knuckles.'

The barb hit every dark place in Finn's soul. He'd never been worth the sacrifice Rupert had made for him. He'd never been worth the sacrifices he'd always wanted his parents to make for him.

Hell! A fortnight on this island with Audra and he'd laid his soul bare. He lifted his arms and let them drop. He didn't know what any of it meant. What he did know was that this Greek island idyll was well and truly over. He wanted to roar and rage at that, but he had no right.

No right at all. So he followed Rupert and Audra into the house, and it was all he could do to walk upright rather than crawl.

They went into the living room. Audra glanced from Rupert to Finn and back again. 'I think we need to talk about that kiss.'

Finn fell into an armchair. Was it too early for a whisky? 'It won't help.' He'd broken his word and that was that. He'd blown it.

Rupert settled on the sofa, stretched his legs out. 'I'm interested in what you have to say, Squirt.' He ignored Finn.

'The kiss—the steamy one—it wasn't calculated, you know?'

She twisted her hands together and more than anything Finn wanted to take them and kiss every finger. He hated the thought of anything he'd done causing her distress. *You should've thought about that before kissing her!*

For a moment he felt the weight of Rupert's stare, but he didn't meet it. The thought of confronting the other man's disgust left him exhausted.

'It was Finn who ended the kiss. I wanted to take it to its natural conclusion, but Finn held back because of how much he feels he owes you.'

He sensed the subtle shift in Rupert's posture. 'You know about that?'

She nodded. 'I'm glad you did what you did when you were sixteen, Rupe. It was a good thing to do.' She folded her arms. 'But it doesn't change the fact that I'm furious with you at the moment.'

Rupert stiffened. 'With me?'

She leaned forward and poked a finger at him. 'You have no right to interfere in my love life. I can kiss whoever I want, and you don't get to have any say in that.'

Finn dragged a hand down his face, trying to stop her words from burrowing in beneath his flesh. Rupert knew Finn wasn't good enough for his sister. Finn knew it too.

'I understand the kiss,' Rupert growled. 'I get the spur-of-the-moment nature of being overwhelmed before coming to your senses. I understand attraction and desire. None of those things worry me, Squirt.' He reached for the photos she'd set on the coffee table, rifled through them and then held one up. '*This* is what worries me.'

Audra stilled, and then glanced away, rubbing a hand across her chest.

Finn glanced at it. What the hell...? It was the second photo—the one after the kiss. Okay, there was some heat in the way they looked at each other, but that picture was innocent. 'What the hell is wrong with that?'

Rupert threw him a withering glare before turning his attention back to his sister. 'Have you fallen in love with him?'

Every cell in Finn's body stiffened. His breathing grew ragged and uneven. What the hell was Rupert talking about?

'Princess?' He barely recognised the croak that was his voice.

Her face fell as if something inside her had crumbled. 'Your timing sucks, big brother.'

'You're family. You matter to me. I don't want to see you hurt. Have you fallen in love with Finn?'

Her chin lifted and her eyes sparked. 'Yes, I have. What's more I don't regret it. I think you're wrong about him.'

Finn shot to his feet. 'You can't have! That's not possible!' He pointed a finger at her. 'We talked about this.'

Audra's chin remained defiant. 'We talked about a lot of things.'

They had and—

He shook himself. 'None of what I said means I'm ready to settle down.'

Her hands went to her hips, but the shadows in her eyes made his throat burn. 'I think that's *exactly* what it means. I just think you're too afraid to admit it to yourself.'

He might be ready to put his freewheeling, adrenaline-loving days behind him, but it didn't mean he'd ever be ready for a white picket fence.

Even as he thought it, though, a deep yearning welled inside him.

He ignored it. Happy families weren't for him. They hadn't worked out when he was a child and he had no faith they'd work out for him as a man. 'Look, Audra, what you're feeling at the moment is just a by-product of your excitement…for all the changes you're going to make in your life, and—'

From the corner of his eyes he saw Rupert lean forward.

'And the romance of the Greek islands.' If he called her Squirt now, she'd tell him that was Strike Three and…and it'd all be over. He opened his mouth, but the word refused to come.

Audra drew herself up to her full height, her eyes snapping blue fire. 'Don't you dare presume to tell me what I'm feeling. I know exactly what I'm feeling. *I love you, Finn.*' She dragged in a shaky breath. 'And I know this feels too soon for you to admit, but you either love me too. Or you don't. But I'm not letting you off the hook with platitudes like that.'

He flinched.

Her eyes filled and he hated himself. He glanced at Rupert. The other man stared back, his gaze inscrutable. Finn wished he'd shoot off that sofa and beat him to a pulp. Rupert turned back to Audra. 'When did he start calling you Princess?'

He could see her mentally go back over their previous conversations. 'After that kiss—the steamy one.'

Rupert pursed his lips. 'He doesn't do endearments. He never has.'

What the hell...? That didn't mean anything!

Audra moved a step closer then as if Rupert's observation had given her heart. 'You might want to look a little more closely, a little more deeply, at the reasons it's been so important to you to look after me this last fortnight.'

'I haven't looked after you!' He didn't do nurturing.

'What do you call it, then?' She started counting things off on her fingers. 'You've fed me up. You forced me to exercise. And you made sure I got plenty of sun and R & R.'

He rolled his shoulders. 'You were too skinny.' And she'd needed to get moving—stop moping. Exercise was a proven mood enhancer. As for the sun and the R & R... 'We're on a Greek island!' He lifted his hands. 'When in Rome...'

Her eyes narrowed. 'You read a book on the beach, Finn. If that's not going above and beyond...'

Rupert's head snapped up. 'He read a book? *Finn* read a book?' Audra glared at him and he held his hands out. 'Sorry, staying quiet again now.'

So what? He'd read a book. He'd *liked* the book.

'And that's before we get to the really important stuff like you challenging me to follow a path that will make me happy—truly happy.' She swallowed. 'And don't you think it's revealing that you sensed that dream when no one else ever has?'

His mouth went dry. 'That's...that's just because of how much time we've been spending together recently—a by-product of forced proximity.'

She snorted. 'There was nothing forced about it. We spent three days avoiding each other, Finn. We never had to spend as much time together as we did.' She folded her arms and held his gaze. 'And I know you spent those three days thinking about me.'

His head reared back.

'You spent that time bringing my dream to full Technicolor life.'

He scowled. 'Nonsense. I just showed you what it could look like.' He'd wanted to convince her she could do it.

'And while you're analysing your motives for why you did all those things for me, you might also want to consider why it is you've enjoyed being looked after by me so much too.'

She hadn't—

He stared at her. 'That ridiculous nonsense of yours when we went running... And then making sure I didn't overdo it when we went jetskiing.' Enticing him to read not just a book, but a trilogy that had hooked him totally. 'You wanted me to take it easy after my accident.'

She'd been clever and fun, and she'd made him laugh. He hadn't realised what she'd been up to. She'd challenged him in ways that had kept his mind, not just active, but doing loop-the-loops, while his body had been recuperating and recovering its strength. *Clever.*

'You haven't chafed the slightest little bit at the slower pace.'

Because it hadn't felt slow. It'd felt perfect. Everything inside him stilled. *Perfect?* Being here with Audra...? She made him feel... He swallowed. She made him feel as if he were hang-gliding.

She was perfect.

Things inside him clenched up. She said that she loved him.

'You're planning to move to the island too. Don't you think that means something?'

It felt as if a giant fist had punched him in the stomach. He saw now exactly what it did mean. He loved her. He wasn't sure at what point in the last fortnight that'd happened, but it had. *She said she loved him.* His heart pounded. With everything he had he wanted to reach out and take it, but...

He glanced at Rupert. Rupert stared back, his dark eyes inscrutable, and a cold, dank truth swamped Finn in darkness.

Acid burned hot in his gut. Rupert *knew* Finn wasn't good enough for his sister. Rupert knew Finn couldn't make Audra happy…he knew Finn would let her down.

A dull roar sounded in his ears; a throbbing pounded at his temples.

'I have a "truth or dare" question for you, Finn.'

He forced himself to meet her gaze.

'Do you or don't you love me?'

The question should've made him flinch, but it didn't. He loved her more than life itself. And if he denied it, he knew exactly how much pain that'd inflict on her. He knew exactly how it'd devastate her.

He glanced at Rupert. He glanced back at her. She filled his vision. He'd helped her find her dream, had helped her find the courage to pursue it. That was no small thing. She would lead a happier life because of it. And he—

He swung to Rupert, his hands forming fists. 'Look, I know you don't think I'm good enough for your little sister, and you're probably right! But you don't know how amazing she is. If I have to fight you over this I will, but—'

Rupert launched himself out of his seat. 'What the hell! I *never* said you weren't good enough for Audra. When have I ever given you the impression that you weren't good enough?'

Finn's mouth opened and closed, but no sound came out.

'When have I ever belittled you, made light of your achievements, or treated you like you weren't my equal?'

Rupert's fists lifted and Finn kept a careful eye on them, ready to dodge if the need arose. He'd rarely seen Rupert so riled.

'That's just garbage!' Rupert slashed a hand through the air. 'Garbage talk from your own mind, because you still feel so damn guilty about me giving up that stupid prize all those years ago.'

Rupert glared at him, daring him to deny it. Finn's mind whirled. He'd carried the guilt of what Rupe had sacrificed for him for seventeen years. He'd used that guilt to keep him on the straight and narrow, but in the process had it skewed his thinking?

'But you ordered me to keep my distance from Audra. *Why?*'

'Because I always sensed you could break her heart. And with you so hell-bent on avoiding commitment I—'

'Because of the promise he made to himself when he was eighteen,' Audra inserted.

'What promise?' Rupert stared from one to the other. He shook himself. 'It doesn't matter. The thing is, I never realised Audra had the potential to break your heart too.'

Finn couldn't say anything. He could feel the weight of Audra's stare, but he wasn't ready to turn and meet it. 'You saved my life, Rupe.' Rupert went to wave it away, but Finn held a hand up to forestall him. 'But Audra is the one who's made me realise I need to live that life properly.'

Rupert dragged a hand down his face. 'I should never have interfered. It wasn't fair. I should've kept my nose well and truly out, and I hope the two of you can forgive me.' He looked at Audra. 'You're right to be furious with me. It's just...'

'You've got used to looking out for me. I know that. But, Rupe, I've got this.'

He nodded. 'I'm going to make myself scarce.'

She nodded. 'That would be appreciated.'

He leaned forward to kiss the top of her head. 'I love you, Squirt.' And then he reached forward and clapped Finn on the shoulder. 'I'll be back tomorrow.' And then he was gone.

Finn turned towards Audra. She stared at him, her eyes huge in her face. 'You haven't answered my question yet,' she whispered.

He nodded. 'All my life I've thought I've not been worthy of family...or commitment. I never once thought I was worth the sacrifice Rupert made for me seventeen years ago.'

'Finn.'

She moved towards him, but he held up a hand. 'I can see

now that my parents left me with a hell of a chip on my shoulder, and a mountain-sized inferiority complex. All of my racing around choosing one extreme sport after another was just a way to try to feel good about myself.'

She nodded.

'It even worked for a while. Until I started wanting more.'

Her gaze held his. 'How much more?'

He moved across to cup her face. 'Princess, you've made me realise that I can have it *all*.'

A tear slipped down her cheek. She sent him a watery smile. 'Of course you can.'

A smile built through him. 'I want the whole dream, Audra. Here on Kyanós with you.'

Her chin wobbled. 'The whole dream?'

She gasped when he went down on one knee in front of her. 'At the heart of all this is you, Princess. It's you and your love that makes me complete. I love you.' He willed her to believe every word, willed her to feel how intensely he meant them. 'I didn't know I could ever love anyone the way I love you. The rest of it doesn't matter. If you hate the idea of me opening up a hang-gliding school I'll do something different. If you'd prefer to live in the village rather than on the plot of land I'm going to buy, then that's fine with me too. I'll make any sacrifice necessary to make you happy.'

Her eyes shimmered and he could feel his throat thicken.

He took her hands in his and kissed them. 'I'm sorry it took me so long to work it out. But I realise now that I'm not my father…and I'm not my mother. I'm in charge of my own life, and I mean to make it a good life. And it's a life I want to share with you, if you'll let me.'

Tears spilled down her cheeks.

'Audra Russel, will you do me the very great honour of marrying me and becoming my wife?'

And then he held his breath and waited. She'd said she loved him. But had he just screwed up here? Had he rushed her before she was ready? Had—?

She dropped to her knees in front of him, took his face in her hands and pulled his head down to hers. Heat and hunger swept through him at the first contact, spreading like an inferno until he found himself sprawled on the floor with her, both of them straining to get closer and closer to each other. Eventually she pulled back, pushed upwards and rolled until she straddled him. 'That was a yes, by the way.' She traced her fingers across his broad chest. 'I love your dream, Finn. I love you.'

He stroked her cheek, his heart filled with warmth and wonder. 'I don't know how I got so lucky. I'm going to make sure you never regret this decision. I'm going to spend the rest of my life making you happy.'

She bit her lip. 'Can…can you take me back to your plot of land?'

'What, now?' Right this minute?

She nodded, but looked as if she was afraid he'd say no.

He pulled his baser instincts back into line and hauled them both upright. Without another word, he moved her in the direction of the car. From now on he had every intention of making her every wish come true.

Audra stared at the amazing view and then at the man who stood beside her. She pointed towards the little bay. 'Do you think we could have a jetski?'

'Will that make you happy?'

'Yes.'

'Then we can have two.'

She turned and wrapped her arms around his neck. He pulled her in close; the possessiveness of the gesture and the way his eyes darkened thrilled her to the soles of her feet. 'I want you to teach me to hang-glide.'

His eyes widened. Very slowly he nodded. 'I can do that.'

She stared deep into his eyes and all the love she felt for him welled inside her. She felt euphoric that she no longer had to hide it. 'Do you know why I wanted to come here this afternoon?'

'Why?'

'Because I want *this* to be the place where we start our life together.' She swallowed. 'I love your vision of our future. And this...'

He raised an eyebrow. 'This...?'

She raised an eyebrow too and he laughed. 'Spot on,' he told her. 'The practice has paid off.'

Heat streaked through her cheeks then. His eyebrow lifted a little higher. 'Is that a blush, Princess?' His grin was as warm as a summer breeze. 'I'm intrigued.'

Suddenly embarrassed, she tried to ease away from him, but his hands trailed down her back to her hips, moulding her to him and making her gasp and ache and move against him restlessly instead. 'Tell me what you want, Audra.'

'You,' she whispered, meeting his gaze. He was right. There was no need for secrets or coyness or awkwardness. Not now. She loved him. And the fact that he loved her gave her wings. 'I wanted to come here because this is where I want our first time to be.' She lifted her chin. 'And I want that first time to happen this afternoon.'

His eyes darkened even further. His nostrils flared, and he lifted a hand to toy with a button on her blouse, a question in his eyes.

She shook her head, her breath coming a little too fast. 'No more kisses out in the open, thank you very much. I bet Lois Lane is still lurking around here somewhere. And one set of photographs in circulation is more than enough.'

He laughed.

She glanced down the hill at the outbuildings. 'Why don't you walk me through your plans for our home?'

He grinned a slow grin that sent her pulse skyrocketing, before sliding an arm about her waist and drawing her close as they walked down the slope. 'What an excellent plan. I hope you don't have anywhere you need to be for the next few hours, Princess. My plans are…big.' He waggled his eyebrows. 'And it'd be remiss of me to not show them to you in comprehensive detail.'

'That,' she agreed, barely able to contain her laughter and her joy, 'would be *very* remiss of you.'

When they reached the threshold of what looked as if it were once a barn, he swung her up into his arms. 'Welcome home, Princess.'

She wrapped her arms about his neck. *He* was her home. Gazing into his eyes, she whispered, 'It's a beautiful home, Finn. The best. I love it.'

His head blocked out the setting sun as it descended towards her, and she welcomed his kiss with everything inside her as they both started living the rest of their lives *right now*.

EPILOGUE

'GO! GO, *PAIDI MOU*!'

Audra laughed as Maria shooed her in the direction of Finn, who was waiting beside a nearby barrel of flowers in full bloom. The town square was still full of happy holidaymakers and *very* satisfied vendors.

'You listen to my wife, Audra,' Angelo said with a wide grin. 'Your husband wants to spend some time with his beautiful wife. Go and drink some wine and eat some olives, and bask in the satisfaction of what you've achieved over the last three days.'

'What *we've* achieved,' she corrected. 'And there's still things to—'

'We have it under control,' Maria told her with a firm nod. 'You work too hard. Go play now.'

Audra submitted with a laugh, and affectionate pecks to the cheeks of the older couple who'd become so very dear to both her and Finn during the last fourteen months since they'd moved to the island.

As if afraid she'd change her mind and head back to work, Finn sauntered across to take her hand. As always, it sent a thrill racing through her. *Her husband.* A sigh of pure appreciation rose through her.

'You make her put her feet up, Finn,' Maria ordered.

He saluted the older woman, and, sliding an arm around Audra's shoulders, led her down towards the harbour. Audra slipped her arm around his waist, leaning against him and relishing his strength. They'd been married for eight whole months, but she still had to pinch herself every day.

Standing on tiptoe, she kissed him. 'I think we can safely say the festival went well.'

'It didn't just *go well*, Princess.' He grinned down at her. 'It's been a resounding success. The festival committee has pulled off the event of the year.'

She stuck her nose in the air. 'The event of the year was our wedding, thank you very much.' They'd been married here on the island in the tiny church, and it had been perfect.

His grin widened. 'Okay, it was the second biggest event of the year. And there are plans afoot for next year already.'

He found a vacant table at Thea Laskari's harbourside taverna. 'I promised Thea you'd be across for her *kataifi*.'

They'd no sooner sat than a plate of the sweet nutty pastry was placed in front of them, along with a carafe of sparkling water. 'Yum!' She'd become addicted to these in recent weeks.

'On the house,' Ami, the waitress, said with a smile. 'Thea insists. If we weren't so busy she'd be out here herself telling everyone how fabulous the festival has been for business.' Ami glanced around the crowded seating area with a grin. 'I think we can safely predict that the festival cheer will continue well into the night. Thea sends her love and her gratitude.'

'And give her mine,' Audra said.

She did a happy dance when Ami left to wait on another table. 'Everyone has worked so hard. And it's all paid off.' She gestured at the main street and the town square, all festooned in gaily coloured bunting and stall upon stall of wares and produce. Satisfaction rolled through her. It'd been a lot of work and it'd taken a lot of vision, but they'd created something here they could all be proud of.

'*You've* worked so hard.' Finn lifted her hand to his mouth and kissed it, and just like that the blood heated up in her veins.

'I heard Giorgos tell Spiros that next year the committee needs to market Kyanós as an authentic Greek getaway. With so many of the young people leaving the island, most families have a spare room they can rent out—so people can come here to get a bona fide taste of genuine Greek island life.'

She laughed. 'Everyone has been so enthusiastic.'

'This is all your doing, you know?'

'Nonsense!'

'You were the one that suggested the idea and had everyone rallying behind it. You've been the driving force.'

'*Everyone* has worked hard.'

He stared at her for a long moment. 'You're amazing, you know that? I don't know how I got to be so lucky. I love you, Audra Sullivan.'

Her throat thickened at the love in his eyes. She blinked hard. 'And I love you, Finn Sullivan.' This was the perfect time to tell him her news—with the sun setting behind them, and the air warm and fragrant with the scent of jasmine.

She opened her mouth but he spoke first. 'I had a word with Rupert earlier.'

She could tell from the careful way he spoke that Rupert had told him the outcome of the court case against Thomas Farquhar. She nodded. 'I had a quiet word with Trixie.'

Finn shook his head. 'I can't believe you're becoming best friends with a reporter.'

'I believe it might be Rupert who's her best friend.' Something was going on with her brother and the beautiful journalist, but neither of them was currently giving anything away. 'She told me the pharmaceutical company Thomas was working for have paid an exorbitant amount of money to settle out of court.'

'Are you disappointed?'

'Not at all. Especially as I have it on rather good authority that Rupert means for me to administer those funds in any way I see fit.'

He started to laugh. 'And you're going to give it all to charity?'

'Of course I am. I want that money to do some good. I suspect Thomas and his cronies will think twice before they try something like that again.'

They ate and drank in silence for a bit. 'Everyone is meeting at Rupert's for a celebratory dinner tonight,' Finn finally said.

'Excellent. It's so nice to have the whole family together.' She'd like to share her news with all of them tonight. But she had to tell Finn first. 'Do you ever regret moving to Kyanós, Finn?'

His brow furrowed. 'Not once. Never. Why?'

She shrugged. 'I just wanted to make sure you weren't pining for a faster pace of life.'

'I don't miss it at all. I have you.' His grin took on a teasing edge. '*And* I get to hang-glide.' He raised an eyebrow. 'We could sneak off to continue your training right now if you wanted.'

She'd love to, but… Her pulse started to skip. 'I'm afraid my training is going to have to go on hold for a bit.'

He leaned towards her. 'Why? You've been doing so well and…and you love it.' Uncertainty flashed across his face. 'You do love it, don't you? You're not just saying that because it's what you think I want to hear?'

'I totally love it.' She reached out to grip his hand, a smile bursting through her. 'But I'm just not confident enough in my abilities to risk it for the next nine months.'

He stared at her. She saw the exact moment the meaning of her words hit him. His jaw dropped. 'We're…we're having a baby?'

She scanned his face for any signs of uncertainty…for any consternation or dismay. Instead what she found mirrored back at her were her own excitement and love. Her joy.

He reached out to touch her face. His hands gentle and full of reverence. 'We're having a baby, Princess?'

She nodded. He drew her out of her seat to pull her into his lap. 'I—'

She could feel her own tears spill onto her cheeks at the moisture shining in his eyes. 'Amazing, isn't it?'

He nodded, his arms tightening protectively around her.

'And exciting,' she whispered, her heart full.

He nodded again. 'I don't deserve—'

She reached up and pressed her fingers to his mouth. 'You deserve every good thing, Finn Sullivan, and don't you forget it.' She pulled his head down for a kiss and it was a long time before he lifted it again. 'And they lived happily ever after,' she whispered.

He smiled, and Audra swore she could stay here in his arms forever. 'Sounds perfect.'

She had to agree that it did.

* * * * *

Keep reading for an excerpt of
Runaway Temptaion
by Maureen Child.
Find it in the
Texas Cattleman's Club: Bachelor Auction anthology,
out now!

One

"I hate weddings." Caleb Mackenzie ran his index finger around the inside of his collar. But that didn't do a thing to loosen the tie he wore, or to rid himself of the "wish I were anywhere but here" thoughts racing through his mind. "I feel like I'm overdressed for my own hanging."

Caleb wasn't real fond of suits. Sure, he had a wide selection of them since he needed them for meetings and business deals. But he was much more comfortable in jeans, a work shirt and his favorite boots, running his ranch, the Double M. Still, as the ranch grew, he found himself in the dreaded suits more and more often because expansion called for meeting bankers and investors on their turf.

Right now, though, he'd give plenty to be on a horse riding out across the open range. Caleb knew his ranch hands were getting the work done, but there were stock ponds to check on, a pregnant mare he was keeping an eye on and a hay field still to harvest and store.

Yet instead, here he stood, in the hot Texas sun, in an elegant suit and shining black boots. He tugged the brim of his gray

Stetson down lower over his eyes and slanted a look at the mob of people slowly streaming into the Texas Cattleman's Club for the ceremony and reception.

If he could, he'd slip out of town. But it was too late now.

"You're preaching to the choir, man."

Caleb nodded at his friend Nathan Battle. If he had to be there, at least he had company.

Nathan settled his cowboy hat more firmly on his head and sent a frown toward his pretty, very pregnant wife standing with a group of her friends. "I swear, I think Amanda really enjoys it when I have to wear a suit."

"Women'll kill you." Caleb sighed and leaned back against his truck. As hot as he was, he was in no hurry to go inside and take a seat for the ceremony. Given a choice, he'd always choose to be outside under the sky. Even a hot and humid August day was preferable to being trapped inside.

"Maybe, but it's not a bad way to go—" Nathan broke off and asked, "Why're you here, anyway? Not like you've got a wife to make you do what you don't want to do." As soon as the words left his mouth, Nathan winced and said, "Sorry, man. Wasn't thinking."

"No problem." Caleb gritted his teeth and swallowed the knot of humiliation that could still rise up and choke him from time to time. The thing about small towns was, not only did everyone know what everybody else was doing—nobody ever forgot a damn thing. Four years since the day his wedding hadn't happened and everyone in Royal remembered.

But then, it wasn't like he'd forgotten, either.

Amazing, really. In the last few years, this town had seen tornadoes, killer storms, blackmailers and even a man coming back from the dead. But somehow, the memory of Caleb's botched wedding day hadn't been lost in the tidal wave of events.

Nathan shifted position, his discomfort apparent. Caleb couldn't help him with that. Hell, he was uncomfortable, too.

But to dispel the tension, Caleb said lightly, "You should have worn your uniform."

As town sheriff, Nathan was rarely dressed in civilian clothes. The man was most comfortable in his khaki uniform, complete with badge, walking the town, talking to everyone and keeping an eye on things. He snorted. "Yeah, that wouldn't fly with Amanda."

A soft smile curved his friend's mouth and just for a second or two, Caleb envied the other man. "When's the new baby due again?"

"Next month."

And, though he knew the answer already, Caleb asked, "How many will that make now?"

Nathan grinned and shot him a wink. "This one makes four."

A set of four-year-old twin boys, a two-year-old girl and now another one. "How many are you planning, anyway?"

Nathan shrugged. "Who says there's a plan? Mandy loves babies, and I have to say I do enjoy making them."

Marriage. Family. All of that slipped by him four years ago. And now that Nathan had reminded him, Caleb idly wondered how many kids he and Meg might have had by now if things had gone the way he'd expected. But the night before their wedding, Meg had run off with Caleb's brother, Mitch. Now the two of them lived on the family ranch with their set of twins. Three years old, the boy and girl ran wild around the ranch and Caleb put whatever he might have felt for kids of his own into those two.

There might still be tension between him and his brother, Mitch, not to mention Meg. But he loved those kids more than he would have thought possible.

"Mitch and Meg still out of town?" Nathan asked, glancing around as if half expecting to see them walking up.

"Yeah. Visiting Meg's family." And Caleb had been enjoying the respite.

"That's one way to get out of going to a summer wedding."

"Amen." Caleb loosened his tie a little. Felt like he was beginning to melt out here in the sun. He spared a glance at the sky and watched a few lazy white clouds drifting along. "Who plans a wedding in August, anyway? Hotter than the halls of hell out here."

"You know how the Goodmans are," Nathan answered. "The old man figures he knows everything and the rest of them—except Brooke—just fall in line. Probably his idea to hold it in high summer. No doubt he was aiming for it to be the talk of the town."

That sounded like Simon Goodman. Though the man was Caleb's lawyer, that was more from inertia than anything else. Goodman had been Caleb's father's lawyer and when the elder Mackenzie died, Caleb just never bothered to change the situation. So his own inaction had brought him here. Truth be told, Caleb usually avoided attending *any* weddings since it inevitably brought up old memories that he'd just as soon bury.

"Anyway," Nathan said, pushing past the uncomfortable pause in the conversation, "I'm the town sheriff. I'm sort of *forced* to be at these society things. Why the hell did you come?"

Caleb snorted. "Normally, I wouldn't have. But Simon Goodman's still the ranch attorney. So it's business to be at his son Jared's wedding." And he made a mental note to do something about that real soon. He shrugged. "If Mitch and Meg had been in town I'd have forced my brother to go instead of me. But since they're gone, I'm stuck."

Served him right, Caleb told himself, for letting things slide. He never should have kept Simon on. He and Caleb's father had been great friends so that didn't speak well of the man.

He'd let the lawyer relationship stand mainly because it was easier than taking time away from work to find someone new. Between running the ranch and expanding the oil-rich field discovered only twenty years before, Caleb had been too damn busy to worry about a lawyer he only had to deal with a few times a year.

Looking for a change of subject, Caleb said, "Since you're here, that means the new deputy's in charge, right?"

Nathan winced. "Yeah. Jeff's doing fine."

Caleb laughed. "Sure, I can hear the confidence in your voice."

Sighing, Nathan pushed one hand through his hair and shook his head. "With Jack retired, I needed a deputy and Jeff Baker's working out. But he's from Houston so it's taking him some time to get used to small town living."

Caleb had heard about it. Jeff was about thirty and a little too strict on the law and order thing for Royal. The new deputy had handed out more speeding tickets in the last six months than Nathan had in years. Folks in Royal hit an empty road and they just naturally picked up speed. Jeff Baker wasn't making many friends.

"Hell," Caleb said, "I've lived here my whole life and I'm still not used to it."

"I hear that," Nathan replied, shifting his gaze to where his wife stood with a group of friends. "But I've been getting a lot of complaints about the tickets Jeff's handing out."

Caleb laughed. "He's not going to slow anybody down."

"Maybe not," Nathan agreed with a nod. "But he's going to keep trying."

"I expect so," Caleb mused, then glanced over at Nathan's wife who was smiling and waving one hand. "I think Amanda wants you."

Straightening up, Nathan gave a heartfelt sigh. "That's it, then. I'll see you after. At the reception?"

"I don't think so. Soon as I'm clear, I'm headed back to the ranch."

Another sigh. "Lucky bastard."

Caleb grinned and watched his friend head toward the Texas Cattleman's Club building. The place was a one-story, rambling sort, made of dark wood and stone, boasting a tall slate roof. It was a part of Royal and had been for generations. Celebrations of all kinds had been held there and today, it was a wedding. One he'd have to attend in just a few minutes.

Shelby Arthur stared at her own reflection and hardly recognized herself. She supposed all brides felt like that on their wedding day, but for her, the effect was terrifying.

Her long, dark auburn curls were pulled back from her face to hang down to the center of her back. Her veil poofed out around her head and her green eyes narrowed at the gown she hated. A ridiculous number of yards of white tulle made Shelby look like a giant marshmallow caught in netting. The dress was her about-to-be-mother-in-law's doing. She'd insisted that the Goodmans had a reputation to maintain in Royal and the simple off-the-shoulder gown Shelby had chosen wouldn't do the trick.

So instead, she was looking at a stranger wearing an old-fashioned gown with long, lacy sleeves, a cinched waist and full skirt, and a neckline that was so high she felt as if she were choking.

"Thank God for air-conditioning," she muttered, otherwise in the sweltering Texas heat, she'd be little more than a tulle-covered puddle on the floor. She half turned to get a look at the back of the dress and finally sighed. She looked like one of those crocheted dolls her grandmother used to make to cover up spare toilet paper rolls.

Shelby was about to get married in a dress she hated, a veil she didn't want, to a man she wasn't sure she *liked*, much less loved. How did she get to this point?

"Oh, God. What am I doing?" The whisper was strained but heartfelt.

She'd left her home in Chicago to marry Jared Goodman. But now that he was home in Texas, under his awful father's thumb, Jared was someone she didn't even know. Her whirlwind romance had morphed into a nightmare and now she was trapped.

She took a breath, blew it out and asked her reflection, "What are you doing?"

"Good question."

Shelby jumped, startled by the sudden appearance of Jared's mother. The woman was there, behind her in the mirror, bustling into the room. Margaret Goodman was tall and painfully thin. Her face was all sharp angles and her blue eyes were small and judgmental. Her graying blond hair was scraped back from her face into a bun that incongruously sported a circlet of yellow rosebuds. The beige suit she wore was elegant if boring and was so close to the color of her hair and skin the woman simply disappeared into her clothes.

If only, Shelby thought.

"Your veil should be down over your face," Margaret chastised, hurrying over to do just that.

As the veil fell across her vision, Shelby had a momentary panic attack and felt as though she couldn't breathe through that all-encompassing tulle curtain, so she whipped it back again. Taking a deep breath, she said, "I'm sorry, I can't—"

"You will." Margaret stepped back, took a look, then moved to tug at the skirt of the wedding gown. "We're going for a very traditional, chaste look here. It's unseemly that this wedding is happening so quickly. The town will be gossiping for months, watching for a swollen belly."

Shelby sucked in a gulp of air. "I've told you already, I'm not pregnant."

"We'll soon see, won't we?" One blond eyebrow lifted over pale blue eyes. "The Goodman family has a reputation in this town and I expect you to do nothing to besmirch it."

"Besmirch?" Who even talked like that, Shelby thought wildly. It was as if she'd dropped into a completely different universe. Suddenly, she missed Chicago—her friends, her *life*, so much she ached with it.

Moving to Texas with a handsome, well-connected cowboy who had swept her off her feet had seemed like an adventure at the time. Now she was caught up in a web that seemed inescapable. Her fiancé was a stranger, his mother a blatant enemy and his brother had a way of looking at Shelby that had her wishing she'd paid more attention in self-defense class.

Jared's father, Simon, was no better, making innuendoes that he probably thought were clever but gave Shelby the outright creeps. The only bright spot in the Goodman family was Jared's sister, Brooke, and she couldn't help Shelby with what was about to happen.

Somehow, she had completely lost control of her own life and now she stood there in a mountain of tulle trying to find enough scraps of who she was to cling to.

"Once the ceremony is finished, we'll all go straightaway to the reception," Margaret was saying.

Oh, God.

"You and Jared will, of course, be in the receiving line until every guest has been welcomed personally. The photographer can then indulge in the necessary photos for precisely fifteen minutes, after which you and Jared will reenter the reception for the ceremonial first toast." Margaret paused long enough to glance into the mirror herself and smooth hair that wouldn't dare fall out of place. "Mr. Goodman is an important man and as his family *we* will do all we can to support him. Is that understood?" Her gaze, hard and cold, shot to Shelby's. "When you've returned from your honeymoon..."

Her stomach sank even further. She wouldn't have been surprised to see it simply drop out of her body and fall *splat* onto the floor. Her day was scheduled. Her honeymoon was scheduled and she had no doubt at all that her *life* would be carefully laid out for her, complete with bullet points.

How had it all come to this?

For their honeymoon, Shelby had wanted to see Paris. Instead, Jared's mother had insisted they go to Philadelphia so Shelby could be introduced to the eastern branch of the Goodman family. And much to her dismay, Jared was simply doing as he was told with no regard at all for Shelby. He'd changed so much since coming back to Texas that she hardly recognized the man anymore.

Margaret was still talking. Fixing a steely gaze on the mirror, she met Shelby's eyes. "When you return to Texas, you will of course give up your ridiculous business and be the kind of wife to Jared that will enable him to further his own law career."

"Oh, I don't think—"

"You'll be a Goodman," Margaret snapped, brooking no argument.

Shelby swallowed hard. When they'd met in Chicago, Jared had talked about his ranch in Texas. He'd let her believe that he was a cowboy who happened to also have a law degree. And yes, she could admit that the fantasy of being with a cowboy had really appealed to her. But mostly, he'd talked about their having a family and that had sealed the deal for Shelby.

She'd told herself then that she could move her professional organizer business anywhere. But from the moment Jared had introduced her to his family, Margaret had made it clear that her "little business" was hardly appropriate.

Shelby met her own eyes in the mirror and read the desperation there. Maybe all of this would be easier to take if she was madly in love with Jared. But the truth was, she'd fooled herself from the beginning. This wasn't love. It couldn't be. The romance, the excitement, had all worn off, like the luster of sterling silver as soon as it was tarnished. Rather than standing up for himself, Jared was completely cowed by his family and that really didn't bode well for Shelby's future.

Margaret checked the slim gold watch on her wrist, clucked her tongue and headed for the door. "The music will begin in exactly five minutes." She stopped, glanced over her shoulder and added, "My husband will be here to escort you down the aisle since you don't have a father of your own."

Shelby's mouth dropped open as the other woman left the room. Stunned, she realized Margaret had tossed that last bit with venom, as if Shelby had arranged for her father to die ten years ago just so he could disrupt Margaret Goodman's wedding scenario.

She shivered at the thought of Simon Goodman. She didn't want him anywhere near her, let alone escorting her, touching her. And even worse, she was about to promise to be in Simon's family for the rest of her life.

"Nope, can't do it." She glanced at her own reflection and in a burst of fury ripped her veil off her face. Then, blowing a stray auburn lock from her forehead, she gathered up the skirt of the voluminous gown in both arms.

"Have to hurry," she muttered, giving herself the impetus she needed to make a break for it before it was too late. If she didn't leave now, she'd be *married* into the most awful family she'd ever known.

"Not going to happen," she reassured herself as she tentatively opened the door and peered out.

Thankfully, there was no one in this section of the TCC. They were all in the main room, waiting for the ceremony to start. In the distance, she heard the soft thrum of harp music playing as an underscore to the rise and fall of conversations. She could only guess what they'd all be talking about soon.

That wasn't her problem, though. Clutching her wedding gown high enough to keep it out of her way, she hurried down the hall and toward the nearest exit.

She thought she heard someone calling her name, but Shelby didn't let that stop her. She hit the front door and started running. It was blind panic that kept her moving. After all, she had nowhere to go. She didn't know hardly anyone in Royal besides the Goodman family. But she kept moving because the unknown was wildly better than the alternative.

Her veil caught on one of the porch posts and yanked her back briefly. But Shelby ripped the stupid thing off her head, tiara and all, and tossed it to the ground. Then she was off again, tearing around a corner and running smack into a brick wall.

Well, that's what it felt like.

A tall, gorgeous brick wall who grabbed her upper arms to steady her, then smiled down at her with humor in his eyes. He had enough sex appeal to light up the city of Houston and the heat from his hands, sliding down her body, made everything inside her jolt into life.

"Aren't you headed the wrong way?" he asked, and the soft drawl in his deep voice awakened a single thought in her mind.

Oh, boy.

Subscribe and fall in love with a Mills & Boon series today!

You'll be among the first to read stories delivered to your door monthly and enjoy great savings.

WE SIMPLY LOVE ROMANCE